Victoire was not certain what had brought her awake. Much as she wanted to peek through the bed-curtains, she dared not.

Another noise. She recognized the sound of faint footsteps, and she slipped her hand under the pillow, searching for her charged pistol. Her fingers closed on the butt and she felt a surge of excitement.

Quelling her fear, Victoire sat up slowly, taking care to make no sound. She pulled the pistol out and reached for the bed-curtain.

"That will do," she said as she flung the curtain back. The pistol was steady in her hand. She blinked against the darkness, able to make out little more than a vague shape in the open door of the armoire.

The man swore as he swung around and fired . . .

Other Mme. Vernet Investigations by
Quinn Fawcett
From Avon Books

NAPOLEON MUST DIE

Prologue

❧

THE BEACH WAS bright and wide, even in the darkness. To the captain's experienced eyes the swirls that hid among the waves in the Channel warned of shallow water and sandbars. It was slack tide, a dangerous time to land, but the men on the British sloop *Duke of Cornwall* were more concerned about the heavy cover of clouds that added to the darkness of the night than the ocean. Secrecy was needed on this mission more than safety.

The landing party was a strange one, composed as it was of six officers from the only unit the king could order into action without the precession of Parliament—the Honourable Artillery Company, also known as the Royal Horse Artillery. They were now in civilian dress—all volunteers—and in the company of fourteen nervous and arrogant Frenchmen intent on avenging their martyred King Louis XVI and restoring the monarchy; their first victim was to be Napoleon Buonaparte himself. Even though he had made many such clandestine voyages to the French coast, Captain Wakefield had been nervous about transporting this mixed lot; he could not but notice that every man among them had that fixed light in his eyes that was found only in the gaze of fanatics.

"We're going to have to come about here," the captain announced as he signalled the helmsman. "Beyond this point it's tricksy."

The senior officer, Colonel Sir Magnus Sackett-Hartley, hooked his thumbs into his belt, squinting into the dark. "I hear breakers."

"As well you might," said Captain Wakefield nervously. "This is a bad stretch of coast here." He watched the jib luff and barked an order to one of his crew. "None of that, not in these waters."

"They won't be expecting us, then," said Sackett-Hartley, who seemed to be in command of the passengers, with satisfaction.

1

"That they will not," the captain agreed sourly. "And who's to blame them, I'd like to know? You've got no business trying to land, not here at this time of night." He scowled at the Frenchmen gathered on deck, and said to Colonel Sir Magnus Sackett-Hartley in an undervoice, "I can understand about them, sir, but, you pardon my saying it, this ben't your fight."

Colonel Sackett-Hartley laughed. "I come by it, through family tradition, I'm afraid. My mother was Lady Laetitia Blakeney; her older brother made something of a habit of rescuing nobles bound for the guillotine, back during the Terror. He's quite old now, retired to the country where he writes execrable verse."

Captain Wakefield shook his head. "Sounds right daft."

"That he is," Colonel Sackett-Hartley declared with evident pride. "Which means I shall be hard-put to equal him."

The sloop pitched and everyone on deck scrambled for footing as the boom swung ominously. A sailor rushed to secure the sail.

"We'll be back here in twenty days," Captain Wakefield said. "Between Dunkerque and Veurne, by road. They call this inlet the Ram's Head, because of how it's shaped. Don't say the name of the place. You don't want to warn the Frenchies." He looked uneasily at the aristocrats, waiting for one of them to protest.

"Ah," said d'Estissac for all of them. "These are Frenchies to us, as well. They are not true Frenchmen. They have all become Corsican pirates."

There were mutters of approval.

"Well, whatever they are, good luck to you against them." He exchanged a halfhearted salute with Colonel Sackett-Hartley. "We'll be back every ten days for six months, unless we're fired on, and then we will return in the next ten days." He indicated the two boats being lowered. "Off you go. Try not to get caught."

"It is unthinkable," said La Clouette, the youngest of the group, an angular youngster not quite eighteen.

"We will suc-ceed because we must," declared Brezolles, unable to stop his stammer. "We must."

"Still," said Captain Wakefield.

Four of the sailors were uncoiling the ladders for the landing party, and a young lieutenant was giving their packs one last inspection. Satisfied, he stepped aside for the men to take up their supplies. "The guns are all French, the rest of the supplies have French stamps. Your jackets are from Rouen; say you bought

DEATH WEARS A CROWN

A Mme. Vernet Investigation

QUINN FAWCETT

AVON BOOKS ◆ NEW YORK

DEATH WEARS A CROWN: A MME. VERNET INVESTIGATION is an original publication of Avon Books. This work has never before appeared in book form. This work is a novel. Any similarity to actual persons or events is purely coincidental.

AVON BOOKS
A division of
The Hearst Corporation
1350 Avenue of the Americas
New York, New York 10019

Copyright © 1993 by Bill Fawcett & Associates
Published by arrangement with Bill Fawcett & Associates
Library of Congress Catalog Card Number: 93-90327
ISBN: 0-380-76542-X

First Avon Books Printing: October 1993

AVON TRADEMARK REG. U.S. PAT. OFF. AND IN OTHER COUNTRIES, MARCA REGISTRADA, HECHO EN U.S.A.

Printed in the U.S.A.

RA   10   9   8   7   6   5   4   3   2   1

them in the marketplace, if there is a question. The money is French and Dutch."

"I know," said d'Estissac shortly.

"You will have at the most two opportunities to assassinate Napoleon. The first group has the greater chance; the second is there in case the first is unable to accomplish the task," the lieutenant went on. "You cannot hope that you will be lucky enough for more than that. You will be on your own. You may not approach the English here officially. Should you be taken, be very sure you are not questioned. No one should attempt to rescue a captured member of this force, but silence him with a leaden ball."

The sloop rocked and dipped in the swell, wallowing as the waves struck her athwart her beams.

D'Estissac held on to the rail, his manner unconcerned. "We have been through this already." He stared from Captain Wakefield to Colonel Sackett-Hartley. "We are ready, mon Colonel."

As he started to salute, Sackett-Hartley stopped him. "From here on, it's Magnus, remember, Magnus Hartley."

"And the *d* is gone from my name," said d'Estissac softly. "But we will get it back."

"No doubt," said Captain Wakefield, who thought the whole project was reckless and ill-conceived.

"Each of you has gold," the lieutenant went on. "Use it wisely."

"We will," said Cholet. He picked up his pack, the first one to do so.

This proved a signal for the rest, who now slung the packs over their shoulders and made their way down the ladders into the boat.

"Remember," called Captain Wakefield. "Build a small fire at the end of the spit over there, on the west side of the inlet. Twenty, then every ten days."

The last of the Frenchmen got into the boats with the officers of the Horse Artillery, and both groups began to row toward the hidden shore, guided by the sound of breakers.

Captain Wakefield ordered his men to stand off from the coast a short distance where he lingered, the sound of breakers no longer demanding his attention. He listened for shouts or shots or alarms and was satisfied when he heard nothing.

"Well," he said softly to the Honourable Artillery officers, "I'll either bring your coffins home, or transport all your fellows and all your horse-drawn cannon and your traveling smithies to sweep the way clean to Paris." He smiled at the prospect, his weathered skin showing deep, hard wrinkles although he was only thirty-six. He ordered the *Duke of Cornwall* to head for home.

1

❧

ALL BUT THE most expensive inns in Calais were filled and so Inspector-General and Madame Vernet spent the night in Bourbourg, at a hostelry called the Botte d'Or, whose blackened beams had first been set in place while the Spider King ruled.

"These sheets are musty," said Victoire as she pulled back the coverlet. "Smell the mildew in them. Thank goodness I brought our own along. I wish I had brought blankets as well." She sniffed at the bedding and began to tug it off the sagging mattress.

They had been traveling for more than four days and she ached all over. Ever since her miscarriage of six months before the constant jarring of coach travel had bothered her though she steadfastly refused to admit it. Vernet had been uncertain about permitting her to accompany him, and she wished to provide him no excuse to send her home. "How does the innkeeper continue in business with such a place, and with such accommodations."

"Because of people like us. But we cannot afford—" he began.

She nodded. "Yes. And I am the one who ordered this economy, so it is wrong for me to complain. But still." She sighed and looked at the worn sheets, shaking her head as she heard the soft sound of a tear as she pulled the old, stained linen free. She flung the sheets in a heap in the corner and turned to her own traveling cases to take out her own sheets.

Vernet came toward her as she took out the clean, embroidered sheets. "Let's not stay here. Let's find a decent inn."

"Where?" she asked mildly. "In the clouds, perhaps?" She put the sheets down on the bed, then paused to unbutton her capped traveling coat before spreading out the first. "We are already farther from the coast than we ought to be. If we go inland again, you'll be criticized because you will appear lax, and we ought not to . . ."

5

Finding her work impeded by her coat, she dropped it over a sagging chair. Immediately a large brown-and-black cat hurtled around the chair—he had been curled asleep behind it—and yowling his protest, leaped onto the armoire.

"What the Devil!" Vernet burst out, about to throw a pillow at the outraged creature.

Victoire laughed unsteadily. "Well, at least we can be certain that there are few mice," she said, and went to open the door to let the cat out. "We ought to be grateful for such consideration. Now it is only a matter of bedbugs and rot." She continued with her self-appointed task, smoothing the lower sheet and beginning to tuck it under the mattress, feeling unpleasant grit against the rough hemp that supported it.

Vernet's eyes were cast down. "I hate it, having to stay here."

Victoire recognized that look, and she set about banishing it at once. "If we don't spend the night here, you'll not be able to pay for your new uniform. This is inconvenient; the uniform is necessary. Therefore we will remain where we are." Once the upper sheet was in place she sat on the bed and was not astonished when it sagged alarmingly. "Tomorrow we'll depart early, and we will look for a proper inn to stay at, one nearer the coast."

He nodded. "Yes. As you say." He regarded her face for several seconds. "You think I don't know what a treasure I have in you, Victoire. But I do. I would not have advanced this far if not for you. I know that I am a fortunate man."

One of Victoire's many annoyances with her fair coloring—decidedly out of the fashion—was the ease with which she blushed, and never more so than now. She did her best to look sensible while her cheeks flamed. "Now, Inspector-General Vernet, you must not flatter me. It will turn my head."

"I'm not flattering you." He smiled, mischief in the curl of his lip. "I am stating nothing less than the truth," he declared. "You are more observant than I am—"

"Because I am not as often under fire," she interjected calmly, though her disastrous cheeks remained bright. "Bullets are distracting."

He would not be deterred. "You are clear-headed, reasonable, and intrepid. And I don't care a fig that you have yellow hair. Let the others sigh for onyx, I prefer gold and topaz. And more fool they for choosing simpering misses who know only how to sigh." He opened the door as she began to put the coverlet in place again. Luckily they had brought their own pillows, she thought.

"I'll arrange to have the landau ready at seven, if that is satisfactory?"

She frowned. "I suppose so. We don't want them to be loading and harnessing in half-light." While she listened to Vernet descend the rickety stairs, she sighed and stared at the three-candle tree on the commode cabinet. It truly was a dreadful place to stay the night. But Victoire was a soldier's wife and she had followed the drum to worse places than this. She put her hands in the small of her back and pressed firmly, trying to ease her aching muscles. It offended her that as minor a task as making a bed had the capacity to tire her.

It was very disheartening, having to travel this way, she thought. Victoire did not want Vernet to know how distressed she felt, as he was already upset at the stringent economies that were forced on them by the high cost of keeping up correct appearances in Napoleon's Paris. There were missing slates on the roof of their cramped house, and the housekeeper complained that the kitchen was woefully old-fashioned. If it were not for the money her father had left in trust for her, they could not have managed at all. "A few more years," Victoire said softly to her uncertain reflection in the single, speckled mirror. "Just a few more years."

There were hurried steps, and Vernet came back into the room. "All set up. The landau will be ready in the morning at seven. Our cases are to be at the door twenty minutes before the hour." He took off his hat and held out his hands to her. "Tomorrow we will look early, and then I will go about my work and you can have a day to read."

She shook her head, a few blonde strands escaping from the simple knot at the crown of her head. "I am not a porcelain shepherdess, to be cosseted."

"I wouldn't bring a porcelain shepherdess on such a journey," he said. "Or most of the other places we've gone. But I can tell you are weary of traveling."

She did her best to make light of it. "And I thought I had disguised it so well."

"Oh, you have," said Vernet. "But I see how you stretch when you think I am not looking, to relieve the ache in your back." He sat down on the bed and pulled her down beside him, surprised at the sway of the mattress beneath them. "This is terrible," he protested as he looked around more carefully.

"We have been in less desirable places, as you yourself admit," she said quietly. "There is a roof over our heads, no sand, no wounded men, no vermin, no enemy soldiers."

He put his arm around her shoulder. "You can't be sure about the last," he reminded her. "If the rumors we have heard are right, there are indeed British agents and ambitious Aristos landing in the area to spy on our fleet."

"This is a reasonable place to do it," said Victoire as if it were obvious. "The fleet is accessible and England is very near." She leaned against him, her short corset pressing against her ribs. "Ah, I will be glad to get out of my stays."

"Truly," he declared, teasing in his voice. "I'll be glad, too."

She looked once around the dark, musty room. "Well, at least we will be warm enough," she said, making the best of it.

"I'll see to that," he agreed. He touched the lacing at her back. "One of these days we'll be able to afford a 'tire woman for you." He unfastened the concealed knots closing her dress. "You should have a 'tire woman, and a butler and all the rest of the staff. But I do not want to give up my job."

Victoire shook her head, trying unsuccessfully not to smile. "I'm not as helpless as all that, husband." She moved so that he could unfasten the rest of the dress, lifting her hands so that he could lift it off her. Sitting in her slip and corset, she was suddenly chilly. "Hurry," she recommended. "I want to get warm."

"Good," he responded, the warmth in his voice becoming passionate. He fumbled with the fastenings of her corset, and while she removed it, and her slip, he set about tugging off his own garments, tossing them onto the chair over Victoire's coat. Their nightclothes he would retrieve later.

They dived under the covers in unromantic haste, then snuggled close together, shivering a little.

"The landlord would be appalled if he could see us," whispered Vernet.

"Then it is just as well he can't," Victoire answered. "Not everyone has to wear clothes to bed all the time."

"I didn't unpack my robe," Vernet pointed out.

"Worry about it in the morning," she suggested, and opened her mouth for his kisses. He was as good and necessary as bread and as luxurious as those outrageous emeralds Josephine was sporting two weeks ago. She felt sustained by him, and nourished. Victoire relaxed into his arms, chuckling once as the old bed groaned and sagged. Thank goodness, she thought, that Vernet was not one to rush.

They made love without haste, concentrating on enjoyment

instead of their depressing room and frustrating situation; there would be time enough for such worries in the morning, Vernet insisted as he pressed closer to her, smiling as they kissed more deeply. She urged him nearer still, and moved to the least-lumpy part of the bed with a grin. This insouciance was still a novelty—for some time after her miscarriage they had made love rarely and with such careful attention that in the end they had more comfort than pleasure, and no amusement. Now at last the laughter had come back to their passion, and the sense of fun that had so delighted her from the first.

Before they drifted into sleep, Vernet remarked, "I have been thinking; I used to condemn every official who ever took a bribe. I thought it was because of them that there was corruption. But now it is clear to me that the bribes were offered, and that was the real perversion, not their acceptance."

Victoire, her head resting on his shoulder, asked, "What made you think of that?"

"Oh, one of Berthier's staff was caught taking bribes, and he's to be put in prison. It turns out the fellow has a large family and a crippled brother to care for, and he hasn't been able to afford ..." He ended in a yawn. "The man who bribed him knew he was in need, and knew also his salary was not sufficient to keep him out of debt. Who is to blame him for taking what was offered?"

"By the sound of it, Berthier," said Victoire, more dryly than she had planned.

"Perhaps," he allowed. "But I am in sympathy with the poor man. I think he was put in an untenable position." He rubbed her hair, now loose and tangled.

"And you worry you could be tempted yourself," she said, recognizing that tone of self-doubt that occasionally came into his words.

"I do not think I would do so now. But we know how little money there is, and if we have more expenses, it would be harder to refuse advantage." He adjusted his arm to serve as her pillow.

She knew better than to be shocked by his doubts. She kissed his jaw. "You know your situation and you know what you may have to face. You've already made up your mind to maintain your integrity, so you are less likely to be persuaded against your will than many another." She paused, and went on drowsily, "I think most men stumble into corruption. They do it, for novelty and gain, with never a thought to what it means."

"You're very harsh," Vernet teased her gently.

"Not harsh, Lucien," she said, about to tumble into sleep, "practical."

"I don't see why I can't go with you," Victoire protested as she stowed the last of their luggage in the room they had taken at the Garçon Rouge in Dunkerque, an inn catering to traveling merchants and minor officials. It was a significant improvement over the Botte d'Or and charged accordingly.

"The waterfront is not a friendly place, my love, not in these times. There is a great deal of danger there." Vernet realized as soon as he said that he had made a mistake. He tried to minimize it. "An armed man in a uniform commands more respect than a—"

"And makes a better target," she said with asperity. "I will not be a foolish companion, my dear, and you should know that by now." Her manner was cajoling but there was firm purpose in her blue eyes.

"It isn't safe," Vernet insisted. "That would mean I would be worrying about you when I ought to be doing my work instead. It would be an unnecessary risk, Victoire. You could be set upon or threatened, and then how would I be able to do my duty?" As appeals went he did not have a very good opinion of it, but to his surprise, she nodded.

"All right. I will remain here and see to having our laundry done. But if you are not back by sunset, I will find the local officers and sent out a search for you."

He chuckled and shook his head. "I am only going to the quays, to find out if there are any rumors there of ships landing in the night."

Victoire threw her hands up in dismay. "You set an impossible task, and you know it. There are always ships landing in the night. There are smugglers up and down this stretch of coast. Frenchmen smuggle in cloth from England and the English smuggle in brandy from France. It is a game. Everyone is aware of that. They aren't going to end good business just because there is more war coming." She gave him a look of exasperation. "What sort of notion do you have? They will tell you lies, my dearest, just lies, as they always lie to officials."

"Perhaps, but I am required to try, in any case." His mouth twitched into a smile. "How will I explain to Berthier if I have nothing to report?"

"I will explain it to Berthier," said Victoire in a tone there was no disputing. "And he will listen to me."

"Now there's a threat that will shake him," said Vernet with fondness. He was more cautious of Napoleon's right-hand man than Victoire was, for she had crossed wits with him on more than one occasion and come out the winner.

"I doubt it," she answered, and gave him an affectionate shove in the arm. "Well, I suppose I cannot convince you that I will be safe in your company; be about your duty, then."

He put his arms around her. "Have a care while I am gone," he said, and kissed her with a mixture of affection and passion.

When she moved free of his arms she made a gesture of impatience. "I am staying here so that you will not worry for me. Therefore, do not worry."

He grinned. "All right."

"And since I can't go with you, tell me everything— everything!—when you get back." This last order was given with a smile, but Vernet saluted smartly.

"Oui, ma Colonelle," he said, using the nick-name he had come to use for her.

She gestured toward the door, watching him as he reluctantly left her to arrange for the laundress to wash their clothes.

The quay was largely deserted, for most of the local ships had been out after fish since dawn. On the other side of the quay a half-dozen lobster boats waited, secured to stanchions with fore-and-aft painters. On this side most of the fishing craft were out in the North Sea. The two remaining boats tied to the quay showed signs of age and damage. Aboard one, a lean, salt-hardened man labored to replace the boom of his mainsail. He swore with vigor and variety as he worked, which covered the sound of Vernet's approach.

"Good afternoon, my good fisherman," he said, trying to sound friendly in spite of his uniform, for the fishermen of this region were as apt to curse a soldier as help him.

The man stopped his work, straightened up, and glowered in Vernet's general direction as he shaded his eyes with his big, hard hand. "If you say it is," he grumbled.

"I say that it might become so, if you will hear me out," said Vernet, who had learned in the last two hours that he had to offer these taciturn fishermen good reason to speak to him. He took a gold coin from his wallet as if it meant little to him, though in fact he could not easily spare such a sum. "I am Inspector-General Lucien Vernet, of the Gendarme Nationale. If you have the information I seek, the afternoon might well be profitable for you."

This caught the fisherman's attention and he left off his task.

"What might your interest be, then?" he asked, moving carefully nearer the quay.

"I am investigating a landing here, a night landing from England. Not one of the usual landings, something else." Vernet said it directly and without any hint of condemnation. He had made that mistake with the first man he approached and had been greeted with stony silence for his trouble. "It is important that we learn if English soldiers have been sent ashore."

"English soldiers?" the fisherman asked with greater interest and feigned ignorance. "What would English soldiers be doing in France?"

"They might well be planning to sink the fleet we are gathering, or so it is feared," said Vernet, knowing that although the fisherman might dislike men in uniform, he would hate the English and anyone who damaged ships.

"Ah!" said the fisherman, and stared off in the direction of the bow of his craft. "English soldiers."

"And French Aristos," added Vernet with emphasis. "Who want to bring down Napoleon and—"

"That's nothing to me. All of them collect taxes, my fine soldier-boy, and taxes are what matter to men like me." He pulled at his grizzled chin, where a two-day stubble grew. "English. English," he mused.

"That's right," said Vernet, holding up the gold coin again.

"There is a rumor," said the fisherman at last as he made up his mind. "Mind you, it's only a rumor, but this morning I heard it from the lobstermen as they came in from the night. They go to their traps at night, many of them."

And they exchange more than lobsters, thought Vernet, keeping this to himself. "What is their rumor?"

"Well, they said there was a sloop come in above Malo-les-Bains and below De Panne. I can't swear there was one because I didn't see it, but three lobstermen swore to it, and they're not ones to make up stories." He folded his arms. "That's the rumor, and you may make of it what you will."

"Who would know if the sloop was English?" Vernet persisted, the gold coin still visible.

The fisherman pursed his lips. "You might try the Père Antoine. He holds Mass at midnight for the lobstermen. He might have seen something. His church is over there, Saint-Pierre-le-Roc. You talk to him." He lifted his chin. "Is that worth anything to you?"

"We shall see," said Vernet as he tossed him a coin, wondering as he did how he would explain it to Victoire, for they were running short of money already.

Vernet paused outside the ancient church. Something felt wrong. He wasn't sure what, but after so many years on campaign, the Inspector-General had learned to trust his instincts. Perhaps he should have followed the example of the other four Inspector-Generals and traveled about with a full patrol in attendance. Then it was hardly likely anyone would speak to him if he had.

Cautiously Vernet moved into the shadows of a nearby wine-seller's booth on the far side of the small square and directly across from the church. The proprietor stared at the gold braid and Gendarme uniform of his visitor after assuring Vernet that he had paid his taxes and was a loyal Buonapartist; he was silenced by an abrupt gesture.

A short while later Vernet was able to determine what bothered him: three men stood at separate sides of the square, exchanging covert glances. All were tough-looking, dressed poorly for this prosperous fishing port.

Several minutes passed and at the nod of the largest, all three entered the church. Vernet was certain they were not going to worship.

When they did not emerge immediately Vernet decided to get closer and discover what they were about. This was the first sign of anything unusual he had seen in Dunkerque; he had to investigate for that reason alone.

Moving slowly, Vernet kept his hand on his pistol as he approached the church's large wooden doors. He was less than a dozen steps away when they crashed open and the three men came rushing out, each holding one of the golden vessels from the altar.

Bellowing his rage and brandishing a long brass candle-snuffer, a red-faced man in clerical robes ran a dozen steps behind them.

Vernet drew his pistol and fired at the closest thief, only seeing the long dagger the man was carrying as he did. The steel blade had been extended like a rapier to wound Vernet. But the ball struck home and the dagger clattered to the paving stones a few paces away as the man crumpled.

The other two thieves pulled to an abrupt stop at the sound of the shot. The presence of the impressively uniformed Gendarme officer was not part of their plan. The priest quickly dispatched the closest of the brigands with a sharp blow to the head with the candlesnuffer.

Caught between the two threats, the third thief turned and ran along the front of the church and disappeared down its side. Vernet hurried after him, only to find the man had run into a cul-de-sac. The back of the alley was blocked by a story-high wall.

The thief spun in panic and slashed out with the short fisherman's knife; it was a nasty blade, curved, commonly used for gutting and scaling fish. Fortunately Vernet was too far away and the blow passed harmlessly in front of him. In the man's other hand was the gem-encrusted gold chalice from the altar, worth more than the thief could earn in a lifetime; he was dressed in a tattered and stained shirt and pants such as were used in the white uniform of the Guard Nationale. Vernet reckoned this man was a deserter and so doubly desperate to escape from a member of the Gendarmes: the punishment for desertion was hanging.

They paused for a moment, Vernet with his sword raised and the thief looking desperately for escape.

"Surrender," Vernet ordered. His sword had more than a foot of advantage in reach over the dagger.

The thief seemed to realize this and his hands sagged. Both men started to relax and Vernet was already forming the question he would ask when without warning the deserter threw the chalice at his face.

Taken off-guard, Vernet staggered back, fumbling with his free hand to catch the sacred vessel before it struck the paving stones.

Seeing his chance the thief tried to rush past, switching the knife to his left hand and swinging the blade to force Vernet further back as he passed. Vernet fell against the weathered stone wall of the church and brought his sword around in a rapid slash intended to strike a glancing blow to his opponent's chest; the thief's own desperate rush drove the edge deeply into his neck, partially severing his head. The man dropped, twitching.

Irrationally, all Vernet could think of as he retrieved the chalice was to avoid getting any blood on his uniform or Victoire would have a difficult time cleaning it.

By the time the city watch had arrived, Vernet had returned the chalice and the priest had given absolution to the last of the thieves. The blow from the thick brass pole, or his fall to the paving stones, had cracked the skull of the man the priest had struck.

The local corporal's outrage over the slaughter in his street gave way to careful respect when he recognized the uniform of an Inspector-General. He was even more grateful when Vernet allowed him and his patrol to take credit for stopping the theft. It was not that Vernet cared whether anyone in Paris heard of this exploit, but Victoire would worry if she learned of his encounter. Miraculously his uniform, the last of his good ones, was neither cut nor stained.

To Vernet's frustration the watch knew all three men, local brigands whom they had long sought. But the priest was most effusive in his thanks and so was more than willing to answer the Inspector-General's questions.

"And that is all you have learned in three days?" Victoire said in surprise as they dawdled over their luncheon. Vernet seemed more excited than the information he had gathered warranted, but she said nothing.

"The priest was the most helpful—I'll give that fisherman his due," Vernet continued, unaware that he was fiddling with his wine cup. "Père Antoine said that he had seen muffled lamps out to sea at two in the morning, east of where the lobstermen lay their traps." He had a bit more of the lamb after he had offered it to Victoire. "I tried all yesterday to find someone who could tell me more than the priest, but either they do not know or they will not tell. One of the lobstermen threatened to set his crew on me if I did not leave them alone."

"Gracious," said Victoire with more indignation than astonishment. "What did you do to them?"

"I reminded them that there were penalties for aiding the enemy, and that made them hesitate, as you may well imagine." He cut his meat carefully, looking around the small dining room of the Garçon Rouge as he did to see if any of the other four occupants were listening to him.

"And then?" she demanded.

"And then I said that they might be rewarded if they had useful information. They had nothing to tell me." He looked at the bread, and cut one more slice for himself. "I will speak to a few more of them, but I suppose I have learned all that I am going to learn already." He stared toward the window where the sunlight caressed a small garden. "It troubles me that there has been only the one landing."

"That you have discovered," Victoire amended.

"True enough," said Vernet. "But if there had been more, if there had been English soldiers about ... Père Antoine must have said something. He is for Napoleon and does not want to see another king in France." He smiled a little. "For an old man—he must be fifty-five at the least—he has very forward-looking ideas. But he tells me that if half the people hereabouts would just as soon have the king again as Napoleon," he scoffed. "They are ignorant."

"Then you must hope that Père Antoine will help them to learn better," said Victoire at her most soothing.

"At least they trust him enough to tell him of ... odd events," said Vernet, a displeased frown in his eyes.

"And he has heard nothing of strangers in the area?" asked Victoire thoughtfully.

"So he says," Vernet answered. "If they are hidden, they have excellent protection. But that would mean they are not able to move about, which seems to defeat their purpose."

"And what purpose is that?" Victoire turned her acute blue eyes on her husband and had more of the lettuce cooked with vinegar.

"To spy on the fleet, or damage it. Or to disrupt the negoti-ations." Vernet spoke firmly, but managed to keep his voice down.

"Are you certain of that?" She did not give him a chance to answer. "Two days ago I might have said the same thing myself but now I am not so sure."

"But of course that is their purpose. Think, my love. They landed here, near the border of the Lowlands." He leaned for-ward, his handsome features intent.

For once Victoire was not distracted by his arresting good looks. "And that, too, is odd, when you think of it," she mur-mured.

"How do you mean?" he asked. "What else could it be?"

"That is the heart of it. We have been expecting the enemy to do what it is convenient for us that they do, and that may be a mistake." Victoire had another bite of the baked apple that ac-companied the lamb. "I find this very puzzling," she admitted. "Very, very puzzling."

"Why?" asked Vernet, knowing his wife was more clever than most. "What puzzles you?"

"Well," she said slowly, and paused for another sip of the red wine that was served with the meal, "I cannot help but suppose that we are wrong in our thinking."

"How wrong?" Vernet inquired, watching her with fascination. "What is wrong?"

She did not answer at once, and when she did, she sounded distant. "It bothers me that they chose to land here. The border with Holland is near, true, but . . . but so is the road to Paris. What if the English are not here to compromise the negotiations or to destroy the fleet? What if they have other mischief in mind?"

"What could that be?" Vernet set his utensils aside and gave her his full attention.

"Perhaps they are after more important targets," she mused. "Perhaps we are limiting our expectation of danger when we must not. These men could be more desperate and ambitious than we have given them credit for being. Let us suppose that they are capable of far more traitorous acts than we have presumed." She paused for a moment and sipped wine while her thoughts formed into words. "They may seek to damage the Consulate or even Napoleon Buonaparte himself." Victoire took a deep breath as the full implications of what she had just said struck her; she steadied herself and went on. "We have been assuming all along that these few English are here because they want to end the negotiations with Holland: there were too few of them to do much to the fleet. That is our assumption, and it is a mistake to assume anything. Events have shown that what we expected has not occurred. Therefore we must begin again, and avoid the error of deciding in advance what their purpose may be. Let us reconsider what we know, not what we suspect. We know that a sloop from England landed and that a small party of men came ashore. Père Antoine says that some of them spoke French and some spoke English, for he heard them as he returned from blessing the lobstermen's boats. You say that he estimates a party of twenty."

"That is what he guessed," said Vernet, trying to match her precision.

"If they were determined to damage the fleet, they might have done it more easily landing in Holland, at Zoutelande, or perhaps at Oostende in Belgium. There would be fewer restrictions on them, and they would not be at risk as they are here." She began to move her first finger on the tablecloth as if writing. "But suppose they are not interested in the negotiations or the fleet. Twenty men are a small force for such a task, but if they were sent here to lead a rising of the remaining Aristos, or as assassins—"

"Victoire! For Saint Dennis!" He looked around to be certain they were not overheard and encountered one startled stare from a ruddy-faced dealer in leather goods.

"Sir," said the merchant's agent, his broad features darkening, "it is hardly fitting to speak to your wife in such a tone."

Vernet realized it was his own outburst that had caught the man's notice, and he made a gesture of agreement. "I offer her and you my apology."

The merchant's agent nodded twice and returned to his cheese.

Victoire had been speaking softly, but she lowered her voice. "Let us suppose that there are no other landings to concern us." She watched him until he nodded. "It would appear that this may be a scouting mission, but if it is, they are not scouting here, or someone would have seen something. So we have to consider the possibility that they are not here at all."

"And how do you propose we find them?" he asked her.

A fine vertical line formed between her pale brows. "It would probably be wise to warn the mission in Holland, and your superiors in Paris. That for a start, at least. If it turns out that the English have merely gone to ground here, then they can be apprehended by local officials. But if they have left this area, we must assume that they are bound for other places. Why come to France unless their target is in France?" Her question hung between them.

"I take your point, my love," Inspector-General Vernet said to his wife. "All right. I will spend one more day in a search for the English. I want to find them. Père Antoine should be able to tell me something. If there is no more information, then I will do as you suggest." He reached across the table and laid his hand over hers. "I do not want to seem to be an alarmist."

"That may be sensible," she said slowly. "But do not delay in dispatching warnings if you do not locate at least one or two of the English in the next twenty-four hours. It would be unwise not to alert—"

"Yes, yes," he said, agreeing with her, little as he wanted to. He wanted the time not only to search for the English, but to examine the implications of the theory Victoire had just put forth. It was one thing, he decided, to apprehend spies. Assassins were another matter entirely.

By the middle of the afternoon Vernet's feet hurt and he was worn out as he trudged up to Saint-Pierre-le-Roc. Hours of questions and small bribes had done nothing but confirm what he had learned already. He was growing bitterly disappointed and apprehensive, for increasingly he thought that Victoire's suspicions—which he had hoped were absurd—were becoming more probable.

Père Antoine greeted Vernet warmly, saying, "Napoleon may dislike religion, but I warrant he knows the value of parishes like this one, and relies on us to aid him in his reforms." There was an appreciative twinkle in his brown eyes. "It is always prudent to value those who advise the community, isn't it?"

"I suspect my wife would agree with you at once," said Vernet, his face remote as he thought about the situation they were in, and gave Victoire's suggestion about the invaders another unwelcome consideration.

"What troubles you, my son?" asked Père Antoine as they entered the little church, a relic from a thousand years ago.

On the walls were faded, ancient frescoes for the Stations of the Cross, the plaster crumbling with decay and age. He knelt and crossed himself and waited while Vernet, belatedly, did the same. "Something *does* trouble you, doesn't it?"

"It troubles me," said Vernet, "that I can find no sign of the English, and no whisper of them, either," he admitted as he followed Father Antoine in the general direction of the confessional. "I have been looking, but there is not a hint of them anywhere."

"Perhaps they have accomplices," said Père Antoine diffidently.

"I thought that myself, at first, but there would still be signs. There would be children displaced in a house, or an increase of errands. Someone would suddenly need to purchase more bread, or had more for the midden, or there would be strange events noticed by someone, if only a jealous neighbor. And there would be speculation, people guessing about the unexplained occurrences. It is difficult to keep secrets in places like this. You are too near the sea and sailors, and—" He waved his hand to indicate that such things are often in the air.

"I would agree," said Père Antoine. He led Vernet behind the altar to a small door that led into a small sitting room. "Please come in." He stood aside to let Vernet enter, indicating one of the two upholstered chairs.

Vernet felt a bit too tall and too bright for the room, and he strove to compensate by choosing the smaller of the chairs. Ordinarily he would have waited for the priest to be seated, but clearly Père Antoine was reserving that honor. "Well, I am grateful you are willing to talk with me," he said, finding the moment suddenly awkward.

"It is my duty and my pleasure." He drew up the larger chair and sat at once. "I would hate to see France under English rule. It has never succeeded, having the English here. We on this stretch of coast have known it since Queen Eleanor eloped with King Henry." He looked around with satisfaction. "Saint-Pierre-le-Roc saw those unhappy times, and ones earlier than that."

"Of course," said Vernet, wondering if this was leading anywhere.

It was. "There is a fisherman who worships here. He has an English wife, the daughter of a sailor who has carried . . . night cargos for many, many years. The English wife is often visited by English. She knows all of them, all the captains and all the navy men who seek to end the smuggling. Even she knows nothing of the English you seek."

"Ah?" said Vernet, to encourage Père Antoine to continue.

"She has said that her brother and her husband have been bothered by others. And she has been slighted in the market. The people blame her for you asking questions." He folded his hands in his lap and looked over at Vernet. "You must understand that she is not one to complain for no reason. Like many of the English, she is stoical in her behavior, not like some Frenchwomen, who would be in tears and filled with outrage if any of the townspeople behaved so badly."

"And she tells you that she knows of no reason for this to happen?" Vernet prodded.

"That is the gist of it, yes," said Père Antoine. "I have asked her if she has received any visitors from England in the last month, and she declares that none have come in over three months. She is not a woman who lies easily or well, and so I believe what she tells me."

Vernet heard this out. "Would she talk to me?"

"She would, but it would not be a good thing for her. It would give rise to more speculation that could cause more of the townspeople to turn against her, and in times like these, such rejection can be very cruel. If she were not English, I would not be concerned for her, but as she is . . ." He opened his hands to show that he could not regulate the attitudes of the whole of Dunkerque.

"You indicate her father . . . smuggles from time to time," Vernet said carefully. "Have I understood you correctly?"

"You have," said Père Antoine without discomfort.

"Is there any way I might arrange to speak with him?"

Vernet asked, thinking that if the daughter did not have answers for him, her father could.

"I will ask her to get a message to him. That is the most I can do." He paused as he got up from the chair and took a turn about the room. "She is a good woman, for all she is English, and she does not deserve to suffer the odium of the town."

"I would not want her to," said Vernet at once. "The Gendarme Nationale does not want to embarrass honest citizens."

"Certainly not," said Père Antoine. "But if care is not taken, such things can happen, can they not?"

"Sadly, yes," admitted Vernet, wishing that Victoire were with him to talk to the priest, for he suspected she would know better how to learn more of the Englishwoman married to the French fisherman.

"There is something that I cannot discuss, for it is of the Confessional and there is a sacred seal on it. However, I can tell you that I have heard the Confession of a Frenchman who came here by sea and who has never set foot in this church before. He is worried for his soul, because of what he has come to France to do." Père Antoine coughed. "That is more than I should tell you or anyone, but I fear if I do not say something, this man might bring great sin upon his soul."

"Because he is a spy?" Vernet demanded.

"I cannot tell you that," said Père Antoine. "But the sin he contemplates is not a minor one, and he is determined upon it."

Vernet scowled. "The seal of Confession is sacred. You would be excused if you said nothing. But it is important that you spoke, and I thank you for it."

Père Antoine motioned Vernet to rise. "Your work is very important to the country, and I respect your goals. Surely when a man is in danger of damning himself, if a word can help to save him, there is sin in silence if it is not the silence of the Confessional. I pray I have done the right thing and that God will forgive me my sophistry now. You seem a man of principle, which is not encountered as often as one would like. I will do what I can, Inspector-General Vernet," he promised. "I will send you word at the Garçon Rouge if I discover anything that may be of use to you."

"I will be grateful for any assistance you give, mon Père. In these times we must rely on the good-will of the people of France."

Père Antoine shrugged. "There is nothing remarkable in that," he observed. "The soil of France has tasted English blood before. This will not be the first time, nor, I suppose, the last."

"What we must hope is that there will be no French blood spilled. Enough young lives have been lost already." Vernet bowed slightly. "I am most appreciate, Monsieur le Prêtre. With help such as yours we may yet foil the English plots."

"As God wills," said Père Antoine, as he sketched a blessing in Vernet's direction. "I will pray for the welfare and accomplishment of your mission, the success of Napoleon and France."

Although Vernet muttered assent as he closed the door behind him, inwardly he doubted that God had much to do with what was happening on this part of the coast of France.

2

❦

SOMEWHERE IN A room not far from the Prime Minister's home, three men met. One was a high official in the government. The second had served as a general in the British army before retiring and was known to be the personal friend of the king of England. The third had once been a king, but now lacked a nation. Carefully the latter two gentlemen told William Pitt, Secretary of War, of their plan. Before the statesman could react the general assured him that there was no way the men in France could be linked to anyone in his government. There was an uncomfortable silence.

It was unlikely that Pitt could protest a plan that obviously had the approval of King George. Still there was a chance that due to the irrational gentlemen's code of diplomacy Pitt would be outraged. That could embarrass very many important men and end with a short note to the French ambassador.

Unused to waiting for another's approval, Louis shifted uncomfortably in his chair. He exchanged a worried glance with the general and then turned to Sir William Pitt again. The Prime Minister was smiling.

As he sanded the eighth dispatch, Vernet looked around their room for a place to set it while it dried. Most of the bed was already taken, with seven of the large vellum sheets drying there already. He swung around in the straight-backed chair and looked toward his wife. "Is there any—"

She reached out for the dispatch and slid it expertly to the top of the armoire. "This will do," she declared, and continued to darn his cuff.

"I think that will alert most of them," he said as he leaned back, tipping the chair precariously onto its two hind legs. "If there are any questions later, I can declare that I thought it best to be prepared when it was not necessary instead of unprepared when it *was* necessary."

"It will be necessary," said Victoire grimly. "I am more con-

23

vinced than ever, husband, that these English are not interested in anything on this coast. Everything you have found out supports that view."

"Then at least we have given the warning," said Vernet, not as convinced as Victoire. "And if we are in the wrong—"

"You may blame me. Berthier will, in any case," she said, with a quick, wry chuckle. "Tell him that I insisted, and he will rub his chubby hands together and turn his oyster eyes to the ceiling."

"Victoire!" he protested, fondly scandalized by her description, knowing it was accurate and therefore the more deplorable.

"Yes, it's not a very flattering portrait, and I am in charity with him these days. But you will admit that he's not a very prepossessing figure." She began blind-stitching the darning into the line of the seam.

"He is utterly devoted to Napoleon," Vernet reminded her.

"He certainly is," said Victoire at once. "And he's as incorruptible as any man in high rank can be. You see, I'm aware of his excellent qualities. But I do not think him a very ... personable fellow."

"You mean unlike Murat?" said Vernet, not without a twinge of jealousy, although he knew it was wholly unfounded.

Victoire smiled. "Well, it would be very difficult not to be swayed by Murat, if one were swayable, and he were inclined to attempt to sway," she said with her usual candor. "But he is a married man, and I am a married woman, and so I will admire his features and the cut of his uniforms and the size of his vocabulary, and occasionally we will flirt outrageously for entertainment, but there's an end to it." Suddenly her eyes were serious. "Without him, I would have died in Egypt."

"Without him, you might not have been in such danger," Vernet reminded her. "But you are right. He provided you excellent protection when I could not, and for that I am grateful. And you did the same for him, in Italy."

Again she chuckled. "An honorable debt."

"Of course." He rocked the chair forward and stood up. "I will have to hand these off to riders this afternoon if they are to be delivered in a timely manner." He reached for one of the vellum sheets and began to fold it, then set it on the table near the standish.

"Tell them it is urgent," she recommended as she made a concealed knot in the thread, then cut it with her teeth.

"Naturally. And I trust it will not be lost with all the others that are urgent," he said, beginning to sound weary. "One more day here—two at most—and then we must return home." He cleared his throat. "I wish that Englishwoman would come to talk to me."

Victoire set Vernet's jacket aside. "Do you think she might talk to me instead? It is not the same thing as speaking to a man in uniform. A comfortable chat with a merchant's daughter; it might cause her to speak freely."

"I don't think she would be more forthcoming. You know what these coastal towns are like, and how private the people can be." He glanced in her direction. "You remember that she is already regarded as a foreigner, and so she will not want to be seen talking to someone like you, simply because you are not from Dunkerque. But I thank you for making the offer, my darling. You already do more for me than most men could have from ten wives."

As always, she found this effusive praise embarrassing. "Well, that's as may be, but where your clothes are concerned, I do not seem to manage all that well." She shook her head as she regarded the jacket. "I don't know how much longer I can darn the collar and cuffs. I've done my best, but it is apparent that there have been repairs."

Vernet sighed. "And I will have to have a new dress uniform if I am to attend the two receptions that are planned—the one for the Swedes and the one for the Austrians. I can't go looking bedraggled or threadbare, not to such functions."

"No, of course you can't," said Victoire with a slow sigh. "I would not want you to, Lucien, but it is not easily arranged."

"Captain Sommenier has run into debt, just keeping himself properly uniformed. His family lost everything in the Revolution and they cannot give him any help but their excellent reputation," Vernet went on. "He has not been able to afford . . ."

"Anything," said Victoire for him.

"Essentially, that is so." He had finished folding the dispatches and now set about writing the directions on each of them before sealing them. "But it is the price demanded by advancement in these times."

"It is an invitation to trouble," said Victoire darkly.

"Hardly that," said Vernet as he continued his task.

"Oh, yes," said Victoire. "If you force your men to live beyond their means, you are making it necessary for them to compromise themselves. You know how you feel about those who take bribes, and you admit that some were not in the wrong as much as they were desperate."

"Yes," he said cautiously.

"And therefore, it is an invitation to trouble, because this policy turns honest men into desperate men," she said at her most reasonable. She watched him write, and then said, "Tomorrow morning I want to take a turn around the town before we leave. I haven't had much opportunity to see the place."

Vernet nodded, a bit distracted. "Very well, I'll arrange an escort for you."

"Oh, that's not necessary. I won't go anyplace dangerous," she promised him blithely.

"You must forgive me if I doubt that," he said over his shoulder, his smile affectionate. "You did not think going up the banks of the Nile was dangerous."

She smiled back. "Actually I did, but I thought not going was more dangerous," she said, and then her expression grew more somber. "I have my grandmother's writing set at home, you know the one, very old-fashioned. I never use it. It is made of gold and should bring a good price—enough to purchase a dress uniform, at least."

Vernet stopped writing. "I cannot ask you to do that," he said very softly.

"You are not asking," she pointed out. "I am telling you that I can get the money for the uniform without either of us being forced to borrow."

"But it was your grandmother's," Vernet protested, feeling wretched.

"And now it is mine, and I am sure she would understand why I wish to sell it. She was a sensible, practical woman, and not one to stick at niceties. I will sell it, you will have the uniform, and there may be enough for me to afford a new lace robe for my green ballgown. It will make the whole dress look new, especially if I change the corsage with new embroidery, and perhaps a few of those seed-pearls from my mother's wedding dress. We will both look very smart." She favored him with a determined nod. "It is the most sensible thing to do, Vernet, and you know it as well as I do."

"I don't like to see you selling such things for me," he said stubbornly.

"Well, I am sure that is very honorable of you, but just at present it is not very practical, and it is more sensible to use good sense." As far as she was concerned it was settled. "You will not disgrace yourself, and we will keep our heads above water for a little while yet. In the meantime, you might arrange to speak to Fouche. He may be able to do something for you."

"Fouche is a very busy man, and his hands are full," said Vernet, who hesitated to involve the former teacher who was head of Napoleon's spies. The man was notorious for his greed and self-aggrandizement. And he used people in his shadow-filled world; to deal with him even once as a supplicant often meant you were never again free from his demands. "I do not like to make such petitions to men of such high position."

"Well," said Victoire in her most heartening manner, "if we do not do something, we are going to run out of items to sell or pawn, and then we *will* have to petition someone, perhaps a magistrate of the court instead of Director Fouche."

"That is a gloomy prospect," said Vernet.

"Then put your mind on other things," said Victoire. "For brooding will not change anything. You are among the highest law officers in France and that gives you many social obligations. Your successful investigation, however, might bring you one of those many bonuses Napoleon hands out, which is far more to the point." She regarded the pile of dispatches. "You had best take those at once."

"Of course," said Vernet. "First things first."

As in most fishing towns, the market in Dunkerque opened before dawn and was bustling as the sun rose. Farmers brought their produce and stock to trade for fish and the specialties of the town; fishermen coming in from the sea brought live lobsters and other bounty. It all offered a wonderful opportunity for haggling and gossip.

Victoire had dressed in her plainest clothes and had borrowed a cloak from the maid at the Garçon Rouge and bought a small woven basket, so that she looked much the same as most of the women who attended the market. She had tucked her fair hair under a starched matron's cap and affected a strong Rouen accent whenever she stopped at a stall to ask a price.

The Englishwoman was easy to spot, for in spite of her French dress, her face was the milk-and-strawberry of true English girls. She had large blue eyes and faded brown hair under her hat, and her apron came from Suffolk, which was obvious from the style of smocking. For some time she sat alone, making no effort to converse with the women in the stalls on either side of her. Occasionally she exchanged a greeting with one of the buyers at the market, but otherwise she kept to herself.

Once she identified her quarry, Victoire did not hurry, for that would not serve her purpose. She approached the stand where the Englishwoman sat indirectly so that her true mission would not be obvious.

"When was that caught?" Victoire inquired, pointing at a bug-eyed fish lying on a slab. Very few of the fish in this stall had been sold, and Victoire suspected the reason was that the townspeople were keeping their distance from the Englishwoman.

The Englishwoman looked at her, a little startled at the accent. "Last night. They are fresh, all of them. They were caught and wrapped at once in straw, as you can see."

"What is the price?" Victoire asked.

"Two sous," said the Englishwoman. Her French was practiced but there was a tone to it that was ineffably English.

"Two?" Victoire inquired as if she thought the sum outrageous; it was expected as part of the dealing.

"Two," the woman answered, a bit more firmly. "It is fresh. No one brings fresher fish than my husband and his brothers. You may sniff it for yourself if you have any doubts."

"It would be hard to distinguish that fish with so many others around," said Victoire, waving a hand to the rest of the market. "The whole of this quarter of the town stinks of fish."

"I no longer notice," said the Englishwoman, a little spark of interest in her eyes now.

"So I would suppose," said Victoire, then dropped a slight curtsy. "I am Madame Vernet, Madame, and I am new to this place. I was hoping that I might come to know some of the women here, but they . . ." She let the phrase trail away to nothing.

"They are used to their own society," agreed the Englishwoman. "I know how difficult it can be to gain their friendship, and how little it requires to jeopardize it." There was a trace of bitterness in her voice now, and she tried to laugh to cover it. "I am English, you see, and they do not often permit me to forget it."

"You must be lonely," said Victoire with sympathy.

"There are times when I am. At other times fishermen come from home, and I do not feel so isolated." She sighed. "It has not happened much, recently."

Victoire did her best to appear surprised. "But English, in this part of the coast, surely there are many English here?"

"Not these days," said the Englishwoman. "They prefer to deal with the Dutch, for there is less interference."

"But . . ." Victoire chose her words very carefully. "I was told that often there were mariners here who carried secret cargo from France to England. A merchant I knew at home said he made a good profit on brandy sent to England clandestinely."

"Oh, that happens," said the Englishwoman, coloring a little. "But it is very dangerous now that the French have become more strict in . . . in so many things." There was a slight hesitation. "It must be for the good, of course."

"But I know how it is to be in a foreign place without the company of your own people," she said with sincerity. "How unfair to someone like you."

The Englishwoman smiled uncertainly. "My father might say so," she ventured at last. "But it is the way of the world, now that Napoleon is reigning here."

"Reigning?" Victoire asked, startled at the woman's choice of words.

"What else would you call it, now that he is First Consul and there are no others."

Victoire nodded, agreeing in spite of herself; she shifted the topic a bit. "If you could tell me, how much traffic of that sort goes on about here?" She saw the Englishwoman stiffen, and went on, "I'm curious because the merchant I knew made some claims that I find hard to believe."

"There is money to be made," said the Englishwoman, her face clouding. "But the risks are great."

"The merchant made it seem as if it were just a game. You know, saying that they would make the run at night without any lights, and there would be signals and transfers, sometimes at sea, sometimes in secret harbors." She was able to make it seem as if she longed for such adventure, which was nearer the truth than she wanted to admit.

"I have heard that the patrols of the French and the English both have been increased. If your merchant friend thinks it a game, then he is being a fool," said the Englishwoman. "No one carries special cargos for the sport of it, not these days."

"And what of other cargos?" asked Victoire innocently, concealing a frisson of danger. "Is everything done so honestly, even by the honest merchants?" She laughed at her own impertinence. "Your pardon, Madame, but it seems to me that those who are the most sanctimonious about minding the laws are merely the ones who have found a successful way to cheat."

The Englishwoman made a very French gesture of contempt. "It is all the navy now, in any case. They are everywhere, stopping honest fishermen and looking for spies and all the rest." She looked around nervously, and added in an undervoice,

"They say that there are fishermen who do that, too, but I know of none. And I would if they lived in Dunkerque."

"Of course you would," said Victoire as if the notion had just occurred to her. "I suppose you know all the English."

"Not all, but I know enough," she said obscurely. Then she sighed. "If war comes again, no doubt my husband will be detained because of me."

"Surely there is not going to be real war," prompted Victoire.

"It is coming," said the Englishwoman heavily. "It is in the air, like the smell of fish."

"Ah," said Victoire. "Perhaps you know more than most, living where you do and being English. I pray that we will not fight, for I hate to see our fine young men die." Her smile was roguish. "There are so many better things for young men to do."

It took the Englishwoman a short moment to answer. "My father says it'll not come, and my brother thinks it will not, but they are wrong." Her face darkened. "I have spoken to others, and they are afraid."

"Afraid?" Victoire prompted. She had sensed she was being watched, but she could not determine where the watcher was; it made her nervous.

"Fisherfolk do badly when navies battle. They are all troubled because once the guns sound, they will have to find other waters." She wiped her face with her apron.

"What woman does not fear for her men when there is war?" Victoire said this with great feeling, and added, "It's unfortunate that powerful men cannot find other ways to agree."

"Amen," whispered the Englishwoman. Then she smoothed her apron. "The price could be a single sou, since you have just come here."

Victoire realized she had learned all that she would be able to from the Englishwoman, and so she reached into her reticule and retrieved the coin. "Done!" she cried, and handed over her basket.

"Come again some time, Madame . . . Ver . . ."

"Vernet," said Victoire. "And perhaps I will." She took the basket back, and dropped the Englishwoman a sociable curtsy. "God send you a good profit and calm seas."

The Englishwoman smiled, and ducked her head politely.

As she made her way back through the market, Victoire decided she would ask the landlord at the Garçon Rouge to prepare the fish with a caper sauce.

* * *

They were almost ready to depart for Calais; Vernet had supervised the loading of their luggage and was now making a last check of their room to be certain that nothing had been left behind. He glanced at Victoire as he rummaged in the armoire. "You are satisfied then, that the woman knows nothing of the English landing?"

"Quite satisfied," said Victoire. She automatically smoothed the bed cover and then added, "I gave her every opportunity to reveal something about English landing here, but there was no suggestion of it in anything she said. I doubt she is clever enough to dissemble so expertly. Which, when you come to think of it, is all the more reason to be worried."

"Truly," said Vernet, closing the armoire. "There should be answers to my dispatches waiting for us by the time we reach Calais. Then we will decide what is to be done."

"Or it will be decided for us," said Victoire fatalistically, and followed her husband out to the waiting carriage. As she handed a doucement to the ostler, she remarked to Vernet, "I hope that someone has the good sense to pay attention to your warning."

"You mean to *your* warning," he said with a wink.

"It had best be your warning, or they will not heed it at all." She took her place in the carriage, wishing that she had a softer pillow for her back. But that would be a foolish extravagance, she reminded herself, and she had endured far worse than sore muscles in her travels. Her physician had said that it would require time for her to recover completely from the miscarriage, and that in time her muscles would be as strong as ever.

"Victoire?" Vernet asked as they set out. "Are you uncomfortable?"

"Only a little," she lied.

"At least there is one response," said Vernet as he came to their room in the Lanterne in Calais. "Bernadotte has sent this." He held out the response, which he had opened already. "Read it, and tell me what you think. He is suggesting—which is as good as ordering—that I go to Antwerp. He wishes me to act at once. Apparently he thinks that if the spies have landed, they are seeking to disrupt the negotiations to unite the Republics of France and Holland."

Victoire took the sheet and read it. "Ah. I see this is another man who consults his wife. You noticed that he indicates that his wife Desirée believes that the spies are bound there, and she has convinced him of it. I hadn't realized he relied on her so much. Look there: 'My dear wife wishes to preserve the safety of France as ardently as I do, and for that reason I am accepting her good counsel. She has much knowledge of these affairs and her mind is as keen as any man's. Therefore I will be guided by her and advise you to proceed as soon as possible to Antwerp.' Antwerp." Victoire shook her head.

"What is it?" Vernet asked, recognizing Victoire's expression of doubt. "What makes you question the orders?"

Victoire did not answer directly. She tapped her finger on the vellum. "Something is not quite as it should be, but . . . I am curious as to why . . ." Her words trailed off as she lapsed into deep thought.

Vernet sighed. "I suppose you will tell me when you have worked it through?"

Her smile was quick but preoccupied; already she was caught up in assessing the letter. "Naturally."

"Naturally," Vernet echoed with an affectionate gesture of resignation.

3

❧

IT WAS A small inn, far from prosperous. The innkeeper had inherited it from his father and somehow kept it open throughout the Revolution and the invasions that followed, though just barely. Now taxes threatened what the combined armies of three kings had failed to do—force him to close. He was therefore more pleased than annoyed when a party of twenty men woke him after midnight, demanding rooms and a meal. The landlord set about making them welcome, opening the taproom to the travelers while he filled the ewers in the guest rooms. He was bustling for the pantry to put together a cold supper for his guests when he realized some were speaking English, and was foolish enough to comment upon it.

They buried the innkeeper under his own midden pile.

There were half a dozen Gendarmes waiting for Vernet first thing the next morning; he hastened away with them for a day of conferring and evaluations, which left Victoire with little to do but darn socks and think. She kept to their room, half-listening to the bustle in the inn yard as she strove to turn the collar of his second-best uniform just one more time.

It was dusk by the time Vernet came back, apologizing as he opened the door. "I had no idea we would require such a long discussion, but there—"

"It is not important," said Victoire, who had not risen from the end of the bed where she sat. "I am pleased to have had the time to think. Truly, Lucien, I have put the hours to good use, I think." She indicated the uniform tunic. "And I do not mean that."

Vernet shook his head. "It is bad enough that you have had to pass the time alone, but you have had to have such thankless chores, as well."

"Never mind," she said, assuring him more emphatically. "I am certain that a little darning will not destroy my eyesight or

33

my fingers. And what I have decided is more important than darning, in any case."

"How do you mean?" Now he was curious, and he dropped his cap on the bed as he sat down in the single chair provided.

"I mean that I have considered that reply sent from Bernadotte, searching for what has rankled," she told him. "And I am more perplexed by it than ever." She looked at him, trying to discover if he wanted her to go on.

"Why is that?" asked Vernet, willing to encourage her.

"It bothers me that spies would enter France to disrupt negotiations in Holland. We have both remarked upon it. It is difficult and dangerous to land in France, but relatively easy to land in Holland. So if the negotiations are their destination, it makes no sense that they would go to the risk of landing here rather than sailing quite properly into a northern port in Holland, where there would be no trouble for them. Do you follow my thoughts?"

"So far," Vernet told her.

"They exposed themselves, these supposed spies, for no reason. Which means that they are fools. Which I do not believe." This last she said darkly. "If it's the fleet they seek, then it makes more sense that they are here, for Antwerp is a goodly distance from the fleet. But Boulogne-sur-Mer is south-west of here, and why would spies wishing to work against the fleet not attempt to land closer to it, if they are willing to risk landing in France at all? It is true that Boulogne-sur-Mer is directly on the road from here, but it's also a day by coach. Why would they not attempt to get as near to the fleet as possible? It would be more sensible to land here at Calais than at Dunkerque."

"I agree with you," said Vernet, listening attentively.

"Therefore, I come again to the fear that the spies are bound for Paris." She rose to her feet and began to pace. "You see, if they are going to Paris, then they might well want to land here, away from the Marine guards at Boulogne-sur-Mer, and not so near the border with Holland that they might encounter patrols there. They could travel to Paris quickly, but avoid the main road from here, and therefore not be subject to much inquiry. They might even—if they are very sly—come by way of Lille and Saint-Quentin. Those roads are not watched as the Calais-Amiens-Paris Road is, or the coast road, for that matter."

"It would take them longer," Vernet pointed out.

"Yes, perhaps. But they would have to hide a great deal on the main road, and I reckon that on the lesser roads they would not have to be so much on guard. Either way, they'll not reach

Paris quickly, but by coming on minor roads, they will arrive without anyone the wiser. Then they will be free to do whatever they came to do while we guard ships and diplomats." She stopped, looking out the window. "I listened today, and I think I heard more than four languages spoken in the inn yard. There was a fuss made over an English merchant, and soldiers came to search his luggage, and were not polite about it. The man was very put out, for he was only carrying goods to his factor in Paris, but they singled him out because they noticed him. His accent and his clothes made him conspicuous. That was what finally convinced me that they are striving to be invisible."

"And do you think they will succeed? Is it possible they will reach Paris, and Napoleon?" asked Vernet, feeling the first real grip of apprehension. "Surely no Englishman could get close enough—"

"That is assuming that the English ship carried only English; that is another question that I cannot dismiss," she reminded him. "There is some guess that there could be Frenchmen among them, Aristos seeking to return. If there are as many Frenchmen as English, then they will not be easily apprehended." She gave him a quirky smile. "And if that is what they have done, I will have to tell you that they are more subtle than I thought they were."

"But what you say is so complicated," protested Vernet.

"Only to our eyes, and only because we have to guess so much. For those men we are seeking, it is not complicated at all. We must not forget that." She cocked her head to the side. "What do you think?"

"I think," he said wearily, "that I had better go to Antwerp. I have only just convinced the Ministry of Police that we may have spies in Antwerp. I don't think it would be prudent to change quite yet. Bernadotte would not like me to act counter to his orders."

"No," she said. "He expects you to go to Antwerp." She looked Vernet directly in the eyes. "Therefore I should go to Paris."

"Victoire!" he objected. "I want you to come with me." He half-rose as he spoke.

She moved away from him. "I have given this my careful consideration. I believe it is necessary that I make the attempt to discover if the Englishmen have gone to Paris, and what their goals are." Her stance was very firm; Vernet recognized the stubborn set of her shoulders.

"And who do you think you will be able to convince in Paris?" he asked, not entirely without ire.

"I don't know. I don't know if I am correct in my thinking. But there are those who have some respect for my methods, and they might hear me out." She did not raise her voice but it was apparent that she had made up her mind.

"So you say," he countered.

"Berthier will give me his full attention, and so will Fouche, if I can get his attention at all. Both of them know in what danger Napoleon stands at all times." She came and stood directly in front of him. "And this way, whether you are on the right track or I am, one of us will be, and the promotion you seek will not be lost."

"Always practical," he said in aggravation.

"I am tired of darning your uniforms and living like paupers so that you can maintain your career, Lucien. If you are worthy of advancement—and you most truly are worthy—then it is time you were paid according to your worth which requires another promotion." She put her hands on her hips and all but dared him to argue with her.

"I don't want to be away from you, Victoire," he said softly.

"Nor I from you," she responded at once. "But we must think of what we seek and turn our efforts toward it."

"I understand," he said. "I do not want to agree, but—" He gestured his capitulation. "You will go to Paris, then, tomorrow?"

"While you go to Antwerp," she said. "There is a diligence leaving for Boulogne-sur-Mer at ten, and I'll purchase a seat on it, and go from there to Paris. The travel is not very grand, but it costs little, and that must be a virtue." She put her hands on his shoulders. "I will call on Bernadotte as soon as he is back in Paris, so that he'll know you are pursuing his orders."

"And you will tell him what you're doing?" asked Vernet.

"Possibly," she said after a short pause; she had felt a twinge of fear that troubled her. "Possibly not. It will depend on what I am able to discover."

"I will prepare dispatches for you to carry, then," said Vernet. "Since you're determined to do this, I'll make the most of it."

"Good," she approved, leaning down to kiss him gently.

"There is nothing good about it," he grumbled as he put his arms around her. "I am doing what I can to make the best of a bad situation."

"It will be better when you have demonstrated your devotion

to Napoleon and received your reward." She let him pull her down on his lap. "You will be able to afford all those little luxuries—"

"To say nothing of necessities," he interjected.

"—we have both missed, and you will not have to accept bribes in order to pay for your family." She leaned back as he kissed her and reveled in the new-born passion he showed.

"If I have to leave you," he said a short while later, already a bit breathless, "I want to make the best use of the time we have."

"Very wise," she murmured provocatively, and reached to unfasten her lacings. His hands were already there.

Colonel Sir Magnus Sackett-Hartley sat on the back of the cart as it trundled through Ressons-sur-Matz, his hat pulled down low over his forehead, his clothes smelling of cattle, for there were three young calves tethered in the cart, on their way to market.

"A fine way to return home," complained La Clouette from the front of the cart where he sat next to d'Estissac. "First we scurry through the night like rats, kill a harmless innkeeper like brigands, and now we plod along like peasants." Of the twenty men who had come ashore six nights before, this group was composed of eight of them. The other twelve had taken the more direct but more dangerous route along the coast to Boulogne-sur-Mer and south to Abbeville and Beauvais.

"You had best hope everyone believes we are peasants," remarked Cholet, who was walking beside the cart on the side opposite to Pasclos. "If they do not believe us, we will not accomplish our mission."

"I think we were wrong to divide into two groups," said La Clouette, finding something else to complain about.

"We voted for it," said Lieutenant Edward Constable, one of two Englishmen in this group of the spies. "You were for it, as I recall." He spoke French adequately, sounding faintly Belgian, but did his best not to speak at all.

"That was when we landed," said La Clouette.

"You were for it yesterday, or so you claimed," Sackett-Hartley pointed out. His French—thanks to his aunt—was excellent, and he spoke it without hesitation or effort.

"I had not thought it through," La Clouette whined. "I was afraid we would be noticed if there were too many of us, but I hadn't realized how exposed we would be, or how difficult our task could become. What if the others are caught?"

"We must trust them to keep silent, or make certain of their silence ourselves," said Cholet.

Brezolles looked around the square. "I will want to p-pray in church," he remarked to no one in particular.

"But how will we know we are safe?" La Clouette went on, paying no attention to Brezolles.

"We will know if the others join us in Paris," said Sackett-Hartley. "Until then, we will have to pray for them, and hope that God and luck are on our side." He indicated the village well. "We'd better fill the bladders here. Otherwise we might become thirsty on the road."

"What about buying a bottle or two of wine?" suggested d'Estissac. "I haven't had wine since the night after we landed."

"The villagers will expect us to drink something other than water," Cholet remarked. "They'll pay less attention if we purchase a few bottles."

"All right," said Sackett-Hartley. "Buy wine and bread and cheese, like any other farmer bound for market. And tell them that we are delivering these animals to the best inn at Creil; they might well believe it." He jumped off the end of the cart and trudged along beside it as they neared the well.

"I hate looking this way," muttered La Clouette. "I do not like to be mistaken for one of these louts."

"You had best hope that you are," said Cholet softly. "Or we will not arrive in Paris to do our work." He felt in his pocket for coins. "Bread, cheese, and wine," he said loudly enough to be heard by some of the villagers lingering on the street. "We will have meat later."

"When these beasts are delivered," added Sackett-Hartley, affecting a strong Artois accent. "They will feed us well."

"So you think," said Pasclos.

"We made a bargain," Sackett-Hartley declared.

"So we did," affirmed d'Estissac. "And he will uphold it." He looked around the square. "A pleasant enough place."

"Truly," said Cholet, and started toward a stall-fronted stop where cheeses were laid out. "Will two be enough for us, or should I purchase three?"

"Three," called Pasclos, and nodded to one of the townspeople. "I'm hungry."

"So am I," called Sackett-Hartley.

"Then four cheeses," said Cholet. "Possibly five."

"I'll see to getting wine," Pasclos volunteered, and noticed out of the corner of his eye that four old men sitting around a table near the well were listening intently.

"Make it hearty," Sackett-Hartley ordered.

"Naturally," said Pasclos.

"I think of our ... c-companions," said Brezolles. "I wish I knew th-they were making good prog-gress."

"They will do as they must," said Sackett-Hartley, more curtly than he liked.

"But still—" said Brezolles, and broke off as if embarrassed.

"We'll find out about their success when we see them again," Sackett-Hartley assured the young man, and frowned as he thought of the other twelve members of their mission who were—or ought to be—on the coast road, bound for Paris.

"Let's get our chores done," said La Clouette, for once not adding a complaint to his suggestion.

They set about refilling the water-bladders. Constable made sure the old Percheron pulling the cart was given water and a large handful of grain. There was nothing unusual about them, or so they all hoped. "Do you think the others will—" began d'Estissac, only to have Sackett-Hartley cut him off.

"We have the contract, and the innkeeper will honor it, no matter what other farmers bring him." His eyes shot warnings at the Frenchman. "Besides, our calves are the best. He would not have given us the order for them if he thought otherwise."

"That's so," said d'Estissac, chastened.

"And do not forget it," said Sackett-Hartley.

Cholet and Pasclos brought their purchases—Les Aix had gone for the bread, still as tongue-tied as he had ever been—but did not hurry to resume their travels.

Brezolles, who at twenty-five was increasingly haunted by memories of his escape from Paris at the height of the Terror, turned to Sackett-Hartley. "I w-would like a little t-time to pray while we're here. The ch-church is just there."

Sackett-Hartley did his best not to sigh, for Brezolles had been stopping in churches since they landed in France. "Don't be long about it, if you feel you must," he said, trying to be pragmatic and kind at once.

"I won't." He managed a twitch of a smile. "I k-keep thinking of your unc-cle."

"So do I," Sackett-Hartley assured him. "He set a splendid example. I regard him as my mentor."

"He did so much for my family." He looked around, suddenly uneasy as he realized that they might be overheard.

"As you did for him, I'm certain," said Sackett-Hartley smoothly.

Brezolles walked away, hurrying toward the church.

Sackett-Hartley watched him and frowned. Brezolles was getting jumpy, reacting with anger and suspicion when anyone questioned him. He hoped that there would not be any incidents here, for villagers remembered incidents with strangers. He turned away as he heard d'Estissac call out to him. "What is it?"

"Do you have the name of the man we are to contact upon our arrival?" It was an innocent enough question, but nonetheless Sackett-Hartley stiffened.

"Most certainly," he said, trying to appear relaxed. "You worry too much, cousin."

"Well, there is much at stake here." He nodded toward the cart. "Especially for the calves."

"Yes, indeed," said Sackett-Hartley, trying to behave as his uncle might have in just such a situation. "In these times there is always something to worry about." Then in a lower voice he added, "But our friend has said he will watch for any problems and assist us in eliminating them." They all had been told that a high government official would do his best to assure they were not interfered with. He spoke more loudly, "But our concern now has to be selling the calves in the most profitable manner."

"And we'd best worry about them," said d'Estissac. La Clouette was devouring a large hunk of bread, chewing with determination.

Sackett-Hartley glanced at Lieutenant Constable, noticing that he was fretful. "Do not worry, we can afford more cheese."

"Good," said Lieutenant Constable.

Sackett-Hartley took the food Cholet offered him, and then helped himself to a deep pull on the bottle of wine that was passing among them. "The thing is," he said when he was through and had handed the bottle to Constable, "we have to keep moving. For the landlord as well as the calves. Time is important."

Les Aix watched the square narrowly. "It is troublesome, having to depend so much on a man we don't know." He glanced at Sackett-Hartley. "Or is it?"

Sackett-Hartley had occasional doubts himself, but he was not about to reveal them to this company. "We have nothing to fear."

"Either he will buy the calves, or we will sell them to someone else," said Cholet, making a covert warning of this to the rest.

"Very true," said d'Estissac, his words muffled by cheese.

"Should have been a priest, Brezolles should," grumbled La Clouette, but no one listened to him. "He's got no business coming on a mission like this."

Sackett-Hartley frowned as he watched for Brezolles, and wondered again if La Clouette was right: had it been wise to bring him on this mission? He had been asking himself what his uncle would do in his position, and so far he had not been able to figure it out.

Vernet handed the four sealed dispatches to his wife, and shook his head regretfully. "I wish we didn't have to separate, Victoire. And I wish it weren't necessary for you to take the risk of carrying these."

"But it *is* necessary," she reminded him as she struggled with the buttons on her capped traveling cloak. It was very early and the dawn light did not reach the rooms on this side of the inn.

"I hope that it is. I hope that it'll prove valuable." His expression darkened. "I don't like it when we are apart. I almost look forward to the days when it will be my rotation to man the desk in Paris. We've spent too much time apart."

"There we are in agreement," she said emphatically. Her eyes brightened. "But it is the work you have chosen to do, and you are now one of the five most important men in the Gendarmes, so we must accustom ourselves to it." She smiled without too much effort.

Vernet shook his head. "Much as I treasure your excellent sense, there are times, dear wife, I wish you had a little less of it."

"To be candid, so do I," she admitted, and leaned forward to kiss him. "Still, it is my nature to be as I am, and I thank God that you do not require I become a simpering echo, as so many husbands do."

"That would be an Herculean task," he said, chuckling at the thought.

"Well, so I think, too, but you've seen how many women become nothing more than dolls for their husbands: pretty, petty, and pampered." She pursed her mouth in distaste. "Or they become all but harlots, the coins in which their husbands trade for advantage."

"Neither is acceptable to me," said Vernet at once.

"It's to your credit." She placed her hands in his. "I wish you

Godspeed, Lucien, and I hope you'll be in Paris again before the month is out."

His kiss was as swift as it was passionate. "There. Now you must hurry or the diligence will be gone."

She stepped back at once. "You're an irritatingly sensible man yourself," she chided him gently. "Take all my love with you."

"And mine with you," he said as he watched her place the dispatches in her reticule as she started toward the door. It struck him afresh that he missed her whenever she was gone.

At Boulogne-sur-Mer the next morning a garrulous widow took a seat in the diligence as it left the inn at first light, and regaled the passengers throughout the morning with recitations of the virtues of her grandchildren in such meticulous detail that Victoire wondered if the children could actually exist. While the widow held forth, Victoire's mood sank, and though she rallied herself inwardly, she could not rid herself of the disappointment and distress she felt whenever she allowed herself to dwell on the child she had lost. Vernet had not chided her for it as many another husband might have done, but she sensed his sorrow in his silence. As the proud grandmother rattled on, Victoire did her best to listen attentively without being seized by regrets. She kept the dispatches she carried in her reticule, and that she held in her lap with both hands.

"They are surely the finest children in Quend," their grandmother affirmed. "All three boys are upstanding lads, bright in their studies and devoted to their parents. The two girls are biddable and so very pretty that even the priest says they were born to break hearts." She looked at the man opposite her, a reedy fellow in unfashionable clothes and the demeanor of a clerk. "What do you think? Am I not blessed?"

"I would suppose that they were beaten every day if they are so pleasant. The children you beat always offer you the best face, that's what I've found," said the man harshly. "After twelve years as a schoolmaster, I have never seen it to fail. So your son must exercise his arm on them often, to have such children."

The widow looked affronted, sputtered that these children were not wild animals needing the taste of a whip to tame them, but perfect and angelic creatures.

"Not in my experience," said the schoolmaster. To the relief of all the passengers inside the diligence, the widow at last fell silent, and remained that way until she was set down at Vron, where all the passengers had a glimpse of her son and one of her perfect grandsons waiting for her in a dog-cart pulled by a stocky spotted pony.

"Father has a temper, that's clear," stated the schoolmaster with authority.

Victoire, looking at the old woman and her family, thought that it was more likely that the widow had filled her empty hours with idealizing her family. She recalled how her father had conveniently forgotten her mother's faults after she died, and eventually had persuaded himself that they did not exist at all.

At Rue the diligence was joined by an escort of Guard—just two tired corporals on horseback—who examined the possessions of the passengers while they had a fast luncheon at the local posting inn. In theory the escort was to provide protection against the robbers who preyed on the coaching routes, but in reality it was to prevent spies from getting to Paris.

These were dragoons, likely sent from some depot nearby. They wore tight cream-colored coats of a style similar to those of the infantry. These differed from the foot soldiers' uniforms in the bright red of their tunics and gray riding breeches tucked into standard black riding boots. Both of the corporals' uniforms were visibly patched and their mounts were second rate. Their high brass helmets vaguely reminded Victoire of those she had seen portrayed as being worn by Grecian soldiers in frescoes on the walls of a Roman villa they had stayed at in the Cisalpine Republic. Along with his sword, each of the two cavalrymen carried a short musket known as a carbine.

When the taller of the two corporals asked to search Victoire's reticule, she hesitated to hand it over.

"Come, Madame," said the shorter, who was enjoying giving orders.

Victoire opened the reticule, saying as she did, "I believe it would be best if you merely looked inside."

"What's the trouble? You have jewels you don't want the others to know about?" asked the shorter as he took the reticule and upended it, letting the contents fall onto the table in the taproom.

"That," she said dryly as the dispatches scattered on the table, "is the reason."

The taller corporal had read one of the addresses and turned pale. "These are not official, are they?"

"They are. I am Madame Vernet, My husband is Inspector-General Vernet." She stood a little straighter.

"On a common diligence," scoffed the shorter corporal.

In spite of herself, Victoire blushed. "It is more fitting for me to travel this way and arrive safely than to demand an escort and make my travels known," she said bluntly. "And it would have been a successful effort if you had not required me to hand over my reticule," she added directly to the shorter corporal, "and if you had respected what I said." She indicated the others watching.

The shorter corporal made the mistake of trying to bluster his way out of the error. "And who's to say that these are genuine dispatches? You say you are the wife of Inspector-General Vernet, but why should we believe you?"

Controlling her temper, Victoire answered, "If you will do yourself the favor of inspecting the seals on the dispatches, you will recognize them."

"Unless the seal is stolen," said the shorter corporal.

Here the taller intervened. He had been inspecting one of the dispatches and now his manner was decidedly more polite. "They are authentic seals, and we've no report of stolen ones," he said as he gathered up the dispatches and placed them—along with a vial of hartshorn, a dozen coins, and a bottle of scent—in Victoire's reticule once again. "Sorry to have done this, Madame Vernet. I guess it was a mistake."

"It certainly was," she said with asperity. "And you may be sure that I'll mention it when I deliver the dispatches." She took her reticule from the corporal. "I want your names and the name of your commanding officer."

The shorter once again blundered. "I don't see any call for that."

The taller said, "I am Corporal Jean-Marie Feuille. He is Corporal Benoit Cruche. Our lieutenant is Yves Durand." He saluted, and glanced at Corporal Cruche to be sure he had done the same.

Grudgingly Corporal Cruche said, "At your service, Madame."

Victoire regarded them evenly, concealing the quiver of apprehension that had taken hold of her. "Belated though it is."

"We have our duty to do," said Corporal Feuille apologetically.

"And I have mine, though you may well have compromised it by this display." She started back toward the diligence. "I trust your mistakes won't be compounded."

"Of course not," said Corporal Feuille. "We will take care to see you are protected, and the dispatches you carry."

"How wise," she said.

When the diligence was under way once again, the schoolmaster gave Victoire a long, critical look. "What an unexpected pleasure it is, Madame, to have a woman of your position in our company."

Victoire resisted the urge to upbraid the man. "I am a traveler, just as the rest of you are," she said in the hope that he would be satisfied with that declaration; she already felt dangerously exposed.

"If that is the fiction you like," said the schoolmaster with a conspiratorial leer. "There must be mischief afoot for your husband to entrust his dispatches to you instead of the soldiers. Has there been bribery or some other act they might wish to conceal?" His eyebrows raised and lowered. "Or is this a matter for discretion, some indication that the wife or daughter of a high-ranking officer has been found in the wrong bed?"

"Nothing of the sort," said Victoire bluntly. "Not that I am privy to what my husband bids me carry," she added mendaciously so that she would no longer be pressed for juicy details.

"We will keep your secret for you, whatever it is," promised another of the travelers, a portly man of middle years who carried a case filled with upholstery material.

This time Victoire did not respond, for she realized that it would be impossible to convince the schoolmaster or the other passengers of the truth—that she was traveling the least expensive way she could because she could not afford any other transportation, and not because she was attempting to deliver the dispatches in secret.

"Your husband must be a very crafty man," said the cloth-factor, his prominent eyes bulging a little. "To think of sending you on such a mission, and by such a ruse."

"He is," said Victoire, watching the other passengers nod, smug in the knowledge that they were now privy to a state secret.

"Do not worry, Madame," said the schoolmaster. "We will not ask you any more awkward questions. We are aware when we ought to keep quiet."

Victoire knew better than to suppose it was so.

4

THE OFFICER WATCHED until the footman had left the room. Then he unfolded the newly cleaned and braid-covered uniform coat over his desk. As he expected, a folded piece of vellum fell onto the desk. Carefully setting the coat aside, he read the note.

It had begun; the sacred mission was under way. He was to watch for anything that might warn the mission had been compromised. Its last line implied he should kill anyone that got too close or threatened the mission. It was signed by the secretary of the monarch, to whom he had once pledged loyalty. He had broken that oath.

Their next posting inn was halfway between Abbeville and Pont-Remy, where they arrived shortly after sunset, the lanterns on the coach doing little to augment the fading light. The ostlers hurried out to greet the passengers and tend to the team, and were at once gratified and alarmed to discover that the Guard escort had assigned itself the task of watching after one of the passengers.

"You must assign her a private parlor; she is the wife of an important officer carrying secret dispatches," ordered Corporal Feuille to the landlord as he entered the Vigne et Tonneau ahead of the rest. "She is under our protection."

The landlord glowered, then wreathed his pliant face in smiles. "Of course, of course, of course," he enthused. "I will tend to it at once."

"And be certain that a servant sleeps outside of her room tonight," said Corporal Cruche. "She has important information entrusted to her that must not fall into the wrong hands."

Victoire looked at the two soldiers in exasperation, and said to them as calmly as she could, "It might be wise not to discuss my mission." The fear that she had succeeded in mastering reasserted itself.

"You may rely on our discretion," said Corporal Feuille, bowing to her a little as he stood aside to permit the other pas-

46

sengers to enter the inn. "We have been warned about the danger of too much loose talk, and we are guarding against it."

"Do you think so?" Victoire asked, but the question was lost in the general babble of arrival.

Within the hour all the passengers had been assigned rooms and had their luggage deposited in the proper chambers while the landlord presided over the taproom, serving generous amounts of red wine to wash down the lamb stew he offered his guests.

Victoire dined on collops of pork cooked with mushrooms in a heavy wine sauce in the isolation of the private parlor; there had been no mention of cost, but she knew it would be more than what the others were paying for their simpler fare. "I am convinced your intentions are good," she remarked to Corporal Feuille, who had appointed himself her servant for the evening, "but I fear that you are doing little more than making me conspicuous."

"Permit me to be the judge of that," said Corporal Feuille.

"Are you convinced the isolation is necessary?" Victoire inquired as she took a long sip of wine and listened to the rumble of conversation echoing in the corridor.

"Most definitely," said Corporal Feuille. "We have little say as to who comes to the taproom, but here we are entitled to admit no one but yourself." He was proud of this stratagem, and it showed.

Victoire realized that she would not be able to change his mind easily, and so she tried a different tack. "But who's in the taproom you could suspect?"

"There are travelers," he said obscurely, and made sure her wineglass was full.

"Hardly astonishing in a posting inn," said Victoire, and sighed a little when she realized that Corporal Feuille had not recognized the humor of her remark.

"You speak truly, Madame Vernet," he responded earnestly. "We have searched their luggage, but there is nothing that cannot be properly accounted for. Even the musician has his instrument with him, a horn. He says he earns his bread with it. The landlord has agreed to charge him less if he will play tonight."

"A musician," said Victoire, who thought that there were few groups of people more harmless to the Republic than musicians.

"He is bound for Paris. He carries a letter engaging him to play at the Hotel de Ville. He claims he has recently come from England, where he was engaged by the manager of a theater there, but that might not be the truth, musicians being what they are." He watched her eat, unable to wholly conceal his own hunger.

"There is no reason to suspect him, is there?" she inquired, and continued to eat.

"No, nor the three men traveling in their own carriage. They have bona fides from the magistrate at Dreux, who states that they are traveling on business for the town. That accounts for their two out-riders, their coachman, and servants. One of them is an English valet. We took care to be certain he is a true valet, and not a rogue intent on deceiving us." He was proud of himself and expected praise.

From the taproom came the sound of a horn playing a series of hunting calls, and then the first phrases of a concerto by Mozart. Without the orchestra, the music seemed strangely disembodied.

"I see," she said. "And how did you arrive at that conclusion, pray?"

"We asked about the care of coats and the proper way to shine boots. The valet knew it all, and the latest fashion in tieing neck cloths. He offered to show us how the Beau Monde was done."

Victoire took another slice of bread and considered everything she had heard. "How many are there in the party, in total?"

"Oh, possibly ten or eleven," said Corporal Feuille. "Corporal Cruche is the one who has elected to deal with the stablehands. He will know more about the coachman and the others." He smiled.

"And that will satisfy you, will it?" she asked, and had another sip of the wine. She sighed, for it was very good, but it awakened again the fear of what it would cost. It was useless to suppose that her guardian corporals would be willing to pay for the position they had imposed upon her.

"It will be within the scope of our duty," he said, his head held very high. "And then I will be able to tell everyone how we have helped to assist an Inspector-General through caring for his wife."

"Quite an accomplishment," said Victoire, making no effort to disguise her sarcasm. "I am impressed."

"And perhaps you will mention the service we have rendered to your husband when you are once again in his company? Tell him of the good service we have rendered you?" The hopeful light in his eyes was almost comical, so eager and openly hun-

gry for advancement that Victoire very nearly granted him a
modicum of support. But he pressed his luck and lost his advantage when he said, "You do understand how we have helped
you, don't you?"

"Oh, I do understand," said Victoire, and finished her supper.

The chambermaid was waiting for Victoire as she went up to
her assigned room. She curtsied and called Victoire "Madame"
a great many times, then indicated the way she had unpacked
all of Victoire's things and deposited them in the armoire. "But
I did not touch the small case, the one you and the soldiers said
I was not to open."

"Yes," said Victoire, aware that the maid would expect a
doucement for her efforts, needless though they were. She
looked at her empty luggage and wondered how long it would
take her to repack it, for she needed only her night rail, her
robe, and the one traveling costume for the morning. All the
rest might better have been left in her luggage.

There was a sound at the door, and she turned to see a stranger glancing in. "Yes?" she said in a tone calculated to halt any
advances and to conceal her apprehension.

"You are the Inspector-General's wife?" the man asked, his
accent striving to be as fashionable as possible. "I am Claude
Montrachet; I play the horn." He lifted the case he carried so
that Victoire could see it. "I'm honored to be at the same inn
as you are, Madame." He bowed slightly, then went off down
the corridor without further ado.

"A nice-spoken gent," said the maid as she watched the musician disappear at the end of the hall. "They're often like that,
aren't they—musicians?"

"I suppose they are," said Victoire, paying little heed. She indicated the bed. "Did you use my sheets, or will I have to
change it?"

"I used Madame's sheets," the chambermaid assured her.
"And I have made sure there are no holes in any of the blankets, or feathers lost from the pillows. The blankets are not
musty and there are no mice in the room."

"Very good," said Victoire, and reluctantly dug into her reticule for two silver coins to hand to the young woman. "For
your good service," she said as she offered them.

The chambermaid curtsied and then did her best to smile.
"Thank you, Madame," she said eagerly. "Thank you very
much." She seemed inclined to linger.

Victoire did not want that, so she yawned conspicuously and

tugged at the fichu she had worn around her shoulders. "Travel is so exhausting," she hinted.

At that the chambermaid curtsied and started toward the door. "Sleep well, Madame. I will be sure you are roused in time to have breakfast before your diligence leaves."

Aware that this service would also require a doucement, Victoire sighed. "Thank you." She trusted that the lack of enthusiasm would be attributed to fatigue instead of the cost.

"My pleasure to serve you, Madame," said the chambermaid as she backed out the room and closed the door.

Victoire sat down on the bed and felt for the money-belt she wore around her waist. It was depleted beyond her expectations, and she began to worry that she would not be able to finish the journey without stringent economies. Perhaps, she thought, she could plead travel sickness at the next stop, and not have to pay for meals. That would save her a little, unless her two self-appointed guardians should override her orders.

Methodically she opened the case and took out the pistol Vernet had given her, wishing it would banish the fright that niggled at her. She charged it with care, then slipped it under the pillows, satisfied that she had taken every reasonable precaution. Next she deposited her reticule under the other pillow, and then she began to undress, shivering a little at the chill in the air. Then she repacked most of her luggage. How very tedious this journey was becoming, she thought as she took down her blonde hair and began to brush it. When that was done she braided it loosely and secured it with a ribband, sighing a little as she turned back the covers and slid into the bed, reaching to pinch out the candles on the stand beside the bed next to the ewer of water before drawing the bed curtains around her. In the darkness she tucked the dispatches into the money-belt that she continued to wear, and wished she were not afraid.

As she lay back she turned her mind to what she would tell Bernadotte and Berthier. With those perplexing possibilities in her thoughts, she drifted into an uneasy sleep.

Two of the men who had arrived in the private carriage were waiting in the stable yard when the kitchen door to the inn opened and Claude Montrachet came out, a pistol instead of an instrument's case in his hand.

"Why the hell why you taken so long?" one of the two men demanded in English that sounded of Northumberland.

"The scullions were still working and I didn't want them to see me," said Montrachet, also in English though his was flavored with French vowels and r's. "And I might ask you why you are here and not farther along the road."

"We had to replace one of the wheelers," said the first man. "It took a day while the horse was traded. In these towns such things can't be hurried."

"You are more behind schedule than ever," said Montrachet, making it an accusation.

"It couldn't be helped," the first man insisted.

"If we're out here too long, we might be noticed. And suspected," the other man declared. "If only those soldiers weren't here."

"They're no danger to us," said Montrachet. "They're all puffed up with guarding that officer's wife." His chuckle was low and unpleasant.

"You don't suppose there's anything to their claims, do you?" the second asked. "Surely she'd have more escort than that if she had anything important with her, wouldn't she?"

"Do you think she really is carrying anything important?" asked the first at the same time, looking around nervously.

Montrachet shook his head. "I doubt even Napoleon's officers are that foolish. But it might be wise to be certain," he added with a significant nod.

"You're not planning—" the first said.

"Let me worry about what I am planning," said Montrachet. "If we can gain useful information before we join up with Sackett-Hartley once more, then we can be of more use to him than we are now." He looked around the inn yard. "In the meantime, you'd better get back to your rooms, unless you have something more to tell me?"

"Nothing much. Our weapons are in the floor of the coach. So far the patrols have not thought to look there." The second man was not as nervous as the first, but he was not at ease, either. "We have a pair of pistols in the coach, in case there are questions about protection, and those the patrols have ignored."

"More fool they," said Montrachet. He held up his pistol, a small masterpiece by Manton. "This is easily concealed in the case with my horn." His face registered distress. "I used to love music. Once we are back in France and in our rightful positions once again, I swear I will have that damned thing melted down for scrap." He spat.

"Hush," warned the second man. "Someone might hear."

"What matter?" Montrachet said, but lowered his voice as he did. He started to smile and then his expression soured. "We should not have been delayed as long as we have been."

"The papers were not ready," said the first man, repeating what had been said many times.

"Still, we should have been in Paris before now. Sackett-Hartley is counting on us to have found a place to live while we complete our mission. He will not be pleased when he learns that we have arrived late." He stiffened as he heard a sound on the other side of the inn yard; he brought his pistol up, motioning his two companions to silence. "Is anyone there?" he called softly in French.

A brindled mongrel with elements of hound, spaniel, and terrier made a tentative approach, scruffy tail wagging uncertainly.

"The ostlers' watchdog," said the second man. "They told me he was fierce."

"Let us not put this to the test," suggested Montrachet. "Very well. I will not meet with you again until Paris." He started away, then turned back. "You will probably want to put up for the night in Beauvais. I will stay in Auteuil or Andeville so that we will not encounter each other again."

The first man nodded. "We will take care to obey you."

"Good. A chance like this, happening once, will deserve no attention, but if it happens again, questions might be asked." Montrachet gestured to the other two. "Your papers are in order now, aren't they?"

"Perfect," said the second man.

"They had better be," said Montrachet, and slipped back into the inn by the pantry door.

The two men regarded one another in the faint light. "What do you think?" asked the second after a short time.

"I think we'd better return to our rooms, or someone will wonder if we're ill and have remained in the necessary house to conceal it." The first indicated the small buildings at the far end of the inn yard. "You had better complain at breakfast. Say you're feeling liverish."

The second shrugged. "If you think it's advisable."

"It will stop questions," said the first, and pointed to the side entrance of the inn, which most of the guests used for their forays to the necessary houses. "Wait three minutes and follow me."

The second shrugged again, this time with a trace of irritation. "I don't know why I should be the one—"

"Because you made the biggest fuss about supper," said the first, and left his companion alone in the inn yard with the mongrel fawning at him in the faint hope of getting a scrap of food.

* * *

Victoire was not certain what had brought her awake, but her eyes were suddenly open though she remained wholly unmoving as she listened intently, her pulse fast and loud. Much as she wanted to peek through the bed-curtains, she dared not.

Another noise, this one sharper without being much louder, caught her attention. She recognized the sound of faint footsteps now, and she slipped her hand under the pillow, searching for her charged pistol. Her fingers closed on the butt and she felt the first surge of excitement over her fright.

There was a faint click and the soft complaint of a hinge—Victoire suspected the armoire was being opened—then the muffled sound of her clothes being searched. It was time to act. Quelling her fear, Victoire sat up slowly, taking care to make no sound. When she had drawn up one leg to give her some stability, she prepared herself. Finally she pulled the pistol out and reached for the bed-curtain.

"That will do," she said as she flung the bed-curtain back. Her pistol was steady in her hand. She blinked against the darkness, able to make out little more than a vague shape in the open door of the armoire.

The man swore as he swung around and fired in her direction. The flame from the barrel of his pistol marked his position. The ball ripped into the bed-curtains above her head.

Victoire fired and had the satisfaction of hearing the intruder cry out, and in the next moment there was the sound of his pistol dropping and a sharp, hissed oath. As her eyes readjusted to the darkness Victoire saw the intruder bend to retrieve his discharged pistol and then break toward the door.

"Come back here!" shouted Victoire, knowing that the two shots would certainly wake most of the inn. *"Stop! Thief!"*

There was a bustle in the next room, and then the sleepy voice of the landlord on the ground floor was heard, demanding that the thief stop.

"Catch him!" Victoire shouted as she clambered out of bed. It was not proper for her to venture out in nightclothes. She compromised by standing in her open doorway and shouting as loudly as possible, "Stop that man! Catch him!"

A door at the end of the hall flew open and one of the passengers, still belting his robe, rushed into the hall. "Thief! Thief!" he shouted.

There were other calls and cries now, so jumbled that Victoire knew no sense could be made of them. She abandoned her place at the door and went to throw open the window and call down to the ostlers. "Stop thief!" she yelled as she saw a shadowy figure flee toward the fruit trees at the back of the inn.

Corporal Feuille, his robe open and his nightshirt untidy, called to her from the door, hefting his carbine. "We are in pursuit, Madame."

"And too late," she amended. "He appears to be getting away," she declared, pointing to where the figure had vanished.

"Corporal Cruche is—" Corporal Feuille began.

Victoire cut him short. "Corporal Cruche is not going to be able to catch him unless he has a horse saddled and waiting." She pulled the window closed as she saw Corporal Cruche in a flapping robe rush out into the inn yard. The fear that had held her vanished, leaving her momentarily weak.

"You can't be sure, Madame," said Corporal Feuille, clearly feeling distressed.

"I have just seen it," said Victoire, resisting the urge to yell at the Corporal. "Where is the landlord?"

"Below," said Corporal Feuille, baffled by the question. "But I assure you that you do not requi—"

"I want all the rooms checked at once. I want to know if one of his guests was in my room," said Victoire with great presence of mind. She stopped at the bed long enough to put her pistol down on the nightstand, then felt in the armoire for her robe, which she drew on as she came to the door, prepared now to face the censure of her fellow travelers. "I think he was wounded."

"Madame?" Corporal Feuille said, following her as she started down the stairs.

"Well, I fired at him, and he swore. He also dropped his pistol, so I suspect he is wounded. That may be of some help when you go to search for him." She was near the ground floor, but she turned and looked back up the stairs, and noticed that half of the guests were out of their rooms, muttering and milling about. "And it would be a good idea if everyone returned to their rooms as well. I might not be the only one who has had a night visitor."

"What do you mean?" asked the landlord, who had heard the last of this.

"I mean that if the man is a thief, he might have taken valuables from others," said Victoire as patiently as she could. "Hurry, man, have your servants speak to everyone." She gestured to the inn. "If the man is a guest, you will find it out quickly. If it is a thief from the outside, perhaps someone in the kitchen or the stables saw him."

The landlord was sufficiently in awe of Victoire's position that he did not hesitate to take his orders from a woman. He called aloud to his cook and the two women who served as serving maids in the taproom. "Hurry. Be up with you and about your searches."

Corporal Feuille had gone back up the stairs in a huff and was suggesting to the guests to report to him all they had heard and seen. He did not tell them to go back to their rooms.

Then Corporal Cruche came puffing in from outside, his rifle held negligently. He looked at the landlord. "The fellow has run off through your orchard, or so it appears."

The landlord looked truly distressed. "Did you follow him?"

"No further than the trees," said Corporal Cruche, and indicated his bare feet. "I should have pulled on my boots."

"So you should," said Victoire, acutely aware of her own bare feet. "Did you see him?"

"Just a man in a dark cloak. He was running fast." Corporal Cruche straightened up as if determined to put the best face on this reprehensible incident. "But as soon as it is light I will try to track him."

"Enterprising," said the landlord, as anxious as the corporal to have it appear that he was doing everything he could to apprehend the criminal. He turned to Victoire again. "You see? They are taking care to respond to the danger."

"They are soldiers," said Victoire testily. She folded her arms, resting them over the money-belt. "It is their task to do this."

"Yes, certainly it is," said the landlord, bent on soothing her. "And Madame, I wish you to understand that considering what terrible thing has happened to you while at the Vigne et Tonneau, there will of course be no charge for your room, for certainly it is my duty to make sure every traveler may stay here without any inconvenience."

"Thank you," said Victoire, relieved in spite of herself, for she was already thinking that there might be other charges made on her account if the landlord decided that the events of the night had been at her instigation.

"It is only fitting. And I pray you will so inform your husband, Madame, when you are reunited with him."

"I certainly will," she said. "And I would like to tell him that the thief was apprehended."

The landlord shrugged. "It would seem that this—"

"You have a dog, haven't you?" asked Victoire, who expected that this inn was very much as all inns were. "Could he not be put to use?"

The landlord waved his hand to show what an absurd notion she had. "He is not a tracker, but a ratter. I doubt he would be able to find a joint of beef in a thicket."

"But why not give him the opportunity," Victoire said, not expecting the landlord to agree. She looked around. "I want two branches of candles in my room while I make a complete search of it."

"Yes," said the landlord promptly. "Yes, indeed. It will be tended to at once." He clapped his hands loudly and summoned one of the chambermaids, who appeared to be half-asleep.

"And you might tell the rest of your guests to do the same," Victoire said, hoping that this time someone would pay attention.

"We will attend to that," said the landlord, with a nod toward the two corporals. "I warrant these two soldiers know the way to manage this best."

She bit back a caustic remark, saying only, "When the maid has brought the candles I would appreciate a cup of chocolate, if you can provide one."

"Certainly," said the landlord huffily, resenting the implication that his inn would not have such a luxury to offer his guests. "I will order it at once."

And normally charge all that he could, thought Victoire as she watched the landlord tromp off toward the kitchen. She hesitated at the foot of the stairs, then started up them, determined to set about her task as soon as possible. The money-belt with its additional cargo of dispatches suddenly felt very heavy.

Victoire's search was unnecessarily thorough, but she wanted it to be understood that she had done everything that might be expected of her. She saw that the ball from the pistol had passed through the thin cloth that hung over the bed and lodged in the wall. The hole was tiny, confirming her impression that the pistol the thief had carried was smaller than even her own. As she repacked her luggage for the second time that night, she declared to the chambermaid, "There is nothing missing."

"Thank God and the Virgin for that." the chambermaid said, stifling a yawn. "I will tell the landlord. He will be gratified."

"So I hope," said Victoire, sitting down on the edge of the bed. She was very tired but so keyed-up that she knew it was useless to try to sleep again that night. Her back ached and she could feel the drag of her muscles. "Where is that chocolate?"

"I will go and fetch it," offered the chambermaid, looking around the room once more. "And you actually shot at him?"

"And hit him, I think," said Victoire as she reached for her pistol, deciding to clean it in the morning, perhaps while traveling.

"How could you do such a thing?" marveled the chambermaid.

"Shoot a thief?" asked Victoire.

"Fire a pistol." The chambermaid shuddered and the flames of the candles on the branch she held quivered in sympathy. "I should never be able to. I wouldn't dare to."

"You might think otherwise if you found a stranger in your room at night."

The chambermaid looked shocked and gestured in confusion. "You are very brave, Madame, braver than any woman I have known, to face a dangerous thief as you did, with a gun, and firing it. I have never known any woman who could do that before. Never in my entire life."

"I doubt that very much," said Victoire with unexpected mildness as she attempted to stop the chambermaid from blithering. "Most women are very brave indeed. They are so brave that they do not know it." She looked away from her things and sighed. "It is possible that the thief was attempting to find something other than money. I am aware of that."

"Madame?" said the chambermaid as she lingered at the door. "You don't mean that he intended to . . . harm you?"

Victoire turned toward her. "Not the way you mean." She waved the thought away. "Go. I want the chocolate, and I need time to think."

"Yes, Madame," said the chambermaid with a hurried curtsy before she hastened away down the stairs.

Victoire stared around her room and sighed. Little as she wished to admit it, she was shaken. Her body was stiff and unwieldy, as if it belonged to someone else and she was only borrowing it. Shock made her slightly nauseated. How could she sleep again tonight? A grue crawled up her spine. She clutched her arms around herself and hung on, worried that she might start to tremble. Beneath her arms she felt the money belt, and for an instant that made her apprehension worse.

What had the man wanted? What was he searching for? Was he truly after money, or had he been seeking the dispatches? How could he know of them, or what they were about? She tried to sort out her thoughts, but those three questions revolved in her mind, fed by her lack of answers. She sank down onto the bed. What would she tell Vernet when she saw him? Would she alarm him unduly if she voiced her suspicions about the thief? She did not want him to add worries for her to the demands of his work, but if she did not warn him, might he not be more vulnerable than if she remained silent?

The chambermaid returned, carrying a tray with a tall pot and a mug upon it. "Your chocolate, Madame." She set this on the dressing table. "And I would probably have cognac if I had been through what you have suffered tonight."

"Hardly suffered," said Victoire brusquely, rising. She could smell the chocolate and it made her very hungry for the drink, as if it were meat instead of liquid.

"The landlord has asked to see you before you depart in the morning. He made me be sure I told you." This was delivered with another short curtsy. "Good night, Madame. Do not fear, you are guarded now. I will rouse you in good time." It was apparent from her tone of voice that she did not relish the prospect of being up again in two hours.

"Thank you," said Victoire as she poured her chocolate.

The chambermaid nodded and was gone again, leaving Victoire to sip her chocolate in the vain hope that it would make her sleepy enough to override the apprehension that filled her.

Both corporals were waiting in the pre-dawn gloom as Victoire descended the stairs, her caped traveling coat closed to the throat and her dashing Hussar's shako held on with a wide satin ribbon.

Corporal Feuille greeted her without effusiveness, his stubble-covered cheeks giving eloquent testimony to his nighttime activities. "The musician is missing."

"The musician?" Victoire inquired. She had a faint headache from sleeplessness and had to resist the urge to demand more information at once.

"Yes," said Corporal Cruche. "He left his horn, but he's gone. He has to be the one who broke into your room last night." He made a disapproving face. "Musicians! They never have any money."

Victoire scowled. "He can't be much of a musician if he left his horn behind. It makes no sense for him to give up his livelihood."

"Well, as to that," said Corporal Feuille, "I have a theory. I think he was planning to return to his own room with whatever he had taken from you, never thinking that you would be armed."

This interested Victoire. "Why do you say that?"

Corporal Feuille could not resist preening. "It makes sense, Madame Vernet. Here is a man of little wealth, making his way to Paris where employment awaits him. He played last night as a way to reduce the cost of his room. And you are a woman traveling alone, for although we are guarding you, at night you must keep to your room yourself." He faltered. "We meant to have a servant sleep outside your door, but . . . but we failed to arrange it. We were . . . distracted." He stared apologetically at his boots, as if uncertain how to account for his boasting and drink of the evening before.

"I am aware of that," said Victoire. "Is that why you think he came into my room? Because I am a woman alone?"

"And because you were dining alone. He might have thought you carried a goodly cache of gold with you." Corporal Cruche's large-featured face revealed that he, too, suspected that Madame Vernet had money at her disposal.

"But why would I travel by diligence if I had funds? Why not try the rooms of the travelers in the coach? They are clearly most prosperous." Victoire was now at the foot of the stairs, glancing around for the landlord.

"But they are armed," said Corporal Feuille. "He would have been foolish to attempt to steal from them. But you, alone, must have appeared to be the easiest source of funds for him."

"I see," said Victoire, who had arrived at slightly different conclusions.

"And the landlord is waiting for you in the taproom. We will come with you if you think it necessary," said Corporal Cruche, who plainly did not want to be bothered.

"That will not be necessary," Victoire told him. "I would rather that you supervise the loading of my luggage."

Both corporals gave her sketchy salutes.

As Victoire entered the taproom, she noticed a mongrel dog lying near the door, the lantern-light falling on his brindled coat; she looked at the animal with curiosity. As she started toward the hearth where the landlord was setting logs on the embers of the night fires, she glanced again at the dog. "You said that he is not used for tracking?"

"For ratting," said the landlord, continuing with his work, his face becoming more visible as the first little tongues of flame lapped the wood. "But by the looks of his muzzle he took a nip at something or someone last night. The poor fellow's been whining and he's got a sore shoulder, that's for certain." Satisfied with the first flames crackling into the new logs, the landlord straightened up and came toward her. "I hope you will accept my apologies, Madame Vernet, for the inconveniences you have suffered here."

"Certainly. I thought I indicated that last night." She did her best to give him a friendly smile, but her mouth felt tight and she knew she would not be able to put the man at ease.

"Last night was a difficult time, and often-times, when the dangers are over and the alarums ended, there are second thoughts." He kicked at the few charcoaled scraps of the previous evening that had slipped onto the flags in front of the fireplace. "I did not want you to suppose that—"

"Under the circumstances I think you managed as well as anyone could expect," said Victoire stiffly. "And I will so inform my husband when I tell him of what transpired here." She reached into her reticule for the coins she had put there. "This is the cost of the room."

The landlord waved the coins away. "No, Madame Vernet, I would rather you did not pay me."

"You did not know this would happen, and therefore you should not have to answer for it," she said reasonably.

"True, but you are a guest in my inn, and you should not be subjected to such abuse. I would prefer you allow me to make this gesture. I do not want it said that I prey on the misfortunes of my guests. I should have arranged for you to be guarded better, but to say truly, I supposed that the corporals were only trying to increase their importance by claiming you carried money and dispatches."

Victoire suspected that the man had spent the last hour preparing to say that to her, and so she regarded him steadily. "There is no reason to fear me, or to assume that my husband would hold you responsible for what occurred. The corporals have more to fear from him than you do."

"But still," said the landlord. "Please do me the courtesy of accepting my hospitality without charge."

She was aware he was serious, but she could not entirely rid herself of the obligations she felt. "Then take this"—she held out a silver coin—"for the chocolate. Will you do that, at least?"

He chuckled and accepted the coin. "Very well." He looked over at the mongrel as it gave a low whine as it turned in its sleep. "Poor old Bouchonie. He's more than ten years old. It's a shame he had to be hurt."

Victoire agreed, adding, "Still, if he bit the man, he had his revenge."

The landlord hitched up his shoulders. "A heavy blow to an old dog, who's to say what it might do to him?"

At that Victoire became inquisitive. "Do you truly think that he bit the man?" What had he said his name was? Mon ... Montra ... something. She shook her head and listened to the landlord.

"I think he must have. No one complained of his biting when they visited the necessary houses; the ostlers have not been bitten. It could be that he caught a rabbit, but why would he be hurt?" He made a gesture of futility. "The dog cannot talk, Madame, so I may only speculate. And my speculation leads me to think that he bit the thief as he fled."

"You may be correct," said Victoire, wondering how she would ever be able to locate a musician without his instrument and sporting a bullet-wound and a dog-bite.

"And I may not," the landlord concurred. He took her extended hand and bowed over it. "I hope that you will not hold this misfortune against my inn, Madame Vernet."

"The inn did not try to rob me," she pointed out. "Rest assured that your reputation will not suffer at my hands, or my husband's." This was clearly what the landlord wanted to be certain of, she realized, and she went on, "Neither of us have any reason to think poorly of you or to question your role in the ... incident."

"You are very gracious, Madame Vernet," said the landlord, bowing to her once more, relief in every line of his body.

"Hardly that," she corrected him. "But I am about to be late, and that would be unfortunate." She had heard footsteps in the hallway and the sound of the ostlers harnessing the team to the diligence.

The landlord escorted her to the door of his inn with a flourish. "I have enough to apologize for," he said with an attempt at gallantry. "So I will not seek to detain you further."

The driver was squinting up at the sky as the eastern horizon brightened to silver and rose. "There'll be wind today," he announced to the passengers gathered in the inn yard. "Best keep your coats about you."

With this unwelcome thought, Victoire permitted the landlord to hand her up into the diligence, and noticed that the two corporals, her self-appointed escorts, were watching with ill-concealed annoyance. Affronted as they were, Victoire hoped that it would teach them to be more prudent in what they said to other travelers. Concealing a shudder at the lingering shock of the night, she took her place in the carriage. They would pass the night in Beauvais, she thought, following the map in her mind. And then one more night—at Argenteuil or Colombes, perhaps—before they came at last to Paris.

Paris, Victoire thought. Home.

5

❧

THE VERNETS LIVED beyond the fashionable quarter of Paris on a cul-de-sac that backed onto a tannery that now served as livery-and-smithy. Their house was narrow and tall, built two hundred years before, like the rest of them in this area, the rooms small and drafty. The ceiling in the kitchen—a woefully old-fashioned chamber—was patched with damp that no amount of reslating the roof could entirely banish. The staircases leaned and creaked treacherously whenever anyone climbed them.

Odette Pilier, the widow who served as the Vernets' housekeeper, met her employer at the door, her black dress covered by a blue apron and her cap askew over chestnut curls. "Good Lord and His saints, thank Heaven you're back again," she cried as she flung open the door for her.

The porter bearing her luggage stood in the street, his small pushcart laden with Victoire's chests. "I'll set these on the step," he said, and went about his task quickly, for he knew he could expect little in the way of favors from someone living in such a house.

Victoire handed him his money and a small doucement, all the while listening to Odette catalogue the various domestic catastrophes that had occurred in her absence. She waved her housekeeper into silence. "Let me sort this out first, and then we will tend to your troubles, Odette."

The afternoon was overcast and stuffy, and the sour scent of drains and old mortar combined to make the street seem more dreary than it was. The work of the blacksmith at his forge sounded like ancient, discordant bells.

"Ah, Madame Vernet, I am so relieved to have you home," Odette sighed. She was only three years older than Victoire, but seemed more, and not just for her widow's black: as a young woman left with no money when her sergeant husband had been killed in battle, she had been forced to come to terms with the world in a way that made her timorous and reserved beyond her years.

"Will you lend me a hand?" Victoire asked as she went to retrieve her luggage. "Between the two of us I'm certain we can manage."

Odette flung up her hands. "You could have had the porter tend to it."

"And he would have charged me for every stair he climbed, and every time he climbed them," said Victoire. "This trip has already been too expensive." She tugged at one of the leather handles on the case. "Help me, will you?"

"If it is necessary," said Odette, capitulating. She came down the stairs and took the other end of the case.

In ten minutes the two women had tugged and dragged Victoire's luggage into the house, and now the cases were standing in the door to the living room.

"We might as well unpack them here. Half my clothes need washing, and the rest will have to be aired." Victoire looked around the shabby room and did her best not to show the disappointment the room often inspired in her. "The cases will need to be stored again, but it will be easier when they are empty."

"You look very tired," said Odette, scrutinizing her employer. "You are not having more . . . trouble, are you?"

"No," said Victoire. "In fact, I think I am much recovered from my miscarriage. But you are correct. I am tired. And I am ill-at-ease." She sank down into her favorite chair and proceeded to tell Odette about her night at the Vigne et Tonneau.

Odette blessed herself and exclaimed in dismay when Victoire described how she had shot the thief.

"At least," she added conscientiously, "I think I did. If nothing else, I scared him off." She bit her lower lip. "But I haven't been able to sleep since that night."

"You must have a care, Madame," said Odette. "It is very bad to keep awake in that fashion. You must let me prepare a tisane for you, something that will soothe you."

"Yes, thank you," said Victoire at once, "but first I need a decent meal, something with taste to it." She pulled off her gloves and stuffed them into her reticule. "And tomorrow I will need to be out in the world, for I have errands to perform for my husband."

Odette looked dismayed. "But madame, you've just been through a dangerous encounter. Surely you need to keep to your bed for a day, to recover yourself." She watched Victoire narrowly. "You admit you are tired, and often this leads to illness."

"Inactivity will do me more harm than good," said Victoire decisively. "I appreciate your concern, Odette, but trust me to know my own limits." She rose and unfastened her caped traveling coat. "I'll be able to recuperate from my journey after I've discharged my husband's tasks." She handed her coat to Odette. "You had better sponge it with vinegar. After all that time in a diligence, who knows what clings to it. And put water to heating. I know I need a bath." She looked down at her lap. "I've had food and drink spilled here for the last four days, and I know it is all sticking to me still."

"Of course, Madame Vernet," said Odette. "A hot bath will do you good, and you'll feel more yourself again."

"I trust I will," said Victoire.

Odette folded the coat over her arm. "I'll attend to it, Madame. But there are a few matters that you must hear of." She pointed to a place near the window. "There is more damp. The carpenter will have to repair it, or there is danger that the window will not hold."

Victoire looked at the place Odette indicated. "You're right," she said with a gesture of resignation. "And something still must be done about the bannister as well."

"Unfortunately," Odette agreed.

"I see," said Victoire, thinking of Vernet's dress uniform and her few keepsakes and antiques. There was a silver-and-garnet brooch that she would not mind parting with, along with the rest; she never wore it, for neither silver nor garnets became her, so there would be little sacrifice in selling it as well as the others. "It must be tended to," she allowed.

"Madame?" said Odette.

"I will make arrangements, do not fear," said Victoire, and turned her mind away from such distressing thoughts. "What's been going on in Paris since I went away?"

This was a topic much to Odette's interest. "The whole world talks of Josephine," she declared. "And she provides much to talk about. All the Buonapartes follow her lead, and her lead is extravagant and scandalous. Young Lucien's marriage is only the most recent occasion for gossip and rumor."

"Um," said Victoire, aware that Napoleon's younger brother had a penchant for the outrageous, and his marriage to the impecunious but beautiful Madame Jouberthon was just the latest action to outrage his sisters.

"They say that her first husband's death has not been confirmed," said Odette, delighted to be shocked by this additional scandal.

"He fled when he went bankrupt, or so I understand. He was supposed to have gone to one of the Caribbean Islands," said Victoire as if this were an everyday occurrence. "Documents do not come quickly from such places."

"No, indeed not," said Odette, and returned to her original subject. "And there is still Josephine. Had Lucien married that ugly Italian woman Napoleon had chosen for him, there would still be more than enough to talk about."

"Truly," said Victoire, though her sarcasm didn't diminish Odette's pleasure in revealing more about the Consul's wife.

"You should see how she has set herself up in the world! The clothes she wears, and the jewels!" Odette's expression of disapproval was marred by the sparkle in her brown eyes. "Imagine, being so indulged," she said as she started toward the rear of the house, where the kitchen was.

Victoire followed along behind. "I know she has a taste for excesses."

"So she has, so she has," said Odette eagerly, opening the door to the kitchen and the servants' quarters: there was space for three, but since the Vernets could afford only one, she was given use of all three rooms as her own, and she had proceeded to turn these little chambers into a neat apartment for herself. "And it appears to be growing with every passing hour."

"That must cause Napoleon some apprehension," said Victoire, knowing it would be her own response to such behavior. "As First Consul, he must be regarded as the example for all Frenchmen."

"As to that, who is to say? He is entitled to have these things, and Josephine is in a position to be his . . . flagship." She chuckled at her own allusion as she put Victoire's coat down over the back of one of the kitchen chairs before reaching for one of four enormous copper kettles, which she took to the pump in the corner of the room. As she filled the kettle with water, she went on. "They say she has spent as much on her jewels as the navy has spent on ships, but I am certain that is only the malicious report of those who are bent on making the worst of everything they can. The First Consul's mother hates her, or that is the talk." Odette was deep-bosomed and strong, but her words slowed as she continued to ply the pump-handle. "They are all becoming very grand now, the group around Napoleon. They are all of them like the old royal court."

"Odette," said Victoire in faint disapproval, for she could not help but agree with her housekeeper's assessment.

"Well, they are," Odette persisted. "And it is enough to make honest men weep to see how like dandies and fops they have become. And these endless family squabbles!" She struggled to lift the filled kettle onto the ancient iron stove, then took down the second kettle and began the process again. "I've seen her once or twice—Josephine, I mean—and she was splendid to behold. A poor man could live half a lifetime on her necklace alone."

"And you don't approve?" said Victoire, and went on without waiting for an answer. "I don't know that I do, either. She is such a frivolous woman, and at the same time her will is very strong. If she ever fixed her attention to some purpose other than amusement, she might be very beneficial to all of France. Or very dangerous."

"She is not the only such woman," said Odette, panting now as she worked.

"No," Victoire said quietly. "Lamentably she is not."

It was shortly after noon the following day when Victoire made the first of her calls at the Ministry of Public Safety, the domain of Fouche. It was in a small building on a street several minutes' walk from the Tuileries. The building itself was one of many dark brick structures with little to set it apart from the counting houses on either side. On a previous visit, Victoire had noticed that residing on a corner and having a wide alley behind, there were almost a dozen doorways on the three accessible sides. At night most would be shadowed or unlit, providing excellent cover for the numerous spies that returned to report to Fouche from nations all over Europe.

Entering the building, there was nothing to show that this was the center of Fouche's web. There was a well-dressed young man behind a desk who greeted Victoire courteously. Not recognizing her, he began a speech she had heard before. From the corner of her eye Victoire noticed three large men whose desks gave them a clear field of fire to all entrances. Each man had opened a drawer which no doubt held pistols.

"I am the wife of Inspector-General Vernet," Victoire announced in her most officious voice. "I have a dispatch from my husband to deliver to Citizen Fouche personally. We have met before and he will recognize me."

The well-dressed young man lost his false smile, but rose

and gestured for her to follow. Behind her, Victoire could hear the sound of drawers closing.

She had dressed for the occasion in her second-best day dress, a handsome, high-waisted afternoon dress in sea-green taffeta with a small, standing ruff of point-lace. She curtsied to Fouché but offered him little more than a perfunctory smile, for she knew that Fouché often regarded courtesy as suspect. "I am sorry to have to interrupt your day, Monsieur le Ministre. If I did not think it important, I—"

"Madame Vernet, I'm always willing to see you when you request it. You are not capricious or one who is seeking favor and advancement." He gestured to the chair on the other side of his writing table.

"There you are not entirely correct," said Victoire in her usual direct manner. She had always found Fouché personally pleasant, but never underestimated the calculated way in which he had risen over all his rivals. "I am a married woman and therefore I'm always interested in the welfare of my husband."

"And the welfare of France," said Fouché without the cynicism that would usually accompany such an observation.

"Yes," said Victoire. "That as well." She got on at once to the reason for her visit. "I know you have received a dispatch from my husband regarding reports of English landing on the coast near Dunkerque. We have reason to suppose that there have indeed been English spies put ashore. There is a possibility that they are bound for Paris rather than Antwerp." She reached into her reticule and withdrew one of the dispatches she had carried. "I have brought this to you from my husband. He describes what he has undertaken, and the concerns we both share for Napoleon's safety."

"Napoleon's safety?" said Fouché, surprised at the turn she had taken.

"Yes. What other reason would the English have in coming to Paris, if not to harm the First Consul? When I arrived I feared they planned an uprising here such as just ended in the Vendée. But the city is too quiet, such things do not spring full grown, as did Minerva. They may be planning to murder First Consul Napoleon, or kidnap him or one of his family. They could want to suborn others of his family." Her expression was somber and she regarded Fouché levelly. "I would like to see the file you have on English spies known to be in France, and the nature of their organizations."

Such a request from most officers' wives would have been met with a firm but polite dismissal from Fouché, but coming as it did from Victoire Vernet, he nodded in agreement, fussing with the folds of his neck cloth; calm in the most difficult of diplomatic circumstances, he was often uncomfortable in social conversations. "Of course. I will have it brought at once. You understand that you will have to examine it here? Nor can you make any copies."

"Certainly," said Victoire at once. "You do not want such sensitive information to leave the building." Her manner was brisk without being unfriendly. "If I notice anything that might lead to discovering this latest English mission, I will inform you at once."

"Excellent," said Fouche, rising in order to summon one of his assistants. "I would like you to bring the file on English spies operating in France," he said, adding, "I would like to have it at once. We will wait for you to bring it."

"At once," said the angular young man who had answered his summons. "Of course."

Fouche returned to his chair, plucking at the ruffles of his cuffs. "May I offer you a glass of wine while we wait for the file to be brought?"

"That's very kind of you," said Victoire, who knew that Fouche served very good wine. "I'd like that."

"Very well," said Fouche, and opened a cabinet near the foot of his desk. "I think that you will find this satisfactory, for you are not one of those women forever drinking tisanes and champagne. I enjoy it myself, but it is not to everyone's taste."

The wine was a Côtes Sauvages, very dark and rich, with a flavor so dense that it seemed chewable. Fouche smiled with understandable pride as Victoire took a second sip.

"This is wonderful," she said sincerely, thinking how much she wished she could afford to offer such a vintage to her visitors. Now that she was back in Paris, she was reminded how important such matters were among the new aristocracy of the Republic.

"Yes, it is. And you have the knowledge to value it," he complimented her, putting his glass down. "I wonder if you would tell whether or not you share your husband's worry in regard to these English."

"Yes, I do," she said, putting her glass aside as well. "If anything, I am more troubled than he, because try as I will, I can think of no reason for the spies to leave the coast if they do not intend to act either directly against Napoleon himself or indirectly, by causing disruption to the negotiations in Antwerp."

Fouche listened attentively. "Perhaps they are waiting to

make some more mischief against the fleet. Already we have enough ships to threaten the Channel. I do understand that is one of your husband's assumptions."

"It was, but is less so now: if that were the case there would be rumors of it, and there are none. Those fishermen along the coast are a greater source of gossip than the most successful hairdresser here in Paris," she said bluntly. "Let the English appear, and they would know of it even if the army did not. And those men guarding the fleet know the ships and fishermen of their area. They would know if there were foreign sailors about." She folded her hands in her lap, her demeanor as modest as she could make it. "My husband has gone to Antwerp, as you are aware, and I am here to serve as his lieutenant, so that if Paris is the destination of the spies, you will not have to wait for word from him to begin a search for them. And we are in agreement that there are spies, and that they must be bound for one destination or the other."

"Your husband is a very sensible fellow," said Fouche.

"He is, isn't he?" Victoire agreed candidly.

"And he is thrice-blessed in you," added Fouche, now fussing with the top button of his swallow-tail coat. "If I were not certain of that, you would not be permitted to examine the file you have requested." He took another sip of wine. "It is a pity that so many of our officers have playthings for wives, or ambitious cats, ready to claw their way to prominence."

Victoire was surprised at the vehemence of his words. "Ministre Fouche, you cannot think that all women are—"

He waved her protest aside. "No, I do not mean that, and you are well-aware of it. I merely observe that most wives are valued for qualities other than the ones you possess, good sense and clearheadedness. And steadiness of temperament." He added this last wryly, for he was known to like the company of volatile women. "Truly, there are officers whose wives are saints, and others who have capable managers and allies in their wives, just as there are some with sluts and slatterns and brood mares. But Vernet has found more than any of the usual admirable qualities of women in you." He finished the last of the wine in his glass. "And you are fortunate that he does not mind your intelligence. There is many another who would."

"I am thankful for his kindness to me," said Victoire, uncertain what other answer to give.

Fouche shrugged. "If he were not kind, he would be truly a fool. I, for one, Madame Vernet, would not like to have you for an enemy."

Her laughter was disbelieving. "I am no one's enemy, Ministre Fouche."

"You think not?" Fouche said, and before Victoire could answer, looked up as the door opened. "Well, let us see this file."

The angular young man stood hesitantly in the door. "The file is . . . is with General Moreau. There is a memorandum left, signed by him." Moreau was a most honored hero who had commanded the Armée du Rhin to victory at Hochstadt not long ago.

"He has taken it with him?" Fouche asked, as if he had not understood. "Did you check the aide's credentials? Confirm his name with Moreau's staff?"

"Apparently they did not. There is no mention of any checks. He took the file. That is all the memorandum says." The assistant looked ashamed. "It was not supposed to be removed, but the aide to General Moreau claimed the general had urgent need of the information."

Fouche's eyes narrowed. "The general said nothing to me."

"The aide said you were not here. That is what he told the clerks, in any case. I wasn't there or this would not have happened." Now the assistant seemed ready to flee. "Should I call upon the general? To request its return?"

"Not on the instant," said Fouche, glancing at Victoire and then back at his assistant. "But perhaps tomorrow, if he has not yet returned it. I will send a note 'round to him, asking that he bring it back."

Fouche said nothing, letting the young assistant blather on. He caught Victoire's eye and shared the hint of a smile.

"He was told the file was not supposed to leave the building," lamented the assistant as if he had been personally responsible for the loss of the information.

"No doubt," said Fouche. "The general is aware of how these things are done." He scowled, then went on smoothly. "The press of events must have demanded he make an exception."

The assistant was pathetically glad to have this excuse to cling to. "That must surely have been the case," he said, his face turning pale with relief.

Fouche waved him away with murmured thanks, then looked back at Victoire, who was listening with close attention. "I know I may rely on your discretion, Madame Vernet," he said pointedly.

"Most certainly," said Victoire at once. "And yet, I must observe that this development is most worrisome to me."

"As it is to me," Fouche admitted, his lips pursing with disapproval and anxiety. "I am surprised that Moreau would behave in this manner. If the man was Moreau's aide, acting at his behest, then it is most unlike him. He is generally a reliable man, and this is not what I have come to expect of him. I will forward what you request once he returns the file." He offered her a second glass of wine, but the gesture was merely a courtesy, and Victoire knew well enough not to accept it.

"You are very gracious, Ministre Fouche, but I have other errands to run for my husband, and they will not wait." She rose and offered her hand to Fouche. "I am grateful for your time and attention. I hope you will review the dispatch I have brought you and will let me know at your earliest convenience any message you would like me to send to my husband."

"It will be my duty and pleasure," said Fouche, kissing her hand. As he rose from his bow, he fussed with his neck cloth, unsatisfied that it was as fashionably tied as he wanted it to be.

"How very kind," said Victoire as she left his office.

Colonel Sir Magnus Sackett-Hartley stood in front of Le Chat Gris and tried not to turn up his nose too much. The tavern was four hundred years old and looked every hour of it: small, dark windows sagged over the narrow street where apprentice weavers trudged home from long hours at the looms.

"The owner knows we're coming," said Cholet, coming up beside him.

"The rest are supposed to be at La Plume et Bougie, near the Université. They should have arrived four days ago, if all has gone according to plan." Sackett-Hartley was used to speaking French now, and no longer feared detection when strangers passed him in the street.

"In the morning, my friend," said Cholet, and signalled to the others. "We have arrived."

Brezolles was the first to object. "But you c-can't mean— This is a-an appalling place," he declared. "Surely we can find b-better lodging than this."

"Possibly," said Sackett-Hartley, "but none safer. The landlord here is in the debt of our ally."

The other six looked dismayed. "What man of high rank would have anything to do with a place like this?" asked La Clouette for all of them.

"That's a foolish question," said Sackett-Hartley. "Men of high rank always keep a bolt-hole or two, if they are wise. My uncle led many to safety from such places as these." He gestured to them to follow him. "We need to hide, and what better place than this?"

Brezolles turned his eyes upward. "We would h-have to be desperate."

"We *are* desperate," said Les Aix.

Sackett-Hartley interrupted this useless conversation. "Remember, we are cousins come here to look for work. We are skilled butchers, all of us."

"So we are," said d'Estissac with a nasty smile.

"None of that," warned Sackett-Hartley as he started toward the door, doing his best to ignore the stench of rotting vegetables that pervaded the narrow inn yard.

The interior of the inn was dark and oppressive. Even the taproom had an air of decay about it, from the dark-stained barrels to the worn and ill-used tables to the hearth where two pigs turned on spits and an ancient crone basted them with a mixture that stank of dill.

"Welcome to Le Chat Gris," said a scrawny youth who appeared in the hallway. "Are you looking for lodgings?"

D'Estissac answered for all of them. "Yes, we are. We were told that Jacques at Le Chat Gris would have room for us."

"Who told you that?" the youngster asked, his eyes widening with shock. "A friend who wears blue, who told us that there is room here," said Sackett-Hartley, using the recognition code. "Tell the landlord."

The boy hurried away, shouting as he went that there were patrons arriving and that the landlord was needed.

A door opened at the end of the hallway and that worthy presented himself. "I am Jacques Panne. And you are the cousins?"

"The butchers from the north," said La Clouette, completing the code. "Our friend in blue sent us here, because you have room."

Panne came toward them, a slab of a man with unruly shoulder-length gray hair and an air of perpetual disgust in his manner. "You have the money?"

Sackett-Hartley pulled out the purse and handed it over. "Our friend in blue said that this is the price. One month for all of us. If we must remain longer, you will have the same again."

"If you have to stay longer, the price will be higher," said Panne. "I have my skin to think about." Nevertheless he took the purse and gave the eight strangers a rictus smile of fallacious welcome. "The boy will show you where you are to sleep. Supper is at sunset. Wine will cost you extra "

"I wonder if he is as generous with his high-ranking ally?" speculated Lieutenant Constable in a tone just loud enough to be heard.

"Enough of that," Sackett-Hartley ordered, and said to Panne, "Very well. I'll give you money toward wine, and then we need not haggle about it." Panne accepted the half-dozen silver coins without any visible reaction. "The house at the end of the next street is empty. It has been secured by the friend in blue, paid for a month. Your friends have the key, or so I was to tell you."

"You're very good," said Sackett-Hartley automatically. "Let us put our things away and then we will have some of that pork you are cooking." He did not like the aroma coming from the hearth, but he was hungry enough to ignore the overpowering dill.

With an insultingly low bow, Panne led them toward the rear of the building.

I did want to confide my fears to Ministre Fouche, my dear husband, but I will confess to you that I cannot like it that the file was missing. It might be that there is no reason for my worry; General Moreau may well have an excellent reason for removing the file, and it could be that the precautions Fouche has instituted are too stringent. I do not know for a fact that there was much danger in Moreau's removing the file. However, I am left with the sense that the information in the file would be better protected within the ministry than in the care of Moreau. If the file has not been returned by the end of the week, I will regard that as a very troubling indication.

Victoire sat at her writing table and stared down at her letter to Lucien. Had she told him enough to alert him without creating unnecessary anxiety? She frowned and went on.

I have also spoken with Berthier, and he is willing to consider my warnings. He has assured me that he will present me with any news that comes to hand that might resolve the questions I have put to him regarding the activities of English spies in France. I am satisfied with such an arrangement, for then neither his men nor I will waste time duplicating one another's efforts.

That was appropriately straight-forward and she felt better for having stated it so clearly.

Odette appeared at the door of her withdrawing room. "Madame Vernet?"

Victoire looked up. "What is it?"

"There are callers," said Odette with a gesture of discomfort. "They have asked to speak to you."

"Who are they?" asked Victoire, aware that Odette was not comfortable about the visitors.

"General Bernadotte and his wife," said Odette. "They say they have been remiss in not coming before now." She gestured to show how helpless she felt. "I've put them in the parlor, but what am I to do?"

Victoire rose and placed a blotter over her unfinished letter. "I suppose then that I must do the proper thing." She had never felt the shabbiness of her house as intensely as she did at this moment. "What do we have in the house to offer them?"

"There is wine, and I have some rolls we did not eat at breakfast. I could serve them with a comfit—there is some left." She was close to blithering.

"That would be very acceptable," said Victoire, knowing it was not truly what either Bernadotte or his wife Desirée would expect. Still, it was polite enough that it would not insult the unexpected guests. "Serve some of that new honey, as well."

Odette waved her hands in protest. "But Madame Vernet, that was supposed to be for the dessert when your husband returns."

"I know." Victoire sighed. "Still, it can't be helped. We will buy more honey when he comes home."

"Very well," said Odette, and went to inform the guests that Madame Vernet would be with them directly.

General du Corps Jean Baptiste Jules Bernadotte was a handsome man, with regular features and a large, straight nose that constantly made him appear to be leaning into a wind. His wife, the former Desirée Clary, was a pretty, petulant woman with large eyes, flawless skin, and a languorous manner that could become ferociously energetic in an instant. Her hair was fashionably cropped, curling tendrils falling artlessly around her face. She was dressed at the height of courtly style in acres of tissue-fine rose-hued fabric that clung suggestively to her body whenever she moved. A wrap of India silk was draped over her shoulders. Her reticule was covered with splendid beadwork that matched the beadwork on the corsage of her dress.

"What a pleasure to have you once again in Paris, Madame Vernet," said Bernadotte as he bowed over her hand. He wore the white uniform of a Cuirassier, even to the heavy leather boots and pants designed to deflect a sword stroke or bayonet. Across his chest was the most colorful of the many decorations Napoleon had awarded him; the effect was both martial and impressive. "You must not think us remiss for waiting until now to call upon you."

"Not at all," said Victoire, wondering what Bernadotte and Desirée were doing calling on her at all.

Bernadotte kissed her hand and then waited for Victoire to touch cheeks with his wife. "We had intended to be here two days ago, shortly after you returned, but the press of my work, you know—"

Desirée brushed her cheeks against Victoire's and murmured a greeting. She was still very young, having been sixteen during her brief but notorious affair with Napoleon; she was almost twenty years younger than the handsome, round-faced Gascon, who had already been a hero of the Republic while she was still a child.

"I'm sorry I was not waiting to greet you when you arrived," said Victoire as she indicated to Desirée a place on her threadbare sofa. "I have not been much in the way of receiving afternoon callers."

"No, I gather not," Bernadotte remarked. "You have given yourself other tasks. You are always active on your husband's behalf; we are all aware of it. I have heard that you have already passed on dispatches to Fouche and Berthier."

"How devoted you are," said Desirée.

"I hope I am a dutiful wife," said Victoire, more puzzled than ever. She took her place in her favorite chair and left Bernadotte to stand or sit as he wished.

"Oh, it is very well-known that you are. Inspector-General Vernet is the envy of half the officers I know." He chuckled with an affectionate glance toward Desirée. "What man does not take pride in a wife who has his interests at heart?"

Desirée's expression did not alter as she said, "And for a man like Vernet, a wife who will aid him is very important."

Victoire looked at Desirée and wondered if her comment had been spiteful or merely ill-considered. "He and I both come from families who have made their way in the world. Fortunately there was money enough for training and education by the time we came along. Neither he nor I ever had to face the world without something in our pockets."

"Not so much as once," said Desirée with a charming smile. So it is spite, thought Victoire, wishing she knew why General Bernadotte's wife would have such a harsh opinion of her. "Very true," she said as if she were unaware of the unkindness in the remark. "Which is why Vernet and I must apply ourselves."

"Such a shame when officers are driven to the limit in these ways, don't you think?" Desirée inquired. "I have thought many times myself that I have been fortunate that I was not left without support or a husband. I am not one who could apply herself as I am certain you would, Madame Vernet."

This oblique reference to Desirée's youthful affair with Napoleon took Victoire aback. "I should think that many women feel as you do," she said, trying to discern what it was that these two wanted of her. "Each of us must be aware of at least one woman who has not been as fortunate as you and I, Madame Bernadotte."

Desiree leaned back, sulking, while her husband took up the conversation. "Yes, it is most regrettable that France has seen so many difficult years. But now that is coming to an end, and you must take pride in knowing that your husband has been one of those who has made this possible."

"I am very proud of Inspector-General Vernet," said Victoire. "I make no secret of that."

"Very true," said Bernadotte. "The vigor with which you have pursued his goals is most admirable." He smiled. "I have heard that it is the contention of Inspector-General Vernet that there are English spies newly come to France. Is this so?"

"It is possible," said Victoire carefully.

"And we were informed that there was an attempt to rob you while you were traveling from the coast to Paris. The story is that you took a shot at the man." He regarded her with a mixture of courteous attention and patent disbelief.

"I believe I wounded him," said Victoire with a tranquility that she did not truly possess, still feeling a twinge as she remembered the incident. Victoire smiled gratefully when Desirée made light of the incident.

"It's what comes of staying at a common posting inn," remarked Desirée.

Victoire was determined to show no offense at this observation. "I would like to think so, but I cannot forget that no one is safe from the action of spies."

"Ah," said Bernadotte. "Then this is the reason you have been so much at pains to persuade Fouche and Berthier to be on guard."

"It is one of them," said Victoire and looked up as Odette

came in bearing a tray with refreshments on it. "Pray let my housekeeper offer you something."

Desirée lifted her arched brows. "Isn't it difficult to run a household with only one servant? No footman, no butler—how do you manage, Madame Vernet? I should be lost without my staff of servants."

"It requires effort, as you say," Victoire answered stiffly, and motioned to Odette to carry the tray to Desirée first. "Had I known you would visit, I would have had cheese and fruit to offer you, as well."

Desirée took a small plate and broke one of the rolls in half, putting compote on one and honey on the other. "And a glass of wine; that will suffice. This house is not like some, where you are constantly offered unwanted luxuries and treats that serve no purpose but to make the host appear grand." She paid little attention to Odette.

"I will have the same as my wife," said Bernadotte as Odette curtsied to him.

"For what reason have you given me the pleasure of your company, General?" asked Victoire as courteously as she was able. Her curiosity was getting the better of her now and she did not want to take the better part of twenty minutes in senseless social frivolities.

General du Corps Bernadotte was taken aback at her direct question, but he rallied himself and did his best to respond. "The stories of your enterprise and tenacity have only recently reached my ears, and what I have heard is most impressive. To shoot a robber with your own pistol, to protect your husband's dispatches! And the tales Murat has told of you in Egypt and Italy. Astounding. It appears there is a dark secret in those events, for he is silent afterwards." He paused for a moment to see if Victoire would clarify the mystery. When she didn't respond, he continued. "I must tell you, Madame Vernet, that I am astonished at how intrepid you are."

"I am hardly that," said Victoire, who knew that the word described her precisely. "I am prudent and sensible, which is often mistaken for intrepidity."

"And so modest," said Desirée.

For once Bernadotte appeared embarrassed at his wife's comment. "Desirée, my dear, think of how this must seem to our hostess. It is not our purpose to make it appear we do not value her as we ought. Not everyone understands your playfulness." He looked at Victoire with an attitude of eager inquiry. "Are you still convinced that there are English spies coming to Paris?"

"I see no reason to change my mind," said Victoire as Odette poured her a glass of wine.

Bernadotte chuckled again. "But Madame Vernet, even suppose this were true, what would be their purpose in coming here? It is very dangerous, isn't it? For what reason would they risk so much?"

"I don't know, not beyond a few assumptions," Victoire confessed. "And that is what bothers me."

After the couple had left, Victoire wondered at their motives. Bernadotte was an old companion of Napoleon from Italy and was rumored to be in line for further honors after the coronation. He was said to be ambitious and the situation in France was far from settled. One general had taken over command of the country: did Bernadotte hope to do the same? There had been that trouble in 1802 when several members of Bernadotte's staff had plotted to take over the government. Nothing had been found that implicated Bernadotte but the conspirators had included his aide-de-camp. Since then he had refused all posts that took him away from the city. Had Bessieres sent him? Had Desirée, Napoleon's spurned mistress, convinced him to come? Had General Bernadotte been politely offering his assistance or checking to see how much Vernet knew? The questions continued endlessly, unanswered.

6

❦

CLAUDE MONTRACHET STOOD in the entrance to the empty house that had been provided for them. "We can't take the chance of staying here, not all twenty of us; in fact, none of us at all should live here," he told the two men with him. "We'll have to have a guard here all the time, but otherwise, we cannot afford to put all of our group under one roof. It's too great a risk if anyone should suspect us." He opened the door, wincing a little as he turned his wrist, where the impressions of teeth were fading at last.

"It is adequate," said one of his companions who had been with the private coach at the Vigne et Tonneau. "The other end backs onto the churchyard of Saint Rafael the Archangel. It is a very old building and there are only two priests there. They will not pay much attention if we cut through their—"

"But we will not do that unless it is utterly necessary," said Montrachet. "We have to be circumspect, and that means that we do as little as possible to draw attention to ourselves." His other arm was in a sling and as he turned, he brushed that arm against the wall. He swore with vigor and variety.

"The bullet wound has not yet healed?" asked the second companion, who had also been at the Vigne et Tonneau.

"It is improving," said Montrachet between clenched teeth. "If I ever get my hands on that woman, she will regret having that pistol."

"An amazing thing, the way she shot you," said the first man unwisely.

"You're an idiot, Bouelac," said Montrachet in his most conversational tone. "It was luck, only my ill-luck, that kept her from putting the ball through her own flesh."

Bouelac and the other man exchanged glances and wisely kept silent.

Montrachet made his way down the hall, looking critically at the wet patches as he went past them. "It smells of mold," he remarked as he looked into one small room.

"The house is old and so near the river it is damp," said Bouelac.

"True enough," said Montrachet. "But I will want someone—a carpenter, I suppose—to inspect these rooms for rot, and do any truly necessary repairs. It won't do to have the place collapse around us while we're here, and I don't want to burn it to the ground if the chimneys aren't safe."

Bouelac sighed and said, "Have you talked to Sackett-Hartley about this?"

"It isn't his decision. This is my part of the operation, not his. I know Paris. He's English," said Montrachet. "He thinks he is avenging the Terror."

"And we are not?" asked the second companion.

"No, Toutdroit, we are not." Montrachet stopped and turned back to regard the two steadily. "We are here to establish ourselves in our rightful places, not to demand recompense. If we do that, we will fail, for that would admit that there is recompense for what was done to our families, and none can be possible. Therefore, we have no reason to seek it. If we act for our own advancement, and to restore our positions in the rightful order, we will succeed." He indicated the house. "See that a carpenter inspects it and that it is put right."

"And if Sackett-Hartley questions this?" asked Bouelac.

"Send him to me," said Montrachet. "He is not so blind that he will not understand me." He resumed his inspection, saying little to Toutdroit and Bouelac, who trailed behind him.

At last they were done, and as they made their way back to the front door, there was the sound of someone coming into the house.

Montrachet motioned to the other two to hide behind him in the alcove as he drew a pistol from his belt.

Footsteps echoed along the narrow hallway, and then a voice called out, "Claude, it is Jean-Armand." D'Estissac did not raise his voice but the sound of it carried easily.

Montrachet sighed. "Here, my friend," he called out and came out of the alcove where he had hidden. "A good thing you identified yourself," he went on, cocking his head toward the pistol in his hand.

"I should think so," said d'Estissac, pretending to be frightened. "We've been keeping watch over the house from the church," he went on by way of explanation. "When Les Aix saw you enter, he sent for me. He didn't know it was you."

"Very sensible," said Montrachet, shoving the pistol back

into his belt. "I trust that you are well. There was nothing in your note that said anything untoward had occurred."

"No, nothing after that innkeeper and that was to his misfortune, not ours," said d'Estissac. "You have not been so fortunate, it seems." He gestured toward the sling.

Montrachet hissed with exasperation. "Yes. It is true." He did not want to go into details. "But the wound was a minor one, hardly more than the dog-bite I sustained the same night. I will be recovered shortly."

"Very good," said d'Estissac. "We had better arrange a meeting for all of us very soon, now that we're all here. Sackett-Hartley suggested tonight."

"Tomorrow," said Montrachet, and added vaguely. "We need time to prepare."

"All the more reason to meet tonight," said d'Estissac.

"I don't think so," said Montrachet. "I leave it to you to explain this to Colonel Sir Magnus Sackett-Hartley." He said the name as if it left a sour taste in his mouth.

"Are you certain that is what you want?" asked d'Estissac. "The longer we delay, the greater the chance that we will be found out."

"One day is not going to make a difference," assured Montrachet with such finality that the other three men made no effort to counter it.

"Very well, tomorrow," said d'Estissac after a short hesitation. "If that is what you think we must do."

"It is," said Montrachet, and looked around the narrow hall in satisfaction. "Toutdroit will watch here tonight, and tomorrow we'll work out the appropriate schedule for all the rest."

This time d'Estissac did not question the order: if Sackett-Hartley did not like Montrachet taking over in this way, he would have to settle the question with Montrachet himself.

The sergeant who waited in the door looked ready to fall asleep. His horse, waiting at the curb, appeared more exhausted than his rider. He saluted Odette and asked for Madame Vernet. "I know it's early," he said. "But the letter I bring is from her husband. I have been in the saddle since three in the morning, and I am ready to find my bed. Pray accept my apologies for coming at this hour."

"Oh, yes," said Odette, and stepped back into the house, calling up the stairs to Victoire. "A letter from Inspector-General Vernet. The sergeant is worn out."

Victoire, who was still abed, looked up from the file she was reading—Berthier had supplied it to her the night before—and called out, "Take the letter and give the poor man something hot to drink before he goes on his way." She was already reaching out for her peignoir, wrapping it around her before she slipped out of bed, taking care to put the file beneath her pillows.

Odette had opened the door to the sergeant, saying, "If you will follow me, my mistress instructs me to give you something to drink, something hot."

"Thanks," the man muttered as he went along to the kitchen with Odette.

Victoire donned her very sensible slippers and tied the sash of her peignoir. It was not at all proper that she greet the messenger en déshabillé, but she was not about to take the twenty minutes it would require to make herself presentable. This man was a soldier, she told herself, and she was a soldier's wife and neither of them need stand on ceremony. Thus reassured she hurried down to the kitchen, coming through the door just as the kettle on the stove began to thrill.

The sergeant looked around, blushed, and got to his feet in the same moment. He half-saluted. "The dispatch is—"

"In my servant's care, yes, I know that," said Victoire quickly as she reached out to take the sealed packet of papers Odette offered her as she looked for the India tea.

"I'm afraid that it must be tea," she said to the sergeant as she prepared the pot. "We have no beer and—"

"Tea is welcome, the stronger the better," said the sergeant. He smiled wearily and sat down again, apologizing as he did. "I am about to fall over, and that is the truth before God."

Victoire regarded him for a short while. "Yes, you must be exhausted. All the more reason to have the tea before you go, and to take with you a note for your commanding officer to express my gratitude for your dedication to duty." She had already broken the seals on the dispatch and was now fumbling with the pages, her hands suddenly clumsy as she tried to read the crossed lines in her husband's angular scrawl.

"You're most gracious, Madame Vernet," the sergeant said to her.

"Odette, I am going to write a note for the sergeant to take with him. I leave you to look after him." Victoire started out of the kitchen door, then paused. "I will need no more than ten minutes."

The withdrawing room was chilly and subtly damp, but Victoire ignored these discomforts as she closed the doors and hurried to her writing table. She sat down and spread out the sheets, reading them as quickly as she dared, promising herself to peruse them at length as soon as the sergeant was gone.

The trail leading to spies in Antwerp, if there ever was such a thing, has long gone cold, and I am forced to accept the possibility that the spies are making their way to Paris, as you suspected from the first. Yet I feel that my time here has not been entirely wasted, for I have learned a great deal more about the danger in which France now stands. It will take a few more days for my work here to be completed, but when it is done, I will not delay an instant returning to you, my dearest. You have put me on the alert and for that reason I am going to take extra care to settle my work here before I come again to Paris. I do not want the ghosts of neglect to rise to haunt me. I will elaborate on that when we can speak together privately, for these reflections do not belong in missives such as this. But to alleviate any concerns you may have, I will tell you that your deductions have proven yet again to be most perceptive.

"Well, at least they were once we discovered that we were entertaining the wrong assumptions," Victoire murmured as she read. "But we had to be sure, Lucien."

Your account of the events at the Vigne et Tonneau very much shocks me, my treasure, and I am filled with misgiving in regard to your safety. That you should have been subjected to such a dreadful occurrence shames me deeply, for I cannot but believe it would not have happened had you been with me, or had you been accorded proper escort, which you did not have. It may be as you say was decided, that the man was only a thief; others have suggested this to you. But in the event that he was something more, and therefore worse, I implore you to be more cautious than is your wont, to guard yourself at every instant. I am disgusted that French soldiers were so foolish as those corporals you described to me, and I will see that they are reprimanded for their conduct. Do not think to protect them from the consequences of their stupidity, my dear, for they are dragoons and must learn to bear the responsibility that goes with such work.

In regard to the circumstances regarding the foreign musician, I must ask you, my treasured wife, not to attempt to find the man. I know your character, and it would not astonish me to learn that you had already determined to see if the miscreant had actually come to Paris. I am not certain that such a desperate man would stop at threats. And if you wounded him as you say you think you did, he will have no charity to offer you but what comes with lead balls. You must not expose yourself to such danger again. It is appalling enough that you were at risk once; it must not happen a second time.

The rest of the letter was filled with details of what he had investigated, and Victoire knew she would need time to reflect upon what he had told her. She folded the dispatch and placed it in the concealed drawer of the writing table. Then she drew a sheet of paper from the central drawer—the one that was supposed to be seen—and took out her standish and pens. It required no more than a few seconds to compose the note in her head, and she wrote it quickly, sanding the ink carefully. As soon as she was satisfied it was dry, she rose and folded the sheet in half once, then returned to the kitchen.

The sergeant had finished about half a mug of tea and was listening to Odette fill him in on the gossip about Napoleon's brother's marriage. He rose as Victoire came into the room, and said at once, "The tea has revived me, Madame Vernet."

"Then thank my housekeeper, for she is the one who made it for you," said Victoire, and held out her note. "Give this to your commanding officer with my thanks, if you will. You may read it if you like."

The sergeant shrugged as he took the paper. "I cannot read, Madame Vernet. That is one of the reasons I have been put on messenger duty."

Victoire's tone was dry. "How sensible of the army." She glanced over at Odette, then looked back at the sergeant. "I fear that I must excuse myself once more. My husband has requested certain things of me that I must tend to at once, and therefore I will have to dress at once and prepare to depart within the hour." She did not pause to give any further instructions to Odette but hurried away to dress, planning already to speak first to Berthier before she called upon Ministre Fouche.

Lamplighters were making their nightly rounds by the time Victoire returned to her house. She was worn out, her back and feet were aching, but her mind was filled with a variety of notions that held her attention and doomed her to an evening of restlessness as she struggled to make sense of all she had gleaned in a day of reports and interviews.

Odette had made them a supper of thin-sliced liver cooked quickly in wine and bacon-grease with shallots and mustard. As she served it, she apologized. "It should be something grander, I know, but the cost—"

Victoire held up her hand. "I am very pleased with your economies, Odette, and you have no reason to be ashamed of this fare. I am sure my father had such food all through his youth, and my mother as well. Besides, my physician has said that liver is useful to women seeking to . . . to get pregnant." She cut a sliver for herself; since the meat had been cooked quickly it was quite tender. "I am certain I will enjoy this. And we will save the joints of beef and rolls of pork for when there are guests who expect fancier fare."

Odette sighed. "You are kind to say so, Madame Vernet, but I cannot like having to feed us as if we were all peasants." She looked around the kitchen. "Just as it is not fitting for us to have the meal here."

"But it is sensible," said Victoire, who was not nearly so displeased with the arrangement as Odette was. "We do not have to squander wood to heat the dining room, we need not bother with two sets of dishes, and we have the opportunity to converse, which is the most useful of all."

"If only things were not so expensive," said Odette quietly.

"I share your qualms," Victoire admitted. "When I look at what Vernet is paid and the money I inherited, and then realize the demands made on it, I despair. I think if my mother had not enjoined her diamond earrings and tiara to be sold only to preserve the life of one of my children . . . not that I have any to save as yet." She quickly dismissed that thought. "And my father's will left a trust to his grandchildren, as well. There is no way to break it until I have reached the grand climacteric without living children, which is many years away."

"Madame!" said Odette, embarrassed at so personal a revelation.

"Ah, pay no mind; I am only thinking aloud. I don't intend to impose on you." She reached to pull out her chair. "Come. I'm tired and hungry, and this food will end one of those two."

"I suppose that is true," said Odette.

Victoire indicated the two other chairs in the kitchen. "Draw one of those up and let us have this excellent supper."

Odette realized that she had been outmaneuvered. "If you insist, Madame."

"What do you think I have been doing these last five minutes?" she asked with a laugh. "Pour some of that red wine, too, the plain, not the fancy. Save the best bottles for company. We will have the Saint-Etienne." She took one of the good-sized rolls and broke it in half. "And tomorrow, let us have that good bean soup, with the minced ham in it. I am very fond of it."

"If it is what you want, Madame Vernet," said Odette carefully, for she was aware that the main attraction of the soup was that it was inexpensive and very filling.

"Soldiers' food for soldiers' wives," said Victoire, cutting more liver. "Pour the wine and sit down."

In the corner the kitchen cat gnawed on a slice of liver, purring and growling at once.

"The cat has killed two rats this week, and several mice; I have rewarded him," said Odette as if to defend the animal.

"Every kitchen needs a cat," said Victoire, and grinned in the direction of the large tortoise-shell tom. "I suspect he is as good a guardian as a dog could be." She paused for just an instant, remembering whom the last dog she had seen had bitten. "Please, Odette, sit."

This time Odette did as told. As a small token of defiance, she did not remove her apron, and was shocked when she saw that Victoire did not care. "Was it a difficult day, Madame?"

"Yes, but it was fruitful," said Victoire, giving every sign of enjoying her supper. "I had quite a long talk with Berthier, and he has not reassured me at all. He is very nearly convinced that I have a point in my concerns, and since Egypt he has occasionally been willing to give my warnings serious consideration. I have laid it all out before him, with my reasons for my apprehension. Between the file missing from the Ministry of Public Safety and what I have learned today, I am beginning to fear that these spies have aid in very high places. And that troubles me."

Odette stared at her. "When you say that the spies have aid, do you mean that there are men in the government who are helping them?"

"Yes, I am coming to think there must be." She leaned back. "Consider how matters stand: these spies must have reached Paris by now, if Paris is their destination. Yet they have not struck yet, which means that they are not here to strike at random, but have certain specific plans. Which must mean that they have people in Paris who are helping them. And in order to protect their actions, at least one of those people must be high enough to—"

"To lose files, and give misleading information!" said Odette, who had caught the direction of Victoire's notions.

"That is how it appears to me," said Victoire. "And I am trying to sort out who in the government would seek to aid such men as these spies must be. General Moreau should be beyond question. He is one of the most honored of our generals. And now he claims to have never seen the missing file. It would mean little if they were aided by Royalists, for most of them are known and their activities watched. So it does not seem likely that any of the Royalists would be able to perform the necessary tasks to misdirect official attention." She took a long sip of wine. "Therefore I must conclude that the spies have other supporters, men of power who have the ability to do the things the spies require in such a way that no comment is made."

"And the missing file?" asked Odette.

"That is clumsy, if it is truly part of the scheme." Victoire shook her head. "And it gives me to wonder if there is more than one person in the government who has made common cause with these English spies. If I knew to what end, I would be more able to assess the peril." She gestured her frustration, flinging her napkin halfway across the kitchen. "I haven't enough information, and if I make too many surmises, I risk overlooking pertinent clues." She had confided as much to Berthier while she was with him, and had had the satisfaction of obtaining his promise to keep her informed of any irregular conduct of the men around him.

"Then what more can you do?" asked Odette, eating with less gusto than Victoire.

"I don't know. I have to think about it," Victoire answered. "Perhaps when my husband returns he and I will be able to work it out between us." She resolutely put the matter out of her thoughts. "More to the point, however, is what we are going to do about the ball given by the Swedes at the end of next week."

"Is it essential that you go, Madame Vernet?" asked Odette.

"Now that Bernadotte and his wife have called on me, I don't see how I can refuse. It would be rude beyond anything to say that I cannot attend the Swedish ball when Bernadotte is their protégé. And that means doing something about one of my gowns. I cannot afford a new one, but if I purchase cloth for a new slip—a satin, perhaps—we can take one of the other robes and furbish it up somehow, can't we?"

"I suppose so," said Odette uncertainly, who had already helped Victoire to refashion more than four frocks to appear new.

"There may be something in my mother's trunks. They are in the attic, aren't they? If we look through them, we may come across something we can use." Victoire had another bit of wine. "Those dresses of hers are more than twenty years out of fashion but if we choose carefully, we may be able to use the fabrics, at least."

"It seems as if we are robbing the dead," said Odette sadly.

Victoire shared her uncertainty. "I know, I know, Odette. But it is how things are. With the carpenter wanting payment for repairing the windows and the staircase, I cannot find the money to purchase new ballgowns. I have already given up the hope of anything new for the Grand Reception, which is going to annoy Vernet when he learns of it. But it was rotted window frames or new gowns. So let us plan to raid my mother's chests." She felt the cat butt his head against her leg, and she reached down to scratch his head.

"We will do whatever we can. If you can find satin in a color you do not usually wear, that would help," said Odette, doing her best to make reasonable suggestions. "A rose, perhaps, or even a puce, if it—"

"Not puce," said Victoire emphatically. "I look as if I have succumbed to sunstroke in puce. But you may be right about a rose. I have not worn that shade very often—I do not think pale hair goes well with rose; it is a color for women with dark hair and pale skin—but it may be possible to find a color that will not make me look like a country milk-maid."

"There is a mercer at Saint-Sulpice, and occasionally he has very good fabrics for far less than you would pay for the same on the other side of the Seine." She pursed her lips. "I will go with you tomorrow morning, if that suits you."

"Yes, it does," said Victoire, who disliked shopping intensely, and never more than when she had to be so frugal. "I am most grateful for your help, Odette, and I realize that you deserve more than my thanks for this service."

Odette blushed. "If you had not employed me, Madame Vernet, I do not like to think what would have happened to me. I could not go back to my family, for they cannot provide for my brothers and sisters. My husband's family lost everything in the Revolution; he told you that before he died. So I would have been without any means if you—" She broke off. "All my brothers save the oldest have had to leave home and seek their fortunes. Two have gone to America, and I do not think we will ever see them again. There is only land and money enough for my oldest brother at home."

"And the others have gone to the army," said Victoire.

"Against my father's wishes," said Odette. "His dislike of the First Consul grows fiercer every day. He has declared that if France is to have a king, it had better be a proper Bourbon and not a Corsican upstart." She stared down at her hands as if her father's opinions might have stuck to her.

"Many another shares his sentiments," said Victoire. "I heard two men in the street today, and they were both decrying the opulence of Napoleon's court. The two men claimed that the Revolution had done nothing but brought a new crew of luxurious pirates to the throne." She coughed gently. "There are such complaints everywhere. I have heard that there was a small uprising in Normandy, not a month ago, of Normans seeking to restore the king to power."

"My father was not a revolutionary, but he said that the king had forgotten the people and his fate was because of that omission. Now he says that Napoleon is worse then the kings ever were, for the kings of France kept to France and did not career all over Europe in search of glory, but were content to summon glory to them." Odette sighed in confusion. "I have tried to reason with him, but he never listens to what women say. All he wishes to hear is that I have found another husband."

Victoire knew enough of Odette's past that this recitation could no longer shock her, but rather than being relieved, she felt responsibility more keenly. "If I knew of a suitable man, Odette, you may be certain that I would—"

"I know, Madame Vernet, and I thank you for your concern. There are other employers who would be at pains to keep men away from me, so that I would continue as housekeeper." She lifted her chin. "My sister works for one such; only two weeks ago she complained of it to me when she was allowed to visit for the afternoon. I did not know how to advise her. She sees men only at church, and then with an escort of other servants. But she has her sights on advancement by marrying the chef or the butler."

"Your sister is not very wise," said Victoire.

"Still," said Odette, "what else is she to do?"

For once Victoire had no answer, and so she changed the

subject. "How are we to deal with the demands on officers when the costs of these functions continue to multiply."

"We will think of something," said Odette, deliberately echoing Victoire's determined optimism.

In the mirror Victoire's reflection was slightly blurred due to the age of the glass. She took a step back and surveyed the ballgown she wore, her eyes narrowing critically to detect any obvious signs of refurbishment. The slip was long, falling from the high waist in thick folds of peau de soie in a color between rose and lilac called "Whispers." The robe over it was of heavy silver Belgian lace edged in silver and gold beading in a leaf pattern that was repeated in the silken shawl she wore over her shoulders. The silver velvet corsage was also beaded, and the lace tulip sleeves were lined in satin. Old-fashioned diamond drops hung from her ears, and a small tiara fronted the elaborate knot of fair curls on the crown of her head. She wore long white gloves and wished that she had a bracelet to clasp around one wrist, for as it was the gloves served only to indicate the scarcity of her jewels.

"It is very elegant, Madame Vernet," said Odette, who had buttoned her into the dress. "I don't think anyone would recognize what you have done. The lace is unusual, but I don't suppose anyone would suspect it came from your mother's old petticoat."

"I hope not," said Victoire earnestly. She reached up and adjusted the tiara, thinking to herself as she did that if there were no condition on her inheritance of it, it would be the next of her heirlooms to go, and the last of any significant value. As it was, she would be able to wear them until they were passed to her daughter.

"That ballgown of your mother's was very useful. All that silver lace, and the velvet." Odette had helped Victoire cup up the wide-skirted dress and the elaborate lace petticoats, and together they had pieced them into the lace robe and velvet corsage where the beading concealed much of the odd assembly they had done. "They don't make much of that style of lace anymore, do they?"

"No; the fashion has changed," said Victoire with a slight frown.

"Perhaps you will renew the fashion," said Odette. She tweaked the back of the robe where it fell in a short train. "Try not to let anyone step on this. I don't think the piecing will hold."

"Nor do I," said Victoire, and wrapped the shawl around her shoulders a second time, thinking that she would be pleased when fashion dictated something a trifle warmer for correct evening wear.

"The coach will be here in ten minutes, Madame," said Odette as she glanced anxiously at the clock. "With just the one footman."

"Don't start on that again, Odette," said Victoire without heat. "A coach is an extravagance, and two footmen would be completely unreasonable. Besides, I do not expect to be waylaid by highwaymen in the middle of Paris."

"There are others who could attack the coach," said Odette darkly.

"But they will not, not tonight. Fouche has put men on the street to ensure public safety. The Swedes have insisted on it. Not that I blame them, of course, but it is perhaps too much caution. Besides, these autumn nights are getting cold, and no robber wants to let his fingers get so stiff he cannot pull a trigger." Victoire reached for her reticule—it was her best one, with beading and pearls worked all over it. "But I am pleased you are concerned for my safety."

"If Inspector-General Vernet were here—" Odette began.

"Well, he is not. And I am capable of fending for myself, after all," said Victoire, suppressing a pang of loneliness. "He will be back by the first of the week, and then you need not worry so much that I might be waylaid."

"And are you carrying a charged pistol?" asked Odette, not entirely in jest.

"No, but I must suppose the footman will," said Victoire, unflustered. "And the coachman may well be armed, too." She took a last look at her reflection, then started toward the door. "You need not wait up for me."

Odette shook her head. "I will meet you when you come in, Madame, no matter what the hour. You cannot get out of those clothes without help, and after all the work we have done these last three days, I will not let you tear that lace, which you will unless I help you."

Victoire knew she was right. "Very well," she said, and started down the newly repaired stairs.

"It is a pity, Madame, that you cannot wear that dress on more than one occasion," said Odette as she watched Victoire descend.

"It certainly is," said Victoire with feeling.

* * *

Victoire completed her deep court curtsy to the Swedish Ambassador, and as she rose noticed the fixed expression in his prominent blue eyes. He must be exhausted with greeting so many guests, she thought to herself. I wonder if he will remember anyone? She accepted the soft-voiced pleasantries and answered with some equally inane, then passed on to Bernadotte, resplendent in his court uniform. Again she curtsied, but not as deeply as she had to the Ambassador. "Good evening, General."

"Good evening, Madame Vernet," he responded, bowing to kiss her hand. "You are an elegant sight. How very kind of you to come."

"You are very gracious," said Victoire. "I was surprised when your invitation came, for this is a very grand occasion. It is an honor to be included." She knew it was what he wanted to hear; she curtsied again and went on to Desirée. "Good evening, Madame Bernadotte."

"Madame Vernet," said Desirée, a faint twist of annoyance in her smile. "How kind of you to come."

"The kindness, Madame, was your invitation," said Victoire in proper form. "I am most appreciative that you would remember me."

"A pity your husband is not here," said Desirée, and she could not entirely conceal her spite. "But that is the fate of an officer's wife, isn't it?"

"Very true, but he will return shortly." Victoire said, telling Desirée what most certainly she knew.

"How fortunate. Such an attractive man ought not to be left alone too long." She looked sly as she motioned Victoire away so that she could greet the next man in line.

7

✤

NAPOLEON ARRIVED AMID a flurry of slamming doors and scurrying servants. Behind him were several generals, including Moreau, St. Cyr, Pichegru, and Ney, whose height and bright red hair made him easy to identify. Victoire had seen most of these men at various events she and Vernet were now required to attend.

Napoleon moved rapidly through the crowd, aides dashing competitively about to bring him a drink or sweet-meat. With him was his step-son Eugene, who had much of his mother's dark beauty but none of her wit. The generals, Victoire was told, had been with Napoleon to Berthier's estate hunting rabbits. They stood quietly near the entrance and sipped claret. For all the rushing about him, Napoleon managed to give the impression of calm among the chaos. He had something to say to each of the important men in the room. Roustam-Raza, his Mameluke guard, hovered a few steps behind him.

The tall Egyptian looked about the room and then smiled as he saw Victoire. Then he returned to staring threateningly at everyone who approached Napoleon.

As always, Napoleon's visit was brief: the First Consul's party was leaving less than twenty minutes after it arrived. From the alcove Victoire watched as the illustrious group vanished, leaving a great vacancy in the entrance to the embassy. She noticed a spot of wax on her corsage and sighed; it had dropped from one of the hundreds of candles in the tremendous chandeliers overhead. She tried to work it off with her fingernail but without success. So preoccupied was she that she did not notice the approach of a handsome, dark-haired man of moderate height in a magnificent dress uniform.

"Nothing damaged, I hope," said General Joachim Murat, bowing slightly to her.

Victoire looked up sharply. "Murat," Victoire was delighted to see him. "How are you, my friend." She curtsied and held out her hand to him.

"Well enough," said Murat with a hitch to his shoulders before he brushed the back of her gloved hand with his lips. "I did not realize you would be here."

"Meaning that this is a trifle above my touch. Yes. It rather surprised me, as well, but after General Bernadotte and his wife did me the honor of calling on me, I could not refuse the invitation." She said it very calmly, and Murat's brows rose speculatively.

"Well, well, well," he said. "I wonder what they're up to now?"

"Exactly so; it strikes you as suspicious as well," said Victoire. She gave him an ironic smile. "I do not grasp why they decided to invite me."

"Your husband is not back in Paris by any chance, is he?" asked Murat.

A liveried servant went by, a tray bearing glasses filled with champagne held aloft. Murat took two glasses and handed one to Victoire.

"Thank you," said Victoire. "No, my husband is not yet back in Paris, which gives me pause. He is expected shortly, but . . ." She indicated that she was alone with a gesture of her free hand.

"Perhaps they are hoping that you will be their advocate with him," said Murat, touching the rim of his glass to hers. "Do you know why they should want an advocate?"

"No; but I suspect you're right, it is something like that, but I cannot think why they need my good opinion, or why they want to influence my husband." She sipped the champagne, then looked over the rim at him. "Your wife is here, of course."

"Just at present she is talking with Pichegru. You can see her, over there in the dress with the green velvet train." He looked at her then directed his gaze toward the entrance to the ballroom. "She is irked because her brother would not stay. She wants to be Napoleon's favorite, so that the whole world knows it."

"It would not hurt you if Napoleon gave more time to your wife, for you would share in the sister's favor, wouldn't you," said Victoire, who had always found the First Consul's sisters puzzling women. "That family is worse than the Consulate."

Murat shrugged philosophically. "It is why Napoleon has such skill in the Consulate, I suspect. The family has been superior training. At the moment the quarrels are about Lucien marrying the widow, but in a week or a month or two it will be something else. At least Pauline has a favorite now, and so she is not running through the generals and Marshalls with her usual abandon."

Victoire nodded. "How do you like being a Buonaparte by marriage?" It was a tactless question, but she hoped that Murat was enough her friend that he would not require her to be more diplomatic.

"It is not quite what I expected it would be," said Murat candidly. "Not that it hasn't some very fine aspects to offer. It is very flattering to have Caroline dote on me, but there is a price to her adoration: her ambitions are as tremendous as her brother's. I don't mind that in a leader like Napoleon—in fact, I think ambition is a most desirable attribute in such a man—but in a wife . . ." He looked directly at her. "The trouble is, Victoire, that I find her desire for advancement and power very seductive." He hesitated. "At least I am still ambivalent about it. I fear the day when Caroline will have persuaded me with her promises of position and glory."

Victoire regarded him very seriously. "I do not wish to speak against your wife, but if she awakens that sort of appetite in you, Murat, she has done you no service."

"If I cannot achieve it, possibly." Murat lowered his voice. "That is the trouble, good friend. Why not seize the day, take the golden cup? I look around me, and the generals are all scrambling to reach the heights. Look at Bernadotte and the Swedes, and he is not the only one. Napoleon has it in him to offer crowns to us now, and if he is giving them out to his relatives, why should my wife and I hang back?"

"Murat!" whispered Victoire, shocked.

"Those are the notions I regret." He glanced around. "You must tell me, Victoire, if I go beyond the limits."

"You are sensible enough to know for yourself," she said at once.

"I would like to think so, but I begin to suspect it may not be true, and so I ask you to be my good angel. God knows you have been so before." His blue eyes grew distant. "In Egypt, and two years ago. No one could ask for a stauncher friend than you. If ever there were anyone trustworthy for this task, it is you." His expression lightened. "And you are less impressed with rank and finery than any woman I know. You have never been dazzled by splendid uniforms or fine titles."

"I should hope not," said Victoire with asperity. "Murat, what is the matter with you? Are you consumed with melancholy?"

"That is the quality I mean—your dedication to seeing things as they are." He smiled at her, not the gracious political smile he used with most people, but with mischief, as if he were still an impish seminarian.

"You are making too much of a practical turn of mind," she said, having no other way to acknowledge what was to her profound praise.

"No, I am not. It is your greatest virtue and most tenacious sin," said Murat, finishing the last of his champagne.

"For heaven's sake, Murat," she said, growing confused. "What a capricious mood you are in tonight."

"Actually, I'm not," said Murat. "But I am bored with these grand functions that eat up so much time. It takes me back to the days when I was in school, and we had to memorize page after page of Greek and Latin. There came a point when I would have preferred to learn German, just for variety." He found a small table and there he put his empty champagne glass. "Since it would be very unwise of me to avoid these receptions and balls, I put my mind to my task, and rejoice when we have the opportunity for a little conversation."

This assurance did not satisfy Victoire. "Murat, what is the matter?" she insisted.

"I've told you," said Murat. "And I have never been more serious in my life." He indicated the room with a wave of his hand. "This is a very heady brew, and few can resist it. I am putting my faith in you, Madame Vernet. I am asking you— very humbly, whether it seems so or not—to help me keep from being entirely sucked in."

Victoire regarded him seriously. "All right, if that is what you truly want, I give you my word I will do what I may to warn you if I perceive you are too caught up in the life of the court."

"It is not a court quite yet but it is getting there," said Murat. He cleared his throat. "We've been talking long enough—much more and tongues will wag, which will not do either of us any good." He lifted her hand and bowed over it. "I will visit you day after tomorrow, in the afternoon, if that is convenient?"

"Certainly," said Victoire. "Will your wife be with you?"

"I think not," said Murat. "I chose the day she is engaged to spend the afternoon with her family." He started to move away from her, his political smile fixed firmly over his teeth.

"But Murat—" Victoire protested, then stopped. She realized he had been right when he warned her that they could create comment—it had happened before. She moved out of the alcove and looked around the ballroom.

More than twenty couples were dancing, but the greatest number of guests were busy with conversations. A dozen high-ranking officers in elaborate dress uniforms stood around the Ambassador, seeking to establish a place with the Swedes, who were much in favor with the First Consul.

"Well, and what do you make of it?" said Marshall Louis Alexandre Berthier as he came up to her, bowing before he took her hand. He was rigged out in all his finery, which served only to make his lamentably blocky figure and plain face the more noticeable.

Victoire's greeting to him was not so cordial as the one she had given Murat. She curtsied and accepted his pro forma kiss on her hand. "I haven't seen enough to come to any conclusions," she answered.

"Oh, I doubt that, Madame Vernet; I suspect you draw conclusions in your sleep," said Berthier. "You make more conclusions, and more accurately, than most of the men working for me." He paused. "Your husband isn't back, so it would not be proper for me to ask you to dance. So let us agree to stand and talk for a moment."

"All right," said Victoire, her curiosity piqued.

Berthier moved a little closer, shoving his hands deep in his pockets. "I have spoken with General Moreau. About the file he took from Fouche's Ministry." He cleared his throat nervously. "He has said it was returned."

"Oh?" said Victoire.

"He told me he no longer has it." Berthier coughed diplomatically. "It would hardly be suitable for me to question the word of a fellow officer, but it troubles me that there is no record of the return of the file at the Ministry."

"Yes, it is troubling," Victoire agreed. "Fouche does not tolerate sloppiness."

"No, he does not." Berthier began to stroll toward a group of officers; he motioned Victoire to come with him. "Therefore I ask myself what can have occurred. I will take advantage of this meeting to find out what you make of it."

Victoire took up the question at once, her light-blue eyes brightening with interest. "First, it may be that General Moreau is not telling you the truth. He may or he may not still have the file. If he does not have the file, it is possible that he returned it to Fouche, or that he gave it to someone else. Or it may be that he destroyed it. If he returned it to the Ministry, it may be that someone there purloined it, or that its return was not recorded, or recorded inaccurately. Or it is possible that Fouche is lying, and that he does indeed have the file and is seeking for some reason to cast doubts on General Moreau."

Berthier was able to smile at Victoire's quick summing up. "This is what I enjoy about you, Madame Vernet—this ability of yours to consider everything."

"Hardly everything," said Victoire. "But it is a stimulating exercise, and one I, too, enjoy." She had the last of the champagne Murat had offered her. "Give me a little time, and I will be able to prepare a more complete assessment."

"That is the very reason I am talking with you now. I do want your thoughts on this question, and as soon as you are able. But," he went on, lowering his voice, "I do not want you to discuss this with anyone else."

"By anyone else, do you mean Fouche, or do you include my husband as well?" Victoire asked, not quite friendly.

"I mean Fouche and any of the other officers. Your husband, naturally, is exempt from any restrictions I impose. It would not be fitting for me to place such restraints on a wife in regard to her husband." His frizzy hair made a sort of halo around his large, square face as he stopped in front of a large sconce of candles. "I will send a messenger to you in a few days—let us say three days—and you will hand him your summation. Is that satisfactory?"

"Do you want me to sign this summation?" Victoire inquired.

"I will leave that to you. Whatever you believe is most wise will be acceptable to me." He bowed to her without taking his hands from his pockets. "I am pleased to have seen you here, Madame Vernet, and I look forward to another conversation with you in the near future."

"Thank you," said Victoire automatically, noticing that Berthier was becoming ill-at-ease. "I wish you good evening, General Berthier." She glanced around to see if there was any obvious reason for his discomfort but could discern nothing out of the way.

Berthier was already heading toward the door, looking around as if he feared he was being pursued.

The rest of the evening passed quickly, a glittering blur of polite conversations and whispered gossip. Murat did not approach Victoire again, and no other officer singled her out for anything more than compliments to be passed to her husband upon his return.

* * *

Claude Montrachet faced Colonel Sir Magnus Sackett-Hartley across the single plank table that, along with two stools and a mattress, had been installed in the rented house. "I say you are wrong."

"You are taking too great a risk," said Sackett-Hartley. "No matter how great the gain could be, you stand to lose your men, and that is not a wise trade."

"It is necessary," Montrachet insisted stubbornly. "If we do not act, we will lose the advantage we have gained."

Sackett-Hartley threw up his hands in dismay. "What advantage is that? This house? Our quarters at the inn?" he demanded. "You seem to think that just because we have been able to reach Paris and have not been discovered in little more than a week, that we are therefore secure. I don't think we can afford to make that assumption."

"You are too cautious," said Montrachet. "I have been able to attend several grand functions already. Now that I have another horn, I have access through the little consorts who provide entertainment for those around the Corsican. There would be no difficulty in getting a few more of our men into such an occasion. It would be an easy matter to conceal a weapon, and then wait for Napoleon's arrival." He folded his arms—he no longer wore a sling—and glared.

A slow drizzle was falling, not enough to make noise, but everything had turned dank and cold; the low fire in the single hearth made little headway against it.

"Very sensible, killing the man in the middle of all his officers, with all his supporters around him. That's supposing that it would be possible to attack him at all, for someone would likely throw himself in front of the fellow to protect him. Whether we succeeded or not, how should any of us escape?" Sackett-Hartley was not impressed with what Montrachet proposed. "Or do you think we would have the opportunity to turn our weapons on ourselves?"

"That is a possibility," said Montrachet stiffly.

"If you think that it would be possible, you are forgetting the company—they may wear satin and gold braid, but they are soldiers, those men around him, his generals." He faced Montrachet, growing more annoyed. "Napoleon is guarded by his Grenadiers, the Consular Guard, even at balls. And there is that Mameluke, as well, the one from Egypt who is always with him. They say the man sleeps across the door of Napoleon's bedchamber. Do you suppose that anyone could get off more than one shot in such a gathering?"

"I think there would be sufficient confusion to make it worth the attempt; it is better than waiting for the perfect opportunity to present itself," said Montrachet firmly. "You credit these upstarts with too much sense and purpose. If anything should happen to Napoleon, there would be such confusion that I venture to guess that we could all escape before we were detected. If you are not willing to try, you and your lot can continue to hide at Le Chat Gris, and slink back to England when I and my men have done what we have sworn to do."

"We don't know enough, not yet," said Sackett-Hartley, switching to English as his emotions grew more heated. "We don't know what the Ministry of Safety knows, we don't know if our allies have been able to remove all mention of the men with us. If anything remains in the files, it will be an easy thing for Fouche's people to recognize and detain all of us. And you know what that will mean."

Montrachet's lip curled with contempt. "Why do you assume we must fail? If your uncle had been as timorous as you are, he would have been useless."

Now Sackett-Hartley was angry. "My uncle succeeded because he would not be led to foolish bravado. He had daring, but that is not recklessness. You are mistaking a grand gesture for a triumph, and that way lies ruin for us all."

"Do you think so?" Montrachet laughed. "What a fool you are."

"Because I am circumspect? You think I am a coward because I will not be so imprudent as to undertake the hazardous action you have decided you want?" He paced the length of the room. "You have not heard from our allies, and yet you think you can proceed without their help. I do not agree, and I will advise those seven men with me to have nothing to do with so ill-conceived a scheme as yours." He turned on his heel and started toward the door. "I am not going to help you bring us all to execution, not if there is anything I can do to prevent it."

"The Frenchmen will see it my way," said Montrachet confidently.

"Ask them," Sackett-Hartley recommended.

"You may be sure that I will," said Montrachet, and watched as Sackett-Hartley slammed out of the ancient house. When the Englishman was gone, Montrachet drew up one of two three-legged stools in the room and sat down. He reached inside his coat and drew out a large, sealed envelope. Smiling, he opened the envelope and drew out the thick folds of paper that had once been in Fouche's files. With mental thanks to General

Moreau, he unfolded the pages and smoothed them out on the plank table. Taking his time about it, he started to read.

When Murat, now serving as Governor of Paris, came to the Vernets' house, Odette presented him with a variety of little cakes, a pâté in the Norman style, and two kinds of cheese, along with a deep red Côtes du Rhone that had an aftertaste of raspberries. She knew he was quite busy preparing the city for the Coronation Napoleon had ordered, less than two months off, and wanted to show him her best. There were rumors that even the Pope would attend.

"This is quite good," Murat approved as he helped himself and glanced at his hostess. He was in uniform, but not one of the very grand dress ones he often chose to wear to impress others. "And if I know how things are with you, you've sacrificed supper for the next two or three days to provide this for me."

Victoire gave him a shocked stare. "How can you say that?"

"I can say it because it is the truth." He poured wine for both of them. "Give me a little credit, Madame Vernet. You and I have been through too much together for you to deceive me on this point. Between our narrow escape on the Nile, the problem in Italy, and that intrigue two years ago, there is a tie holding us." He cut a slice of cheese. "I noticed your ballgown the other evening."

"What was wrong with it?" Victoire asked, chiding herself for giving away so much.

"Nothing, if one did not observe it carefully. In fact, it was a most ingenious creation. I admire your skills and your audacity. But if you continue to use old lace and old velvet, someone other than myself will notice eventually, and that will not redound to your advantage." He took a bite of the cheese. "This is excellent."

"What do you mean, old lace and old velvet?" she challenged.

"I might not have noticed," said Murat in an abstracted tone. "But my grandmother made lace, you see, and I remember those patterns she used to do. The lace you wore was like that, and much heavier than what you would buy today. Therefore, I surmised that you had raided your mother's closets, as it were, and had made up the dress that way."

"There are people who still make the old lace patterns," said Victoire without conviction. "They sell them more cheaply because they are not in vogue, and I like them quite as well as the current modes."

"There are dolts out there who might believe that farrago, but I am not one," said Murat. "It won't fadge, my friend." His smile took the worst sting out of what he said. "I know your circumstances are straitened. If you think——"

Victoire interrupted him. "Did you mention this to anyone?"

"No. Why should I? But I remarked upon it to myself because it confirmed what I have suspected this last year and more—the station granted your husband forces you to live beyond your means, Madame, through no fault of your own, and you are suffering for it." He put his wineglass aside. "And that saddens me; I am concerned for you."

"It vexes me," said Victoire, abandoning her affronted manner. "But what am I to do, Murat? The fact of the matter is that Vernet's salary does not cover the expenses of being an Inspector-General, and my inheritance is barely adequate to keeping this house. With the cost of everything rising, what are we to do?"

"Vernet is not in a position to borrow, is he? I understand he is a younger son." Murat helped himself to one of the little cakes.

It was apparent to Victoire that Murat had made himself familiar with the facts of their lives. "His father could not afford to leave him much, and what there was is entailed. It provides him a little income each year, but——"

"Fouche does not like to hear high officials have run into debt. He fears that makes them subject to bribes and other temptations." Murat had a bit of pâté. "Is this your recipe, or did your housekeeper supply it?"

"The recipe is my mother's," said Victoire.

"It is wonderful." The compliment was sincere but it was also clearly a delaying tactic while Murat achieved the best position. "Fouche has asked many of us to see that some officers resign rather than risk having them compromised. They were of lower office, still . . . I don't want to alarm you, but it could happen to Vernet if matters continue as they are."

"I am aware of that," said Victoire, watching Murat narrowly. "Why do you mention this? If you want to offer Vernet another position, I warn you that he will not accept. This is the work he wants to do, and unless——"

"I don't need him on my staff, even if he were inclined to accept such an offer, which I doubt he would," said Murat at once. "He is at best an adequate horseman. Though it served him well enough against that traitor in Egypt. No, that was not what I intend for him, or, more correctly, for you." He looked directly at Victoire. "I propose to extend you a loan, a sizeable one."

Victoire straightened in her chair. "A loan, Murat? In exchange for what?"

"Oh, don't poker up like that, Victoire," said Murat with a chuckle. "I've had too many opportunities to compromise you already to need to bribe you now, were that my intent."

As much as Victoire wanted to be offended, she could not manage it. She pressed her lips together, but a smile escaped out the corners. "All right, you are not trying to corrupt me," she allowed. "I'll give you that much."

"Good," he approved. "Now, about the loan. It will be private, between you and me. I will not ask any collateral, and there will not be demands imposed on you later. You have my word on that. But there is something I expect in exchange, and I do not expect you to refuse me: I do want to be kept informed if there are any activities against me."

"But I do that already," said Victoire, thinking back two years ago. "And I would continue to do it; you do not need to offer me money."

"But you need money. And your husband is an honest man. There are too few of those in the world." He had more of the wine. "Listen to me, Victoire. There are too many men coming to the government who are there for their own advancement before any attempts at justice. Those men who, like your husband, are trying to maintain the ideals on which the Republic was founded are being driven from position by these hyenas, or are succumbing to other influences through bribes and coercion. Therefore it is necessary that Vernet and those few like him be supported in their work. And to that end, I will underwrite his work through the loan I extend privately to you. If you like, you need not tell him about it, or say that it was a legacy from a relative."

"I do not like to lie to Vernet," said Victoire stiffly.

"It is up to you, however you handle it," said Murat. "But do not refuse out of hand, not with the changes that are coming to France. France needs men like your husband, and I would not like to try to find my way through this Consulary snakepit without an occasional timely warning from a friend I can trust."

"You are bribing me, in fact?" she asked, intending to be playful but not succeeding.

"That isn't what I would call it; I have said it is a loan," Murat told her as he cut another slice of cheese.

"But you say nothing of repayment. You mean that you will not require me to repay you? You are actually making a gift which you are rendering tolerable by calling it a loan?" Victoire asked, color mounting in her cheeks.

"Madame Vernet, both you and I must hope that your husband's services will bring him better fortunes than what he now enjoys," said Murat. "And you are not without resources of your own."

"You expect me to break my father's trust in order to repay you?" Victoire demanded. "Murat, this is ludicrous."

"I expect nothing of the sort," said Murat bluntly. "I expect you to be the sensible woman you are and agree to take the money. I will put it in writing that I will ask nothing of you than what you already provide. I will stipulate that you must leave my heirs the money in your will, if that makes you feel less burdened by the loan." He poured a glass of wine for her. "Victoire, you are not a married hussy who seeks to make her husband's promotions on her back, and you are not a puppeteer pulling his strings. You are a good wife and for that alone I would admire you. But I owe you my life, for Egypt and two years ago. How can I, in honor, see you floundering and not do what I can to help you?"

She accepted the glass of wine he handed to her. "I would hardly call it saving your life."

"I would, and I was there," said Murat dryly. "Little as you may think there is reason for it, you have my gratitude for heroism that most soldiers would envy." He touched the rim of her glass with his. "If you want to be my friend, let me discharge some of the obligation I have to you through this loan."

Victoire sighed. "The trouble is, you make it all seem so sensible," she protested. "I shouldn't listen to you—we both know that—but I cannot help feeling persuaded by all you say. Those years of education have stood you in good stead, Murat."

"A rueful compliment if ever I heard one," said Murat, smiling a little. "Tell me you will accept my loan, then, and then let us settle for a comfortable gossip. I haven't been able to do that for weeks."

"I ought to tell you no," said Victoire slowly. "I know I ought to, but—"

"But you are a sensible woman, and you know that it is better to have money from me than leave Vernet exposed to bribes and the possibility of losing his post." His dark-blue eyes glistened. "I have said that you are a woman of rare perspicacity. And you have demonstrated it yet again."

"Vernet won't like it," Victoire predicted, then recalled their conversation of a month ago. "But he might prefer this to running the risks you mention."

"He is a reasonable man, your husband. So handle this in any way you wish, Madame, and let us then forget about it." Murat gave her one of the little cakes. "For heaven's sake, eat something, Victoire. I am beginning to think that this is all the food you have in the house."

"It's not quite that bad," she confessed.

"How reassuring," he said without excusing his sarcasm. "Why didn't you tell me about this? Why didn't you inform me?"

"It isn't your concern, Murat," she said bluntly.

"And why not?" he asked. "Because I am married to Napoleon's sister? Because we are not relatives? You are my comrade-at-arms, and that bond runs deeper than blood." He seemed almost angry. "Let me do something virtuous for once, will you?"

"I've said I'll accept the loan," she said grudgingly.

"As you would have a rotten tooth drawn," Murat responded at once. "You know it is the sensible thing to do, but you loathe doing it." He put his wineglass down. "The draft was deposited to your account by my advocate before I came here. According to what the banker was told, an uncle left it to you. That is all he knows and all he will be able to find out, I've made certain of that. For you did have an Uncle Remi who has been dead little more than a year, didn't you? You will discover that the money appears to have come from him." The admission was not contrite. "It is an accomplished thing."

Victoire wanted so much to be outraged, to upbraid Murat for such presumption, but try as she might, she could not muster the necessary indignation. She began half a dozen expostulations but abandoned them almost at once. Finally she took a long sip of wine and did her best to organize her thoughts. "When did you decide to do this?"

"At the Swedish reception," said Murat. "When I realized how badly you needed my help. That I might finally pay back part of what I owe you. I must admit it is a relief to be able to do so." He went on in a more distant tone. "You know, I've seen a man die of poison before. I watched that Italian officer suffering so terribly, and felt helpless. If you had not warned me, I would have died the same way. There is not money enough in this world to pay for being spared that." He regarded her steadily. "Are you angry with me?"

"I should be," she said. "I know it is very improper of me to accept this money, and I know that Vernet will be shocked." She reached out and took a slice of cheese for herself. "But I cannot conceal from you what relief it is to know that we will not be ruined."

This time Murat chuckled. "It is also a great relief to me, Madame."

She answered his grin with one of her own. "You are much too clever, Murat."

"Would that it were so," he answered with a pretense at humility. "Let us say that I am wise enough to realize when I am likely to be out-gunned by you, and therefore have the sense to prepare."

Her expression grew more serious. "I hope that it will be possible to explain it to Vernet so handily."

"Do not doubt it," said Murat. "You and I are not the only ones in Paris to have such a bargain. Do not doubt that Vernet knows it. And if this is not sufficient assurance for you, have him talk with me, and I will give him whatever guarantees he wishes to ensure your protection." His manner changed again, now becoming more worldly. "I have little enough to be proud of in my life—and do not remind me of the cavalry charges I have led, for that is not virtue—but this is one thing I can do that is not tainted with the lust for power or glory. It would please, though likely astound, my old instructors at the seminary."

Victoire frowned though she spoke lightly enough. "It would be uncharitable of me to deprive you of an opportunity for virtue, is that your argument?"

"It is," said Murat. "And so I will tell Vernet, if he taxes me with my arrangement with you."

"Vernet knows of our friendship and trusts us both without question." Victoire fixed him with her stare.

Joachim Murat smiled. His reputation with the ladies, before Caroline, had been considerable. But there had never been any question of his behavior toward Victoire. "Very wise of him."

"Very well, I capitulate," she said as she passed him the wine to refill his glass. "And I hope that neither of us will have cause to regret this."

8

❦

INSPECTOR-GENERAL LUCIEN Vernet arrived home a week later; it was a deceptive autumn day with bright sunlight belied by a chill wind and deep shadows that leached the heat out of the air. He entered his house at mid-afternoon to discover his wife and their housekeeper in deep conversation with a carpenter and his assistant.

"What a scene to greet a man," he said. "What disaster threatens us now?"

"No disaster," said Victoire, turning to him with delight. "And less than ever now that you are home."

He had put down the case he was carrying, and held his arms open to her. "Ah, Victoire!" he exclaimed as she ran to him.

The carpenter stared at them curiously, but he remained discreetly silent beside Odette.

"They are staring," whispered Victoire between kisses.

"Let them," answered Vernet. "They might learn something."

"Perhaps I ought to come back tomorrow," suggested the carpenter, looking at Odette for an answer.

She shook her head. "No. Let us withdraw to the kitchen and review what we have discussed with you. Madame and I have already gone over what is required." She cocked her head toward the embracing couple. "He is a returning soldier. Neither of them will have any attention to spare."

"No doubt you're right," said the carpenter, and resigned himself to an hour in the kitchen with the housekeeper.

As soon as the two were gone, Vernet lifted Victoire into his arms. "I have missed you. I could not miss food and drink more."

She wanted to give him a bantering answer, but the words stopped in her throat and she put her arms around his neck. "I thought I would perish of missing you."

"You had better not," he warned her, starting toward the stairs, and remarking as he started upward, "Ah. The bannister is repaired at last."

"It was necessary," she said, paying little attention to this domestic detail. "If you'd sent a messenger ahead, everything would have been ready to welcome you."

"I'd rather surprise you," said Vernet, shoving his way through the door into their room. "Look at the welcome you've given me." Playfully he tossed her onto the bed.

"It is hardly a welcome yet," she said, and reached out to him again, this time with passion in her eyes. "Let me show you what welcome is."

He was pulling at his pelisse, discarding his uniform hastily as she worked the fastenings holding her muslin housedress. When he was down to shirt and unmentionables, he reached for her again. "By God and Saint Michael, Victoire, you grow more intoxicating to me with every passing day."

"Then you should come home more often," she said, attempting to pull her dress over her head without standing up.

"Let me do that," he offered, and took the bodice in both hands, tugging upward.

Then she was in her slip and corset, and she reached to pull his shirt out of the waistband of his unmentionables. "And take off your boots," she recommended.

He sat down at once and obliged her, tossing the boots across the room before he turned to wrap her in his arms again. "Take the pins out of your hair." He had already pulled one out of the neat coronet of braids she wore. "And loosen it."

"If you will take the rest of your clothes off," she bargained as much to get her breath back as to take her hair down.

"Agreed," he said, and rose to pull off his unmentionables. Now he was in his underwear and she could see clearly how excited he was.

She had her hair down and had unfastened the lacings of her corset. With two expert wiggles, she was out of her clothes entirely. "Come. Warm me." In spite of the desire gathering in her, the chill of the room intruded.

"Very well," he said, and cast the last of his garments aside as she flung back the bedding.

His body was familiar and strange at once, but his ardor propelled them together with feverish intensity. The sharpness of their need left little time for subtlety. There were not enough ways to touch or taste or unite them that fully gratified them as they came together; they strove a second time and finally a third before the frenzy left them.

* * *

"I am perplexed," Vernet admitted two days later as they sat together in the withdrawing room, listening to the sound of hammers and saws in the parlor. "I don't like this covert arrangement, but—" He indicated the house. "The work is required, and how else could it be done?"

"I know of no way," said Victoire. She stared around the room. "Murat told me that the bank has nothing that would link the money to him. And it is true that my Uncle Remi might have left me something—had he anything to leave." Her brows drew together. "I have tried to think of a way to return the money without exposing him and myself to the sort of attention that would embarrass all of us, and I have yet to hit upon the means."

Vernet nodded. "Your friend Murat appears to have anticipated everything." He slapped his hands together. "Well, I won't say that the money isn't welcome; it spares me from having to compromise my position. But it could prove—"

"I don't think Murat will say anything, to anyone," said Victoire. "I have given this my close consideration, and I believe he meant what he said to me. I know that his wife would not approve of the loan, and no doubt Napoleon would dislike having one of his Inspectors beholden to a Marshall, and so I think Murat will keep his word, and the matter will remain private." She studied an old print hanging on the far wall as if she had never seen it before. "I was afraid of what you would think of me, Vernet, when I told you of this. I was afraid you might suppose that I had entered into a clandestine—"

"Affair?" Vernet finished for her. "There are many husbands who might be excused for thinking such things of their wives, especially with a man like Murat, so handsome and powerful. His escapades once were the talk of Italy, and then he was just a wounded General du Brigade. There are men who would encourage their wives in such things. But those women are not you, Victoire, and I know it. So does Murat, it appears."

She continued to stare at the print. "I would despise myself if I thought you suspected, even for an instant, that I would—"

"'Well, I do not suspect you," Vernet interrupted her. "I know you are loyal to me and faithful to your vows." He reached over and took her hand. "It bothers me that you were so reluctant to tell me of this. I know it is awkward, but the fact that you admit you hesitated, that causes me grief, for it seems that you do not have the reliance upon me that I have reposed in you."

Her answer was delayed as a fury of hammering sounded on the other side of the door.

"That was not why I hesitated," she said when the drubbing stopped.

"It may not be the entire reason, but it was part of it, most surely," said Vernet. "I can see it in your eyes." He rose and took a turn about the room. "You could have kept it from me, couldn't you?"

"No," she answered.

"Murat provided the means—he cloaked the loan." His tone was not accusing but there was something hard at the back of his eyes. "You could have remained silent and let me believe what the banker said."

"No," she repeated. "I could not."

His face softened. "No," he agreed. "And that is why I know that there is no reason for me to doubt you or suspect your motives." He came back to where she sat and drew her up out of the chair. "You would no more permit me to be deceived than you would let Murat be poisoned."

"You make it sound so dire," she protested, but without the same pragmatism she might have used for another issue.

"Not dire, my love. It is what I value in you, and why." He bent to kiss her, and she responded to the surge of passion that went through him. "Sadly, I have an appointment with Fouche in an hour," he said as he stepped back from her. "If I did not, we might well be back in bed. Again."

"There is always this evening," she whispered.

"After the banquet, I fear," he said reluctantly. "I am bidden to Pichegru's for an officer's banquet. It is expected to continue until ten." He gestured his resignation. "I must not refuse to attend. There are too many men coming who have asked to hear about the state of affairs in Antwerp."

She knew this was true but could not disguise the disappointment she felt. "Perhaps tomorrow morning we might rise late."

"It is possible," he answered. "If my duties do not require me to report at first muster."

"Heaven forbid!" said Victoire.

"Amen," answered Vernet. "But tomorrow afternoon I am released from duty at four. That will give us all evening, and leave time for supper, as well." Anticipation shone in his eyes. "Will you be willing to wait until then?"

"If I must," she said. "But I warn you, these few hours will be harder to endure than all those weeks we were apart. It is one thing to miss you when you are in Antwerp, and quite another thing when you are in Paris." She reached out and touched his face. "I don't think I will ever grow tired of loving you, Lucien."

"That is reassuring," he said. "For I know I will never grow tired of you."

At the soirée the guest of honor was Count Jean Rapp. The able if rather stolid soldier had been with the infantry in Egypt, an exceptionally honest and dependable general. Napoleon noticed these qualities and had recently been sending the often-wounded Rapp as his representative to sensitive but not complicated negotiations. Most of these were with the many small German states that stood between France and Prussia.

So the company was mostly military men and their wives, although some of the more important ministers and a few favored intellectuals were included, along with the great actor Talma, who held court so graciously that most of the ambitious men around him regarded him with veiled outrage. Count Lazare Carnot—much to everyone's surprise—had put aside his well-known distaste for Paris and the Consulate and presented himself in the very elegant drawing rooms of Viscount François René Chateaubriand and his wife Celeste.

Here everyone was fashionably unfashionable, dressing with studied restraint, taking care not to flaunt their wealth or position, deliberately wearing few jewels; there were no elaborate coiffeurs; as it was late afternoon, most of the women were dressed in promenade frocks instead of ballgowns, and the men wore parade instead of dress uniforms. This liberal attitude of restraint was reflected in the guests, several of whom were at odds with the Consulate.

This was just to Victoire's liking, for it promised stimulating conversation and the chance to observe the machinations of power. She had worn a pretty walking dress in pale-blue sateen with a half-robe and corsage of dove-gray that complemented her light-blue eyes without making her appear washed-out. Her hair was in a braided coronet without any curls around her face. She had new kid boots of gray that buttoned almost to the swell of her calf. She left her walking coat with the footman, though the room was chillier than was comfortable.

"I am going to try to talk with Carnot," Vernet said to Victoire shortly after they arrived. "He may not want to talk to me, but possibly he will have information for us, or would be willing to make a few educated guesses. Wish me good fortune." He kissed her hand and wandered away through the crowd.

It did not take very long for Victoire to get her bearings. She started toward the buffet, taking care to greet every woman she knew, but allowing herself to be drawn into conversation with none. Most of the conversations she heard related to the upcoming Coronation of Napoleon as Emperor of France. Not all were approving and Victoire wondered if Fouche had any agents among the crowd. Lost in this thought she was startled when a small, middle-aged woman with intense eyes and the manner of a street-seller reached out and grabbed her arm.

"Madame," exclaimed Victoire, louder than she intended. Then she recognized the woman and her shock ended. "Madame LeNormande," she said, dropping the older woman a curtsy.

"Madame Vernet," she answered, ignoring the others stand ing around her and paying no notice to the astonishment her ac tion caused. Madame LeNormande was a striking woman, seeming by force of character to be taller and more impressive than she actually was, for she was slight, of no more than average height, and was rumored to wear spectacles when alone. She was somewhere between thirty-five and forty-five, her hair negligently coifed and fading. Her black eyes were keen and intelligent.

"It is surprising to see you here," said Victoire. "I did not think you enjoyed these entertainments."

"I don't," said Madame LeNormande curtly, paying no attention to the dismay this announcement caused in the women around her. "But I realized that it was important I attend, so here I am."

One of the women gave Madame LeNormande a reproachful stare. "You had not finished my fortune," she complained.

"Ah!" Madame LeNormande made a quick, dismissing gesture. "Your husband will be in high favor until 1817, at which time he will fall. You will be taken in by your oldest son and his family, and will live with them quite comfortably for the rest of your life. You will have eight grandchildren, and two of them will prosper in America." She spoke quickly and without much interest. Then she swung back toward Victoire. "You, Madame Vernet, do not have such a life. Pray remove your right glove."

In the three years since she met Madame LeNormande, Victoire could not make up her mind about the woman: many of those around Napoleon—and Napoleon himself—swore by her predictions and said that she had the gift of prophesy. That might be true, thought Victoire, but she has the conduct of a charlatan; yet the woman was so accurate that she had twice been confined to the Bastille for her predictions. She tugged off her glove and reluctantly held out her hand, her eyes on her palm and not on the woman proposing to read it.

Madame LeNormande stared first at Victoire's wrists. "There are three, and possibly a fourth." She pointed to the lines just below Victoire's hands. "These are the bracelets, and it is these, not the lines in the hand that reveal longevity. It would appear that you will live for sixty, perhaps seventy years at most, if you do not encounter a fatal accident. You have the capacity for . . . let us say sixty-five to sixty-eight years of life, and all but the last will be passed generally in good health, unless you should bring misfortune upon yourself. Your hands are well-formed, not too broad, the fingers slightly longer than the palm. You will not be content to sit at home, and you will deal directly with those you encounter." She then peered down at the palm itself. "You are a woman of rare intellect. You see this line? It is the indication of the mind. It shows that you are a very thoughtful woman, most observant and of great mental capacity, for the line goes all the way to the edge of the palm, and it is very straight. You are not often distracted by melancholy and you do not permit yourself to become lost in cloudy theories." She touched the deep line that curved around Victoire's thumb. "A very active and changeable life, Madame Vernet. You have seen much excitement and you will see much more. You have a hunger, a need for excitement, I think, very like what I see in the hands of some men. You have had narrow escapes, and there are more to come, which is why I have warned you about the risks of fatal accidents. You could well press your luck too far, and then you would suffer for it. Your activities may take you into strange places and stranger company."

"Isn't she marvelous?" murmured one of the women watching the reading.

"I'm afraid to show her my hand," whispered the woman beside her.

Madame LeNormande went on as if no one had spoken. "You are a very constant friend, loyal and persevering. Your husband is very fortunate in you, for you are trustworthy and without guile. But you are loyal also to your friends, and the time may come when this is not as comfortable an arrangement as it is now, for your family and your friends may be at cross-purposes. You have very strong passions, Madame Vernet, but they run deep and are not easily touched. Beware those who fear your passions." She continued her examination. "You are independent in your methods and accomplish the most when left to your own devices. Your faith has not survived this rigorous strengthening of your mind, but in time you may discover it again. You are articulate except in the presence of true beauty and true ugliness. And you need privacy, with your husband and alone. It is possible that you will have a second marriage late in life, or possibly some other very enduring relationship. You will have three children, I think, but I doubt all three of them will live through childhood. But there are at least two grandchildren, and so I suppose at least one of your children will thrive."

"I have no children, Madame LeNormande," said Victoire stiffly.

"There are three in your hand, Madame Vernet," the fortune-teller countered. "And two grandchildren at least." Victoire tried to draw her hand away, but Madame LeNormande turned it over and studied the back as well. "More traveling, of course. I am sure you are aware of all the travels in your life. And beyond that, I see that there is much danger around you just now. You are not aware of it, and it is possible you will not recognize it at first. Let me warn you that when you think you have rooted it out, yet half the plant will flourish again unless you are vigilant." She held Victoire's hand between her own palms. "You are set on the course, Madame Vernet, and you see your way, or you think you do. But you do not often consider treachery, and how easily it can smile." She released Victoire's hand very suddenly. "There," she announced.

"There?" Victoire repeated, uncertain what she ought to do next.

"That is what I can tell. Except that you have skill for botany." She made a motion of dismissal. "You may put your glove back on. If your handsome husband should wish me to read for him, I will. Otherwise, do not approach another seer for at least six months, or you will be given faulty information. That is the way of this gift—it will not be pressed by anyone, and so the First Consul has learned to his grief." With that she turned back to the other women and ignored Victoire completely.

As she moved away, Victoire found herself thinking of the kitchen cat—Madame LeNormande had much the same air about her.

"Oh, excuse me," said a man as he backed into Victoire. "I did not see you, Madame. Pardon me."

"You are pardoned," said Victoire automatically, about to

continue toward the buffet, and was startled to realize that the popinjay was not stepping back. She gave him a pointed look. "Please do me the courtesy to move aside, Monsieur."

"Pray, not yet." The man was not going to be put off. He bowed over Victoire's hand with a flourish. "I am Querelle," he announced, as if his name should mean something. Then he beamed down at Victoire, and continued in calculatedly mellifluous tones and with an imitation of good manners. "This is a most fortunate accident. I am delighted to have this opportunity to make your acquaintance, Madame Vernet. Having heard your praises sung by so many, I have been curious to meet you."

"I was unaware I had any reputation at all," said Victoire firmly, although it was less than the truth. She wanted nothing to do with this preening dandy who affected all the highest kicks of fashion and was so studied in his graciousness that he succeeded in being the more offensive.

"But you do, my dear Madame Vernet, most assuredly you do. Permit me to inform you that even the great Berthier speaks of you with respect for your conduct and your mind. You do not need the ravings of that charlatan"—he cocked his head in the direction of Madame LeNormande—"to confer notice." His smile widened and gestured to show he was comparing her to everyone attending the soiree. "Who has not heard of your steadfast loyalty, and your dedication to the First Consul? They say you helped stop a gunman from shooting him in Egypt. A feat indeed! When he becomes Emperor, it is known that your actions will carve a place for your husband. And it is said that General Murat owes you his life too. How many can make such a claim on so gallant a soldier? Your husband is fortunate above all reckoning. There are those of us who have not the admirable services of such a wife, and we must advance on our own wits."

This was more offensive than the last; Victoire wanted to twitch her skirts out of the way so that they would not brush against the man. "It is not fitting to say such things to me, Monsieur Querelle."

There was no alteration in Querelle's false affability. "You are convinced that you have protected Vernet, aren't you? It is your purpose in life, and you have served him with such determination. Wouldn't it be a shame to have it all be for nought?" He chuckled. "You think you have discovered all, and that you have performed your duty. What consolation it should be. But you reckon without others more clever than you." He gazed over her shoulder toward the tall windows. "To have spent so long and done so much, and yet have it be for nothing." He shook his head. "There are many who will be distressed for you, Madame Vernet, when it becomes known that your much-vaunted methods have failed." He made a little bow and strolled away.

Victoire stared after him, thinking that Querelle was boasting, but of what? And why? She wanted to find Vernet and inquire who the man was and in what relation the two stood, but knew that this was not the place to ask such questions. She continued to the buffet, trying to concentrate on the impressions she had gained of the man in their brief and unwelcome encounter.

At the buffet she helped herself to one of the stuffed eggs, then selected a braised mushroom wrapped in bacon. As she ate, she continued to watch. Somewhat later she noticed that Querelle was deep in conversation with General Pichegru, who was preparing to leave, for one of the footmen followed him about with a gray campaign cape over his arm. Whatever the dandy Querelle was saying caused Pichegru some satisfaction, for he nodded and made a sign of approval to Querelle, and then took Querelle's hand: Victoire had the impression that something had been exchanged, for Querelle hastily disengaged his hand and slipped it into his coat, glancing around as he did so.

"A vastly pretty entertainment," remarked a low, sinuous voice from the corner of the buffet table. "Wouldn't you agree?"

"Extremely pleasant," said Victoire, alarm coursing through her. She turned and made herself offer a curtsy to Charles Maurice de Talleyrand-Périgord.

"The food is excellent," Talleyrand observed.

Victoire hoped he would not ask her to sit with him. What was it about the short, lame man that distressed her so? She could not put a name to it, but whatever it was it clung to him like an odor. There were those who said Talleyrand was like a snake, but that seemed to her to malign the reptiles. Belatedly she realized she had to say something. "Chateaubriand has always been at the forefront of elegance."

"Very true," Talleyrand agreed, and smiled at Victoire. He was more of a dandy than Querelle, except in one particular, for although the fashion had changed, Talleyrand still wore his hair powdered. "So very well-considered," he went on, indicating the other guests. "Just the right mix of staunch Napoleonists and detractors." He laughed once. "In these changing times it takes skill to achieve such a perfect balance, so that one does not appear to toady to the First Consul but is not branded a dangerous radical."

"As you say," Victoire remarked stiffly.

"But no English. That is the one failing, and one that could yet prove costly," Talleyrand said. "No one believes that we must have peace with England if Napoleon is to prevail."

"I know you have warned him of this many times," said Victoire, unable to relax.

"The more who know of it, the better," Talleyrand stated as if he were addressing a crowd; a few heads turned but he gathered little attention. "Someone must persuade Napoleon that this must be our goal—a lasting peace with England. He has ceased to listen to me on the matter, but there are others who understand, and I hope that they will prevail over the shortsighted fools who do not appreciate our situation. Otherwise in time they—the English—will come against us, and all of Europe will suffer for it."

"How could they prevail, if they were foolish enough to make such a move now that the First Consul has—" Victoire began, then interrupted herself so as not to encourage Talleyrand to continue.

"The English are not fools, Madame Vernet," said Talleyrand with a slight inclination of his head. "They are a patient people, enduring and constant. We will never be able to make the Germans one with us without conquest, and Europe lies open to us. But England has the sea to defend her, and we know to our sorrow that they are tenacious enemies." He grinned once, but there was no humor in it.

"As you say, Excellency," Victoire said, using the title Talleyrand had when he was Bishop of Autun; this was not quite an insult but she hoped it would discourage the man. Then she saw Vernet making his way toward her through the crowd. "Excuse me, but I see—"

Talleyrand was not fooled; he regarded her lazily. "You know, Madame Vernet, there are few members of this government who have wits enough to match with yours or your husband's. It is a pity that you do not realize it yet, for you are one of the few opponents worthy of my steel. Not many could offer you the sport I can." The innuendo in this invitation was so blatant that Victoire wished she had sufficient credibility of reputation to permit her to slap his smiling face; to make matters worse, she had somehow lost track of Querelle.

"You are very generous to say so," she told him, and gave

her attention to Vernet. As he came up and led her away with a nod to Napoleon's Foreign Minister, she said in an undervoice, "Thank goodness. Talleyrand makes my skin turn cold."

"I know what you mean," Vernet said when he was certain that Talleyrand could not overhear them. "I find myself hoping that I will discover a link from him to the English spies. For all his talk about peace with England, I cannot suppose he will do nothing to further his cause. So far there is nothing, but . . ."

Victoire shook her head once. "He is venal, completely venal. And worse than venal."

"And, I suspect," Vernet added, "proud of it."

Only later, as they were leaving, did Victoire remark on Querelle's obnoxious manner as they donned their coats; Talleyrand's miasmic presence had diminished the impression Querelle had made. "Who is this creature, Vernet? I do not like him."

"He is one of those who rose in Paris by toadying to the right people. Considering how tumultuous the Directoire was before the general brought stability, it was quite a feat. During the Terror he was nowhere to be found. Then when there was wealth and power to be had, his kind appeared. The ministries are full of them. Of such men Querelle is among the most successful. He has friends in very high places, high enough to keep my office from inquiring as to certain matters relating to him only a few months ago. It's odd, though, his talking with Pichegru. Considering that Pichegru is still somewhat under a cloud, I'm surprised that Querelle would bother with him. Querelle is an opportunist, my love. Right now Pichegru's friendship is not an asset—hardly the associate Querelle seeks out. It isn't his usual style." He handed a small doucement to the footman and helped his wife down the stairs.

"His usual style is affected and sycophantic, if his behavior at this soiree is an indication," Victoire decided aloud.

"He can be, but he is gaining importance, nevertheless. Don't underestimate his ambitions." Vernet signalled for their hired carriage.

Victoire frowned. "I inferred much the same thing from what he said to me. He is spiteful, isn't he?"

"I have never known him to be so, but it wouldn't surprise me," said Vernet as he held the door open to allow Victoire to climb into the carriage.

"Do you think he could be up to something?" she asked as she took her seat and tightened her coat around her.

"You mean, do I think he might be acting against the First Consul?" He tapped on the roof of the carriage to signal the coachman to drive on. "It is possible, I suppose. He is just brazen enough to ally himself with those opposing the Empire." He scowled at his own words. "But he is not so important. He has little impact; nowhere near the power of someone like Talleyrand, though he may aspire to such position. Oh, he is protected by his patron, the Swedish consul, but if he acted against Napoleon, his patron would throw him to the mob."

"Then he is either very clever or very stupid," said Victoire thoughtfully.

"And you suspect the worst of him?" Vernet suggested.

"I don't know yet," said Victoire. "I will have to learn more before I am certain. Why would he draw my attention?"

"Why bother? The man is a fop and a boor. There are better things to occupy you, Victoire, since I will be away for a week."

"I think it very unfair of Berthier to send you off again so soon," Victoire said, pouting a little. "Surely you could have refused the assignment?" She said it the way Desirée might, very coquettish and pouting.

"You know the answer to that better than I do," Vernet said, smiling ironically. "Napoleon himself has asked me to protect those men who are preparing the first of a special type of boat, the very existence of which would end the peace with the British, if they knew of it. This may be what our English spies are seeking. And it would be a disaster should they even suspect such things exist. It is my duty to protect the boat, much as I would rather bide with you. Besides, spoiled women make for harried men, my love, and well you know it."

She could not deny his good sense. "Yes, I do know it, and I am proud that you are being given such important work to do. But I cannot pretend I wouldn't like it better if the important work was in Paris."

At that he laughed. "As would I. Let's make the best of the time we have together." He leaned back and pulled her close to him. "I want to spend hours and hours and hours in bed."

"Asleep?" she inquired provocatively.

He grinned. "I hope not."

"Odette," said Victoire the next morning as she came into the kitchen shortly after Vernet had left for the week, "do you have an old dress, a very old dress, something that you would not like to wear in public? Perhaps what you wear to wash the walls or—"

The carpenters had arrived a short time before and the house rang with the sound of hammers and saws.

Odette paused in kneading bread dough and stared, apprehension hidden in her eyes: she knew Victoire too well to believe that the request was wholly innocent. "Why on earth, Madame—"

"I have something I must do, and I do not want to draw attention to myself. If I dress like a poor person, with a shawl over my head and a ragged dress, no one will look at me and I may go about my task without undue notice." She smiled as if this were a regular part of her routine. "May I borrow such a dress?"

"It will be too large for you," Odette warned her, as if this would persuade her to abandon whatever she was planning to do.

"So much the better," said Victoire eagerly. "Then it will serve to make me appear more desperate. I think I will put some ash on my face, as well." Her blue eyes were sparkling. Perhaps, she thought distantly, Madame LeNormande had been right about that, at least: Victoire did hunger for adventure. "Odette, the house is going to be too noisy for me to think, let alone accomplish anything. I might as well give myself the chance to test a few of my theories while the carpenters are so busy."

"Madame Vernet," said Odette firmly, "does the master know of this? It would not be fitting for you to do anything so . . . irregular."

"Nonsense," Victoire said heartily. "I have already ridden camels through the Egyptian desert in Egyptian clothing. What is so shocking about so mild a disguise as an old, ill-fitting dress?" She sat down at the kitchen table and helped herself to an apple. "I am bound for Les Invalides, and those rough soldiers are not the best company. Therefore I will make it appear I am nothing they want, and I may pass safely among them."

This argument was more successful; Odette gave an understanding sigh. "Soldiers might know you, Madame Vernet."

"Not in shabby clothes with a shawl over my head and ashes on my face. They won't look at me, and if they do, they will not know me." She said it with great conviction, warming to her project. "I will not be anything that interests them, and so they will ignore me and I will be able to do the things I must."

"And what things are those, Madame?" Odette inquired with exaggerated politeness.

"It would be better if you didn't know," said Victoire candidly. "Just be satisfied knowing that I am working to protect the interests of the First Consul in what is a dangerous time."

Odette resumed her kneading. "All right. When I have set this to rise, I will find the dress for you. I warn you that it is filthy and it smells."

"Wonderful!" Victoire exclaimed. "Then with my pale coloring I will not have to use anything more than ashes to complete my disguise." She got up, taking another bite of the apple. "I am going upstairs to change. Bring the dress up as soon as you can. And thank you, Odette. Thank you."

"Um," said Odette dubiously as Victoire hurried out of the kitchen.

It was nearly an hour later when a stooped figure left the rear of the Vernets' house; her dirty dress sagged on her frame and the heavy woolen shawl over her head was moth-eaten in several places. She carried a sack slung over her shoulder, and as she went, she called out, "Rags! Any rags!" in a strong Norman accent.

It took her some time to reach Les Invalides—for she did not approach the place directly, but arrived by a circuitous route that would confuse anyone who watched her. She sat down outside a draper's shop and spent a while investigating the contents of her sack as a cover for her watching for Querelle.

He emerged an hour later, dressed more lavishly than was called for. His driving coat had five capes and his hat was worn at a rakish angle. As soon as he stepped into the street, Victoire closed her sack, slung it over her shoulder, and hoped that Querelle would not summon a carriage. In this luck was with her, for Querelle started off on foot with a swinging stride that suggested he intended to walk.

Victoire had to struggle to keep up with him, but fortunately his dress stood out enough that she could fall as much as half a block behind him and not lose track of him. At last she saw him enter a discreet doorway guarded by a tall African in elaborate dress. Querelle was no stranger here, for the black man greeted him familiarly and said something about Sophie waiting for him. Not far from the door, Victoire sighed and turned away, planning to try again tomorrow.

It was four days later—a Monday—when her persistence at last paid off. With Vernet away she had become increasingly active in order to keep from missing him, so she set about her self-appointed task as soon as she rose. She arrived earlier than usual outside Les Invalides, two shawls gathered around her against the morning drizzle. She had left Odette to deal with the carpenters and hurried along to what she thought of as her watching post, more to relieve herself of the sense of loss than to keep track of Querelle. Vernet would not be back until Thursday, and from what she had been able to coax out of Berthier, he might be sent to Orleans shortly as well.

For once Querelle emerged dressed pretty much the way most of the men on the street were, in unremarkable clothing and without his fashionable hat. This alerted Victoire as much as the unusually early hour of his departure, and she stumbled along behind him, making sure to keep to the opposite side of the street from where he walked, to be less obvious. This time his destination was not a brothel or a gambling club, as it had been before, but a small inn on the Left Bank, a place called La Plume et Bougie, frequented by men visiting the Université and those who preyed on the innocence of scholars.

While Victoire huddled near the doorway, Querelle made his way into the taproom, slapping down a coin on one of the small tables and calling for hot wine as he took off his coat and hung it near the fire to dry.

The landlord complied at once, offering to have his cook prepare a meal for him, while Querelle refused. "I am waiting for a friend," he declared. "The man is staying here, or so I understand."

"What is the name of this man who is staying here?" the landlord inquired.

"Oh, he knows I am to meet him this morning," said Querelle lightly. "I want to have something to drink before he and I begin to talk." He sat down and favored the landlord with a faint, superior smile. "Doubtless he will be here soon."

"Will he?" muttered the landlord as he took the coin from the table. "Your wine will be brought directly."

"Much appreciated, on such a day," said Querelle with a gesture toward the door. "A warm fire with hot wine. In drizzle this is heaven."

The landlord glowered at this effusiveness, then went to draw a tankard of wine for heating.

Left to himself, Querelle looked around the taproom with an expression of distaste. He sniffed in disapproval and brushed at his sleeve as if to rid it of any taint of the inn.

Taking a chance, Victoire edged through the door, then crept into the taproom as if seeking the warmth of the fire—which was only partially a ruse, for her clothes were damp and she was starting to shiver. She pulled a coin from her sack and held it out as the landlord brought the hot wine to Querelle, demanding in a cracking, Norman-accented voice to have hot wine, too. She took care to keep her shawl drawn close around her head to hide her features, although she suspected that Querelle would pay very little attention to her in this disguise.

The landlord took the coin, but shook his finger at Victoire. "You can't stay in here for long, Auntie; you'll stink up the place and drive my customers away."

"I paid you," she said belligerently.

"And you will have your wine, and then you will have to go." The landlord shook his head and fetched a second tankard.

Three men had come into the taproom while the landlord delivered this warning, all of them looking expectant. One of the men was in his late thirties and walked like a soldier, but the other two were younger, seeming more studentlike than soldierly.

"I believe you are waiting to see us," said the older man. "I am Etangherbe." He held out his hand to Querelle. "The others are at the house."

"Ah," said Querelle, rising to shake Etangherbe's hand. "I'll have to wait to see your leader."

Toutdroit made a hesitant offer. "I can go fetch him, if you like."

"That will conclude our business more quickly," said Querelle, for the first time betraying signs of nervousness. "It might be best if you get him."

"Bring him here," said Etangherbe quickly. "The other place must remain secret for now."

Querelle nodded. "It's better that way," he agreed promptly. "Very well, and tell him that there is some urgency." This last was said with a self-important sneer.

Etangherbe cocked his head. "He's aware of that, Monsieur." He chose a table near Querelle's and sat down.

Victoire slipped into the fireside nook and pulled her shawls more closely about her, as much to hide her presence as to get warmer.

The landlord came back into the taproom and demanded what the new arrivals would drink, and accepted their orders for hot wine with grim satisfaction. He glanced toward where Victoire sat and shook his head in annoyance.

"I've been in contact with one of your friends," said Querelle when the landlord was gone. "You are aware of your friends, aren't you."

"Of course," said Bouelac, too quickly.

"We know as much as is wise for us to know," said Etangherbe, with a warning glance at Bouelac. "Which should be the watchword for us all."

"Certainly," said Querelle confidently as he took a first sip of his hot wine. "In days like this, hot wine thaws everything."

"Especially the tongue," said Etangherbe, looking at Querelle.

This had no effect on Querelle, who went on, "The time is nearing when you'll be able to undertake your task. You must feel very proud, knowing that you'll be the instruments of liberation. It will be the hour of vindication for everyone."

"Not if the whole world knows of it," said Etangherbe. "Jesu et Marie, what is wrong with you? Keep your mouth shut."

"Why?" asked Querelle. "We know our purpose and we share the goal. It is good to be able to speak of it from time to time. Don't tell me you speak of anything else in that secret house of yours." He glanced in Victoire's direction. "That's a street crone, a rag-picker. She probably doesn't understand anything we say. And if she does, who would she tell? And who would listen to her." He laughed at the absurdity.

"There is a landlord here, as well as that woman, and he would not be lightly dismissed if he brought complaints against you." Etangherbe looked disgusted. "So keep your own counsel, Monsieur, for the cause we all share."

"Oh, very well." Querelle looked truculent but fell silent.

"As soon as our leader returns, let us go to one of our rooms in this inn. We'll be able to discuss matters more safely there," said Etangherbe as if to coax a child out of the sulks. "Whatever message you carry, it is too important to risk it being exposed. That woman may not know anything, but if there is paper she can—"

"You are very cautious," said Querelle, and pointed to Victoire. "You there, you rag-picker . . ."

Victoire turned slowly. "You want to speak to me?" she asked in a falsely high voice, making her Norman accent as thick as possible.

The landlord returned with a tankard of hot wine, which he held out. "Where is the money, Auntie?"

Victoire tossed two coins to him. "There, and no thanks to you."

Bouelac chuckled and said, "An Auntie like you, you must

want that wine badly. There's nothing else to warm you, is there?"

As much as Victoire wanted to demand of the fellow what he meant, she kept silent and covered this by taking a long draft of the wine. It truly did spread welcome warmth through her and the heat of the tankard was wonderful to feel. Her fingers tingled as the cold diminished and her fear increased.

"Leave her alone," recommended Etangherbe. He rocked back on his stool. "Don't give her any reason to remember us. It would be foolish."

Querelle shook his head. "You are too easily frightened," he declared. "You think that such a woman as this has any knowledge of us, or will be able to recall this day when another week has passed?" He strolled over and looked down at Victoire.

She drew back, afraid that he would recognize her. "I'm a widow-woman," she whined. "I don't bother nobody."

"Of course, Auntie, of course," Querelle soothed her with condescension, taking care not to get too close to her. "You are a sensible country-woman, aren't you?"

Victoire crossed herself. "As the Saints know," she said, making herself appear more countrified than ever.

"And you would do nothing to hurt good men, would you?" Querelle persisted.

"Nor anyone else, with my soul to answer," she said, keeping her face turned down.

"Oh, yes." Querelle smiled and glanced toward Etangherbe before he went on. "But what if they offered you gold coins; important men from the Préfecteur. What would you tell them?"

Victoire spat as she had seen old village women do in her youth. "I'll say nothing to cockerels in uniform."

Bouelac sniggered, and the landlord bringing two tankards laughed aloud.

But Etangherbe watched her narrowly. "What do you expect her to tell you, you fool?" he asked Querelle, and came toward Victoire.

A spurt of alarm shot through Victoire, sharpening her mind and her senses so that the very odor of the hot wine stung her nose. She backed toward the nook, gesturing them to move back. "I don't want trouble. I had trouble all my days and I don't want no more of it. As I am a good Christian woman, I'll not speak against you."

Querelle stood straighter, as if he had vanquished an enemy. His voice was threatening. "See that you remember your promise, Auntie, or we will find you, and there'll be more trouble than you ever dreamed of. Who will care what happens to one old rag-picker?"

"Put her out of the house," said Etangherbe. "We'll pay the landlord for the tankard. We won't have to bother with her."

"But—" Querelle protested; he was enjoying the opportunity to bully someone.

"She's only seen the four of us," said Etangherbe reasonably. "If she sees the others, then she'll be more dangerous to us, no matter what she tells you. I know these creatures, and they are as false as cats."

"Monsieur!" Victoire protested.

"That's being a little extreme, don't you think?" asked Bouelac, his face paler than it had been.

"Peasants turned my family over to the Revolutionary Tribunal at Lyons," said Etangherbe. "They promised to protect them and then they betrayed them, and were well-paid for their treason. She will do what she thinks will best serve her advantage."

Victoire cringed, and only part of it was acting. "No, no, I'll speak to no one but the priest." She hated saying that, but it was what a rag-picking widow would do.

"She's just a rag-picker," said Bouelac.

"She could be your Judas," said Etangherbe. His features were growing harsher and his eyes fixed on Victoire in a way that made her flinch.

Querelle took Victoire by the shoulder, his fingers digging in. "Come, Auntie, it's time you were gone. We don't want to have any dead bodies around this inn, and if you stay much longer, that is bound to happen." He handed her a franc. "Use this for more wine." He looked at the others. "To speed her forgetting."

"Thank you, Monsieur," she muttered, allowing herself to be propelled toward the door.

Just before Querelle reached for the latch the door swung open and Toutdroit came through, followed by the man he had been sent to fetch.

Victoire stopped in her tracks. Querelle swore under his breath, then shoved her forward again. "Hurry up, Auntie. You want to be out of this place."

"Yes, yes," she said, trying not to run into the newcomer.

"Wait," said the man, reaching out to seize Victoire's arm. "What is this?"

"A rag-picker," said Etangherbe, rising in respect to the leader of their group. "She is leaving. We were just showing her out."

"Um," said the man, looking once at Victoire as he came a step further into the taproom where his face caught the light.

It was all Victoire could do not to gasp in recognition. She bent her head more fully and attempted to continue toward the door, still clasping the tankard and wondering if she could use it as a weapon.

The hand on her arm grew tighter and she was tugged into the doorway. "A rag-picker?" said the leader as he stared down, scrutinizing her. "I don't think so, not with those hands." He reached out and pulled the shawl from her head. "Flaxen hair, not gray." He chuckled without a trace of mirth. "I never thought Nemesis would be so fair a goddess," he said as he took her chin in his hand and forced her face upward.

9

❧

VICTOIRE LOOKED UP into the hot eyes of Claude Montrachet. For an instant she considered throwing her wine in his face, but immediately thought better of it. Had he been alone it might have been worth the risk, but with so many others, she realized the gesture would be dangerous and futile. She stood very still and waited for what he would do next; beneath her ire she was terrified.

He surprised her by releasing her and offering her a slight bow. "Madame Vernet. What an unexpected ... ah ... pleasure."

"Madame Vernet?" said Querelle in astonishment.

She decided to match the leader's manner; she dropped her Norman accent and offered him a very little curtsy, saying, "Monsieur Montrachet."

"How reassuring that you have not forgotten me, brief though our encounter was. As you see," he went on with ironic gallantry, "I have recovered from the wound you gave me at the Vigne et Tonneau."

"All your friends must rejoice," said Victoire directly, masking the dread filling her.

Etangherbe had come nearer. "Do you mean this is the woman who shot you?" He stared at her. "This woman? You said she was an officer's wife—"

"Alas, it is so," said Montrachet, his voice hardening. "And she has yet to earn my pardon for it."

"But what is she doing here?" asked Toutdroit, very much puzzled.

"We will have to find out," said Montrachet, with such grimness that Victoire felt the hair on her neck stand.

Querelle moved closer to Victoire. "This is not Madame Vernet," he blustered. "I have met Madame Vernet. She is young and pretty in a vapid, pale way. This woman is more than forty—look at her face."

"Wash away the grime and you will see how young she is."
Montrachet stared at her. "You are ever the thorn in my side."

"I regret," said Victoire without a trace of contrition.

Montrachet moved away from her. "Don't underestimate her.
I made that mistake once and paid the price for it." He regarded
her as he chose a stool and sat down. "What are you doing
here, Madame Vernet? Why have you done this?"

"Madame Vernet is married to Inspector-General Vern—"
Querelle began.

"I know who her husband is," said Montrachet. "And that
gives me to wonder all the more." He kept his coat on but
pulled off his gloves. "Under the circumstances, I believe I deserve some answers."

"Unfortunately, I must disagree," said Victoire, feeling her
mouth go dry.

Montrachet shook his head. "Not this time, Madame. You're
alone in a room full of men. Think of what could happen to
you here. Between us, we could insure that your husband
would never want to touch you again. We could destroy your
reputation and wreck his honor."

Victoire was all too aware of those sickening possibilities;
she said nothing but she breathed a little faster and felt her
pulse in her temples. It was an effort to keep her fear from
showing, but she steeled herself.

"Montrachet!" exclaimed Etangherbe.

"Oh, we will not resort to such methods. Not yet." He
showed his teeth to Victoire. "We'll not use them unless you
make it necessary, Madame, and then we will naturally lament
the necessity."

"How considerate," said Victoire before she could stop the
words. It galled her to say anything to Montrachet.

"But what are we going to do with her?" asked Toutdroit as
he closed the door to the taproom. "And for God's sake, don't
let anyone see her."

"No, we ought not to do that," said Montrachet. "That would
be stupid, would it not?"

"What's she doing here?" demanded Etangherbe.

"The very question I have been asking myself," said Montrachet in a measuring tone. "And I don't like the answers I have
come up with." He looked at her with narrowed eyes. "If
you're here for your husband, he's sent you on a hazardous errand, Madame. And if you are not, then you are unpardonably
foolish."

Victoire was able to keep herself silent.

"Why would your husband be so careless of you, do you think, Madame?" he asked, his voice becoming malignly flirtatious. "Has he so little regard for you that he permits you to undergo danger on his behalf? Again?" He regarded her, his eyes fixed in the middle distance. "Obstinate, are you?"

"She's an officer's wife," said Querelle nervously as he considered their position. "She isn't street trash or a brothel woman. It could go hard for us, if—"

Montrachet laughed harshly. "On two of his campaigns, the Corsican encouraged his men to rape. How could he object if we followed his example? How could her husband blame us?"

"You aren't going to—" Bouelac protested.

"I told you all," Montrachet cut in, "not yet. But it may come to that, if she remains intractable." He looked back toward Victoire. "Or is that what you are hoping for, Madame? Your husband is not enough for you? Perhaps you would like a better-born lance in your sheath?" Montrachet reached down and ran his hand along her side, brushing the back of it against her breast before wiping his hand against his jacket as if it were soiled.

This almost goaded Victoire into an angry retort, but she realized that was what Montrachet wanted, an excuse to do more to her, and worse. She set her tankard down and folded her arms.

Montrachet gave her a little time to answer, then shrugged and continued. "We have to know what your mission here is. We have too much at stake to permit you to withhold anything from us. You must understand that I am perfectly sincere in this, Madame. You are our captive, and you will help us."

"Lock her up and use her," suggested Etangherbe. "We can bargain with her, gain her husband's help in return for the safety of his wife."

"Possible," said Montrachet speculatively. "Yes, that's one way to turn this development to our advantage."

Querelle stepped forward. "She's a friend of Murat's, everyone knows that. He has money, and he's closer to Napoleon than her husband." The way he said this was so salacious that Victoire felt heat mounting in her face.

"A friend of Murat's?" echoed Montrachet nastily. "And what does your dear husband think about that association, Madame?" He came toward her and tweaked one of the straggling locks of blonde hair. "His wife is the only light-haired Buonaparte! Perhaps Murat has a weakness for yellow treason?

What an honor for you, Madame, to have the protection of such a man as General Murat."

"I could carry word to Murat, telling him what would happen to Madame Vernet if he doesn't assist us; Murat wouldn't hesitate to do what he could to rescue her," said Querelle, who was eager to have the endorsement of the handsome Gascon. "Murat is an important man. His assistance would mean everything. My superior would be delighted if there was a way to suborn Murat. We could get much closer to Napoleon with Murat aiding us, and there would be a better chance for our safe escape when the work is done. The thing would be assured if only Murat could be compelled to help us."

"Will you be quiet?" complained Montrachet. "You are revealing too much." He cocked his head toward Victoire. "You are a very clever woman, Madame Vernet, and you're apt to make connections that would displease us. Until you're willing to cooperate with us, you'll have to be kept apart from us, so that you won't learn more than you have." He signalled to Toutdroit. "Take her up to the attic. There's an old servant's room up there, under the eaves. It will do for the time being. Lock her in and be sure the door is double-bolted."

Toutdroit took Victoire by the arm. "Those rooms have no heat."

"No, they don't," agreed Montrachet. "And it is cold today. Tonight there will be frost. In damp clothing, such as the dress Madame Vernet is wearing, a person might freeze to death in a frost." He gave Victoire a long, hard look. "Unless she's willing to trade information for a blanket or two? And something hot to eat?"

Victoire looked at Toutdroit. "Show me the way, Monsieur."

Montrachet laughed. "Oh, very good, very good; worthy of a hero in a story." He clapped three times. "Brava, Madame."

As Victoire was taken from the taproom she heard Etangherbe say, "Sackett-Hartley isn't going to like this."

"Be damned to Sackett-Hartley," Montrachet responded as Victoire was shoved in the direction of the flight of stairs. "He still thinks he is carrying on his uncle's work, more fool he."

Now who, wondered Victoire as she climbed the stairs ahead of Toutdroit, is Sackett-Hartley? And what had he to do with these men?

It took an hour for Victoire to make a thorough search of her improvised prison. She was shivering from either the damp chill or fear after just a few minutes even though she had kept moving, using the action to keep her fear at bay. The room was small, with a single window over a cobbled courtyard. The steep roof brought a sharp angle to the ceiling, and after ascertaining that the window could provide nothing but a fall, Victoire began to feel her way along the beams, searching for soft wood that would indicate poor slating above. From the condition of the rest of the inn she suspected that the slates were not well maintained. There was a single metal tub in one corner that had probably once been used for the servants' bath lying abandoned, but other than that the chamber was empty. Think, she ordered herself repeatedly. Think. Think, or succumb to the paralyzing embrace of despair.

"When would Odette begin to worry?" she asked herself as she continued her inspection. And with Vernet gone to Amiens, who would she contact? She knew she had to rely on her housekeeper and at the same time she was apprehensive, for it was not easy for a servant to make herself heard. Who would listen to Odette? These and other more dismal thoughts kept her occupied while she felt her way along the beams of the pitched roof.

After more than two hours she found what she was looking for. By that time she was so cold that her teeth were chattering and her muscles were beginning to ache. Already there was a knot in her shoulders that felt as if she had a cobble-stone under her skin, but dread kept her moving as her strength waned. She tapped the boards crossing the beams and noted with satisfaction that in a section near one side, where she could just barely reach the ceiling from the floor, they had a definite spongy texture. She poked at the boards and was rewarded with a spatter of pulp and splinters falling into her face; it was what she wanted. Without doubt she would be able to pry her way through—if she did not succumb to the cold first. And if no one came to disturb her. The thought of Montrachet returning to the inn and discovering her escape attempt was more chilling than the unheated room, and spurred her on.

Victoire's fingers were bleeding and her knuckles skinned by the time she succeeded in breaking through the wood to the slates above, where the biting, sodden wind slapped at her and threatened to break her hold. As she clenched her teeth and stretched higher, she felt the first of the slates loosen, shift, and then fall, skittering down the roof to smash into the wall of the building next to La Plume et Bougie. Relief and hope surged through her with such force that she felt tears on her face. She looked out into the gray sky and mizzle, and had to stop herself from whooping with joy. With renewed purpose she went back to work on the hole she had made, driving herself to find purchase on the slates to shove them, to pull down more of the rotted timber until, after two hectic hours of effort and constant fear that the innkeeper would hear the clatter of the tiles falling, she had widened the gap to an aperture large enough for her to squeeze through.

With great care, Victoire went to the tub and rolled it carefully over the floor, trying to make as little noise as possible. When she had got it beneath the hole she had made, she turned it upside down and climbed on top of it, thrusting her head and shoulders through to the outside where the dank cold waited.

She hesitated as she worked her arms through, all the while praying that Montrachet would not choose this time to return and resume his questioning. She tugged and pulled and strained, and dislodged another dozen slates before she was able to haul herself through onto the roof. She winced at the thunderous echo of the slates as they crashed into the courtyard. Her hideous dress tore and the rotten timbers clawed at her; she endured the pain grimly, determined to get out.

Once she had her feet braced against the hole, she reached upward toward the crest of the roof where the chimney pots poked into the lowering fog. She secured a grasp at the top and began her climb, reciting the prayers of her childhood as she slithered away from the hole. Pressed flat against the steep angle of the roof, she inched upward, never looking down; she was frightened enough and did not want to increase the terror that was holding her. Finally she reached the level center of the mansard roof, where she sat, one arm around the base of the warm chimney, gathering heat and catching her breath as she planned how she could continue her escape.

The carpenters were leaving for the day when Vernet returned home, pale from long hours on the road without rest; he greeted the workmen, then hurried to the withdrawing room in long, eager strides, calling for Victoire as he went. To his surprise the room was cold and dark; the lamp was unlit and there was no sign of his wife. He removed his cloak and dropped it over the bannister as he started up the stairs, wondering if she might be there. "Victoire," he called as he opened the door to their bedroom, disappointed when he saw no light there, and no sign of his wife.

"She isn't back yet," answered Odette from the foot of the stairs. "I have been waiting for the last three hours, and she has not returned." She watched Vernet come back down the stairs. "She left shortly after first light this morning."

"Left?" said Vernet, frowning as if the word itself were unfamiliar.

"She was . . . she was following someone, someone who has made her suspicious." Odette crossed herself and put her hand over her mouth before she went on. "Oh, dear. I told her I would say nothing, but you see, I am so worried."

"Following someone?" Vernet questioned, more perplexed than before. He was having trouble listening to Odette, for there seemed to be a sudden ringing in his ears. He spoke his jumbled thoughts aloud. "Who should she be following, and why? What was she suspicious of, that she had to follow this person? Whatever possessed her to undertake something like this?"

"I don't know who the man is, precisely," said Odette quietly as she started back toward the haven of her kitchen, Vernet tagging after her. "She said that she had to find out what the man was up to, and so she . . ." This was becoming very difficult for the housekeeper. "She was certain that the man was doing something wrong. That was why she concealed her identity, to keep from alerting him. She borrowed an old dress of mine, a very old dress, and disguised herself as a rag-picker. She put ashes on her face and covered her head in a shawl."

"What on earth for?" Vernet stared at Odette in disbelief. "This is nonsense, Odette, complete nonsense."

Odette nodded. "So I thought, but—"

"What could she mean by doing this? She is a woman of good sense, and why would she do such a capricious thing? What reason could she have for this?" Vernet demanded irately as he became indignant. "What absurd start has she—"

"She began four days ago, following the man. She was certain that the man was going to meet enemies of the First Consul, that he was only waiting for the opportunity to pass important information to . . . She told me that this man had not yet carried his message to . . . I don't know who she thought he would carry the message to, only that she was certain he was carrying it. She said she saw him take . . . I don't know . . . at the soirée you attended." She stared toward the old-fashioned stove, where a capon broiled. "Oh, I am so glad you are back, Inspector-General. I was beside myself, not knowing who to turn to, and—"

"I don't understand any of this," said Vernet, his face darkening with anger and anxiety. "I don't believe that my wife would do something so . . ." The words trailed off as he sat down. "What can have happened?" he asked in sudden consternation.

"I don't know," said Odette. "That's the worst part. I thought earlier that she had taken shelter from the weather and would return. But the time for that is past. Then I thought someone must bring word, and I have been watching for . . . No one has come."

"Sacré bleu," whispered Vernet as the enormity of what Odette was telling him sank in. "Do you mean that she is out there still, in her disguise?"

"I . . . I hope so," said Odette.

The full implication of Odette's answer was staggering to Vernet. He gripped the kitchen table, then mastered the dread that threatened to overcome him. "I will need to know everything you can tell me. At once. And then I will visit Fouche and Berthier. And Murat," he added after a slight hesitation. "She must be found."

"Please God," said Odette in a fatalistic voice, and resigned herself to betraying Victoire's confidence, for the thought of harm coming to Victoire was more terrible to Odette than Victoire's annoyance.

In this part of Paris the houses leaned close together and Victoire was able to make her way from rooftop to rooftop the length of the block where La Plume et Bougie was located. She went carefully, holding on to chimneys and dormers and the occasional tree-branch, all the while fearing to hear the outcry of discovery. Her dress was clinging to her in the damp, weighing her down and making her fret with every small jump she encountered. Would she be able to cross? Would the dress drag her down? Would someone see her and give the alarm? There, at least, she had some luck: it was growing dark and the slow rain made people passing on the road below unwilling to look up; she remained undetected as she was made increasingly clumsy by exhaustion and the sodden dress. At every moment she feared the outcry of her captors.

At the end of the block she discovered she could not climb down, and the distance across the narrow street was too great for her to attempt jumping. After a short, frustrated moment, she decided to continue on to right, and hope that at the next corner there might be a way to descend safely to the street.

Her purchase on the roofs was becoming more precarious as the thickening fog made every surface slick and dangerous, and so she searched as she went for some safe opportunity to get down. She found it when she had nearly reached the next corner of the block: there was a house, older than the rest, with a bakery and a pantry behind the main building. There was no light in any of the windows she could see, and no smoke rose from the three chimneys of the place. Victoire ground her teeth together and made herself continue. As she reached this ancient house, she slithered her way down the tiles to the base of what had once been a watchtower but was now nothing more than a masonry stump on the side of the house. From there she was able to make her way down over the rough stones to the low roof of the bakery, doing her best to ignore the further damage all this did to her dress. Here she made a last swing away from the eaves and hung from her arms as she gauged the distance to the stones below. Satisfied that she was in no serious danger, she let go, and tumbled the short distance to the ground.

As she straightened up, assessing the extent of damage done to her dress, she gathered her shawls around her ruined clothes and looked about the courtyard for the gate she had seen from the roof. She moved toward it at a clumsy run, her knees stiff, her back and shoulders sore. Her vision swam and she blinked in the darkness to clear her eyes. She grabbed the latch and slipped into the alleyway, and from there, she made her way to the street. In spite of her fatigue she felt renewed determination and growing anger. She had to stop Montrachet and Querelle. She was so tired her arms were shaking.

It was her plan to trudge home, trusting to her disguise to protect her and her steady activity to keep her warm enough to avoid the worst of the cold, but after going half a dozen blocks, she realized that it would not be possible for her to go so far before she collapsed. Some other haven must be found.

Another thought occurred to her: Montrachet knew who she was; undoubtedly once her escape was discovered he would send his men to intercept her before she ever reached her door. With Vernet gone, Odette, too, would be in danger if Victoire attempted to enter the house. Then all her striving would be for nothing, or worse than nothing. Choking back a sob of rage and fatigue, she forced herself to start looking for a place she could hide.

Two blocks later Victoire found what she sought—a livery stable, the forge damped for the night and only a groom to tend the horses. Locating an alcove near the stable gate, she slipped inside it, out of the weather, and set herself to watching. She hid in the shadows, waiting as the groom downed the greater part of two bottles of wine and making her plans as she fought off the chill drowsiness that threatened to overcome her.

When the groom had got to the stage where he not only could not remember the words, but the tune as well of "Sur le Route," she crept out of her hiding place, and keeping to the shadows, made her way back through the stalls to the rear of the stable, where four taffy-gold Belgian draft horses were confined. Like most of the coldbloods, the horse in the stall she chose was enormous and friendly. He nudged Victoire and sniffed at her, letting her lean against him to absorb his warmth.

"Do you mind?" she asked softly, "if I share the stall?" It was a pity, she thought, that she could find nothing to eat, but the nearest food was in the basket beside the drunken groom, and she could not take the risk of stealing any. Odette would worry, but she was too worn out to attempt anything before the morning.

The Belgian whickered and went back to lipping the last of the hay in his manger while Victoire made a nest for herself in the straw.

"I don't know what more I can tell you," Vernet said to Murat as they sat in the Marshall's carriage, bound for Fouche's ministry at a brisk trot that was only possible at this late hour of the night, when the streets were clear of traffic. He had found Murat at a fete given by Josephine, a company so grand that Vernet had felt ashamed to intrude: only his frantic concern from his wife gave him the incentive to send a note with the footman to Murat. "Our housekeeper told you everything she told me, and I . . ."

Murat nodded once, his mouth in a tight line. "You need not remind me of your wife's determination. I've seen it for myself." He was resplendent in a dress uniform of white-and-gold, the fabric cut to make the most of his shoulders and the turn of his calf; his dark brown hair was cut in the Classical style, similar to Napoleon's. But while the First Consul affected the mode to conceal increasing baldness, Murat was blessed by thick, glossy waves, and he was vain as a girl about them. At the moment his hair was in disorder and he paid no attention to the damage the swaying carriage was doing to the swags of braid across his chest. He glowered; his manner was brusque in a way that would have surprised his wife. "She's a wonder, Madame Vernet is, but I can think of few women who are as fixed in their purpose as she."

"True," said Vernet quietly.

"It's unfortunate that she did not let anyone know the subject of her investigation," Murat said a bit later as the carriage neared the Ministry of Public Safety.

"But she didn't," said Vernet, who was doing his best to keep from giving in to despair.

"You know," Murat said after a short, thoughtful pause, "it could be that she is keeping away for a reason other than the one we both fear."

Vernet was ready to cling to any hope that would banish the hurt consuming him. "How do you mean?" he demanded.

"Well, if she found out something that made her think she might put you in danger, might she not stay away?" Murat made his expression as convincing as he could, but he saw that it was not enough.

"She didn't expect me back for another two or three days," said Vernet. "There was no pressing reason to protect me."

Murat went on doggedly. "But perhaps if she was captured, they did not know who she was, or if they are suspicious of her, she wants to make certain there is no connection made between her and you." He leaned forward as the coachman reined in his team at the door to the Ministry of Public Safety.

"Why?" asked Vernet bluntly.

"Who can say?" Murat countered. "But it is the sort of thing she would do, isn't it, if she was worried that you could be drawn into hazards by her actions."

"It is," Vernet allowed as the door was open and the steps let down by the footman. "But if that's so, then she is dealing with very dangerous men." The worry which had begun to lift from his countenance returned at once.

"Possibly so," said Murat as he motioned to Vernet to get out first. "But it would mean that she is acting with her usual prudence, and that is encouraging."

"Assuming that she is able to act, that she is free to act, and that she still is able to . . . to have her wits about her," Vernet said. He stood aside for Murat. "What I cannot make myself believe is that—"

Murat laid a hand on his shoulder to quiet him. "Actually, Lucien, neither of us knows anything. We are indulging in speculation so that we will deceive ourselves into doing what we can to help her." He turned to tell his coachman to get the team out of the weather, then pointed Vernet in the direction of the Ministry. "And the first thing we can do is speak with Fouche. After that, we ought to consider going to Berthier, and then we will have to decide who best to address next." He consulted the watch hanging from his satin waistcoat. "Given the hour, we'd better plan to deal with Berthier first thing in the morning. It is already nearing eleven and by the time we are through here, it will be too late to rouse the man."

Vernet paused as he started up the steps. "Yes. That's sensible; the hour is too late to make much difference tonight. You're right, but—"

"Yes, I know," said Murat as he followed Vernet up the stairs.

10

❧

VICTOIRE AWOKE TO a loud shout and the sight of a pitchfork leveled at her chest; a boy of about nine in smock and culottes stood over her, blocking her access to the Belgian draft horse as if he feared she would vault onto the placid creature and flee. "You get up now," he ordered in a frightened treble.

"If you will move that pitchfork I will certainly do so," said Victoire as reasonably as she was able. In spite of the scrapes and hurts and complaining muscles, she pulled herself to a sitting position, keeping a handsbreadth away from the tines.

The stable boy stared, for in spite of the ruined clothing and distressing appearance, he recognized her accent as good and her manners as better than what was usually found in these streets. "All right, Auntie," he said, taking a step back, but holding the pitchfork at the ready. "You tell me what you're doing here in D'or's stall. Then I'll decide what to do."

"I was seeking shelter for the night," Victoire said quietly. "As you see, I have nothing to protect me from the cold and rain." She was thinking rapidly, sizing up the boy and trying to decide how best to win him over.

"Your dress is tattered," the boy agreed without relinquishing his weapon.

"And my hands are cut," she appended, holding them out to show the bruises and blood. "I have escaped from danger." She remained sitting, afraid that if she stood up the boy might do more than threaten her with the pitchfork.

"Or the beating of someone you cheated," suggested the boy. He used one hand to wipe his ill-cut hair out of his face. "How do I know you are not a thief, or worse?"

"You know because a thief would conceal injuries from you, and would try to flee, which I have not done," said Victoire calmly.

"Do you think so? When my master comes we'll see what he thinks." His jaw set firmly.

"And when will that be?" she asked. "If he is coming, let it be soon. He may be more understanding of the peril I face."

"My master will be here at noon: he is delivering a matched pair to Inspector-General Suchet." He said this with pride, then stared at her in speculation. "What danger could a woman of your sort be in?" For a youngster there was an unexpected worldliness in his question. "Tell me that."

"Fine," said Victoire, and quickly thought of an acceptable version of the truth; she sensed the boy's keen sensitivity to lies. "I am a soldier's wife, and my husband is posted elsewhere." That much was true. "I have been hounded by his enemies." While that was not quite as true, it was not entirely a lie, either. "His enemies are also enemies of the First Consul," she went on again, returning to the whole truth. "And it is necessary that I . . . I warn him of these enemies."

The boy scoffed. "You, warn Napoleon himself?"

Victoire had anticipated this, and decided to try the one ploy that had occurred to her the night before while she fell asleep trying to puzzle out how to report what she learned without going near her house, Fouché's ministry, Berthier, or Murat, all of whom she feared were under observation. "No, of course not." She hoped she sounded as modest as the boy thought correct. "But I do want to reach the Mameluke who guards him. You know, the tall man in the turban, the Egyptian?" She saw skepticism dawning in the boy's face again, and she hurried on, "My husband and I were in Egypt with Napoleon, and my husband came to know the Mameluke. His name is Roustam-Raza, and he was a gift to Napoleon, to serve him all his life." Again this was the truth, and she hoped it would be enough.

"What would he want with you?" demanded the boy.

"He would come to help me—"

The boy threw his head back and laughed. "Right, a man like that listening to a woman! They say those Egyptians keep their wives in pens, like ewes. What would he want with you?"

"—and he could warn Napoleon of his enemies," said Victoire, refusing to give in, then realized that her stubbornness was turning the boy against her. She faltered. "I know I must look like a drab, and I can understand why you would not trust what I tell you. But think of this, I beg you: what if everything I have said is true and the First Consul is really in danger. What if his enemies succeed against him because they were unknown? Would you be able to bear it, knowing that you might have given the warning, and did not?"

"You never could do that," he said, but less confidently.

"Not without your help, I could not," she said with utter sincerity.

The boy's eyes had become large and intent. "Could it be so?"

"Yes," Victoire stated. "It is so. Napoleon's enemies are real." She saw the single, slight nod the boy gave. "With his Coronation approaching, those who oppose him are likely to strive to act before he can be crowned."

"We have had a king before," the boy said.

"Not like this man," corrected Victoire. "Consul for Life or Emperor, Napoleon is France, and his enemies are the enemies of France."

"You don't talk like the women who gather rags. You sound like the fancy ones who ride in the carriages." The boy narrowed his eyes as he considered what she said. "You are some man's mistress and he has grown tired of you."

"It is possible, but I am not. My husband is an officer on Napoleon's staff. He often works with Fouche and Marshall Murat."

This reference to the Governor of Paris had the desired effect. "Very well," he said. "If I am to go to this Egyptian, how do I know you will not flee when I am out the door and I will receive nothing but a thrashing for what I have done?"

"I will give you my word that I will remain here unless the First Consul's enemies find me, and if they do, I will find a way to leave a message on this stall. I will scratch out the word for enemies," she offered.

"Which you could do in any case," said the boy cannily. "And my master here would dismiss me for being taken in." Nevertheless he motioned to Victoire to get up. "This Egyptian will know not to beat me?"

"If you bow to him this way"—she performed a sala'am as she had learned it in Egypt—"and say that you are the messenger of Madame Vernet, he will hear you out." Then she remembered the locket she wore, and struggled to unfasten it, flinching at the hurt in her torn fingers. At last the clasp opened and she pulled the chain from around her neck. "Here. Show this to him after you greet him. He will recognize it. And you may keep it as payment. It is gold."

The stable boy seized the locket and stared at it, suddenly avaricious. "Real gold?"

"Real gold," she affirmed. "And if you think to keep it and do nothing, remember that locket would then be worth thirty pieces of silver."

"Ah." The boy looked up sharply. "All right," he said, his sense of adventure winning out over both greed and apprehension. "Show me how to do that again, and I will do this errand for you."

Victoire sala'amed again, very slowly. "Do this, and give him the locket and the greetings of Madame Vernet. Go to the coaching door of the Tuileries and ask one of the footmen to fetch him."

"Why should they do that?" asked the boy suspiciously.

"Because you will give them this," she said with a sigh, and handed over her last two coins. "And you will say you bring word from an Egyptian veteran."

The boy thought this over. "All right. But if they do not do this, I will not stay to be disciplined." He looked over at D'or. "He's branded, and if you take him, my master will set the bailiffs on you."

"I will not take him," Victoire promised.

"What is the name of the Egyptian again?" he asked.

"Roustam-Raza. He is a Mameluke." She repeated this. "If you say his name, the footmen will be impressed."

"Right." The boy nodded, repeated the name, and finally lowered the pitchfork. "You had better be here when I return, with or without this Mameluke."

"I will, or there will be something scratched on the wall," she said, sinking back down into the straw again, thinking that while the boy was gone she could make herself useful by cleaning the stall and bringing fresh bedding. "If I am gone more than three hours, you had—" he started, doing all he could to appear threatening.

"You will be back in less than two," said Victoire, hoping it was so.

The stare the boy gave her was unconvinced, but he left the stall, flung the pitchfork tines first into a mound of hay, and went on his way whistling.

Victoire took a long, uneven breath and glanced over at the Belgian. "Well, D'or," she said, "I suppose we have to wait."

The massive horse favored her with a friendly but uninterested stare.

Claude Montrachet concealed his growing anger in a sneer. "What's the matter with you, Sackett-Hartley?" he asked as they paced the tiny inn yard at Le Chat Gris. "You're squeamish as a girl about this incident. It's not as if we murdered her or sold her to a brothel. What is one woman, or a dozen of them, or a hundred, compared to our cause? We did the reasonable thing, under the circumstances. Don't you appreciate the stakes here?"

Colonel Sir Magnus Sackett-Hartley paced along beside him, shaking his head. "I am surprised you ask such an inexcusable question. We aren't here to terrorize helpless women, Montrachet. We're supposed to be ridding the world of a tyrant, or had you forgot?"

Montrachet rubbed his arm where the bullet had left a furrow. "I would not call Madame Vernet helpless. She found us and no one else has. I'd rather have half the police in Paris on my trail than that woman."

"Then it is a question of revenge? You wish to dishonor her because she shot you?" Sackett-Hartley said contemptuously. The clouds of the night before had gone and in their place was a dazzling autumn day with bright skies and a brisk wind that snapped color into cheeks and turned shadows cold. Sackett-Hartley squinted as much against the brilliant light as against Montrachet.

"That has nothing to do with it," Montrachet said darkly. "She defied us and she will stop at nothing to ruin everything we must do here."

"You make her sound worse than a troop of cavalry. Isn't that a little extreme? She is not the enemy," said Sackett-Hartley. "She is the wife of an honest officer. She is the epitome of those we have come to aid." Had he been French he would have waved his arms for emphasis, but being English he merely nodded once. "What harm can she do us, in any case?"

"She knows who I am, and she can identify me; and make no doubt about it, she will. She is not one of those shrinking females who are afraid of making accusations. Not she," said Montrachet heavily. "And her husband is an Inspector-General. If he brings a complaint, he will be heard. Such men are both judge and accuser."

"Assuming that the woman can persuade him that she has not been compromised. No man wishes to be shamed by his wife." His eyes grew distant. "My uncle carried the rumor of his wife's shame until he was able to vindicate her honor."

"Your uncle? This has nothing to do with your uncle!" Montrachet rounded on him. "What is the matter with you, Colonel? You are not such a naif as you pretend. You cannot be." He indicated the inn. "You are the one who insists that you and your men stay here instead of sharing duties at the house with the rest of us. You are the one who has contingency plans for escaping France if we cannot safely reach the coast. You are the one who has arranged for the guns and money, and you have no direct contact with Querelle, let alone his superior. What makes you so meticulous in these matters and fails you when confronted with the opposition in female form?"

"I wasn't confronted by her," Sackett-Hartley reminded him with heat. "Had I been here, this whole disgraceful episode would not have happened."

Montrachet came to a halt and stared contemptuously at Sackett-Hartley. "We're here to kill Napoleon, and anyone who tries to prevent us from doing it. Yet you balk at locking one woman in a room."

"Which she escaped from," said Sackett-Hartley. "Which shows poor judgment on your part, Claude."

Montrachet gestured his increasing disgust. "If you're unwilling to do what must be done, then you can say nothing against those of us who are." He started away from Sackett-Hartley. "We will discuss this when you're more rational."

At that Sackett-Hartley reached out to restrain Montrachet. "We will settle it now. I'll not have your pride compromising our mission, or leading us into disgrace."

Montrachet looked at Sackett-Hartley's fingers where they closed around his forearm. "Take your hands off me. At once."

Sackett-Hartley refused. "This is going to be resolved now."

"So be it," said Montrachet, breaking away from Sackett-Hartley and brushing his sleeve as if to rid it of contamination. "It is resolved. You will do your part and I and my men will do ours. But once Napoleon is dead, I swear you will meet me for what you have said today."

Sackett-Hartley came to attention and gave Montrachet an exaggerated salute. "You may expect my seconds to wait upon yours," he said. "Monsieur le Duc."

"You despicable—" said Montrachet as he turned on his heel and strode away.

It was less than two hours later when the stable boy returned, strutting as he escorted the tall, turbaned Mameluke Roustam-Raza. He made certain that as many of the denizens of the neighborhood as possible saw his companion, then entered the livery stable, calling out in a cracking tone, "Madame Vernet, this is Jean-Adam."

Although the stable boy had not told Victoire his name, she recognized his voice and came out of the stall at once, just as Roustam-Raza stepped through the tall doors.

"Blessings upon you, my old friend. May you live all your life the honored servant of Allah, and may you have your rewards here on earth as well as in Paradise," she said with a curtsy in her awkward Egyptian dialect.

Roustam-Raza sala'amed to Victoire at once—far better than Jean-Adam had managed it—and wished her long life and many sons in his native language, continuing in French, "What has become of you, Madame Vernet?"

"A great deal," she said. "And I hope you have brought me some food, for I think I could faint with hunger." She laughed a little, which served to alarm Roustam-Raza.

He turned to Jean-Adam. "Here is money. Bring us food at once. Hot food," he added as he gave the stable boy three gold coins. "Have some for yourself."

Jean-Adam took the money, his eyes bright. "At once. There is a bakery in the next street, and a maker of sausage." With that he scampered off, eager to be about his errand so that he could boast of his exotic and illustrious companion.

"That is a good boy," said Roustam-Raza. "He has a little imagination—just enough to understand danger—but not too much, to make him afraid." He dragged a sawhorse nearer to where Victoire stood and sat down as if the device made a comfortable seat. "What has happened?"

"I'm not entirely sure," said Victoire, and began to recount her activities since the soirée at the Chateaubriands' fashionable home. "It was seeing Querelle talking to Pichegru that most bothered me. Why should such a man as Querelle allow himself to be seen with Pichegru? And when I saw something pass between them, I feared that there might be treachery in it."

"Why would you think that?" asked Roustam-Raza. "A man, with another man, there are many reasons for notes to be exchanged."

"For men like Querelle, there can be no reason but advancement. If that advancement is through covert and devious methods, it is probably the more exciting for him." She sighed. "I've been thinking about everything I observed yesterday, and the more I think of it, the more it troubles me." She folded her damaged hands and walked down the row of box stalls. "I have thought about all I heard, but it was not enough for me to be certain."

Roustam-Raza indicated her clothing. "Tell me why you resorted to this? You must have feared discovery to dress in this way."

"Oh, yes," she said. "I thought that Querelle would not

bother to look at a rag-picker." She cracked a single laugh. "And I was right as far as it went. If Montrachet had not come I would have got away handily. But I did not count on finding Montrachet again, not after what happened at the inn."

"What are you talking about?" pleaded Roustam-Raza, who was becoming very confused. "Who is Montrachet? What about the inn?"

Victoire glanced over her shoulder toward the door, then said, "Yes, I suppose it does need more explanation than what I have provided." She stopped walking and composed her thoughts. "You knew that Vernet was sent to the coast where he discovered rumors of a landing of English spies—"

"With your help, I surmise," said Roustam-Raza.

"When it was needed," said Victoire and paid no attention to the snort Roustam-Raza offered in comment. She told him what they had learned, of how she had come back to Paris by diligence, of Corporals Cruche and Feuille, who bungled their attempts to protect her, of the musician Montrachet breaking into her room, and her action against him. "I had feared something could happen, so I had kept a charged pistol by me."

"Naturally," said Roustam-Raza sardonically.

She described the shot and Montrachet's escape, then began to discuss the most recent developments in Paris. "It was seeing Querelle with Pichegru that startled me, for Pichegru is beyond the pale just now. You are aware of that, of course."

"He's under suspicion," said Roustam-Raza.

"Exactly," Victoire confirmed. "That's what rankled: Querelle with someone out-of-favor. Ordinarily such men are avoided. So why would a man like Querelle be willing to approach him, and at such a gathering, where it could be noticed by those he wanted to impress."

There was a noise in the doorway as Jean-Adam returned, trailing a squad of apprentices and other curious youths. He carried a basket over one arm and a bottle of wine in the other hand, and as he started through the door, he turned back to his goggling audience. "You see? The First Consul's dervish, just as I said."

Roustam-Raza was about to upbraid the boy for his error when he saw Victoire signal him to silence. Slowly the Mameluke rose and offered the watchers a deep sala'am, which sent most of them scattering.

Jean-Adam grinned in delight as he stepped into the barn. "So. Here is bread, still hot, and cheese and butter, and broiled sausages, also hot. And wine." This last he held up as if it were a trophy. "Andre the wine-merchant is a pig, but he has the best wines. He gave this to me for nothing, because of the Mameluke."

Victoire did not know how to explain to Jean-Adam that Roustam-Raza was a devout Moslem and did not drink. Besides, she was ravenous, and the sight of food so near made her giddy. "Thank you," she said, with a warning sign to Roustam-Raza to remain silent until all the boys but Jean-Adam were gone.

"And I thank you," said Jean-Adam, beaming. "No one in this street has ever had such a visitor. My master will be able to say that the First Consul's Egyptian servant came here. It will make him very happy."

"How grand," said Roustam-Raza gravely. He returned his attention to Victoire with unseemly haste. "But you've sent for me, not for your husband or Murat."

"My husband is out of town until tomorrow—" Victoire began.

"He returned last night," Roustam-Raza corrected her, "and has been knocking on doors all over the city."

Victoire blushed, hating her fair skin for giving her away so utterly. "How does it happen he came back early?"

Roustam-Raza made a gesture of uncaring ignorance. "He is back, and he and Murat have been insisting that a search be mounted for you. Therefore everyone in Paris is up in arms, Madame Vernet."

Jean-Adam stared at the two with rapt fascination, drinking in all they said. His young, clever eyes shone.

"That's unfortunate," said Victoire, and hurried on to explain, her mouth watering as the scent of hot sausages went searching through the air. "It might well put the conspirators' superior on the alert, which will make him all the harder to catch. I am troubled by everything I have discovered about this conspiracy." She looked down at herself. "I think I must ask you to arrange for me to see Napoleon as soon as possible."

The stable boy gasped.

"Late this afternoon it would be possible," said Roustam-Raza in a thoughtful way. "I believe he will have returned from his hunting by then and will not yet have to be ready for his evening banquet. He has a fitting with Bastide at four, who is cast into gloom if Napoleon presents himself two minutes late—he is a most down-cast tailor. And as I recall, Constant will need to put him in order at six to have him presentable by seven. So if you will meet me at five, I think it can be arranged."

Victoire nodded. "Good. In the meantime I shall strive to put myself into better fettle." She tugged her shawls around her shoulders as she reached for the bread. "Pardon me, Roustam-Raza, but I must have something to eat."

"Frenchwomen eat when they wish," said Roustam-Raza philosophically. It had taken him some time to get used to this custom, for among Egyptians, men completed their meals before women were allowed to dine on their left-overs. "It will not offend me."

"Good," she said, tearing into the bread. She picked up one of the little sausages in her fingers and popped it into her mouth, blowing against its heat. As soon as she had swallowed, she said, "I want you to arrange for more guards on the First Consul. He is vulnerable to attack as he is. I will explain the reason to him myself, but I'm relying on you to put the guards on notice of the danger."

"He will not like it," Roustam-Raza warned.

"Possibly not," said Victoire as she reached for another sausage; it tasted better than anything she could remember eating in the last three yeas. "But he will like even less being killed by his enemies, which I suspect is what may happen if we take no precautions."

"He still will not like it," said Roustam-Raza fatalistically. "But it will be done. You are correct to say it is essential."

"Thank you," said Victoire as she pulled off another mound of bread and spread it with butter. "I haven't been this hungry in more than two years," she said as she chewed.

"You were locked up then as well, I recall," said Roustam-Raza, noticing how amazed Jean-Adam was. "Listen to me, boy," he went on to the youngster. "You are hearing things that stable boys ought not to know. If I learn that you have repeated any of this, I will return and you will regret speaking."

Jean-Adam went pale.

"But if you keep your silence and show that you are reliable, then there may come a time when I might recommend you for advancement." He said the last very quietly. "A trustworthy servant is a treasure—an untrustworthy one is a traitor."

"I . . . I will say nothing," said the boy, hoping it would be true.

"See that you remember this," said Roustam-Raza, and once more gave his attention to Victoire. "I will take you to your house, Madame Vernet, and I will make the arrangements that need to be made. At five this afternoon I will expect you, at the side entrance, so that we may be more private." He looked around the stable and at last his eyes settled on D'or. "That one. I want that one harnessed to a wagon, a wagon where Madame Vernet may rest and have her luncheon as I escort her to her husband."

"D'or is—" began Jean-Adam.

"I will pay for her use. Name any reasonable amount." He was already reaching for the wallet hanging from his sash. "I will have one of the Consular Guard bring them back before the end of the day."

"But . . ." Jean-Adam knew he was not supposed to rent out the horses, that only his master could do that. At the same time he could not resist the temptation. "All right," he said. "If you will repeat that in front of Marie and Paul, I will strike a bargain with you."

"Marie and Paul," said Roustam-Raza, wanting more information.

"He wants witnesses, so that his employer will not beat him," said Victoire as she swallowed the wine. "His employer may return before the horse is brought back. It's a reasonable request, my friend."

Roustam-Raza considered it. "Very well," he said in a measured tone. "I will do it. Let us summon these people at once."

Victoire put her basket aside reluctantly, but the worst of her hunger had been satisfied and now she was prepared to concentrate on making her plans.

"I'll get Marie and Paul," said Jean-Adam. "They're just over the road."

"Fine," said Roustam-Raza, and watched as the stable boy rushed away. "And while he's away, we will make our arrangements. The wagon is necessary. You will be able to ride unseen, Madame, which is desirable."

"I agree. We don't want anyone to know that I have returned home; it's probably being watched. The men know who I am and it's not difficult to find out where we live, not with Querelle to assist them." She picked up the basket and did her best to straighten her rent and bedraggled clothes. "I think it would be wiser if we went to my house by the rear entrance, as if we were tradesmen."

"Tradesmen? I fear, Madame Vernet, that we will have to find you another escort, one who can pass unnoticed." Roustam-Raza indicated his Egyptian dress and his turban. "Do you suppose anyone would think me other than I am?"

To the Mameluke's surprise Victoire nodded emphatically. "Yes. And ordinarily I would share your worry, for it would be a very bad thing if anyone learned I had returned until it suits our purpose. You are right, you are a very identifiable figure. And, yes, I think I may have hit upon a plan that will work." She rubbed her hands together. "We make you not less than you are, but more," she said.

"How more?" asked Roustam-Raza.

With growing enthusiasm Victoire explained.

The wagon attracted quite a lot of attention as it came down the street, its canvas flaps billowing in the wind, the streamers on the harness of the butter-colored horse composed of brightly dyed woolen braids. Most astonishing of all was the driver of the wagon, who was rigged out in a mountainous turban and enough striped canvas to make an awning—which, up until two hours before it had been; all those who had ever seen Napoleon's Mameluke agreed that he was not half so fantastical as this spectacular creature. The wagon progressed along the street, the driver calling out now and again for Monsieur d'Jaffa in a high, loud voice. Twice the driver stopped and walked up the stairs of the house he had selected. He inquired of the occupant for the house of Monsieur d'Jaffa. Each time he was informed that he had not found the fellow in question, which appeared to cause him great distress, for he would cry aloud to Heaven that he was being deceived.

At the fourth stop—the house of Inspector-General Lucien Vernet—he asked if he might have some water for the horse, for they had been traveling some distance; he explained in broken French that he had a duty to find this Monsieur d'Jaffa and give him a bequest.

"Well, I know nothing about that," said Odette, her recognition of Roustam-Raza well concealed. "But you are welcome to water for the horse. The well is in the back." She hesitated, then said, "Have you tried at Les Invalides? Many of those poor men were in Egypt. Someone there must know where he is."

"No. But you are right. They must know something." He beamed and sala'amed in a way that would have embarrassed his relatives had they seen it. "May Allah thank you for the kindness to my horse."

"Humph," said Odette as she closed the door, then hurried down the hall past the carpenters, toward the rear of the house.

Roustam-Raza, looking unhappy in his ridiculous get-up, was

giving D'or water and screening the rear of the wagon from the street. He looked up as Odette rushed out of the kitchen door, and after signalling to the housekeeper to be silent, called very softly, "Madame, you are home."

Victoire pulled aside the flap and slid out of the wagon, taking care to keep in the shelter of Roustam-Raza's enhanced bulk. She glanced up at him, smiling. "Thank you, and may Allah—"

"Give me your blessing later, Madame," said Roustam-Raza quietly, "when we have completed our tasks and Napoleon is safe from his enemies."

She made a gesture of chastened assent, then hurried into the kitchen door, which Odette held open for her. She resisted the urge to wave to Roustam-Raza as he sighed and led D'or away, for even so minor a movement would attract the attention of watchers, if they had any.

"Heaven be praised," whispered Odette as she hastened Victoire into the large pantry. "I was afraid that the worst had happened to you, Madame. I was certain that you had come to harm." She crossed herself and stared at Victoire. "You *must* have come to harm, to look so."

Victoire's laughter was more nervous than she liked. "It is not as bad as it seems," she declared. "In fact, it isn't bad at all." She looked down at the dress. "But this will have to be disposed of. I think burning it would be wisest, and not because of all the rents and smuts, but—" She put her hand to her brow. Her headache had faded after she ate, but now she was growing so tired that she did not know how she could hold two thoughts together, let alone remain on her feet. "I . . . I'm a little tired," she said.

"You look half-dead," Odette stated. "What happened?" But before Victoire could answer the question, she hurried on. "No. Never mind. You will tell me that later, when you are rested. You must have a bath. You smell quite dreadful, Madame. And your arms, your poor arms! I will find the salve." She put her hands on her hips. "I will bring the bathtub in here and I will see that you are washed, all without the carpenters discovering it."

"Sensible," said Victoire, starting to yawn. She breathed out slowly, without apology, then said, "Roustam-Raza informed me that Vernet has returned early."

"That he has," said Odette with feeling. "And he has been beside himself with worry for your sake. I will send a messenger—"

Victoire gestured no. "We must do nothing to alert the men who are watching this house. If they discover I am back . . ." She sighed. "And I must visit the First Consul at five this afternoon. So you must not let me sleep on and on. Let me get clean, have an omelette, and then rest for a couple of hours. You can dress me and arrange my hair in less than an hour, can't you?"

"Madame Vernet, you cannot expect to be out of bed again before tomorrow morning," Odette declared, taking care not to raise her voice.

Now a little of Victoire's spirit flared. "You are not the only soldier's wife here, Odette. I will not sleep while Napoleon is in danger and there is anything I can do that will protect him." She started to work the buttons down the front of the dress. "So prepare the bath, or I may fall asleep where I stand."

"You husband will want to know you are here," Odette warned as she started toward the door.

"He will learn it soon enough. When I leave to speak with the First Consul, send word to him to meet me there."

Odette tapped the door latch. "And General Murat?"

"Has he been dragged into this?" she asked, and answered her own question. "Oh, yes. That's what Roustam-Raza said. Better find a way to get a message to him, as well, then." She cocked her head. "I will think of some way to get out of this house without anyone noticing." This last was said to the closed door, and the distant metallic clang of the bathtub as Odette began lugging it toward the pantry.

11

❧

LESS FEARFUL OF the connection to the Old Regime than the Director and Consuls that had preceded him, Napoleon had moved into the palace, bringing his bristling energy with him; at the Crown's peak of elegance and power this building and grounds had never seen so much activity.

Louis' army had amounted to almost a hundred thousand men, most on garrison duty: the Republic's army was four times that size. Messengers in the colorful uniforms of the hussars and chasseurs galloped through the gates at all hours of the day or night. A battalion of the Consular Guard infantry in their tall bearskins drilled on the swath of green that once served as a croquet court. Two brass cannon, well-shined and quite operational, reminded all who entered the palace grounds of the "whiff of grapeshot" that began Napoleon's rise to power.

The long, arcing drive that led to the main entrance was crowded with gilded carriages. The entire family had gathered for the upcoming Coronation and vied with each other to be elegantly and extravagantly served.

With over 150 regiments and an equal number of ships, France had almost as many men under arms as all the rest of Europe. Even at night during peace time the palace saw a constant parade of couriers, their arrival time dictated by distance, not the hour. Napoleon Buonaparte himself slept fitfully, more often than not arising hours before the sun to dictate letters and directives to bleary-eyed secretaries.

The straight drive leading to the side entrances of the palace was hidden by a double row of bushes and trees. Along it rumbled carts and wagons laden with the food and luxuries required to maintain a palace housing almost two hundred guests and servants. At the entrance to this tradesman's lane was a guard station, where a sergeant screened each person wishing to enter while four private soldiers searched their wagons or loads. Victoire was pleased to see the care with which the men checked each delivery, but she hoped that Roustam-Raza had ensured her own quick passage through their post. After all she had been through she had no desire to be caught in the long line of carters, tailors, and gardeners awaiting permission to enter, where Montrachet's spies might observe her.

Victoire emerged from the landaulet near the side entrance. It was a cloudy afternoon and a bitter wind was picking up as the ill-defined shadows lengthened; Victoire's caped traveling coat and her warmest afternoon dress—a simple wool twill of green and black with a corsage al hussar and a complicated set of pleats falling from the high waist—were not proof against it. The two hours' sleep she had garnered had been sufficient only to make her aware of how exhausted she had become. Her eyes were hollow and she was pinched about the mouth. There was a scratch along her left cheek and a bruise was forming on her jaw. Giving up on more fashionable modes, Odette had dressed Victoire's hair in a simple braid coronet. "For you may be certain that in spite of his lack of concern for his own appearance, the First Consul is a stickler for everyone else's." These words rang in Victoire's ears as she pulled her coat about her.

It was not Roustam-Raza who came to greet her, but General Joachim Murat, blue eyes thunderous. He bowed to her in excellent form, kissed her hand with absolute propriety, signalled the coachman to take the landaulet into the stable yard, then said under his breath, "What the Devil were you trying to do?"

Murat was dressed in another of his custom-made uniforms; it was loosely modelled on those of the hussars, the light cavalry having by far the most ostentatious uniforms in the army. The pale blue pelisse was lined with a white fur that contrasted well with the deep blue and heavily gold-braided jacket beneath. The gold inexpressibles were tucked into white riding boots.

"I wasn't trying to do—" she began, keeping her voice low, only to be waved to silence.

"Tell me later. Whatever the answer is, it will be outrageous in any case." He put her hand through the crook of his arm and led her into the palace, behaving as if they were exchanging nothing more than pleasantries about the weather. "We were worried nigh unto madness, Madame," he whispered.

"So was I for a time," Victoire said, and raised her voice, "Yes, I am pleased that some of the Swedish ladies are making it more fashionable to be fair, but I will continue to long for dark tresses."

The two officers walking by smirked, saluted Murat, and continued on.

A little of Murat's affronted manner lessened. "Well, at least you've kept your wits about you."

"I'm not a ninny," she snapped in an undervoice.

Murat relented a bit more; he could not contain a rueful smile. "No, you're not that."

"And I know I look a dowd, and my skin is the color of glue, but this cannot wait. Believe me, Murat, I would not have asked to see Napoleon if I were not absolutely certain that he is in grave and immediate danger." She was able to keep from raising the level of her voice, but her face flushed.

"Oh, dear," said Murat shaking his head. "Now they will say that I tried to compromise you and that you have put me in my place."

She looked around and realized at once that Murat was right. "What should I do?"

"Laugh, if you can. Then they will decide I made a remark that was too bold." He continued beside her, his eyes fixed on a point about six strides ahead. His next words were louder. "When I told it to your husband, he thought it funny."

Victoire could not make herself laugh but she was able to simulate indignation. "You military men! There are times I wonder how your families can bear you with your rough humor."

"Sometimes they can't," said Murat, and motioned her to take the next turn. He lowered his voice again. "We will meet Napoleon in an unexpected place."

"That seems sensible," Victoire said. "I know some pieces of this puzzle but not enough of them to make me think Napoleon is protected."

"So I gather," said Murat, and opened the door leading into the music room.

Napoleon Buonaparte was standing beside the fortepiano. In his hands he held a number of papers, none of which were music. He was reading quickly, frowning as he did. As always Victoire was taken by the sheer magnetism of the man. Even when he acted like a petulant child, which she had seen too often in the past years, he had a way about him. She had heard about Napoleon's ability to inspire men in battle from Vernet and caught a glimpse of it as he sat there glancing idly through a stack of papers.

No taller than Victoire, Napoleon was dressed in the plain blue uniform of the Consular Guard. It carried no marks of rank, nor any of the numerous decorations commonly worn by most members of this prestigious unit. If it were not for his height—the minimum height for the guard was six feet, and Napoleon was the single exception to that rule—and piercing eyes there was no way to tell this was the man who controlled the fate of France, and possibly all Europe.

Suddenly he thrust all the papers onto the fortepiano bench and looked up as if he had been startled by a loud noise. "Murat." He strode forward as Victoire curtsied. "Madame Vernet. Roustam-Raza tells me that you have important information." He regarded her with a frown. "You're not in your best looks, Madame."

"No, I'm not," Victoire agreed.

Napoleon signalled to Murat to guard the door. "I want you to stay to hear this. You'll only try to find out everything in any case."

"True," said Murat, and took up his post directly in front of the tall pocket doors, his gloved hands resting on the latches behind him.

"You told my servant that there are spies here in Paris. You claim they are here to kill me. Is that correct?" Napoleon was curt at the best of times and often lapsed into outright rudeness. "You are becoming a harbinger, Madame Vernet."

"Better a harbinger than no warning at all, First Consul," she said with equal directness, knowing that most women would be terrified by now. Truth to tell, she was apprehensive, but had learned from her overbearing father that buckling under such tactics only caused their severity to increase. "Would you rather I keep this to myself?"

"Powers preserve, no," Napoleon expostulated. He frowned down at fine carpets patterned in the Egyptian style. "Very clever, Murat, to choose this room for our meeting," he murmured. "Reminds me of another warning."

From his position at the door Murat chuckled.

Napoleon looked directly at Victoire once more. "So. Tell me how you have arrived at this certainty of yours. Not that half the nobility of France and all of Europe would not be glad of my death."

"I . . . I am aware of my husband's work, of course." She steadied herself and continued. "As you must know, he was sent to the coast to investigate rumors of secret English landings. At the time, it was assumed that the negotiations with the Low Countries were the object of their efforts; either that or the disposition of the fleet. But there was no trace of these men anywhere. Some in the administration probably suspected a hoax or a rumor that had been blown out of proportion. Some inferred this was a British attempt to frighten us into chasing phantoms," she said carefully, aware that the first proponent of this theory was Napoleon himself. "Had I not been attacked at a posting inn near Abbeville, I might have agreed. As it was, I began to consider the possibility that the men who landed were bound for Paris." She paused. "I can explain my assumptions more fully if you like, First Consul."

"Perhaps later," said Napoleon. "Continue."

"As you wish." She went on to describe her encounter with Querelle, her observation of Pichegru, and her subsequent actions. "I did not realize that there was more than one or two men involved, and I did not anticipate that I would have to escape from them." She swallowed hard, her throat suddenly tight. "I believe I would have proceeded differently had I known how many were involved, or how well-organized they are. I've deduced, from what I heard, that there's a group of spies and that they have been in Paris some little time."

"And you say you're certain that there are more?" Napoleon said.

"From what I could gather during their conversations, I must suppose that there are. Perhaps ten or more." She would have liked to sit down. Her bruised leg was getting very sore and being tired only made it worse. But Napoleon was starting to pace, which meant she would be expected to remain on her feet. "I know that they receive messages from someone well-placed in the government and that messages from this person may be carried by Pichegru, and definitely Querelle, to these spies."

Napoleon was looking seriously displeased. "And you do not know who this person is?"

"No, I don't; I can identify only Montrachet and Querelle both by face and name, but as to the others, I can identify face only, or guess," said Victoire. "I could speculate, but that would not be worth much, would it?"

"I suppose it wouldn't," said Napoleon, the speed of his pacing increasing.

"You have the men around you to discover who these traitors are," said Murat. "It could be done very, very discreetly." He paused and when Napoleon said nothing, he went on. "If we detained Querelle—"

"Querelle!" Napoleon exclaimed. "The man is nothing more

than a hanger-on, a would-be general, nothing more. This is idiotic."

"But the fellow *is* an idiot," Murat reminded his brother-in-law.

Napoleon laughed twice in short, harsh barks. "You're a clever one, Murat. Your seminary time wasn't wasted, except for the religion." He swung back toward Victoire. "So, Madame Vernet, do you agree with the Marshall? Do you think we ought to send our own spies out to watch every important figure in—" He gestured as if to include the whole of the Paris.

"I think it would be wise," said Victoire seriously.

"And the utmost folly," Napoleon snapped. "These men do not want to be the object of questions and investigations. At such a time as this, anything of that sort would serve no purpose but to aggravate those men who have served me well."

"I realize that, First Consul," said Victoire carefully. "And I do not disagree with your concerns, but I'm afraid that if you don't begin a thorough investigation, you'll be taking your own life in your hands."

"Ha!" He turned on his heel and went back in the other direction, toward the ormolu harp. "You'll never make a proper general's wife if you talk that way, Madame." He moved restlessly about the room, a faint line between his brows. "Constant is waiting for me. He is annoyed if I make him rush."

"He is a valet, and you are the one who pays him. Let him be annoyed," Murat recommended. "This might well spare Constant the trouble of finding something to bury you in."

Again Napoleon laughed. "All right. You and Fouche work out how you want to look for your high-ranking conspirator. Have Moncey assign General Vernet or one of the other five of Moncey's Inspectors. But do not forget there are many other threats to France as well. This still may be a careful plot to distract us from some other mischief. I give you three weeks to come up with something. If you have nothing by the time of the Coronation, then the matter will be abandoned. In the meantime, put Querelle under arrest and get everything out of him that you can. I want a report on him by this time tomorrow, under seal." He leveled his finger at Murat. "See that there is just the one copy. And this Montrachet, the one who plays the horn, find him and arrest him, and as many of his men as you can discover. Send word by courier to the coast at once."

"Of course," said Murat.

"I want it done quietly; not a whisper. If any hint of this escapes all the rest will go to ground and we may never find them." Napoleon rounded on Victoire. "I am grateful to you for this, Madame Vernet, but I am not pleased."

"Nor should you be," said Victoire. "In your position you cannot wish for covert opposition."

"True. Very true," said Napoleon. "General Murat will escort you home so that those watching your house will be aware of your return but may not—"

Victoire did the unthinkable and interrupted Napoleon. "You mean that you would rather compromise my reputation than put the traitors on alert," she said bluntly.

"Precisely," said Napoleon. "What difference can the opinion of traitors matter? We know the truth, as does your husband."

"This is poor reward for good service, First Consul," said Murat with an edge in his tone. "It is unfair to her and Inspector-General Vernet."

"Sadly, yes it is, but it is excellent protection when protection is more important than gossip." He smiled once. "A few sordid whispers so you may sleep safe in your bed." He looked at the tall clock and shook his head. "You have done us good service, Madame, I know, and it will be acknowledged when it is prudent. In the meantime, bear with matters as they are." He bowed slightly, then left the room by the servants' door.

Murat strolled toward Victoire. "If it means anything, I will try to dissuade him from putting your reputation at risk."

"Thank you," said Victoire. "I would never think otherwise. As long as Vernet understands that I am faithful—"

"He knows you are," said Murat, and added, "He also knows that my care for you is more than brotherly."

"Murat!" she admonished him. "It is also less than overlike."

He flashed her his very best smile. "My dear Victoire, if you had a wife as unfaithful as mine, you would understand Vernet's happiness better than you do. Oh," he went on, "I realize I am no model husband either, but from the first Caroline has set the tone, and . . . and since Egypt, since . . . her death"—he was unable to speak her name—"it hasn't seemed . . . so important."

"It's been more than four years," said Victoire. "Surely after this time the grief has—"

"It could be forty years and I don't think it would make much difference." He gave a short sigh. "I don't know. If she had lived, I would have had to resign my commission. I'd probably have stayed in Alexandria. I wouldn't have my command, or Caroline or . . ." He shrugged. "Sometimes, late at night, I think about what my life would have been had she not been killed. I suppose I would have become a merchant, dealing with Egyptians and Europeans. I like to think we could have prospered."

"Would it have pleased you?" Victoire asked doubtfully; try as she might, she could not picture Joachim Murat as a merchant.

He gave an elegant shrug of dismissal. "It hardly matters. *She* more than pleased me; she satisfied a hunger in my soul I did not know I had. For that I would have carried water jugs in Jerusalem," he said solemnly, then lightened his tone a bit. "And I tell myself that with industry we could have lived very well indeed. I am a sensible man, and I work hard. A place like Alexandria rewards effort and I seize advantage when I may." This time his manner was rueful. "There are those who would say that is precisely what I have done in marrying Caroline."

"Is it true?" Victoire asked, as she had wanted to ask since the wedding.

"More or less." He hitched his shoulder toward the door. "Are you ready to risk the occasional stare, my good friend?"

"Perforce," she answered philosophically as they walked toward the door. "I only hope Madame Murat will not be too distressed."

At this Murat only laughed.

Fouche stared across his desk at Inspector-General Vernet; between them lay the signed statements made by Querelle the night before. "You must have been most persuasive."

"When he realized I was Victoire's husband, I didn't need to lift a finger. The man is a coward, as well as a traitor." The contempt in Vernet's voice was obvious.

"I do not like to think that General Moreau was part of them," Fouche said slowly. "I would like to doubt but I cannot."

"No," agreed Vernet thoughtfully. "That is distressing news."

"I would have preferred to find evidence against Pichegru. I want a letter or a report that links him solidly withe the English spies, but it isn't to be had. Only Moreau was foolish enough to implicate himself, while Pichegru is too canny and is 'taking in the country' until the Coronation. Oh, I realize that this implies his participation, but it isn't enough. He could slip through the net if we act on what has been given. For the time being we must concentrate on Moreau. Once we have him, Moreau must be kept isolated, hidden. Pichegru has been very clever, more than I realized." He tapped the paper with two fingers. "As it is, we will issue the warrant for General Moreau. Perhaps he will turn against the others, and we will get Pichegru that way."

"And perhaps he will not," said Vernet. "I want a warrant for the occupants of the house Querelle describes. With any luck he and his men will be there or at La Plume et Bougie." He straightened in his chair. "I'll need about a dozen men, if Querelle's report is to be believed. I don't want to go against armed enemies with insufficient force."

"A good precaution," said Fouche, and reached for a stack of paper printed with a notice of special assignment. "Take twelve and fill in the names of the men you want."

"Thank you," said Vernet in some surprise. "The foreigners first, I think, and then Moreau. The foreigners are more likely to be watching Moreau than he is to be watching them. We will lose fewer of them if we take them first."

Fouche pulled at his lower lip. "Has your wife read this statement yet?"

"No," said Vernet. "She has not been able to come to the Ministry to read it." He regarded Fouche with uncertainty. "Is this needed? She is very tired."

"No, no," said Fouche, shaking his head slowly. "But I would like to hear her thoughts on this, when she has recovered from her ordeal. She has great perspicacity, your wife, and I cannot help but think that she would discover any flaw in our plans if she had an opportunity to read this material."

"I will tell her you said so," said Vernet, rising and taking the assignment slips. "We will be about our tasks within the hour. I'll send word to the stable now to ready three enclosed coaches." His salute was quick and crisp.

"Good." Fouche offered a slow salute. "Report to me as soon as you have General Moreau in custody."

"I will. Where do you want me to take him?" He paused. "Do you want him brought here?"

"No. Take him to the nearest guard station. I will decide what to do with him while you catch these English assassins and spies." He gestured to Vernet to let himself out.

The old house near Saint Rafael the Archangel seemed vacant from the street, but a thin smudge of smoke from the rear chimney belied its appearance. Lucien Vernet signalled the driver to bring the coach to a halt. "Thank you, good coachman," he called as if he had been a paying passenger; this was a signal to the coachman to turn into the next street and wait. Vernet crossed the street in an aimless sort of way, then stepped into the protection of the eaves of a tobacconist's shop, huddling there against the fog.

The second closed coach stopped two blocks short of the supposedly empty house; the third, Vernet knew, was waiting at the edge of the churchyard of Saint Rafael the Archangel. As Vernet watched the two coaches he could see, men got out and moved into the streets. There was little traffic at this late hour and the fog shrouded everything but what was near at hand.

"Sir?" asked one of the two sergeants with him. "Are you ready?"

"I haven't seen the third group's signal," said Vernet, and pointed down an alley so narrow that only a trim, scarecrow-looking fellow or a child could walk down it. "As soon as they are in place, we will move."

"I'll pass the word," said the Bearnais sergeant, whose name was Dagonie. He had a long stride, one that covered ground without apparent effort.

"Well enough," said Vernet, though he spoke to himself. He peered down the narrow passage, hoping to see the candle he had been promised; all that greeted his sight was a scrawny gray cat with large ears and a scabby tail. Vernet knew that such cats were as wild and fierce as tigers in the jungle.

Sergeant Dagonie appeared again at Vernet's shoulder. "How goes it?"

"No signal yet," said Vernet, who wondered idly if something might have happened to his men.

"Give them time. There's always something going on around a church. They might have a funeral or a wedding," said Sergeant Dagonie.

"True," Vernet allowed.

"No one will be foolish, Inspector-General," Sergeant Dagonie promised him.

"Pray God you are right, Sergeant," said Vernet, then caught sight of the sliver of candlelight at the end of the passage. "There. We're ready."

"I'll signal the men," said Sergeant Dagonie laconically as if he were about to call them to order at muster instead of giving the order to break down doors.

"Good," said Vernet, moving a little nearer the front door of the house.

There was a flurry of movement on the street, and a number of men—until then seeming to be mere passersby—took up the double V formation at the front of the house. Sergeant Dagonie slammed his fist on the door and demanded it be opened, then signalled the nearest of the Gendarmes to break in with the sledge he carried.

From inside there came the sound of sudden activity. Muffled shouts and the pounding of feet intermixed with the blows on the door.

At the third battering the door splintered. Sergeant Dagonie broke the last of the pieces and flung them away, then led his men into the house, his pistol at the ready.

Vernet remained on the street with two privates to keep anyone from attempting to get in or out. He listened to the shouts and cries and clamor, and wished he were inside rather than standing here in the fog. He rested his hand on the butt of his pistol, but that served only to remind him that he was inactive. He sighed.

Finally Sergeant Dagonie's face appeared in one of the top windows. "We have them all, Inspector-General," he called down. "Two tried to get away through the back but they were stopped."

"Excellent," said Vernet, and stepped over the threshold at last. The stark interior did not surprise him, but he hesitated before he went down the musty hallway. "How many?" he asked the nearest private.

"Twelve, sir," said the private, speaking stiffly because he was awed.

"Very good." Vernet peered into the front parlor, noticing that there were only two rickety stools in it, and they were placed near the front windows. Why had the watchers not warned the conspirators earlier?

"It seems they were having some kind of meeting," the private went on, answering Vernet's unspoken question. "There's a room on the next floor, and six of them were still in it. There's a table and chairs there, and two cots."

Vernet nodded. "Good work," he said, and saw the private blush.

At the foot of the stairs Vernet paused. He could hear his men cursing the spies as they bound their wrists and prepared to bustle them into wagons. He swung around. "Don't injure them too badly. We still need information from them."

A corporal with a bruise forming on his cheek looked furious. "They gave us a drubbing back there. I'd like to return the favor."

"No," corrected Vernet. "Your bruise will heal, but that prisoner will never recover from his injuries."

The corporal laughed nastily. "You're right. You're right." He slapped Toutdroit's face. "Your trouble is fatal, isn't it, boy?"

Toutdroit spat but he was pale with dread.

Vernet tapped the corporal on the arm, saying sternly, "Just get them out of here. And see they go unharmed. If anything happens to them you will answer for it."

"You're asking—These men are enemies of the First Consul—" blustered the corporal.

"I am asking you to show that we are not the despots of old, but a nation of justice," said Vernet quietly. "Get them into the wagons. Now."

The other police set about this order, hustling their captives out of the house. Vernet himself was almost to the door when one of the prisoners shouted to him. "We are not here to bargain with you, lackey," he declared contemptuously. "We know that you will kill us no matter what we do. This politeness is nothing but sham, to take us quietly to slaughter!"

A few of the others muttered, and one or two of them struggled more forcefully with the men restraining them, and were rewarded with sharp blows.

"Stop it!" Vernet ordered. "All of you!"

It was a short while before order was restored, and at the conclusion, several of the conspirators were bruised and bleeding, including the one who had begun the incident.

"Now then," said Vernet, adjusting his hat once again. He was breathing a little hard and his knuckles hurt; he had struck Bouelac in the jaw when that young man had futilely attempted a break for the door. "Enough of this."

The man who had spoken first laughed condemningly. "You're the corrupt hangers-on to a more corrupt leader. He is nothing more than a Corsican bandit, and you have all been suborned by him."

"That is enough. If you continue to speak," Vernet said levelly, "I will order you gagged and kept in a solitary cell."

"Vive le Roi! Dieu defend le droit!" cried the man confronting Vernet.

"Not Dieu et mon droit?" countered Vernet sardonically, using the motto of the kings of England with full deliberation. He approached the man. "You are one of those fanatics; it is in your eyes. What is your name?"

The man refused to speak.

Vernet shrugged. "Have it your way. You will tell us eventually. Someone will if you do not—one of your men, the innkeeper at La Plume et Bougie, a witness. We will learn." He made a gesture to his men and the captives were taken out to the closed carriages.

When the house was empty, Vernet signalled Sergeant Dagonie to his side. "Has there been a last search made?"

"There has," said Sergeant Dagonie. "And there will be others here later, to inspect it more completely. It won't be finished until sometime tomorrow, but if we rush the work—"

"I know," said Vernet. "And I want your report to encompass everything in this house. And everything you can learn from the landlord and servants at La Plume et Bougie. Perhaps you will find some who can help you, who noticed who came to the inn or . . . oh, anything out of the ordinary." He stared down the hall once more. "To think that twelve men could come this far undetected."

"It's a frightening thing, that I'll grant you," said Sergeant Dagonie. He followed Vernet out the door to the waiting closed carriages.

As Vernet started to climb up beside the driver, he turned back to the sergeant. "That man, the one who was so insulting? Find out who he is if you can and keep him awake. I want to talk to him later tonight, when he's had a chance to get tired and hungry."

Sergeant Dagonie saluted. "Consider it done, Inspector-General."

Victoire sat cross-legged on their bed, her elbows propped on her knees. Her blonde hair was in charming disorder, and the night-jacket she had dragged around her shoulders for warmth did not hide the curve of her breasts or the slight flush that still remained from their earlier lovemaking. "What more?" she asked, her eyes bright as she looked at Vernet. "Oh, I wish I could have been there!"

"Well, I'm not sure you would have liked it, actually," said Vernet, one hand behind his head on the pillow, the other—the one with the swollen knuckles—tucked under the covers out of sight. "A few of the men have talked. They're hoping it will go more easily for them, I think."

"Will it?" asked Victoire.

"I don't know. That is for the court to decide." He was sleepy now that his long day was over and he had spent almost as much time making love as he had done eating supper; the heightened excitement that had possessed him had faded and the melancholy that sometimes came after he had been forestalled with passion. "It's pretty obvious that someone close to Napoleon really is helping them. They haven't given us enough to get Pichegru, but at least we know more about Querelle's dealing with him."

"Then why not arrest him?" Victoire asked reasonably. "You have Querelle, you have Moreau—"

"It still horrifies me, that Moreau should be caught up in treason." He yawned. "We are going to move him to a more secure prison, and keep a guard at his cell around the clock; he might try to do away with himself, or so Fouche thinks."

"And you? Do you think he might make such an attempt?" Victoire inquired.

"I think it will depend on whether we find out who his superior is," said Vernet.

"And do you or Fouche have any notions about that?" she asked.

"Not yet. Tomorrow, when you come to identify the prisoners, we may have more information." He stretched and shifted position, preparing to fall asleep.

But Victoire had more questions. "Is there anyone more suspect than anyone else?"

"Not yet," said Vernet, no longer concentrating.

"Talleyrand supports alliance with England," Victoire pointed out to him. "It would be very satisfying to discover that Talleyrand was the traitor."

"That's because you don't like him," murmured Vernet, fading into sleep.

"You don't like him either," said Victoire, and would have gone on if Vernet had not begun to snore. She gave him a single, exasperated stare, then pinched out the bedside candles and lay back, her mind fixed on all that Vernet had told her. It was hours before she finally drifted asleep.

12

❦

"THE FELLOW IN the solitary cell, that is Claude Montrachet," Victoire told her husband and Fouche the next morning. She was astonished at the intensity of the revulsion that went through her at the mention of his name. He was the last of the prisoners she had been asked to try to identify, and when she caught sight of him a hard fist closed in her chest. She had been grateful to be taken to the antechamber where she would not have to see Montrachet again.

"The one you shot?" asked Vernet incredulously.

Her face was grim. "The same," she said, and went on. "I recognize a few of the others." She looked around the white-washed walls of the antechamber where they waited. "I will make a statement now, if you like."

"It would be welcome, if you are sufficiently collected in your thoughts," said Fouche, and went to summon his secretary.

Vernet looked truly upset. "I did not realize that . . . It never occurred to me that one of these men might . . . might be the person—"

Victoire laid her hand on his. "He only threatened. We will be certain he is punished, between us." It was not possible for her to smile, but a look of harsh satisfaction came into her eyes. "See that he does not slip through your fingers."

"No fear of that," said Vernet, and leaned down to kiss his wife's hand. "I'm sorry, my love; I had not thought this would be such an ordeal."

She did her best to shrug, then regarded him steadily. "I don't think any of us anticipated this, Vernet." She was about to change the subject, when she recollected something she had been meaning to ask Vernet since the evening before. "Among those arrested is there an Englishman named Sackett-Hartley?"

Vernet chuckled at the unwieldy name. "No, nothing like. Why?"

"Because I overheard mention of him while . . . while they had me at the inn. I got the impression that he was part of the company." She had taken a handkerchief from her reticule and was pulling it between her fingers. "You would think that someone with such a name would stand out."

"Probably one of their contacts, a messenger or a seaman or something of the sort," said Vernet, dismissing the matter.

"Possibly. Or another spy," said Victoire, with the increasing certainty that she was right. "There may well be more of them in Paris, if we do not have this Sackett-Hartley with the others."

"But Victoire," said Vernet at his most reasonable, which made Victoire want to strangle him, "there are so many other explanations. You yourself have said that this company of spies is already dangerously large. Why should there be more of them, when they need fewer in their company as it is?"

She stared at him in exasperation. "Consider, Vernet. We are assuming that they are wholly under the command of their traitorous leader, this unknown high-ranking Frenchman. But it may be that they feared precisely what has happened here, and because of that sent a second ... a second wave of assassins and spies, to take over the despicable task if any mischance overcame them."

"You are making it too complicated, my love," said Vernet. "You are being cautious and prudent, and these blackguards are neither of those things." He was about to expand on this when the door opened once again and Fouche, followed by his secretary, came back into the room.

"And now, Madame Vernet," said Fouche with a slight, formal bow, "let us begin at the beginning, when you accompanied your husband to Calais and Dunkerque." He was not a man who smiled easily but he was able to make his expression appear cordial, and Victoire was willing to take the effort for the deed.

"All right," she said, her throat feeling dry. She did her best to clear it, knowing it would take some fair amount of time to give her statement. "We go back to the beginning of last September."

The carpenters had moved to the higher floor and now the sound of hammering and sawing came from above, making the parlor echo like a manufactory. Victoire sat in a high-backed chair and did her best to concentrate on what Murat was trying to tell her. From his arrival half an hour before the din had been almost continuous.

"It does not look promising for Bernadotte, I am afraid," said

Murat, raising his voice to be heard. "It appears he is implicated." He was in regular uniform today, without the formal excesses he enjoyed on occasion. His boots were glossy with polish and his dark tunic had only a single medal on it, the one he had been given two years ago, shortly after Victoire had saved his life.

"But there is nothing to implicate Bernadotte," protested Victoire. She was wearing a simple housedress chosen more for comfort and warmth than fashion; she had not expected Murat to call upon her that afternoon—or anyone else, for that matter.

"Probably true enough," said Murat, taking another slice of soft Saint-Andre cheese. "But Fouche is more convinced with each passing hour that Bernadotte is his man. Or possibly Desirée his woman."

"Ah!" said Victoire, pouncing. "Is that likely, do you think?"

"More likely than Bernadotte being the traitor," said Murat. "She has never forgiven Napoleon for jilting her. Although why she should feel so singled out, I can't imagine. She is not the first or the last, and everyone knows it. Napoleon takes and discards women all the time. He is not a constant lover, but for Josephine. And even that may change in time." He took a short sigh. "Madame, let me tell you that those carpenters are the very servants of the Devil."

"Yes, I think so, too," said Victoire, and poured more coffee for him. "But they will be finished before much longer, and then this will be a suitable habitation. And since it could not have happened had you not come to my aid, you will have to endure my thanks."

"Readily," said Murat. "I've wanted to tell you how much improved the place is. You need not fear to bring any of Vernet's superiors here; they will recognize the touch of one who has good taste and does not waste the ready." He sipped at his coffee, and when he spoke again he had shifted the subject. "Your report to Fouche makes very interesting reading. I had the opportunity to skim through it, and I take leave to tell you, Victoire, that you are too careless of your own safety."

"Would you not have done the same?" Victoire asked with all the appearance of innocence she could muster.

"I am a soldier of France. I am expected to do such things. And do not plead circumstances to me. I am well-aware that you had not accurately anticipated the number of spies you had to deal with. My objection is that you were dealing with any of them at all. A police agent should have been doing what you did; those fellows are trained to that work and they appreciate the risks." He did his best to look huffy and failed. "I wish you could instill spirit like yours into some of our officers."

"The worried ones, or the malign ones?" asked Victoire audaciously in order to cover her growing embarrassment at his praise.

"Both. All of them." He accepted more coffee. "I had a word with Berthier this morning, about Bernadotte."

"And?" said Victoire.

"And he is inclined to give him the benefit of the doubt for the time being. He has said that if it can be shown that evidence points to another he will gladly do all that he may to convince Napoleon that Fouche, while dedicated and persistent, is occasionally wrong." He selected his words very carefully, and added, *"Faenum habet in cornu,* my friend."

Victoire recognized the Latin warning. "I find it hard to think of Fouche as a dangerous bull, but you may be right. I'll tread carefully. *Dictum sapienti sat est."*

"Precisely." He was silent a short while. "Is it permitted to ask if you have a plan to exonerate Bernadotte?"

"It's permitted," said Victoire with a slight laugh. "And to keep you from being worried I will say that I intend to become more interested in what Desirée is doing. She ought to accept me as one of her court—she is dark-haired and dark-eyed, so what will I look next to her but washed out."

Murat snorted with laughter. "I am very pleased that I am not often on the rough side of your tongue, Madame."

"You've done nothing to put you there," said Victoire reasonably.

"Then I pray God that day never comes. Though there are men who are the more ardent when their innamorate are most arbitrary." He made a rueful gesture. "Only a few of us are fortunate enough to know love that's as kind as it is good." He cleared his throat. "I trust Vernet is aware that he is one of the happy few to have a wife who is his staunchest supporter yet at the same time does not slight the accomplishments of others."

This was too effusive for Victoire to handle, and she turned the conversation back to its original course. "Desirée, to the contrary of your overly perfect model, has chosen to treat many people badly, and she cannot expect to escape unscathed. My only regret is that Bernadotte may once again have to suffer for her actions." She leaned back in her chair, a bit startled by the harshness of her feelings. Until this moment she had been unaware of how deeply offended she was by Desirée's languid condemnation.

Murat regarded her closely but wisely said nothing. He re-filled his own cup and poured more coffee into Victoire's. "This is warm, and it is chilly today."

"Yes," said Victoire, already starting to set her plans. "It is."

D'Estissac sat with Sackett-Hartley, the only two of their group of eight currently at Le Chat Gris. They sat close to the large fireplace, their stools at the edge of the flags of the hearth. Outside it was overcast and sullen; inside it was not much better.

"We will know who is in prison very soon, and what charges have been brought. We will find out if anyone is talking," said d'Estissac as if repeating a lesson by rote. "Then we will be able to make new plans."

"We can do nothing until the others return." Sackett-Hartley sighed and rubbed his eyes. "Until we know what has tran-spired, there will be no point in anticipating developments, for—"

"We had better have some plans for leaving Paris in a hurry," said d'Estissac with asperity. "It could easily come to that, you realize."

"That is supposing that the police have learned about us," said Sackett-Hartley with dogged optimism.

"And what makes you think they have not?" demanded d'Estissac.

"Only my faith in their honor," said Sackett-Hartley heavily. He stared into the fire as if reading omens there. "We are all sworn to the same glorious duty, and I put my trust in our men, that they will not forget what they have sworn to do."

"You are placing your faith in green lads who have never walked a battlefield, and others who are greedy for advance-ment," d'Estissac reminded him. "I have welcomed their ac-tions but I've never fooled myself that there was a bond that went beyond the rewards of killing Napoleon. And you cannot afford to believe anything else, Magnus."

Sackett-Hartley said nothing for the greater part of a minute; his expression was that of a man dealing with necessary nasti-ness. "If they are talking, then we must find a way to leave, and leave quickly. The gendarmes will be after us." Sackett-Hartley bit his lower lip.

"It would mean failing in our mission," protested d'Estissac.

"Of course," said Sackett-Hartley. He rubbed at his stubble-covered chin. "We will also have to contact our ally, and find out what he advises."

"That's not going to be easy," said d'Estissac. "I've tried to reach him twice this morning and nothing. He does not respond to my inquiries. It may be that he is being watched, or . . . There is a reception tonight given by the Corsican's sister Pauline, and all the world goes. If our ally doesn't attend, it's as good as a confession; he will call attention to himself that might—"

Sackett-Hartley cut him short, then raised his hand to signal the landlord for cognac-and-cider. "Nothing so specific, my friend," he cautioned.

"All right," d'Estissac said, realizing that Sackett-Hartley was right. He rose and paced once around the taproom, then came back to the hearth. "There isn't much time. The Coronation is only a few weeks away."

"True," said Sackett-Hartley, once again with a raised warning finger.

"What I cannot grasp is how the gendarmes came to know of the house at all. How did they decide to follow Querelle?" D'Estissac slapped his hand hard on his thigh. "They are not clever enough to have thought it out, not these damned peasant bureaucrats."

"There must have been an informant," Sackett-Hartley muttered.

"Exactly!" said d'Estissac. "You have the right of it."

"But what informants?" asked Sackett-Hartley. "Not the landlord here or at La Plume et Bougie. Not the owner of the house we rented, not . . . I cannot think who would be near enough to us to know what we planned and at the same time ready to betray us to the police."

"What about our superior? Perhaps he decided the cause was lost and has taken this chance to sever all connections with us." The implications of his own observations struck him with force. "It may be that he has found a way to trade all of us for his security."

"I've considered that possibility," said Sackett-Hartley in an undertone. "Whoever this man is, he undoubtedly is in great danger now, as we are. Without the reports from our remaining men, how are we to know whether it is safe to turn to the superior or not?"

"We may have to decide which risk is the greater," said d'Estissac, "and act quickly, whatever we decide. There's no telling when we might be described to Fouche's men, and once they—"

"You wish to go underground, don't you?" Sackett-Hartley shook his head slowly. "You bewilder me."

"I? Why is that?" asked d'Estissac. "Because I know that it isn't safe to remain here? Because I don't trust the whole of our company as much as you wish to? You know what could happen to us if the police start searching. We have no choice but to go to ground until we have word from the superior. I will try to get a message to him again, but I don't hold out much hope of it. I suspect that whoever he is, he has already learned what has come about and has made his own plans to protect himself. It's what I would do in his situation." He got to his feet and stretched as if his muscles were sore. "I don't think Montrachet will speak against us—he's too zealous for that. But a few of the others are not so reliable. And the Inspector-General's wife was here; even if they have already captured everyone she knew of, this place is implicated. I am worried, I admit it."

Sackett-Hartley could not find it in his heart to argue. "Very well. We will leave this place and choose another. We must be inconspicuous about it, and that could prove difficult if the police extend their search. It will take time to find the proper combination of—" He broke off, seeing a flicker in d'Estissac's eyes. "Or have you one picked out?" He knew the answer as he asked the question.

"There's a tavern—not a very good tavern, but a little better than this—near the old Avignon Gate. It's called Le Chevre Chantier, very ancient as you can tell by the name. The landlord is a widow who answers to Isabeau. She's not bad looking and they say she sleeps with a mad dog at her door." He tried to smile at this. "She has two suites of rooms she is willing to let us have at a good price."

"It sounds as if you have some connection with her," said Sackett-Hartley.

D'Estissac nodded. "Her husband's family served my family as coachmen for eight generations." He shrugged. "She is loyal to us, as her husband would have been had he lived."

"She could identify you," warned Sackett-Hartley.

"She can also carry messages, and she will if we require it of her. Have no fear, she is not one to be swayed by fops and sycophants; she knows the old ways were best. She is no supporter of the Corsican—her husband was killed in Napoleon's service and there has not been one sou of pension paid to her, though it was promised to her husband before his wound rotted." He slapped one hand on his thigh. "Shall I tell the others?"

"It would be useful, yes; tell them to be ready to move before nightfall. I suppose we ought to be quit of this place, after all," said Sackett-Hartley, musing as d'Estissac slipped away, "I wonder if my uncle ever had such things happen to him?"

Desirée turned her head coquettishly and twinkled at Bernadotte, as much for Victoire's benefit as for his. "Say you will permit me to have new draperies for the ballroom. It would make all the difference, and it would not be as costly as repainting. It would not take much more than four days to accomplish and it would not make a mess of the place. It's just fabric, Bernadotte, just velvet and damask. The whole room would be changed, don't you see? It would be like the hall of victory on Olympus, where you would ride as Mars, or Apollo. Oh, please, my love. You do not want the Swedes to think you do not value them as you ought."

"No, I don't want that," said Bernadotte, not looking at Victoire as he went on, his Gascon accent stronger than usual. "But it is very costly, the decorations you want, and we cannot easily afford them." His smile was pained. "Velvet and damask may be fabric, Desirée, but they are more dear than fustian and muslin."

Desirée was a clever woman and so she did not pout, but regarded Bernadotte in the manner of one who had been asked to endure serious hardships and was prepared to do so as noble self-sacrifice. "Very well, if it is not possible to have the new draperies, I must contrive other means to make this place appear properly à la mode. If it is what I must do," she said softly, "then I will do it."

"There are other decorations we can have that are not so costly and that will show all the regard for the Swedes they could want," Bernadotte said, moving toward her.

She took a step back. "No, no, I can see how it is, and I must adapt myself to the realities of the world. We are not so favored that we can draw on endless funds. Never mind that Josephine puts us all to shame with her extravagance and her luxuries and her excesses; the rest of us cannot have such opportunities." There was no disguising the malice she felt for Napoleon's wife, nor the envy that consumed her. "It's different for Josephine. She has the treasury of France for her pocketbook."

"Desirée!" protested Bernadotte, who knew his wife too well to be shocked.

Victoire remained very still and hoped that Bernadotte and his wife would forget she was in the room. If there had been an opportunity for her to leave, she would have taken it. But no such opportunity presented itself, so she huddled down on the divan as far as she could and tried not to listen too much.

"Well, she has!" Desirée snapped. "Everyone knows it. She boasts of it. She claims that she is able to have whatever she wants because no one can refuse her, because that would the same as refusing the First Consul, and only madmen do that." Her hands were on her hips and the languid air she affected had vanished entirely. "But do not worry, my husband, I will do as you tell me, and I'll smile as best I can when we are compared to the entertainments offered by Josephine, for well I know that the comparison will not be flattering to us."

While they argued, Victoire studied the man suspected of treason. It still made no sense to her. Bernadotte was the son of a tailor and perhaps the most proper man in Paris. He had spent eleven years in the ranks before being promoted to lieutenant; two years later, after his heroic assault on the woods turned the tide in the Battle of Fleurus, he was a Brigadier General. Yet he could never forget those lean years when he lived on a private's meager pay; he could not understand the excesses Desirée took for granted.

When Napoleon made his bid for power, he approached Bernadotte. The general refused on the strength of his soldier's oath. But he did agree to take no action against Napoleon's followers unless directly ordered to do so. When the coup succeeded, his reluctance was an embarrassment, but Napoleon had been impressed by his integrity and soon restored him to command. Though perhaps in punishment for his earlier reluctance and an abortive effort to actually arrest Napoleon when he returned from Egypt, Bernadotte's corps was given the undesirable duty of suppressing a revolt in the Vendée. Later, several members of his staff were caught in a plot to support another such uprising and only Desirée's pleading had kept Napoleon from acting against him.

In Paris they lived as Desirée felt they should. Their house was larger and closer to the palace than those of Jerome or Joseph, Napoleon's brothers. Desirée threw lavish parties that Bernadotte often left early. He had received many pensions and awards, and there were persistent rumors that much of Bernadotte's wealth had come from rich citizens of the Vendée who were suspected of fomenting revolt, and bribed their way out of suspicion.

"Desirée, please," Bernadotte answered firmly, though they both knew he was begging her to restrain herself.

"And everything we do from that point on will look make-shift and miserly, if we fail to make the right display now. We, my husband, you and I," Desirée went on relentlessly, "will be watched with a jaundiced eye by the Swedes. They will know we did not receive them as they ought to be received, not for the reception we have announced." She turned on her heel and was about to leave the room when she saw Victoire. At once her manner changed and she gave her visitor a bright smile. "Husbands are always the most exasperating creatures, aren't they?" she asked.

"So I believe," said Victoire carefully, trying to sit a little more comfortably so that she would not reveal her distress.

"They are always telling us what we may do and what we may not. It is very bad of them." She tossed her head and looked back over her shoulder. "Bernadotte, you'll have to give me some time with Madame Vernet. If you're determined to place restrictions on me, than I will have to appeal to her good advice to make the best I may from what little you have permitted me to have."

Bernadotte flung his hands in the air to signal his capitulation. "I would not ask this of you, my dear, if our resources were not already strained to the limits. Another festivity and we could face some very necessary economies." He bowed slightly to Victoire, then kissed Desirée's hand. "I have a meeting I must attend. It cannot wait. Pray excuse me; my time is not my own. I don't know when I will be back; before midnight, I suspect." He took one step back. "My love. Madame Vernet, your servant." Then he was out the door.

"He's a great dear when he is pleasantly disposed," said Desirée as if speaking of a favorite pet. "But lately he has been gruff and unpleasant, which does not please me." She stared at Victoire and then gave her attention to the ballroom, which lay just beyond this antechamber. "What am I to do, I ask you?"

"About what, Madame Bernadotte?" asked Victoire, taking care to maintain the correct social manner with her hostess.

"Ah, no such formality between us, I beg you," Desirée urged prettily. "You must be Victoire and I must be Desirée. We officers' wives belong to a society that has different rules than the rest of the world."

"How kind," murmured Victoire, wondering what it was that Desirée wanted of her; she remembered the undisguised contempt Desirée had shown when she and her husband had called at her home, and was more puzzled than ever at this abrupt change in manner.

"We must surely be like sisters," declared Desirée. Whatever it was that Desirée wanted, thought Victoire, it was something very important to her, or she would never consider making such gestures toward her. "What a great honor, Desirée," she said carefully.

"Yes, it is," said Desirée with strange naiveté. "But these are the fortunes of war and the fruits of victory, aren't they?" There was something in her manner now, something sly and insinuating under the excessive sweetness of her conduct.

"If our victory is assured," said Victoire, keenly alert. She could not help but feel she was in the company of a jungle cat, beautiful and sinuous and apparently indolent, who could eviscerate an unwary goat or cow or man in a single swipe of one daggered paw.

"Oh, you're not one of those who still persist in warning Napoleon about hidden enemies, are you? If he had half the opponents some feel he must have, he would be in his grave ten times over and not preparing to be crowned emperor." She had taken a few steps into the ballroom, and she indicated the pale-green-and-gilt decor. "Look at this place! I am ashamed for you to see it, and yet my husband declares that I cannot have new draperies. How am I to entertain here with the room so dowdy?"

To Victoire's eyes the ballroom was extravagantly decorated and of the first style, but she knew that she must not say so. "What were your plans for the draperies? What do you want to do with the room?" It was a safe enough inquiry, and one that would give her a little time to learn the answers Desirée sought.

"You see what they are now, all straw-colored? Against the muted greens, I suppose it would be well enough in the summer, but it is coming to winter." Little as she wanted to remember, she had liked them well enough a year ago when she picked them out; now they looked tawdry to her. "It's dreadful. So I have hit upon the notion of changing the draperies to a dull red and the valences in bronze, with bronze cords and the seats of all the chairs and divans done in the same color. I think it would be truly charming."

"It would be quite remarkable," said Victoire with sincerity, thinking that the ballroom would truly be spectacular with such decor; little as she trusted the purpose, she could not fault Desirée on her vision. "But your husband's right: it would be very dear to have it done in so short a time."

"He wants to disoblige me," said Desirée. "He has decided that he must be the one to decide what will and won't be done in this house, and he's ruled that we will have nothing very new for the reception." She began to pace around the room; it was large enough that this took her some little time. "He's the one who wants to impress the Swedes. He's the one who stands to gain from their favor. He is the one who—" She stamped her foot. "He expects me to smooth the way for him, but gives me no means to do it."

"The First Consul does not require much grandeur," said Victoire, knowing that Napoleon cared little for his own appearance, but also aware that he expected his court to reflect the glory he had brought to France. "If you were to change the valences, wouldn't that be enough for your husband, and the Swedes, and you?"

"Of course not," scoffed Desirée, the color mounting in her cheeks. "I will not say that Bernadotte lost his advancement because of his wife." She strode back toward Victoire. "It's bad enough he has been gone so much on these damned secret meetings of his, but he has left all of the work to me. All of it. But he will not let it be done properly."

"Secret meetings. Is it with the Swedes, I wonder? What could the Swedes have to discuss secretly?" asked Victoire, doing her best to sound disingenuous. She supposed it was the Low Countries that concerned the Swedes—such meeting would be private.

Desirée made a moue of distaste. "Bernadotte can be so disobliging, who knows whom he meets? It's probably someone like Pichegru, someone he knows will do him no credit. It would be the worse for him if it turns out that Pichegru is a traitor, for Napoleon would not forgive Bernadotte for supporting anyone seeking his downfall. And Bernadotte can be a Gascon fool. He does it to spite me, you know." Her lovely eyes narrowed and were no longer very pretty. "He does it to be certain that I never forget I'm here under sufferance, because of that affair with Napoleon."

"You were very young," said Victoire, soothing her. "And Napoleon was more urgent then than he is now."

"He was ardent and insistent. He was determined to have me." It was difficult to determine if she took pride or shame in this admission; perhaps it was some of each. "He was the most dashing man I'd ever met, and the most heartless. He cared more for his desire than for me." Her wordplay on her own name was bitter. She looked around the ballroom. "This and Bernadotte were the sop he gave me in return for everything he did to me."

Victoire had rarely seen such humiliation as there was in the
expression that passed over Desirée's pretty features; she was
troubled by it, and didn't know how to respond. At last she
shook her head and directed her gaze toward the ceiling. "It is
unfortunate that so much love turned out so badly."

For a moment Desirée looked as if she might weep, and then
she changed and achieved a charming shrug. "It's the way of
the world, is it not?" She came up to Victoire's side. "I'll have
the draperies, you know, and I'll give the grandest entertainment that the Swedes have had since they arrived. There are
seven days yet until the reception and ball. The drapers would
have seven days, and the nights if that were necessary. They
could transform everything in the ballroom, just as I want it.
You'll see. Everyone will say that this was the most elegant
gathering other than the Coronation. Everyone." Her smile widened. "Even Napoleon will say it."

With a coldness growing in her bones, Victoire listened as
Desirée went on about swags and sconces and wainscoting; all
the while she wondered if Bernadotte or his wife was the one
she was seeking.

"It's too convenient," said Vernet over supper that night. He
had removed his tunic and donned his dressing-gown, a magnificent new garment of claret-colored velvet edged in quilted
satin. As he sat facing Victoire across their dining table, he
grinned at her and the lines of fatigue began to fade. "I was just
thinking, as I watched you."

"What were you just thinking?" she asked, more curious than
flirtatious.

"That I feel like an eastern potentate." His expression eased
more and he settled more comfortably back into his chair.
"Odette helped, with this sour-cherry duck. It seems Oriental to
me." He indicated the ruins of their meal.

"It was quite delicious," agreed Victoire, who still had a little
on her plate. "But what's too convenient?"

"What?" Vernet inquired, puzzled.

"You said that it's too convenient. I'd like to know what it
is," said Victoire, smiling as she had the last of her wine. "And
why it's convenient."

"Oh, that," said Vernet, retracing his mental steps. "I am
finding it difficult to believe that Bernadotte is the villain
Fouche thinks he is. He's so obvious, and so very exposed. He
was never so foolish in the field, to leave himself so vulnerable.
I have found too much and found it too easily for me to believe

that he is anything more than a handy dupe. I've explained my reservations to Fouche and Berthier, but I don't know. Fouche wants to hold Bernadotte until the Coronation is over but the Swedes would raise a tremendous outcry if we so much as contemplated such a thing. It would be diplomatically distressing for everyone. That is another part of the puzzle: the damage of suspecting Bernadotte is very great, and very obvious."

"Ah?" said Victoire, in order to encourage Vernet to continue.

"You have only to examine the circumstances and it becomes apparent that there are many reasons why nefarious persons might find it useful to direct suspicions on Bernadotte, not the least of which is the embarrassment it would bring to the Swedes, which could result in an international scandal." He drank his wine in one long sip, then helped himself to one of the little rolled pastries Odette had made that afternoon. "Perhaps even forcing them into a formal alliance with England."

"You and Berthier are in agreement about that?" asked Victoire, who recognized the concerns as ones she had heard many times from Berthier.

"Oh, yes. It's Fouche who doesn't believe in making the problem more complicated that it appears to be." He shook his head. "He thinks that the Swedish presence is nothing more than a smoke screen."

Victoire took time to think. "If there were one Swede, that might be reason enough to ignore the Swedish presence. But there is a whole embassy of them, a delegation for the Coronation, and they are directly connected to Bernadotte, his personal guests. I don't think they can be dropped from the equation." She braced her elbows on the table and folded her hands under her chin. "In fact, I think the Swedes might be crucial to the case regarding Bernadotte." She paused to study the pattern of cut-work on the tablecloth. "Of course, there is Desirée, too. She is the other factor in Bernadotte's life, isn't she?" She did not look up.

"What did you make of her this afternoon?" Vernet asked.

"I don't trust her." For a few seconds she was silent. "She makes it very difficult to like her. It is easy to see that she enjoys making Bernadotte dance to her tune, and that she's still, in some way I cannot define, tied to Napoleon."

"You mean she loves him still," said Vernet.

"No; in fact it may be the opposite. I think she may detest him quite profoundly." She saw the startled expression in Vernet's eyes, and did her best to explain. "I think to be made the object of his desire and determination when she was young was too ... overwhelming for her. And when he turned away, as he has from so many, and gave her to Bernadotte, I think she broke, somehow, like a bone in the leg, and never healed properly." She stared into the candle flames. "It's conjecture, but it is possible she would be pleased to have it appear that Bernadotte is Napoleon's enemy, to have vengeance on him."

"On Bernadotte?" asked Vernet, who was having some difficulty following her logic. "Why should she want to—"

"On Napoleon. She wants to wipe her feet on him, I think; on Napoleon." She leaned back. "Gracious. I hadn't realized until now how Desirée had troubled me, or why. I thought she was simply jealous, but I realize now it is more than that. Much more."

"But you're suggesting she might be capable of actual treason," said Vernet, shaking his head.

"It could happen," said Victoire cautiously. "Not as treason, precisely, but something more ... personal."

"And you think that it has happened, is that it?" he inquired.

"I think," she said, frowning with concentration, her gaze at a place distant from their dining room, "that if there is another group of spies we have failed to detect and apprehend—"

"Tales!" Vernet protested. "Merely an attempt to confuse us, and make us waste our efforts looking for chimeras instead of tracking down real traitors. Like Moreau."

"What if they aren't traitors? I know you and Fouche think that the name I heard, the English name, is the name of the ship's captain who brought them here, but I don't agree. I think that Mister Sackett-Hartley"—she handled the English pronunciation as well as she could—"is very real and is still in Paris. And I think we ignore him at our peril."

"I have three men checking out the inns for suspicious Englishmen. But I don't expect much from them. An Englishman in Paris," scoffed Vernet. "We'd find him in an instant. None of them speak good French, and they are so ... so *English!*" He laughed. "Come, my dear. Don't let yourself be taken in by these rumors and all the rest of it." He reached over and touched the place on her jaw where a small cut from her escape had not quite healed. There were bruises on her body still, faded to a sickly yellow-green, like wilting flowers. "We're sensible people, we French. We're not like the Egyptians or the Italians, who see saints and spooks and spies in every nook and cranny. We have a fine tradition of police work in France, and we need to show that it will only improve when Napoleon is emperor. And that, Victoire, includes exercising rational judgment in cases like this one."

"Certainly," said Victoire without heat. "And that is the reason I find it difficult to cast either Bernadotte or Desirée in the role of conspirator. It is so irrational for either of them to undertake so dangerous a venture." She chuckled. "Now, if it were Talleyrand, that would be different; he thrives on the draconian. I could believe he'd encourage a conspiracy, if only to destroy it in order to show how devoted he is to Napoleon and thereby gain the gratitude he does not deserve." Her chuckles turned to laughter. "You need not bother to tell me that this is not sensible, and that I've these suspicions because I dislike and distrust Talleyrand. It's all true, and I own it freely."

Vernet made a gesture of mock surrender. "In that case, Madame, what can I say?" He reached out and took her hand. "All humor aside, my love, no more risks, if you please. I don't like to see you exposed to danger."

"Neither do I," said Victoire with feeling. She pulled her spangled-silk shawl more closely around her shoulders and thought that the room had become uncomfortably cool. "I don't enjoy narrow escapes."

Vernet very nearly offered a sharp answer but managed to hold his tongue. "No, I don't suppose you do," he agreed.

13

⚜

THERE WERE FINE bits of snuff all across Berthier's elaborate neck cloth and waistcoat, and he slapped at them with a plain linen handkerchief as he regarded Victoire seated on the far side of his office. "You have been through this with me before, Madame Vernet, and we do not yet understand one another."

The man who had served as Napoleon's chief of staff and key aide sat in an office in his home near the palace. On the desk in front of him were four neat piles of papers; several bore the embossed eagle emblem of Napoleon across their tops. At least one, Victoire noticed, was headed by the device of the Pope.

When she entered the room Berthier set aside his pen with the look of reluctance. Everyone knew how hard the man worked and for a brief instant Victoire felt guilty about interrupting him for what, she had to admit, were unsubstantiated assumptions. Without facts, Berthier was not inclined to be convinced, and said so.

"General Berthier, I understand your position very well. But I wish you to know that I still don't agree. You say I have no evidence, but neither have you. You've chosen a convenient assumption—that the assassins are routed—and it may not be the safest." She looked demure enough in her mulberry-colored walking dress, her fox-fur cloak folded over her arm, but there was nothing in her blue eyes that was tractable.

"And you persist in these tales of more conspirators," said Berthier warily. "Your husband has a few men watching for your phantom Englishman."

"A corporal and privates, in uniform yet. What good is that?" Victoire protested.

Berthier was not moved. "Do you realize the Pope will arrive here shortly? He left Rome less than a week ago. He is already looking for reasons to withdraw from the Coronation. This could provide him the perfect opportunity to return to the Vatican. If you continue to insist that there are English assassins waiting to kill Napoleon, His Holiness would have the excuse he needs to—"

"I'll not tell the Pope. You have my word on it," Victoire answered quite seriously.

"No." Berthier paused for a long moment and added, "It's absurd." The aide regarded her with open curiosity. "Why are you being so persistent, Madame Vernet, when you know that there is nothing more to support your theory than inconsistencies in the suspect confessions of the spies we have caught? If you were in my position, I'd venture to say that you'd have the same attitude I do: that the prisoners are still trying to misdirect our efforts away from the highly placed French traitor to ephemeral English spies so that the miscreant may have a little more liberty to work his evil."

" 'Work his evil,' " Victoire tried not to sound too annoyed. "A very good phrase, Berthier. You must save it for a more appreciative audience than I provide." She gathered up her cloak. "Very well. If you are determined on your course, it appears I will have to find these Englishmen myself."

Berthier was shocked. "Madame Vernet! Y-You're not to engage in anything dangerous," he protested, stammering with indignation.

"But you are certain there is no danger." Victoire pointed out quite reasonably. "You've said so. Therefore you can have no objection to my project, can you? Rest assured that I'll keep you informed of anything I learn." She swung her cloak around her shoulders, glad of the warmth of it, for the morning was dank, with icy mists hanging near the river in the still air.

"Where are you going?" asked Berthier suspiciously. "I will not have you placing yourself in danger again. I'm still distressed by what became of you on your last venture."

"I escaped," said Victoire coolly. "And I'd do it again if it proved necessary."

"Madame Vernet, you are a resourceful woman. I have no doubt of that. We are all grateful for your past services to Napoleon and France. But, if correct, you are facing men who are growing more desperate by the hour, and they will not hesitate to do you an injury, or worse." He started to rise, then hesitated. "You are not going to try to find them again, are you?"

"These non-existent English spies? Not directly, no," she said with what she intended to be a reassuring smile. "I thought I'd learn what I may about the whereabouts of Pichegru. He would appear to be the most important of all just at present. And he's a genuine conspirator. Wouldn't you agree?"

"Pichegru?" questioned Berthier, astonished and horrified. "But surely, Madame Vernet, you cannot—"

"Yes, I can," interrupted Victoire. "And then I must see my dressmaker for a fitting on my clothes for the Coronation: nothing too grand, you know, but suitable for the occasion." She nodded once to Berthier. "Thank you for listening to me."

"Madame Vernet—" Berthier began, already worried that she was being much too accommodating. She had been right too often in the past to not have aroused some concern in Berthier. But the aide reminded himself of the definite problems he had to resolve in the ten days remaining before the Coronation. "Let your husband and Fouche tend to the conspirators, Madame."

Victoire pulled on her cloak. "You may believe what I've told you: if I learn anything of use, I will be certain to provide you with the information as soon as possible." She let herself out of the door before Berthier could summon up arguments to use against her.

Roustam-Raza was not much more help when Victoire met with him later. "You are being reckless, Madame, very reckless." There was a hint of resignation in his voice. "It is not suitable for you to mount the pursuit of these criminals."

"Would you rather I concern myself only with ballgowns and jewels and which receptions to attend before the Coronation? Or perhaps I should be attending more to the fashionable life, meeting those men who can advance my husband's career if I am charming enough, do you think?" Victoire asked innocently. "I know it would please Berthier to have me wasting my time on such twaddle." She stared across the road toward the gray front of the stables.

"There are fetes and entertainments almost every night now; everyone is busy with them," said Roustam-Raza, who did not entirely approve. "Most of the Marshalls are as preoccupied with their clothes as their wives are."

"Which has become the obsession of half the wives in Paris," she agreed with asperity. "But not of this wife," she went on in a warning tone. "Let others worry about their jewels and the cut of their corsages and the color of their shoes, and whether they dare to darken their lashes with lampblack, or brighten their cheeks with rouge. I'll busy myself with more compelling matters. Someone must find those spies."

"And if they aren't there to be found?" suggested Roustam-

Raza. "There are twelve traitors in custody. Surely not even the
English are mad enough to send more than that?"

Victoire was undaunted. "How convenient it would be if all
our enemies did precisely what we expected them to do, and in
the numbers we thought were reasonable."

Roustam-Raza shook a disapproving finger at her. "You are
being as stubborn as Fouche, Madame Vernet, and well you
know it. It is your way to be determined. You have endured
much, but the danger is over, and you need not fear to find
spies in every closet. With thanks to Allah and your courage,
they are all in custody. You have no reason to be afraid of these
men now."

"Nonsense," said Victoire roundly. "Why must you all persist in seeing females as incompetents? I can recognize danger
as readily as any man, and I do not mean phantasms and spec-
ters of the mind." She indicated the street behind them. "Or do
you suppose I've become foolish?"

"No," said Roustam-Raza. "It would be easier for us all if
you were foolish, but alas, Allah made you with a most unwomanly mind and an inability to sit still." He gestured to
show how hopeless it was to attempt to fathom Allah's wisdom.
"But you are set on a course to prove your point, aren't you?
And when you decide on such a course, you throw prudence
and caution aside in favor of—"

Victoire made no apology for interrupting this tirade. "There
are traitors who are seeking to murder Napoleon. They are in
association with spies who will carry out their plans. I don't see
any error in trying to be certain that their schemes fail." She
had drawn on her gloves; now she lifted her hand to signal a
cab to stop for her. "While the rest of you reassure one another
that no danger remains, I'll do whatever is in my power to stop
any greater misfortune." She saw a cabby draw in at the opposite corner. "We must find Pichegru, Roustam-Raza. And we
must find the Englishman."

Roustam-Raza shook his turbaned head. "But Madame
Vernet, Fouche's report says that—"

"Fouche! Has he followed any of these men? Has he heard
them talk? I'm worn out with Fouche's stubbornness. What if
Fouche is wrong? I have no doubt that my husband, not
Fouche, will receive the blame," countered Victoire before she
crossed the street and climbed into the waiting cab. "An inn
near the Université," she said, loudly enough for Roustam-Raza
to hear. "Called La Plume et Bougie."

* * *

Odette was still tacking sprays of artificial flowers on the shoulder of Victoire's ballgown when Vernet announced that their carriage was waiting. They had been misted with perfume and smelled lovely.

"The Devil fly away with him," whispered Victoire in aggravation, and was very nearly jabbed by her housekeeper's needle. She called out, "Just a few moments longer, Vernet."

"The coachman will not like to keep his team standing," Vernet warned from the floor below. "Hurry."

Victoire met Odette's eyes in the pier-glass. "How much longer?"

"There is one more spray, that's all," said Odette through the pins she held in her mouth. "Two minutes, perhaps three."

"I will be down directly," called Victoire, and inspected herself in the mirror critically, looking for those imperfections that would earn her condemning looks. At least the ballgown itself was acceptable, being another successful product of ingenuity and her mother's old gowns. This one was of heavy bronze silk in a damask pattern, with short puffed sleeves and elaborate beadwork in a pattern of laurel wreaths on the corsage; the artificial flowers were Royaume d'esprit, as delicate and feathery as sun-struck spiderwebs.

Odette tied off the thread and went to work on the last of the artificial flowers. "Don't forget to put your cloak on carefully, or these could be damaged," she warned as she stitched. "They're very fragile."

"I will be careful," Victoire promised.

"And no chasing off across Paris in these clothes. The way you appeared three days ago after that attempt to find the remaining spies . . . That frock cannot be made clean again. I don't know what it is you have on the hem. I have not been able to get it out but I will not dispose of it until I try to clean it. This gown must be for the reception, and not for racing about after spies. I want your word on it." Although this was said in a jocular way, it was clear that Odette was serious. "Be sure you take care with the train, as well. Don't let anyone stand on it if you can help it."

"I'll be careful," Victoire assured, reminding herself that she would have to kick backward whenever she turned or risk snagging her own ankles in the fabric.

"Well, then," said Odette, and set the last stitch. "There. Your gloves are on, your tiara is in place, your choker is fastened, your shoes are without blemish, and that color becomes you, Madame." She reached for the cloak and set it carefully over Victoire's shoulders. "Make sure that you do not get wax on you, if you can. Be careful where you stand, so that the chandeliers—"

"I'll be careful," Victoire said, and hurried out the door, her reticule clutched in one hand along with her long silken fan, her other hand holding her cloak closed.

Vernet was watching for her, one hand on the front latch, his handsome face marred by an impatient frown. "I don't want Murat saying I've done anything to his horses," he muttered as he held the door open for her. "He won't arrive until later in the evening, with Napoleon. If he receives a poor report—"

"He won't," said Victoire, hurrying down the stairs to where the footman waited to hand her up into the carriage. "And I doubt he'd believe it if he received one. He knows you are not inconsiderate."

"I'm not entirely certain I like the loan of the carriage at all," Vernet continued as he prepared to climb into the vehicle behind her.

"Murat was merely trying to help," said Victoire. "As he is with the First Consul tonight he does not need his carriage."

"He has already loaned you money, and he—" Vernet broke off as he sat back against the squabs. "The other day I encountered that painter cousin of mine—yesterday, in fact," he said, deliberately changing the subject.

"Carle Vernet?" asked Victoire, a little surprised that Vernet had abandoned the subject of Murat so abruptly.

"Yes. He was preparing to paint the Polish troopers who have come for the Coronation. I never know what to make of him, or any of that part of the family. They seem like foreigners; we are only second cousins." He straightened the fall of his pelisse, which was stiff with bronze-and-gold braid. "He, well, Carle and Horace are giving an entertainment for David in four weeks, after the Coronation, when they can all display their sketches of the event. He asked me if we would like to attend."

"What did you tell him?" Victoire asked, wishing now she had chosen to wear violet scent instead of jasmine.

"I told him that if our schedule permits we will put in an appearance. I hope that is satisfactory to you," said Vernet. "One does not know what to do when there are artists in the family."

"Ah, but the artists in your family are successful. That makes it much less awkward, doesn't it?" she inquired with a mischievous smile. "It is only the artists who are unsuccessful who are true liabilities."

"Victoire," he warned her affectionately. "Do you think you

can endure an evening with all those fellows? You said you thought David was a pretentious oaf blessed with a steady hand ... you might not want to ... to have to speak to him."

"If it's a large function, I'll not have to do more than nod," said Victoire calmly. "Don't worry, Vernet. I can face your relatives more readily than you, I suspect. And David is so taken with himself that he'll not notice if I have nothing to say to him provided I curtsy when we meet."

The carriage was almost at the Bernadottes' hotel, and its way was impeded by a number of other vehicles all bound for the same destination. The avenue was wide enough for five coaches to travel abreast, so in several places six were jammed together so tightly you could cross the street by walking through them without ever touching the bricks. The coachman swore and the footman climbed onto the roof of the carriage to avoid being struck by the other teams and carriages crowding in on both sides.

"I suppose they will be here tonight," said Vernet distantly. "My cousins."

"How will you know, in this crush?" asked Victoire, who hated this jostling for position. "If you do not want to talk to them, you will have no difficulty in avoiding them." She touched her tiara to make sure it was properly in place. "Madame Bernadotte sent me word yesterday that there will be over two hundred guests at this reception, including Napoleon and Josephine, and Caroline with Murat, and Pauline as well."

Vernet regarded her with curiosity. "She has been very forthcoming with you of late, hasn't she?"

"Desirée? She has. I've not discouraged her," said Victoire. "There's too much to be learned from her, and I am concerned for Bernadotte. Say what you will about his political ambitions, Jean Baptiste Jules has always been kindly disposed to me and to his fellow-officers and their families. There are those who say he is ungrateful and ought not to have been made Governor of Hanover, but—" She stopped herself. "I'm not so sanguine about his wife."

"And you are still investigating him? Or her?" Vernet suggested.

"Until the question regarding Moreau is answered, yes," she said with a trace of defiance. "Fouche may think the matter closed, but I don't agree."

Vernet shrugged. "If you're continuing your inquiries, then who am I to stop you? But as your husband, I trust you will observe due circumspection?"

"I'm not going to embarrass you, Vernet," she reassured at her most heartening, her cheeks suddenly rosy.

"That's not what I meant, and you know it." He reached out and tweaked one of the fashionable curling tendrils of pale hair framing her face. "You couldn't embarrass me if you tried."

"Let's not put that to the test," Victoire agreed, feeling oddly light-headed.

The carriage was at last nearing the covered entrance; six vehicles were ahead of them, but the coachman tapped on the panel to signal his passengers.

Vernet answered the tap with one of his own and gave Victoire an inquisitive glance. "Well? Are you ready? We're almost there."

"More than ready," said Victoire, gathering her cloak with her left hand and securing her reticule and fan with her right. "All they need do is let down the steps." She offered him a tight, anticipatory smile, then said, "I can't help thinking I ought to have brought my pistol instead of my fan." Her chuckle was uncertain. "I suppose my recent escape still troubles me from time to time."

"What would you want a pistol for at a reception?" asked Vernet.

"I don't know—perhaps for those English spies everyone tells me aren't out there. Perhaps because I fear that another attempt will be made to kill the First Consul." She felt the coach move into position. "And perhaps you are all correct and I'm only jumping at shadows." She did her best to show him a reassuring smile. "It's nothing important, I'm certain; otherwise I would have the pistol."

Vernet shook his head in fond disbelief. "What other man has a wife like you?" He reached toward the coach door as it was drawn to a stop and the footman scrambled down from the roof to assist them out.

The Bernadottes' hotel was resplendent, Desirée having her new draperies and valences as well as five enormous chandeliers cleaned and set with new beeswax candles. The servants were rigged out in dull red livery but for the master-butler, who wore a uniform so grand he might be mistaken for one of the admirals or generals attending the reception.

The Swedish delegation was primarily composed of soldiers in their resplendent white-and-blue uniforms. All were covered in medals and decorations, which Victoire found amusing, as Sweden had not had a war since Gustavus Adolphus had died. Just as Desirée had planned, they were dramatically impressive against the dark color of the new draperies. Although Sweden was no longer the premier military power she had been in the Hundred Years War, she remained vital to both France and her enemies. To France she represented a force that could balance the power of the Czar. England had nearly denuded all of her Irish possessions of their once extensive forests, so Sweden was the only European source left for the timber needed to maintain the Royal Navy: Swedish forests provided, at great profit to their crown, virtually all of the timber needed for the masts of all of Europe's navies. Neither France nor England could afford to affront, much less alienate, the Swedes.

Vernet and Victoire surrendered their wraps and their invitation to Bernadotte's servants, Victoire remarking in an undervoice, "I don't know why they always take these away from you just when you want them most. This hallway is drafty as a hayloft."

"You will be warm shortly; these receptions and balls are always overheated." He took her hand and kissed it. "If you remain chilled, I will see you are seated near the fire."

"Thank you, but I am not yet in my dotage," murmured Victoire, but with a trace of wistfulness. She slipped her hand through her husband's arm and took up her place in the reception line, which wound down a long hall to a lavish antechamber where the hosts and the Swedes received the guests.

As a general, Bernadotte had the right to create his own uniform. Tonight he had abandoned the plain infantry uniform he normally wore and sported one made in the same colors and materials as the Swedes, but in reverse, something that obviously pleased the guests of honor. The general's jacket was dark blue and emblazoned with all the honors he had gained, which virtually filled the front of the jacket. The well-tailored unmentionables were the brightest white with a gold stripe down the sides that matched the cuffs and revers of the jacket. Victoire suspected Desirée had had a hand in the uniform's design.

Desirée was equally magnificent: she wore a velvet gown of a red so pure and dark that it seemed black in shadow. On her bosom lay a coronet-shaped lavaliere of rubies-and-garnets set in white gold. Her earrings were ruby baubles, and her tiara had a dozen diamonds as well as eighteen rubies. As Victoire curtsied to her, Desirée offered her cheek. "I am so pleased you are here, Madame Vernet. In this gathering, I am delighted to see a friend's face." She indicated her elderly Aunt Hortense, who served as senior representative of her family. "I have spoken to her of you. You may have to talk loudly, for she does not hear well."

"You're very gracious, Madame Bernadotte," said Victoire in proper form.

"When this reception line is over, you must come with me and drink a glass of champagne. After so many compliments and praises, I fear I'll require your honesty. A woman can become too besotted on flattery, can't she?" Her full lips curved, but the smile never reached her eyes.

"It would be an honor," said Victoire, and continued down the reception line, concealing her growing sense of foreboding. She curtsied to Aunt Hortense and yelled a few polite phrases to her, and then joined her husband just inside the ballroom.

"There is a quadrille forming," remarked Vernet, making it a suggestion.

"Not quite yet, I think," said Victoire, her eyes scanning the room. "I want to have some notion of who is here."

"Because you anticipate trouble?" Vernet suggested with mild disbelief.

"It may come to that," she said, her gaze fixed on Talleyrand, who had just arrived with Fouche.

"But my love," said Vernet, indicating the gorgeous surroundings, "consider this occasion. What spy could come here?"

Victoire was about to give a dismissing answer when she recognized one of the new arrivals. She flipped her fan in the direction of the high interior window that gave onto the hallway and the reception line, where the guests waited to be presented to the Swedish delegation. "That one. Look."

Resplendent in full dress uniform, General Jean-Charles Pichegru stood near the end of the line, unmindful of the stares he was attracting.

Vernet bit back an oath as he recognized the interloper.

"Unless I miss my guess," said Victoire evenly, "those soldiers around General Pichegru are his, not Bernadotte's." She deliberately turned so that she was not staring at Pichegru. She had noticed the bulges inside the jackets of several of the men, which indicated they were carrying pistols. "If he intends to provoke an incident, he has certainly chosen the occasion." She nodded toward Bernadotte. "He must be informed."

"Surely he knows," said Vernet, still watching the general. "How can he not?"

"No, he doesn't know; Pichegru is too far down the hall, beyond Bernadotte's sight. The windows are not visible from the antechamber." She stared down at her shoes. "It's not correct, but you had better inform him so that he can protect the Swedes."

"The Swedes?" Vernet asked. "What of Napoleon?"

On the dance floor a number of sets had formed for the quadrille, and now the seven-piece consort set to playing for them

"Anything causing trouble for the Swedish delegation will be held against Napoleon," said Victoire. "And Napoleon is on the alert; the Swedes are not." She lowered her head. "Take care not to say anything to Desirée."

Vernet stared at her. "What do you mean?"

Victoire spoke hurriedly. "I mean only that Pichegru has come here prepared and he must have carried an invitation to have reached his place in line. If Bernadotte did not give him the invitation, I must ask myself who did." She moved so that she could watch the line more closely. "As Inspector-General, you have a duty to your host, Vernet," she reminded him in the same steady tone. "I'll be sure the doors to the terrace are open." Without waiting for his response, she made her way along the foot of the ballroom toward the four sets of tall French doors on the far side of the room, pausing at each one to open it as Vernet slipped behind the reception line to whisper something to his host.

More couples had formed sets and were joining the dancing. Those guests not dancing gathered into comfortable groups for news and gossip, a few of them taking pains to show off their finery.

Victoire could see Bernadotte stiffen from across the room; as she watched she saw the general turn to the Swedish Ambassador and motion him to move aside. The reception line halted as the Ambassador took a step back and signalled to the rest of his delegation. Beside her husband, Desirée stood in confusion, pouting at this neglect.

At a signal from Bernadotte, a number of servants abandoned their serving work and came to surround the Swedish party and the others in the receiving line. Just behind them were half a dozen Guards in full uniform. Bernadotte whispered something to his wife, then spoke to the Swedes once more.

The guests gathered in the ballroom began to mill as they noticed the unfamiliar activities taking place around the reception's host. The consort faltered in their melody and the dancing straggled to a halt; conversation, until then little more than a low, steady buzz, now became louder and shriller.

"Who would have thought he had the brass?" marveled

Talleyrand at his most insinuating as he appeared beside Victoire.

Victoire made herself show no reaction to this intrusion. She turned and regarded the fop, doing her best to conceal the revulsion she felt. "One can only be astonished," she said, trying to move away.

"I saw you open the doors. An excellent precaution. You are always so perspicacious, Madame Vernet." His eyes lingered on Victoire in a way that made her want to scrub her skin raw to be rid of his gaze. "I have said before that you are most acute."

"How kind," she said brusquely.

"Still," Talleyrand went on, his expression more serpentine than ever, "one wonders how he intended to escape. If, indeed, that is his intention."

"Perhaps he is a diversion, or intends to provide one," said Victoire, again attempting to get away from the sinister dandy.

"Or it may be that he intends to sacrifice himself in protest. Do you think Pichegru is the sort who would immolate himself? Or is he going to try to ruin Bernadotte and the accord with the Swedes?" His laughter sounded like stones breaking. "What do you think, Madame Vernet? You are so often in the right."

"I don't know," she said bluntly. "I wish I did." She made another attempt to break free of Talleyrand only to find that he was keeping limping pace with her.

"A bloodbath here, so that the First Consul arrives to carnage—wouldn't that create trouble?" At last he stepped away. "Whatever is in motion, it is too late for you to stop it, Madame Vernet." He stretched his mouth wide and then bowed.

Victoire continued to move her way through the guests, who were now growing dangerously restive. She wanted to reach the reception line before any of the military men turned the reception into a battleground. Although she did not know what she would do to stop such a disaster, she hoped that something would occur to her.

The Guards and the servants had been formed into a protective escort for the Swedes, and now, with Bernadotte leading them, they hastened toward the nearest of the open French windows. As they made their way through the ballroom, Victoire overhead Vernet call out their destination to her: Sacre Famille, the small twelfth-century church half a block away.

Hearing this, Victoire felt a rush of relief. At least there would not be a pitched battle in the ballroom, and if the

Swedes were taken to safety, there was an excellent chance that Napoleon could be warned in time.

The ballroom was in complete disarray. Only Desirée and her Aunt Hortense remained at the door. Those waiting in line were now confused and distressed, and several of the men had called for arms, their dress swords being good for little more than slicing cake. Pichegru was surrounded by the men who had accompanied him, and most of them had drawn their pistols.

Suddenly there was a running surge of servants from the rear of the hotel, all of them men and all armed with cudgels. They rushed at the men gathered with Pichegru, a few crying aloud.

Desirée stood where she had been left, her pretty face completely unreadable.

In the ballroom a woman screamed, and at that half the company broke for the French windows at a run. The rest were either too upset to act or too confused to know what was best to do. Three of the tall, standing candelabrae in the entryhall were overset, and their light extinguished almost at once, giving Pichegru and his company the advantage of darkness as the servants closed with them.

Desirée tugged her Aunt by the sleeve and drew her into the ballroom, where more of the women had gathered near the musicians.

After a moment's pause, Victoire started toward the hallway, trying to make out what was happening in the uncertain light. For the most part all she could see was a flailing jumble of bodies. Fright warred with curiosity and determination within her. She cursed her elaborate ballgown and long white gloves, wishing now she were dressed for a hard ride or work in the kitchen.

Then there was a shot.

Now several of the women screamed, and Desirée raised her voice. "Pray be calm. The soldiers will protect us," she said confidently, and addressed the master of the consort. "Play that new march that Paisiello composed, the dignified one you were to play for the First Consul's arrival," she ordered.

The violinist stared at her as if she were insane.

"It will quiet these women and keep them from panicking," said Desirée, and indicated her Aunt Hortense, who was breathing in long, shuddering gasps. "Do it now, churl, or—"

The violinist gave a few hasty orders and struck a downbeat with his bow.

As a second shot was fired, the consort made a tremulous beginning to Paisiello's "March Triumphant."

"Good," Desirée approved as the first clarion call of the trumpet sounded over the blows, oaths, and clattering in the hall.

Victoire was now at the doorway; she hesitated going further, for in the darkness she knew that she could come to grief. She heard the music grow louder and grudgingly admitted that Desirée had hit on the way to keep some order.

Another shot erupted, and this time there was the unmistakable cry of a gravely wounded man.

This spurred Victoire to action, and she plunged into the hallway toward the mass of struggling men. She still did not know what she would do when she reached the fight, but she felt driven to act.

A figure materialized from the shadows. "Madame Vernet, is this wise?" asked Talleyrand.

"They have to be stopped," said Victoire, as eager to break away from him as to end the battle. "Someone is badly hurt. You can hear him."

"With music to accompany him," approved Talleyrand, and held out a sabre to her. "It is one of the Cuirassiers'," he explained. "Not for dress. You may need it."

Much as she hated taking anything from Talleyrand, Victoire accepted the long, curved sword. "Thank you."

"Use it well," said Talleyrand. "And do not fear, I have weapons with me." He slid away into the shadows on the far side of the hall.

Victoire stood still for the better part of a minute, wondering who else was skulking about in the darkness. She tried to peer into the niches and alcoves that lined the hall, but could determine nothing; with a stern inner warning not to succumb to an attack of nerves, she closed her hand more firmly about the hilt of the sabre. Then she heard two more shots in quick succession, and she caught up her train over her arm and hurried toward the fighting men.

She had almost reached the chaotic battle when Pichegru's men broke free of the servants, retreating toward the coach entrance of the hotel amid shouts and the ring of steel on steel.

Behind them the sound of the march was growing in volume.

One of the combatants—a servant—was flung back from the rest; he careened into Victoire, all but knocking her off her feet. He muttered an apology and staggered away, one hand pressed to the side of his face where blood seeped through his fingers.

Victoire advanced again, and this time she was able to seize one of the servants by his shoulder and pull him back from the fray. "You'll be shot if—"

She was interrupted by more explosions as Pichegru and his men reached the entrance. There coachmen joined with the servants to attempt to thwart Pichegru's escape, many of them bringing their long whips into play.

There were more discharges of pistols, and one of the coachmen fell dead, while a servant collapsed with a shattered leg.

Two of Pichegru's men were lying on the floor in the hallway, unconscious, bruises already forming on their heads and hands. One of them had a broken leg, the bones piercing his skin and matting his inexpressibles with blood.

Victoire took just enough time to determine that they were still alive, then followed after the retreating men, holding the sabre at the ready.

More of the servants were breaking away as Pichegru's men moved him beyond their reach. Several of them had been hurt in the fight, and now they began to realize the extent of their injuries.

From the ballroom the refrain of the march began again.

At last Pichegru was almost into a waiting carriage; Victoire saw this with dismay, and started to run forward.

Then a foppish, limping man broke from the shadows, a sword upraised. He rushed directly at Pichegru, shouting something that was lost in the chaos around them. Pichegru's men turned on Talleyrand as Pichegru himself fled in the carriage.

Victoire saw one of Pichegru's men take aim at Talleyrand, and she charged him, bringing her sabre down on his arm. The impact of the blow, followed by the tension in the blade as it bit into cloth and flesh sickened her a little, and she stepped back as the soldier tottered, clutching his arm to his chest.

Most of Pichegru's men were breaking away now, some running for the streets, some of them climbing aboard waiting coaches of the Bernadottes' guests, and whipping up the horses to escape.

Ahead on the paving stones Talleyrand sat with his head in his hands, his finery torn and smirched. He winced as Victoire approached him. "I couldn't stop him. Thought I might, but—"

Victoire could only nod. She no longer heard Paisiello's march.

14

❦

VERNET WAS PALE and his visage grim as he returned home. He
removed his greatcoat and called harshly for Odette. The day
was bright and brittle, with a cold wind to make mockery of the
sun, which precisely echoed his state of mind. "Odette!" he
yelled again over the hammering from the floor above.

Victoire appeared in the hallway, coming from the withdrawing room. "You're back sooner than I expected," she said
calmly, noticing how rigidly Vernet was standing.

"It's done," said Vernet heavily.

"All of them?" asked Victoire. "Did none of them speak?"

"Oh, they spoke. Montrachet delivered quite an oration, but
none of it was useful to us, except that it confirmed their conspiracy. He was proud of it." He went toward the living room.
"There is still no sign of Pichegru."

"That should not surprise you," said Victoire, turning toward
the kitchens and calling to Odette to bring cognac before following Vernet into the parlor. "If he has any intelligence, he
will be out of this country as soon as he can."

"There are men dispatched to the borders and the coast
searching for him." He sat down on the new divan. "The conspirators are gone, dead or left the country. Or so Fouche declares. Most of them were very young, hardly more than boys,
and they died bravely, but so uselessly." He glanced toward the
ceiling, where the sound of carpenters continued. "Would you
ask them not to hammer for a while? The sound, after the
executions—"

"If you wish," said Victoire, and went to relay his request to
the workers. By the time she returned Odette had come from
the kitchen with the cognac and two balloon glasses on the tray
she carried. "Let me pour for us," she offered, and motioned to
Odette to leave them alone.

"It's a bad business, but it was managed as well as possible
under the circumstances. Dangerous men like that, we dare not
risk a trial now." He frowned. "Fouche is persuaded that spies

200

like those must be dealt with summarily, as you would in war because they are committing an act of war. But still." He looked over at Victoire and then away again. "We were not wholly unfeeling for their plight. They had Mass and Communion, those who wanted it." He held out his hand for the glass she offered him. "It was very cold, and the wind cut like a sword. They were shot in groups of four; there were six of the groups, between the spies and Pichegru's men who were captured. Most of them—Pichegru's men—were injured. We rounded them up after the debacle at Bernadotte's reception. They were shot first, because they disgraced the uniform of France." He drank half the contents of the glass.

"They revealed nothing," said Victoire, certain they had not.

"No; no, they told us nothing," said Vernet, and drank again, less deeply than before. "The Coronation is slightly more than two weeks away, and—"

"There is still the possibility of treason and assassination," said Victoire bluntly. "Fouche has finally admitted that, has he?"

"Not quite," said Vernet. "But he has redoubled the force assigned to protect the First Consul."

"But you are afraid it may not be enough?" Victoire suggested.

"I don't know," said Vernet, rising and beginning to pace. "I know you've said all along that there are still conspirators at large—"

"And their undiscovered allies close to Napoleon as well," Victoire interjected.

"Yes, yes. Fouche hasn't come to accept that theory of yours, not wholly. He believes that it is Pichegru who was their master, and that once he is apprehended the rest will be caught, assuming there are any of them left, whoever they are." He stopped to stare, unseeing, out the window.

"And you do not believe this," said Victoire.

"Not anymore, no," he admitted slowly. "I want to believe it. I have tried to persuade myself. I'm afraid there are more of the spies or followers of Pichegru's at large, and I am not convinced that they will not make another attempt on Napoleon's life." Now that he had actually said this, he smiled sheepishly. "You've thought this all along, haven't you?"

In spite of herself, Victoire nodded. "It has troubled me."

"I should have listened to you before." He finished the cognac. "Those men, this morning, they were mad with purpose."

"Zealots," said Victoire.

"Zealots," Vernet confirmed. "And they did not seem defeated. That's what has weighed on me since . . . since they were executed this morning. I've been thinking over the way they died, and it was the death of martyrs, not those with a lost cause. It has rankled with me, that . . . that *confidence* they displayed."

"I see," said Victoire, refilling his glass with cognac.

"If Pichegru has fled, it's only because there are others to do his work for him," said Vernet with conviction. "You were right about that. I should have seen it from the first, but Fouche was so determined to . . . Little as I wish to believe this, I know it for the truth." He took another sip, this one quite modest. "I had better not finish this second glass. There is a meeting this afternoon I must attend, and it would not do for me to arrive less than alert."

"This is the preparation for the Coronation?" Victoire inquired. "For Fouche and the rest of you?"

"Yes, and there is another tomorrow. From now until the event, there is something every day relating to it. I must have another fitting of my Coronation uniform tomorrow, though where I'll find the time I haven't decided." He set the glass aside. "Have Odette use the rest in a sauce or something," he recommended.

"I will," said Victoire. "My gown ought to be ready at the end of this week, or so the dressmaker tells me. She has a strict schedule to keep, and I am sure to have the gown by Friday." She looked away, recalling once again how expensive these two articles of clothing were. "A pity we will have only the single occasion to wear them," she said before she could stop herself. "Like wedding clothes, it seems."

"Yes, it is," said Vernet in a practical tone. "But there may be other foreign events that will demand such finery again, and so—"

"And so we will put them in clothes-presses and trust that we can use them again before they are hopelessly old fashioned," she said. "Such is the favor of advancement, my love. And the time may come when we will be pleased to have spent so much."

"Do you think so?" Vernet wondered aloud. "I am appalled at how much we must spend."

"As I am," said Victoire. "However, it is necessary if the others are not to dismiss you." She stepped to the hearth and stared down at the low fire burning there. "Fortunately there will not be another Coronation for a time. We will not have such expenditures next year."

"Let us pray so," said Vernet, and then stood very still, watching her. "You aren't planning to do any more investigating, are you?"

"Not unless something new occurs to me," she promised him, which did not provide the reassurance he sought.

"Promise me you are not going to strike off on your own again. Tell me that you will speak to me before you do anything more to find these spies." His eyes were somber and his expression grave. "If you are right, the men we seek are more desperate than you can imagine, my love, and they would not hesitate to murder you. Since we have not identified their associates, you could be courting destruction if you attempt to find them." He came toward her. "If you'll not protect yourself for yourself, do it for me."

"All right," she said, realizing how deep his apprehension was. "I won't do anything without informing you. Is that acceptable?"

"Not entirely," he said, "but if it's the best concession you offer—"

She shrugged. "It is the best I can do without falsehood."

He bent and kissed her lightly, "Then I accept it with gratitude."

"How intrepid you were, Madam Vernet," exclaimed Desirée as she and Victoire faced each other across the long dining table. Gone was the sensibility and good will of their conversations of a week ago. Now there was combat in Desirée's splendid eyes. "And how fortunate that your bravery brought you such flattering attention." Around them the high-ranking officials and their wives sat, enjoying the lavish meal offered by Napoleon's sister Pauline. "I would never have the courage to face a company of armed men."

"Hardly a company, Madame Bernadotte, and I was far from alone. Your servants had already moved to capture the traitor; I merely observed as closely as I could," said Victoire with a gesture to indicate her lack of need for acclaim. "I find myself admiring your conduct during the trouble. It was a lucky thing that you are not easily distressed. You served to calm many of your guests, and with such presence of mind that your Swedish company were wholly protected at all times. Surely your husband and the delegation must be grateful for your presence of mind."

"You are kind to say so," said Desirée, though her eyes held another message entirely.

"Oh, no. I could never have been so clever as to order the musicians to play. That was a brilliant stroke," said Victoire sincerely. "I suspect that we're more in your debt than we know. A panic at that reception would surely have been catastrophic."

"It may have been what Pichegru sought," said Desirée. "If there had been complete disorder, he might have been able to make an attempt on the First Consul." Her eyes flashed.

Victoire regarded her with interest. "Do you think it would have been possible? There were so many officers in attendance, surely one of them would have warned Napoleon before he arrived."

"It would please me to think so," said Desirée with a wide, false smile. "You would have been at the door to warn him, in any case, wouldn't you, Madame Vernet?"

"Perhaps," said Victoire, wondering what Desirée intended by that observation. "That would have depended more on your servants than on me."

"And Murat as well," Desirée added with a deliberate sting in the words. "Doubtless you would seek to warn Joachim Murat, wouldn't you?"

The use of Murat's first name startled Victoire and she knew that her response would be noted by guests other than Desirée. "I would hope that had it not fallen out so unfortunately that I might have been able to give the warning to everyone accompanying the First Consul," she answered.

"Noble sentiments," said Desirée, and changed the subject to jewels.

The innkeeper at Le Chevre Chantier favored Colonel Sir Magnus Sackett-Hartley with a wide, encouraging smile. "Your ally has sent you word at last."

Sackett-Hartley put down the load of wood he had carried in from the shed behind the inn, and he regarded her with suspicion. The small lobby was deserted, and the door to the taproom was closed, leaving them isolated. "What are you talking about?"

"Very fussy handwriting has your ally, dainty as a woman's," she said, holding out the folded missive with a provocative air. "D'Estissac said there would be a message, and here it is." She ran the tip of her tongue over her parted lips. "If you want to read it, you'll have to thank me for it properly."

"Properly?" he repeated, not certain of her intention, for he had seen her taunt men and then upbraid them for their forwardness. "I'll bow and kiss your hand, if you require it. You have had generous payment already."

"That is not what I meant," she said, and her smile changed, becoming more eager and inviting. "There are many ways to be thanked, aren't there? A man like you, well-set-up and handsome, you must know these ways. I am a widow, and there are times my bed is too empty and cold." She paused, letting her words sink in. "It would be a welcome gesture to have a little of your time, my fine English gentleman."

Sackett-Hartley stared at her, wondering if he had suddenly forgotten all his French. "You cannot . . . surely you do not intend . . ." He stopped, too flustered to continue. What if he had misunderstood her? he asked himself, and this was another one of her flirtatious ploys?

"I mean that I expect you to give me a great deal of pleasure before I give you this message," she said plainly. "And if you do it well enough and I am satisfied, then I'll continue to serve your purpose here, as long as you serve mine." Her eyes were bright, anticipatory. "If you disappoint me, I'll no doubt have to find a way to . . . to achieve other satisfaction and pleasure. There are rewards for those who bring the enemies of the First Consul to light. A poor widow like me, who could blame me for fearing for my life in the company of desperate men?"

Sackett-Hartley regarded her steadily for a short while, then said, "And what is to keep you from informing against us whether you are pleasured or not?"

Her laughter was short and sarcastic. "You are taking quite a gamble, my pretty Englishman."

"And coming to your bed is not a gamble?" he asked, his expression self-effacing. "Madame, consider: neither you nor I have time for courtship. You have danger enough having us here. Why bring more—"

"That is my thought," she interrupted him. "As long as I've taken so great a chance, I wish to be richly rewarded."

"But Madame—" Sackett-Hartley protested.

"Do you not think me fair?" she asked.

"Yes," he admitted at once. "That's never the issue. You are a beautiful woman." He looked directly at her. "It's not a question of your beauty, Madame."

"I'm Isabeau, not Madame," she said gently, and indicated the small room that served for her office. "Come in. We can be private here."

"Madame, it isn't wise," he cautioned her as he followed her into the little room. "You may discover that I'm not to your liking, and what then?"

"Then you will learn what I like," she said, closing the door behind them. "And I'll give you the letter for trying, in any case."

He stared at her, knowing this was folly but letting himself be persuaded by her magnificent figure and beautiful skin. Her face was lovely, he thought, and he had speculated more than once what her tastes and talents might be, and imagined what she would offer him, and how he would take that gift. For an instant, he remembered his uncle, and knew that the dashing old man would not approve. But Uncle Percival was in England and Isabeau was three strides away, and Uncle Percival had adored his wife. "Give me the letter first," he said.

She leaned back against the door. "We will be alone for a short while," she said. "We could make a beginning. And then the letter will be yours."

With a slight shrug, Sackett-Hartley went up to her and with slow deliberation kissed her, pulling her into his arms as she warmed to him.

Fouche shook his head and fussily adjusted the stack of files on his desk. "Madame Vernet, your concern for the safety of the First Consul does you great credit. Doubtless you have demonstrated steadfast purpose better than many of the very highest. But you must see that the measures you advocate are no longer necessary. We have ended the activities of the English and the French traitors, in large part due to your tenacity. There are no dangerous men abroad, not any longer. They've been captured and shot, all, that is, but Pichegru and possibly one or two of his supporters. But we have taken measures to be sure he cannot approach the First Consul."

"The Emperor," corrected Victoire. She had arrived at Fouche's office less than ten minutes before and had been given very little of his time; there was a Coronation rehearsal in an hour and Fouche, along with a hundred others, was required to attend.

"In eight more days, yes," said Fouche. "And we are aware that this could well be a crucial factor in regard to his safety, but I assure you there's no reason for this constant distress you feel."

"I'm not distressed," said Victoire emphatically. "I'm frustrated because no one is willing to take the time to finish this investigation. My husband spends most of his time escorting foreign dignitaries about the city and has neither the time nor the men to pursue the inquiry he began. I cannot locate the officials who can authorize more diligence in discovering the others in this treasonous plot, for they are all being fitted for uniforms or attending banquets or military reviews. Berthier hasn't been at his desk for more than three days." She knew that Fouche would be offended that she had approached Berthier, but hoped that perhaps such a remark would goad him into providing her with the assistance she needed. And, she added to herself, it was impossible to have two words with Murat, who as Governor of Paris was more caught up in the Coronation preparations than any of the rest of them.

"This obsession, Madame Vernet, is not to your credit. You have always appeared to be a woman of sense, which is why I have listened to you when I would not generally give such serious attention to a woman. But now you have let yourself be overcome by your notion that there are more traitors than there are. It is understandable," he went on in a condescending way. "After such harrowing experiences, it is hardly surprising that you should think that the problem is vaster than it is."

"I'm not hysterical or overwrought," said Victoire with admirable calm. "I'm not upset by anything but the stubborn blindness to danger that everyone has adopted." She rose. "I know you're busy and that you gave me this time because you have none else to spare."

"You have duties to attend to, as well, Madame Vernet," said Fouche, doing his best to be courteous to her, for as annoying as she was, she had the approval of Napoleon himself, and the friendship of Murat; Fouche was not so reckless as to risk earning the disapproval of either of those men.

"Yes, I do. And whether it suits you or not, I'll attend to them." She curtsied and let herself out the door, doing her best to control her temper. In the street she summoned a cab, and as the driver drew up, she warned him that his horse was about to cast a shoe. "Off-side front," she informed him. "I can hear it."

The driver stared at her as she climbed into his vehicle. "Where do you want to go, Madame?" he asked, paying no attention to her warning.

She provided her address, then changed her mind. "No, take me to the hotel Bernadotte. Do you know—"

"I know the place," said the driver, whose opinion of his passenger went a bit higher.

"The coach entrance, then, and drive carefully." She leaned

back and drew her coat more tightly around her against the pervasive chill. Her frown deepened as they drew nearer the Bernadotte hotel, and was quite marked by the time she paid the driver and stepped out of the cab. "That shoe's gone," she informed the driver. "Best have it replaced before your horse is lame."

The butler who greeted her informed her that Madame Bernadotte was not home, but if Madame Vernet cared to wait, she should return in half an hour. "She's with her dressmaker," he explained.

"As is all the world," said Victoire. "Yes, I will wait if you don't mind. I'd appreciate a cup of coffee, if you would be kind enough to provide it."

The butler looked a bit put off by the request, then said, "My master is currently having coffee in the library. If it would suit you to join him?"

"Certainly, if I am not intruding," said Victoire at once, pleased to have this unexpected opportunity to speak privately with Bernadotte.

It was apparent that the butler did not approve, but he led Victoire through the hall toward the library, remarking that most of the blood had been cleaned from the floor but that the carpet was ruined by it. "A great loss," the butler declared, "for it was made especially for this passage."

"How unfortunate," said Victoire indifferently, and added with genuine concern, "What of the injured servants?"

"Two were killed, as I suppose you know. One . . . well, the physician is not able to say what happened, but he was struck a number of times on the head, and now he does not seem to be himself. Of course, it may be that he requires more time to heal, but he's very forgetful, which has never been the case before." He closed his mouth very suddenly, as if he thought he had said too much.

"That is sad news," consoled Victoire with feeling as the butler opened the door to the library and announced her to Bernadotte.

The general was seated at one of two long trestle tables, a tray untouched by his arm. Two large volumes of maps were open in front of him; he was startled as he looked up at the butler's appearance. "Who did you say?" he asked. Bernadotte was relaxing in only a dress shirt and uniform inexpressibles; the shirt was plain, but well tailored, which was hardly surprising as Bernadotte was the youngest son of a most successful tailor in Pau, the capital of the most distant province of southwestern France, Gascony.

Until a few months ago Bernadotte had been without any duties or command. Implicated in a plot to overthrow Napoleon, he had been appointed ambassador to the United States, mostly to get him far away from France. But before he could leave to take this station, Napoleon sold Louisiana and the post lost its importance. Without orders Bernadotte had returned to Paris and waited for over a year. Only within the last few weeks had Napoleon needed his services, this time to squire about the Swedish delegation. The activity agreed with Bernadotte and he looked both happier and healthier than he had on his visit with Desirée two months earlier.

When the general saw who the visitor was, he smiled and gestured for her to sit down in the expansive way of most Gascons, which the sophisticated Parisians found laughably provincal.

Victoire curtsied as the butler stood aside. "Good afternoon, General," she said, and approached him, holding out her hand. "I hope I do not intrude."

"No," said Bernadotte mendaciously. "Please do come in, Madame Vernet, and give me the benefit of your conversation for half an hour."

"How kind," said Victoire, admiring the skill with which Bernadotte had so courteously limited her visit.

"My wife might well be back by that time, and would be pleased to see you." He looked away. "You must not be offended by her starts, Madame Vernet. I know that there are times she is . . . difficult, but I assure you she means no harm."

"You are very kind," said Victoire, choosing one of the chairs on the opposite side of the table and sitting. "I have not been distressed by anything your wife has said to me."

Bernadotte motioned the butler to leave, adding, "Bring coffee for Madame Vernet, and perhaps some cheese."

The butler bowed and withdrew.

"Those are magnificent volumes," said Victoire, leaning forward a little.

"A gift from the Swedish delegation," said Bernadotte. "This one is a complete atlas and travel diary of Sweden, and this of France. The maps and illustrations are most commendable." He paused. "I never thought knowing how to speak Swedish would be useful."

"A very pretty conceit, and very appropriate," approved Victoire as she looked at the books, wondering a little how she was going to turn the conversation to the plotters now that she had the opportunity to speak with Bernadotte in confidence.

She need not have worried, for Bernadotte brought up the matter himself. "I cannot flatter myself that you are curious about the Swedish delegation, or that your visit is only a matter of form. I suppose you are investigating about Pichegru, and how he came to be here." He saw her raise her brows. "There is no need to dissemble, Madame Vernet. I know your skills as well as anyone, and I confess I expected to find you on my doorstep well before Fouche's men."

Victoire could feel the flush spread over her face and down her neck. "Dear me, I had no notion that—"

"You have discovered the English conspirators, and you are searching for those in high places who gave them help. And because Pichegru arrived at my reception, you have good reason to suppose I might know something of the matter. Have I discerned your purpose?" He looked weary as he asked, and his large, heavy-lidded eyes seemed to droop.

"That will make my time with you much more productive, and I thank you for your candor, for it makes my situation easier," Victoire replied, abandoning the more indirect examination she might have used. "Do you, in fact, know how Pichegru came to have an invitation to your reception?"

Bernadotte shook his head twice. "I have been troubled by that myself. You may believe me or not, but I did not provide the invitation, and I have not been able to discover who did. You may ask among my guests, if you wish, and you will find that I've been there before you." He sat back and stared at the far wall. "So far I've learned nothing."

"Nothing," she said, nodding. "Does this distress you?"

"Yes," he admitted at once. "I'm faced with suspecting my colleagues of lying, or my servants of duplicity, or perhaps worse than duplicity." He shook his head once, as if to rid himself of lingering doubts. "I trust you'll fare more successfully than I have."

"Thank you," said Victoire. "But I fear that so far I've accomplished very little." She glanced at the door as the butler returned with a serving maid accompanying him, bringing another pot of coffee, a cup, and a plate of marzipan-stuffed pastries.

Bernadotte said nothing while these were presented, and when the servants were gone, he continued. "The event has put a cloud over me; I know that my wife's suffered because of it."

This was a dangerous subject, and Victoire framed her question very carefully, aware of how chary Bernadotte could be. "Your wife has not said much to me concerning the fracas. Has she reached a conclusion of her own, do you think?"

"I think she's pleased that it caused difficulty for Napoleon," Bernadotte said diffidently. "She hasn't discussed it with me except to remark on Pichegru's temerity. She told me that not even Napoleon would be so audacious, and for her, this was a most telling comment."

"Truly," said Victoire, and went on gingerly. "I admired her steadiness during the event. She must be credited with keeping the occasion from degenerating into a rout."

"Yes," said Bernadotte, with the first indication of friendliness. "Steadiness is a very good description of her behavior. She was amazing, wasn't she, telling the consort to play music?"

"She has great presence of mind," said Victoire. "In such an emergency, there are few of us who could keep our heads as well."

"Exactly," said Bernadotte, and in a rush added, "I was so grateful to her that I could not express it but with a gift. I have ordered an emerald necklace for her, to show the depth of my appreciation." He poured coffee into Victoire's cup, then into his. "I never knew what staunch character my wife has until now."

"Staunch character," Victoire echoed. "Yes, that's her nature, isn't it?"

Now that he had started to talk more freely, Bernadotte went on enthusiastically. "I am certain that everyone was impressed by her good sense. As they are impressed with yours, Madame Vernet. I had not seen this aspect of her before and now that I have, my devotion to her is greater. I am so moved by her gallantry." He glanced at Victoire and then away. "You may think that an odd word, gallantry, but—"

"I think it a great compliment, and I am certain your wife is honored by it," said Victoire quickly.

"She was so grand, wasn't she?" This time Bernadotte actually smiled. "Had she planned for the event, she could not have managed it with more grace, could she?"

Victoire regarded Bernadotte carefully. "No," she said after a little hesitation. "No, she could not have done it better had she planned it."

With the Coronation four days away Vernet was gone almost constantly, and Victoire was kept occupied with a long string of social obligations that left her exhausted, and, as she admitted to Odette, "wishing I could say something shocking and rude, just for variety." The carpenters were gone and the house was oddly still in the fading evening.

Odette had finished sweeping the three fireplaces in the house and was about to tackle the tremendous and messy work of cleaning the stove; she slapped at her heavy apron and gestured in exasperation. "Who does not want that from time to time?"

"Ah, but this is so constant," said Victoire, glancing around the kitchen. "The carpenters will arrive here eventually in the morning, and when you finish cursing them, it'll be better." She drew up one of the chairs and sat down. "But I must say that it is pleasant to have a few hours to myself, and the chance to loosen my stays."

Odette laughed, and gave herself a little more time before starting her unwelcome task. "I have hopes that we'll have some winter vegetables this year. I put the seedlings in last month and thus far they are growing."

"Excellent," said Victoire. "You're doing very good work, Odette, and I know I have not noticed it as I ought."

"There's too much occupying your thoughts," said Odette.

"And there will be for some little time to come," said Victoire. "Do forgive me for the oversights I know I have committed." She chuckled once. "It is a compliment to you, in a way, for it means that you are running the house so smoothly that it requires little of my attention."

"It's a pleasure to me." Odette pushed her hair back from her face. "I'd rather be left to do my work properly than have to answer to you for everything I undertake. I know of such mistresses, and I want no part of them."

"And a good thing it is," said Victoire with feeling. "As you haven't one such."

Odette grinned. "So I know." She was about to add a quip when a sharp rap at the back door caught her attention, and she turned toward it in surprise.

"It is late in the afternoon for a tradesman," said Victoire.

"I expect no tradesmen," said Odette, her surprise giving way to alarm. "Do you think—"

The knock was repeated, this time more loudly.

"I think it would be wise to answer the door," said Victoire, rising and starting toward it herself.

Odette quickly moved to lift the latch and peer out into the darkness. "Who is it?" she demanded in a loud tone.

There was little light spilling from the kitchen to the porch next to the pantry, but it was possible to make out a single figure standing in the shadows. A soft voice said, "Is Mad-dame Vernet . . . is s-she here?"

Odette stared at the young man. "Those who seek Madame Vernet do not come to this door," she said at her most imposing.

"Is she here?" the young man persisted. "It is very important."

Victoire had risen and now said, "It's all right, Odette. Let him in."

Disapproving, Odette stood aside. "Enter," she ordered the young man.

Brezolles came hesitantly into the kitchen, like a cat uncertain of his reception.

"Madame Vernet," he said, bowing in good form.

"You have the advantage of me, Monsieur," said Victoire.

"I ought not t-tell you," he said, looking embarrassed.

Odette scowled, but Victoire only shrugged. "If that is how it must be, then—" She indicated one of the chairs. "Be seated, and tell me what you are doing here; why did you want to see me?"

Brezolles ignored the chair. "We want to leave France, most of us. Things have gone b-badly for us."

"Most of you want to leave," said Victoire, doing her best to conceal the eagerness that spread through her.

"Yes. The C-Corsican is too closely g-guarded." His gaze shifted to Odette guiltily. "We want only to b-be gone."

"Who are the 'we' you speak of?" Victoire had been listening to the stammering young man closely, admiring his aristocratic accent, but hearing something else in how he spoke, a subtle shift of rhythm that hinted of the cadences of another language. "The English?" she guessed.

"Two are English," Brezolles said. "The rest are French."

"Aristos," said Victoire. "Those who fled the Revolution."

"A good thing they are gone," said Odette. "They plundered the country."

"The C-Corsican has done worse," said Brezolles, his eyes brightening.

"And you seek to restore the old order?" Victoire asked.

Brezolles straightened up. "Yes," he declared. Then his pride deserted him. "But we c-can't do it now. Most of us want t-to leave."

"Not all," Victoire said.

"No," Brezolles admitted. He looked nervously around the kitchen as if he expected to see soldiers appear.

"You worked with Pichegru and his . . . associates?" Victoire asked. "You are one of those who took me captive?" She had not intended to make this accusation, and the intensity of her feeling took her aback.

"It was Mont-trachet who . . ." Brezolles took a step backward. "I did not like it." He bowed again, this time apologetically. "S-Sackett-Hartley would never have allowed it."

"Sackett-Hartley!" Victoire exclaimed. There was that English name again. Her senses became keener as she stared at Brezolles. "You were not arrested with the others."

"No." He stared down at his feet. "We were not caught."

"How many are you?" Victoire asked.

"Eight. Two English, six French." He cleared his throat as if that could diminish his stammer. "If you would h-help us, I'd tell you where P-Pichegru is."

"And who his allies are?" Victoire asked as she fought off a ripple of dread.

"I reg-gret, I do not know who they are," admitted Brezolles.

Victoire sighed in aggravation, convinced that the young man had told her the truth, for if she were part of such a conspiracy she thought, she would make sure that as many of the conspirators as possible were unknown to one another. "That's very inconvenient," she remarked; there was a ball that night, starting at nine in the evening, and she had to appear there. Failure to be present would be a severe embarrassment to Vernet. No matter what this young man told her, she would not be able to act on what she learned until the following morning, and by that time Pichegru might be gone. "All right. Where is Pichegru?"

"Swear you will help-p us," insisted Brezolles.

"I can't do that," Victoire said reasonably. "You must understand that. But I will give you my word that I will not send soldiers after your company of men." As she promised this, she reminded herself that even had she wanted to summon soldiers it was not likely that they would be available.

"For two days," said Brezolles, pressing for what small advantage he could.

"All right," said Victoire, determined now to find Pichegru herself; without doubt Fouche would refuse to order his men to action on Victoire's request, in any case.

"Two full d-days," Brezolles insisted.

"No soldiers for two days," she affirmed.

Odette crossed herself and muttered a few words.

"Very well," said Brezolles, and took a long breath. "Pichegru is at the old Jesuit rectory near Vincennes. He is using the name Gambais."

"Is he alone?" Victoire asked, feeling her pulse race.

"His remaining men are in the t-town; they won't be there long," said Brezolles. "Two days," he reminded her. "So t-that we can leave."

"Two days," Victoire agreed; if she could find Pichegru, she thought, it would not matter that a few English spies escaped.

Brezolles was sidling toward the door, eager now to be gone. "You g-gave me your word," he reminded her.

"And I will abide by it," she said. As she watched Brezolles open the porch door, she thought of one more thing. "When does Pichegru intend to strike again?"

"I don't k-know," said Brezolles, and pulled the door closed behind him.

Odette rushed to set the bolt in place, then turned to stare at Victoire. "What do you think, Madame Vernet?" she asked breathlessly.

Victoire shook her head slowly. "I won't know until I visit the Jesuit rectory in Vincennes. If Pichegru is there, I can summon Vernet to apprehend him; if not, we should remain quiet. There is always the chance the man was sent to cause me to embarrass Vernet and destroy my credibility. I must assure myself Pichegru is there." She paid no heed to Odette's shocked exclamation, but started to pace the kitchen. "That ball tonight, if only it were not necessary to attend."

"Surely you would not go to Vincennes at night," Odette protested.

"Not tonight, certainly," said Victoire, annoyed. "It can't be helped." But it was possible that she might make an early start, she decided. If she could persuade Murat to lend her one of his light carriages, and if she could get away shortly after sunrise, she might be able to apprehend General Pichegru.

"What is it, Madame?" asked Odette apprehensively.

Victoire made herself stop pacing and offer Odette a reassuring smile. "Wishful thinking, I fear." She touched her neat coronet of braids. "Come. Give me a hand with my hair. The stove will wait."

15

✤

MURAT LOOKED TIRED, and for once he was simply dressed in sensible clothing: woolen breeches and double-breasted riding coat, high cavalry boots, and an engulfing three-caped greatcoat which he wore with the collar up against the misty rain. A low-crowned beaver hat covered his glossy hair. He leaned down from the spider's rear-mounted driver's box and offered Victoire an ironic bow. "I trust your husband will not have my ears for this."

"What are you doing here?" Victoire asked as she gathered her cloak more closely around her. It was not long after sunrise but the rain held the dark, so that lanterns burned at the pantry door of the Vernets' house. "When I asked for the loan of one of your carriages, I never intended that you—"

"Your husband is on station at the palace with an entire company of gendarmes to reinforce the Consular Guard. We were both sure our arguments at the ball hadn't dissuaded you from this dangerous mission. I'm almost hurt you thought I would let you go careering across the countryside after a dangerous criminal with no more escort than a coachman," Murat interrupted her. "What a fine opinion you must have of me."

"I have a very high opinion of your good sense," said Victoire, "and I didn't suppose you would lose sight of it now. I have no intention of storming the ramparts on my own, or fighting the man in single combat. I don't need more than a coachman to determine if Pichegru is truly in Vincennes."

Murat snorted. "Well, you'll have me for escort or you will walk to Vincennes," he said bluntly. "Since you're determined on such an impetuous course—and it *is* an impetuous course—I'll do what I can to keep you from harm. And I'll pray your husband will not call me out for this."

"There is no reason he should," said Victoire at her most reasonable. "A tandem team," she went on, deliberately changing the subject. "You must expect driving some narrow roads."

two-horse team hitched lead-and-wheel instead of side-by-side as a pair was not often seen in Paris.

"I can think of many reasons why Vernet might be upset, and no, I will not be distracted by observations about my horses," answered Murat testily.

Victoire settled herself in the high-wheeled light carriage, taking care to wrap the heavy rug Murat had provided around her legs. "I think you are being much too cautious, and undoubtedly you are absenting yourself from important events," she cajoled. Murat could hardly afford half a day for this gesture. "We could stop at your hotel, and you could—"

"But I won't," he cut her off. "In fact, I would prefer to take a squad of my own cavalry with us, in case these criminals are truly hiding there. But that could mean an argument with Fouche, and just at present I want to be spared that. Besides, their approach would give warning to Pichegru if he truly is at the Jesuit rectory, and that is the last thing we want." He had set his team at a steady trot, heading eastward through the city as the sun strove to lighten the heavy clouds.

"I am confident that we will have the element of surprise, and that more force will not be needed." As she said it, the notion sounded incredibly naive, even to her, but she lifted her chin and added defiantly, "Besides, Murat, you and I have faced far worse than Pichegru before, and won through."

"Madame Vernet," said Murat with asperity, "I don't plan to be nearly killed again for you to prove a point."

"Why should you be? Not that you expected it two years ago, either. But Murat, be sensible. Surely this is much less dangerous than that escapade," she teased, trying to enjoy herself. Little as she wanted to admit it, Murat's company was more reassuring than she had anticipated; now that he was driving her, she began to consider the danger they could encounter, and the adventure. "We are not entering a trap, after all. They do not know we are coming," she said, as much to herself as to him.

"So you hope," corrected Murat as he guided his team around an ox-drawn wagon filled with open cages of lambs, bound for the Tuileries' kitchens.

"I think my informant was desperate enough to keep his word," Victoire declared, recalling the fear she read in Brezolles' eyes.

"I don't know why I ought to believe you," he said. "If they're prepared to be found, we'll have to abandon any hope of capturing them. In fact, if there's any sign of them, we re-

treat instantly and I'll order out the Guard Lancers to capture
them and count ourselves lucky to be out of it."

She turned around as far as the seat would let her, trying to
meet Murat's eyes. "You don't think we're going to find them,
do you?"

"No, I don't," said Murat. "But I think, if they have really
been hiding there, that someone could tell us where they have
gone and what they are planning. And that information,
Victoire, is what I expect we will find. And that is worth a wet
drive out of Paris."

She considered what he said, and allowed inwardly that he
was probably correct. She faced forward again. "I am hoping
for something more—I'd like to know who near the First Consul has been helping Pichegru."

"Need I remind you that's the more dangerous person," said
Murat emphatically, then added, "and I fear, the more crucial."
He went on for some time in silence, his mind on driving, or
so Victoire supposed. Eventually he said, "It is the ally we
must find, not Pichegru. Without finding the hidden traitor, the
known one is useless, whether we capture him or not."

"I would not call Pichegru useless," argued Victoire.

"But you understand me, don't you?" asked Murat.

"Oh, yes," said Victoire, her mind running very fast. "I un
derstand."

Like most church property, the monastery at Vincennes had
been confiscated by the Directoire early in the Revolution. For
a few years it had served as the barracks for a demi-brigade
then it had been converted into an inn for tradesmen and others
who could not afford to stay in high-priced Paris establish
ments.

The former chapel now served as the main room and was
filled with long, rough tables. It was early enough that only
few people were eating and the floor was still stained from the
wine spilled the night before. Victoire's traveling shoes stuc
on half-dried scraps as she waited for Murat to inquire about
the presence of Monsieur Gambais. He returned, taking Victoire
by the arm and hurrying her out of the building.

"The innkeeper thought you were my mistress and we sough
a secluded room," he began in disgust. "And he did not even
know me."

Victoire wasn't sure which annoyed Murat more, the accusa
tion of philandering or the lack of recognition. She remaine
tactfully silent.

"He is still here," Murat informed. "He is in a room alon

the back of the second building. I told the innkeeper he was a distant relative we wished to surprise. I doubt he believed me, but that and a few sous gained us this key to his room." Murat hurried to his spider and lifted one of the seats. Under it was a dark wood box containing two pistols. He handed one to Victoire for charging as he tended to the other. "At Aboukir surprise gained me victory."

"He's not expecting us," Victoire agreed.

"Us?" Murat looked concerned. "Your husband would never forgive me should I put you at risk again."

She could see from the determined set of the Marshall's handsome features that he would not listen to her protests. "We can't have that."

"Then you stay here. Let me handle it," Murat said, a bit surprised at the easy victory; he started toward the old rectory before she changed her mind.

Victoire smiled as he walked away and waited until he was inside the building before moving toward the rear of the building.

The old rectory was surrounded by a shoulder-high wall, now pitted where the soldiers used it for musket practice. The area around the rectory was hard-packed dirt, now smirched with refuse and waste. Victoire stepped carefully, trying to not stain the hem of her woolen traveling cloak. At one point she had to climb over a small wooden fence that formed an enclosure in which sheep bound for Paris could be held. Victoire was shivering—and not entirely from cold—as she rounded the flank of the rectory. She was shocked to see a figure crouched about ten paces ahead of her, facing in the opposite direction. Victoire recognized Pichegru: he held a pistol aimed through the window and as she watched drew back the hammer.

Pichegru had been warned, and now he waited to ambush Murat.

As Victoire raised her own pistol she wondered if she could hit the man at so great a distance. The blighting distress of Murat's danger closed in on her like steel chains. Cocking her own pistol, Victoire took as steady an aim as she could and fired. Her aim was off, too far to the right, and the ball glanced off the wall several feet short of Pichegru.

Chips of brick struck the man on the side of his face and shoulder; he was already turning in response to the report. Howling with pain and rage, Pichegru leveled his pistol at Victoire.

A shot exploded; Victoire flinched, expecting agony.

Instead Pichegru spun away, the pistol blown from his hand by the shot Victoire thought was intended for her. Pichegru stumbled away from her, clutching his arm to his chest. He clambered over the fence and was lost to sight.

Victoire stared after him, and wished for a second pistol. She felt eager and weak at once.

Moments later Murat, a smoking pistol in one hand and his sabre raised in the other, came around the corner. "Are you all right?" he demanded.

"He was waiting for you," Victoire explained in a rush. "He would have shot you."

"Did you not realize that he would fire back if you missed?" Murat asked incredulously. "Any soldier knows to do that."

"I wanted to kill him." Victoire's pulse raced and she fought off the faintness that washed through her.

"So did I," said Murat, offering her his arm. "I think this is a draw for honors, don't you?"

She wanted to laugh but when she did, tears filled her eyes. "We have to find him."

Murat shook his head. "He's long gone. I heard a couple of horses gallop off as I came up to you." He looked at her steadily. "Are you hurt?"

She shook her head, chagrined that he should see her cry. "I'm furious," she said. "I always cry when I'm—"

Murat put one finger to her lips. "I know."

The note was in the same neat, perhaps feminine hand. Sackett-Hartley took it from Isabeau and made a point of kissing her before he broke the seal and spread the single sheet to read.

Arrive at the place before midnight at the animals' door you will be admitted. Take your position in the highest gallery, in case the general should fail, and permit him the first strike. Leave in the confusion when the tyrant is gone.

Your friend

"The animals' door?" Sackett-Hartley wondered aloud.

"Saint Anthony's door," said Isabeau, sliding one arm around him and nuzzling his neck. "Your friend means the Cathedral, doesn't she?"

"Why do you say she?" asked Sackett-Hartley, becoming anxious as he read the note a second time. He moved a few steps away from Isabeau, concentrating on his instructions.

Isabeau came after him. "That's a woman's handwriting." There was a hint of jealousy in her voice.

"Or a very fussy man's," said Sackett-Hartley. "Someone who works all day at a desk, preparing endless reports and other papers." He looked around the small lobby as if he feared being overheard.

"A woman's," she insisted, reaching as if to pluck it from his grasp.

"Perhaps one who was taught in the religious schools and retained their style. More likely a dandy's," said Sackett-Hartley, holding it where she could not reach it. "One of those overdressed fops; they often cultivate feminine handwriting, to make them appear more sensitive and elegant." He paused. "My uncle used to affect that pose—made everyone think he was a trivial sort of fellow—but his handwriting was nothing like this."

"You may be right," said Isabeau, wanting to be convinced. "We will decide it is a lace-and-scent man, wed to his desk. And it is true that I prefer it be a man, Magnus. It would distress me to have a rival."

"You have none, my dear," said Sackett-Hartley, and took a turn about the room. "And forgive me for being distracted. I have been worried for my men, afraid that they might suffer the same fate as Montrachet and his ... And I was beginning to think that we had lost our opportunity altogether. Instead, I find that we are to go directly into the heart of the evil. Waiting is very hard."

She did what she could to console him. "Your associates will be at Isle-Adam by now. There is a ferry across the Oise at Isle-Adam. They will be well-hidden by nightfall, in the care of those you can trust." She rubbed her palm against the back of his neck. "It's arranged and the fee paid. The cooper is ready to help you. You will escape." She said this last sadly.

He reached out and took her hand, kissing it before saying, "Ah, Isabeau, if it were not for this business, I would hate to leave you," he said, and was partly sincere. "But I have sworn to do my duty, and—"

She went on as if reciting a lesson. "The preparations are complete. There will be ten barrels in his load, and all but one will contain lamp oil. It will not be comfortable, but you will be safe, and when the cooper reaches Amiens, your own men will be waiting for you. From there you can reach the coast without trouble." Isabeau watched Sackett-Hartley speculatively, as if trying to discern his feelings

"My uncle endured worse, so I'm told," he said nonchalantly. "Still, two or three days in a barrel . . ." He did not continue.

"You will arrive in Dunkerque without discovery," said Isabeau, her fervor revealing how much she hoped that he would be safe.

"There will be such chaos in France when we succeed that I have no worry of that." He squared his shoulders. "It is getting to that happy moment that worries me."

Isabeau bit her lip to keep from revealing her fear for him. "There is some time yet," she said hopefully. "We can occupy ourselves in better ways than consumed in worry."

He turned to her, his eyes lingering on her breasts and the drape of her high-waisted skirt against her hip. "Truly."

The innkeeper smiled, her large eyes hungry. "There isn't much time left for us, Magnus, and I've not had my fill of you." She indicated the note. "Put that away for an hour and give thought to me. Let me soothe you and turn your thoughts from fruitless worry. Whatever may befall you, there's nothing you can do about it just now."

It was pleasant to be persuaded, thought Sackett-Hartley as he drew the woman into his arms.

All along the newly widened boulevards leading to Notre Dame the traffic was so heavy and so grand that it could hardly move at all. Napoleon's escorts alone had taken up almost half a mile on either side of his coach. They began with a squadron of Cuirassiers, mounted on the largest saddle horses that could be bought in France. They wore silver helmets and bright green, heavy leather coats. When they arrived at the cathedral, the Cuirassiers formed a line on the side of the large plaza across from the cathedral's entrance. They were followed by Pauline in a gilded carriage and her own escort of Dragoons. She was followed by Hussars, looking both noble and rakish with their turned-back yellow pelisses and drooping mustaches.

By the time Napoleon had arrived in the oversized coach surrounded by the Consular Guard, the spectators were forced to one side of the plaza by the mass of cavalry waiting to honor their future Emperor. After the Emperor had entered the cathedral, dignitaries and their honor guards continued to arrive.

Bernadotte arrived with the Swedes. His white-and-gold uniform glittered with the Order of Saint John, presented to him the night before by the Ambassador. He bowed each member of the delegation to his assigned position, then offered his hand to his wife to escort her to her place.

"I think I am going to faint," whispered Desirée. "This crowd . . . it is so oppressive."

Bernadotte looked down at her. "Aren't you well?"

"It is the crowd, it makes me frightened . . . the press inside and the cold outside—" She shuddered, making this common-place movement seductive. "I may have to get some air," she warned her husband as they reached her place. "I'll try not to call attention to myself if I have to step out-of-doors. I'll not disgrace you, my husband."

"My dear . . ." There was nothing more Bernadotte could say. He bowed over her hand. "Do not tire yourself too much. This will not last forever, and we'll depart as soon as it's appro-priate. I hate to leave you, feeling as you do, but I must take my place in the procession."

She motioned him away with an impatient gesture and one hand holding her silken handkerchief to her mouth, her manner distracted, as if she had something pressing on her mind. Bernadotte looked back, concerned, but Desirée was already moving away from him.

Some distance back in the cathedral, Victoire watched the el-egant pandemonium and wondered if it would resolve itself to order as it was supposed to. She admired the staggering ele-gance of the gathering even as she felt herself flinch at the tre-mendous cost of such an ostentatious display. She could not entirely excuse herself from participation. She had spent more than half again as much as she had intended to, and her clothes were restrained compared to many others: her gown, a magnif-icent creation in ecru silk with an edging of bronze-green vel-vet and embroidered on the corsage and train in golden thread; it had cost more than Vernet earned in three months. Her hair was dressed in a knot of curls and fronted with her tiara. Her pearl and-diamond drops hung from her ears, and a neat collier of pearls-and-tourmalines was around her throat. She was not nearly warm enough for the bitterly cold day. Victoire longed for a sensible woolen shawl to wrap around her shoulders, though such a breach of fashion was unthinkable.

But now that the cathedral was filling, it was growing stuffy without becoming hot. Victoire wished for the opportunity to pace, but at so magnificent a ceremony as this, pacing was un-thinkable, not that there was sufficient room to do it. She tried to concentrate on the gorgeous stream of arriving dignitaries, and found her attention wandering. She was still upset at the recollection of the useless talk with the elderly Jesuit who now ran the inn at Vincennes: yes, there had been another man staying there calling himself Gambais, a tall man with an eyepatch; no, he had not come with armed men; no, he had not spoken against the First Consul. He had barely spoken at all. No, Gambais had sent no letters, nor received any. Yes, except for the eyepatch he had looked much like a sketch of Pichegru that Murat had the forethought to bring. No, he had no idea where he had gone.

Murat had searched the room, but Pichegru had removed all his possessions.

A jostling of her elbow recalled Victoire to her present situation. She shook herself mentally, glanced behind her to make sure no one was standing on her train, then moved a little nearer the wall, the better to watch the tremendous crowd crushed into the back half of the cathedral.

The Coronation began with a flourish of trumpets. Then, as was fitting for a military leader, standard bearers, each carrying the flags of their regiments, marched in a double row down the center aisle to exit through small doors at the sides of the High Altar. These were followed by almost a hundred clergy, beginning with the major abbots in the dark brown and gray habits of their Orders. These were followed by priests in white, bishops in white and red, Cardinals in their scarlet capes, and finally the Pope in his purple-and-gold vestments.

During it all a youthful choir and organ filled the cathedral with joyous anthems.

Behind the clergy came dignitaries from all over Europe. Even England's ambassador and several English nobles marched in the procession to take their seats toward the front of the cathedral. Following the foreign delegations were those members of the government that had been honored with a place. Victoire could see Fouché in that company. She wondered if the man, most content when operating in the world of shadows and deceit, was uncomfortable parading before so many important spectators; there was no way to tell from his carefully neutral expression.

The Generals of the Army, resplendent in their fanciest uniforms, came next, Murat, as always, outdoing them all with a colorful ensemble that was topped by a spray of large feathers imported from Africa. Behind them came the Inspector-Generals of the Army, gold braid over the severe blue-and-white dress uniforms of the Gendarme; Victoire was proud and pleased at the way in which Vernet carried himself. As he passed by the pew where Victoire stood, their eyes met. After this the procession continued with the members of the Buonaparte family. From her conversation with Murat, Victoire knew that nearly two hundred more were scheduled to march before Josephine and then Napoleon himself entered.

Desirée slipped out of her place, her handkerchief still held to her lips. No one attempted to detain her and she reached the side door before Pope Pius VII and Cardinal Fesche intoned the first Latin phrases of the celebration.

An armed soldier from the Grenadier Company of the Consular Guard stood next to the old statue of Saint Anthony, his fancy uniform out of place with the firm purpose in his eyes.

"I must get some air," whispered Desirée, and turned her pleading eyes on him.

"Madame—"

"I fear I am going to be sick," she said faintly. "I can't do it here. I would not want to . . . to disgrace the celebration."

From her position farther down the nave, Victoire saw Desirée, and her attention was fixed on Bernadotte's wife.

"Madame!" the soldier exclaimed.

"Just let me have a few breaths of cold, fresh air. I won't bother anyone if I step outside for a short while." Her plaintive tone and her bejeweled loveliness had the effect she intended: the soldier nodded.

"All right," he said, and opened the door just enough to allow her to slip out through it. "Knock twice when you want back in."

"Thank you, thank you," she said as she left the cathedral.

Victoire noticed Desirée's exit, left her place toward the back, and hurried toward the soldier. She was no longer listening to the ceremony, and paying no attention to the curious glances shot in her direction. As she came up to the guard, she said, "Excuse me, Corporal, but is something the matter with Madame Bernadotte?"

The guard looked at her in mild surprise. "Who?"

"Madame Bernadotte. You just let her out . . ." Victoire gestured to the door as the choir swelled in fulsome praise of God and Napoleon.

"Ah, the beautiful lady," said the guard. "She said she was unwell."

"Did she," said Victoire. "That's very unfortunate. If there is any difficulty, send her to me. I'm Madame Vernet, and I will watch after her. I'm eleven rows back in this section."

"That's very kind of you," said the soldier, and moved a little nearer the door.

Realizing that there was not much more she could do without obviously waiting for Desirée to return, Victoire retreated to her place in the ranks, and once again took to scanning the crowd.

Murat and Caroline were easily recognized, being among the favored in Napoleon's company. There was Berthier, managing to look rumpled in his silken finery, and there Talleyrand, his elaborate coat trimmed with profusions of gold lace. Her eyes sought out Vernet, now standing between Fouche and the delegation from the king of Spain; she watched her husband with affection and pride.

When Victoire glanced toward the Saint Anthony door again, no more than five minutes later, she could not see the guard.

Disquieted, Victoire once again made her way toward the Saint Anthony door. As she approached the old statue, she saw that the door was ajar. Puzzled, she stepped through it into the cold wind. The massed formations had left as soon as the procession began, anxious to return to warm barracks and their own celebrations. She saw no one but a gathering of coachmen and postilions huddled some distance away, waiting for the ceremony to be over before they had more work to do. Desirée was nowhere in sight, and neither was the soldier set to guard the door.

Now her bafflement became anxiety. Victoire raised her hand and called out to the nearest of the coachmen. "Have you seen a woman here, or a soldier?"

Two of the coachmen swung around, one of them shaking his head, the other saying, "There was a woman. She helped the general inside, I think. He arrived late."

"The general," said Victoire, certain she knew which general that was. "A man in the uniform of a general officer? Tall and thin?"

The coachman shrugged. "I suppose so," he answered, and looked at the others. "Any of you see him?"

Most denied it, but a young postilion from the Perignon household agreed with the description. "He wasn't in very grand dress, not like the Emperor's group. He was probably embarrassed to show himself in such a poor uniform. The Emperor won't like it."

"Thank you," said Victoire, and started back toward the door, pausing to glance around the foot of the cathedral's buttresses as she went, not truly expecting to discover anything terrible. She was more shocked than she wished to admit when she found the young guard in a heap at the foot of one of the massive supports, his face calm, the front of his uniform soaked in blood from the gaping wound in his neck. The blood was not yet clotted—the soldier had not been dead for much more than ten minutes.

The choir soared into another anthem, making the whole of the stone building ring as with bells.

Victoire stood still for several seconds, then forced herself to take action. She glanced back in the direction of the coachmen, and decided at once to say nothing to them. To raise that alarm now would contribute nothing but turmoil, and that would be more apt to serve Pichegru's purpose than her own. She wished more than ever that she had a shawl or a coat with her; she was becoming cold. She must do something at once, to keep from taking a chill, to prevent a tragedy. She could not linger here staring at the dead corporal. Her jumbled thoughts finally sorted themselves out and she started around the massive flank of the cathedral to the wide square at the front, her keen blue eyes already searching for the familiar sight of Roustam-Raza's turban.

He was standing not far from the enormous doors, his arms crossed and his head lowered. His Mameluke uniform was more elaborate than usual, with swags and tassels and extensive amounts of gold braid augmenting his Egyptian finery. Not far away from him Napoleon's state carriage waited.

"Roustam-Raza," Victoire cried as she hurried up to him. "Thank God I've found you."

"Madame Vernet!" he exclaimed as he scowled at her. "You ought to be inside."

"No, no," she said impatiently. "I need your help. At once."

He regarded her narrowly, too familiar with her skills to disregard her demands. "Why?"

"The Emperor is in danger," she said, and rushed on, "I've found a guard, killed. A door is open, and I fear that Napoleon's enemies—"

"Have entered the cathedral?" he finished for her, one hand going to the scimitar thrust through his sash.

"That is what I fear," she said, and quickly summed up what she had witnessed without distracting blather, "I cannot find Madame Bernadotte, and I cannot tell for sure that she is aiding the traitors, but I fear they entered where she stepped out and if she is not helping the traitors she is in the gravest dan—"

"Take me there," said Roustam-Raza, and strode off more quickly than Victoire could easily follow in her thin kid slippers and fine clothing. She hitched her skirt and train over one arm and hastened after him, ignoring the stares of the coachmen and postilions as they neared the Saint Anthony door.

"You are right," said Roustam-Raza, bending over the guard's body. "He has not been dead very long. He must not have known what was happening, or his face would not be like that. Whoever killed him cannot be far away." He straightened up and motioned to the coachmen. "You!" he cried out.

A few of them had been watching the Mameluke, and they responded with a combination of curiosity and hesitation.

"There is a murdered man here. He must be guarded. I want two of you to watch him until the Gendarmes come to take charge." He motioned the coachmen forward, and as they neared him, he pointed out where they were to stand. "And I want you"—he pointed to the largest postilion—"to carry word to the Guard station, at Pont Neuf. I will take responsibility for this order if there is any question about it from your masters or the Guard." He pointed to the body. "Take care you watch well, lest you end up as he has." With that daunting remark, he swung around to Victoire. "What now?"

"We'd better warn the other guards, and have a look about inside." She saw Roustam-Raza look askance and went on, "You are not here to worship, you are here to protect Napoleon, as you are sworn to do. Allah will forgive you for entering the cathedral. And God will forgive me for bringing you."

Roustam-Raza made an abrupt gesture, then acquiesced. "If it's not sacrilege, I will follow you," he said, and let her lead the way into Notre Dame through the small Saint Anthony door. "Allah is the All-Merciful."

The choir was silent and so the loud chanting of Cardinal Fesche echoed through the cathedral, the sense of his words lost in the dying repetitions of the stone.

"He'll have to get above this crowd," Victoire said to Roustam-Raza, pulling on his sleeve so that he would bend down to hear her. "There are stairs next to that chapel." She pointed toward what was little more than an alcove. "We must look."

"Summon the guards," Roustam-Raza suggested.

"And cause a panic?" Victoire countered. "Let us hope we find a priest, or a sexton." She was already starting toward the narrow stairs. "Be careful. These are steep."

Roustam-Raza made a sound that might have been a protest but he went up the stairs behind Victoire, one hand on the hilt of his scimitar. He had carefully avoided looking at the chapel and altars and made it clear that he would not listen to the choir.

The passageway was narrow and gave onto a galleried corridor running the length of the nave. There were a number of places where a man might take aim over the heads of the crowd, and Victoire rushed to look at each one of them, knowing as she did that there was an equal number of hiding places on the opposite side of Notre Dame, and three levels of galleries above them. She reminded herself that the coachman had seen only one general enter the cathedral. That was a mercy, she thought, for it would be difficult enough to find the assassin. Had he brought others, the task would have not been possible for less than a company of Guards.

Roustam-Raza scowled, coming to the same conclusion that Victoire had. "Madame Vernet," he called to her, doing his best to make himself heard over the sonorous chanting. "We must search better."

"Yes," she agreed, and said, "I will take this side of the cathedral, and you must take the other side. You will have to go back along this corridor, and cross to the other side. Be careful how you go. We are looking for desperate men, and they will not hesitate to kill you."

"Or you, Madame Vernet," said Roustam-Raza very seriously.

"I doubt I am in the same danger you are: you are Napoleon's personal guard, and everyone knows it. I, on the other hand, am Lucien Vernet's wife. Most of these conspirators do not credit women with the same determination as they themselves possess, unless they think the woman is crazy." Roustam-Raza protested that in her case they had likely learn better but she waved this away with a single gesture. "You take the other side, and be quick. The ceremony is a long one, and that is as much to General Pichegru's advantage as ours."

"In what sense?" demanded Roustam-Raza, raising his voice against the renewed exultation of the choir.

"He can move about if he suspects he is being sought," said Victoire. "And he might be able to escape before we can reach him, once he has done the deed."

"Yes," said Roustam-Raza decisively. "Others must be alerted."

"Not yet," said Victoire, hoping that one of the priests or monks living at Notre Dame would assist them. "That would serve only to frighten everyone below and make the celebration a mockery, as well as threaten chaos if there is . . ." She did not want to be distracted by worry about panic in the cathedral "We must find him before we do anything else. That's of the greatest importance. We cannot stop him if we cannot find him and if there is distress or upset, he and his men could easily make good their escape."

"May Allah guide us," said Roustam-Raza defiantly, as if he expected Notre Dame itself to contradict him. Then he turned and hurriedly retraced his steps.

Victoire watched him only for a moment, then hurried on along the gallery, taking as little time as she dared to peer into alcoves and niches and closet-sized chapels, trusting to surprise for protection. She felt apprehension building in her.

The Coronation continued below. Several representatives of foreign nations were making short speeches, presenting gifts many to both Napoleon and Josephine. Others were giving speeches praising Napoleon as a great leader and inspiration most of these came from Frenchmen or the weak German state that lined France's eastern border.

The gifts were followed by a prolonged sermon on the responsibilities of leadership. This was given by the Cardinal, for the Pope's French was not good enough for the task. The Cardinal's voice was high and nasal, and it echoed eerily through the huge cathedral.

Victoire reached the end of the gallery and looked for stairs to the next level, and found them tucked away behind thirteenth-century screen. Taking care to be certain that no one was watching for her from ambush, she rushed upward, doing her best to shut out the enormous sounds that rushed and rang through the cathedral. In the next gallery up, it was more difficult to make out what was happening below. She realized that she was almost directly over the center of the cathedral, and she allowed herself a few seconds to look down on the gold white, and red gathering before the High Altar. To her surprise Napoleon met her gaze and a brief look of concern crossed his face.

At this level there were a number of small balconies projecting out over the nave and transept. The leaf-shaped carving supporting them provided some protection to anyone willing to crouch down. Victoire found herself standing in front of chapel that was little more than a double-width alcove; a tiny altar faced a small, dusty triptych of the Annunciation flanked by Saint Barbara and Saint Veronica; the three woven metal plates of the triptych leaned against the marble of the cathedral wall and appeared ready to fall. Using the chapel for some co cealment, Victoire peered around at the profusion of balconies and projections that were in the greatest number directly above the High Altar. She looked down only once, and had to take hold of the nearest pillar to stop the vertigo that seized her.

It was then that she noticed a shine that did not seem to be part of the stone. It came from the front of one of the little balconies a short distance away. She narrowed her eyes, concentrating and wishing now she had not sent Roustam-Raza away. She dared not take the time to look for additional help. Napoleon was easily visible from that balcony. If she tried to raise the alarm it would do little more than warn the assassin that he was observed. She again saw the metallic sheen of a rifle-barrel. As Victoire watched in horror, Pichegru, in parade-dress uniform with full honors fixed on his sash, rose from his crouch and brought his breechloader up. He was taking aim as the Coronation approached its most compelling moment: the placing of the crown on Napoleon Buonaparte's head. Already the Pope was reaching for the crown.

With horror Victoire realized that this would be exactly when an assassin would strike, robbing Napoleon of his triumph and his life at the same time.

The excitement in the cathedral was increasing, its intensity as palpable as the cold breeze that raced through its lofty galleries. The assembly of distinguished persons was alive with motion and whispers as everyone waited for the historic moment with intense anticipation.

Somewhere down below, thought Victoire, Desirée was waiting with the rest, but what she anticipated was not Napoleon's epitome of glory but his violent death. A sense of helplessness coursed through Victoire, and was banished as quickly as it came. This was no time to despair, she ordered herself, and determined to act. She was prepared to rush the man and fight him if she had to. If Pichegru shot at her, he would have to reload before he could fire at Napoleon, and that would serve to provide warning. She had already faced the man once. Would she be as lucky again? If she attacked him, either or both of them might fall from the balcony to land in front of the High Altar far below. There had to be a better way, one that would lessen the chance of any more bloodshed.

The triptych caught her eye again, and now she reached out for it, taking it down and folding it into a form about the size of a jewelry-box. She hefted it once, and gave a small, experimental swing to her arm. She could throw it as far as she needed to, and with some accuracy. It was heavy enough to in-

flict damage, she decided. Certainly it was enough to leave
bruises and perhaps cause him to misfire. She took it, holding
it in the curve of her arm as she crept nearer, all the while praying that Pichegru would not fire for a few seconds more, until
she was in a position to use her make-shift weapon.

She rounded the end of the chapel, moving as close to the
balcony as she dared. Then she braced herself and hurled the
triptych at Pichegru, aiming for his shoulder to deflect his
weapon.

The triptych struck him at the base of the back of his skull.
Pichegru shuddered, straightened, then collapsed back against
the pillar, his rifle falling against the stone with a clatter that
only Victoire could hear.

16

✤

THE POPE STOOD with the crown poised over Napoleon's head. At that instant the same instinct that gave him an edge on the battlefield caused the Emperor-to-be to look up. He found himself facing Pichegru and the breechloader. All the glory and gaudy finery vanished and the world came down to that ominous barrel and Pichegru's enmity.

Then the Pope shifted slightly and caught Napoleon's attention; the Pontiff was standing just in front of his throne and was about to lean over to place the crown on his head.

Napoleon stood, jamming the crown on his head and shocking the Pope. It also placed the Pope directly between the self-crowned Emperor of France and Pichegru's ball.

Risking a look over the Pope's shoulder Napoleon saw the folded leaves of the triptych slam into the back of Pichegru's head. As the man fell, Napoleon could hear the faint clatter of the breechloader over the music and murmurs of the crowd. As Napoleon watched, Madame Vernet appeared in the balcony. Smiling with relief, he turned his attention back to his Coronation.

Victoire stared in astonishment at the still figure of Pichegru, unable to believe that she had succeeded in knocking him out. Of course she had intended to stop him, but now she was shocked by what she had done. She might feel jubilant later, but now she could see blood matting his hair, and she feared he was severely injured even as she felt blossoming pride in her accomplishment. After a slight hesitation she moved forward to take the rifle and determine how badly the general was injured.

Pichegru was in a heap, his breathing shallow and his face pale and mottled as curdled milk. He made no response when Victoire bent over him, her hands trembling a little as she felt at his nose for breath and then pulled his rifle away from where he had fallen.

The excitement below was growing; the choir sang in soaring phrases and the Pope continued his benediction on the newly crowned Emperor.

What would she do, Victoire wondered, if Pichegru regained consciousness before help arrived? She could not leave him unattended, but she was shrewd enough to know that the general might still be capable of further damage. He had to be immobilized, and she lacked the means to assure that. She looked down at him, her thoughts racing, as she sought for the means to keep him from any action. At last she reached out and pulled at the wide military sash Pichegru wore, a profusion of his medals fixed to the wide band of silk. Victoire tugged at it, and at last pulled it off his shoulder and worked it from under his arm, then struggled to roll the fallen general prone so that she could secure his hands behind his back. She set about tieing his hands with the wide military sash, relishing the irony of Pichegru's capture.

Below the Pope was placing the crown of Empress on Josephine's head. The choir took up another anthem, this one recently composed in honor of the ceremony. Josephine beamed her irregular teeth the only imperfect note in the perfection of her dress and coiffure. Napoleon also smiled with delight. As the Pope moved back, he gently reached over and squeezed Josephine's hand. The affection and joy the two shared was visible to everyone assembled. A few of the less discreet officers in the back of the cathedral actually cheered.

Satisfied that Pichegru could not easily free his hands, she gave her attention to his feet. With an effort she removed his boots, flinging them back into the chapel where the triptych had been, then worked to remove his gartered hose, knotting them together before she secured them around his ankles.

This done, she got to her feet, ignoring the dust and grime that had ruined her gown. She brushed her hands together, looking around for the help she needed. Then, with a sigh, she started away from Pichegru, setting the musket out of sight behind the altar and then going back along the gallery toward the stairs to the next level down.

She had almost reached the place when a sexton appeared, all but running, cutting her off. She was about to order him out of her way when she saw he carried a Wilson pocket pistol, and it was pointed directly at her.

"I regret the necessity," said Colonel Sir Magnus Sackett-Hartley in flawless French, "but I cannot permit you to reach the floor before I do. Please stand aside, Madame."

"And if I refuse?" Victoire asked, wondering if the man was more frightened than he was daring.

"Then I regret I will be forced to stop you, Madame." His answer was cool and without a trace of fear.

Victoire stared at him, memorizing his clean-cut features and his fine manner. "How many of you are there?"

"Not enough," said Sackett-Hartley. "My shot went wild—"

"Your shot?" Victoire repeated, aghast at this revelation. "You fired?"

"When Pichegru failed to, yes," he said. "The choir covered the sound." He motioned her back with a flip of his pistol. "And I had just the one for the Ferguson."

At another time she might have admonished him for his lack of foresight; now she could only be grateful that the English assassin—for surely this must be the English assassin she had been seeking—had been so sure of himself that he had not brought more than a single charge for his rifle. "And the pistol?"

"I have two of them, both charged. I don't want to shoot you, Madame. It would require a ball I cannot easily spare, not and keep one for myself." He studied her a moment, intense concentration in his manner, and then his expression shifted, became strangely cordial. "You are the one Montrachet caught, aren't you? He spoke of a fair woman, not yet thirty, with bright blue eyes. He said you had a most unwomanly lack of fear." His eyes smiled appreciatively. "Surely there cannot be two of you. You are Madame Vernet."

"I am," she said, unwilling to deny it, even to an enemy.

"At another time I would be enchanted, Madame," he said with a slight bow. "As it is, I am saddened that we meet under these unhappy circumstances."

"But as it is you're going to shoot me?" she said, not quite able to keep the quiver out of her voice.

"Hardly that, Madame Vernet; not if I do not have to." Sackett-Hartley actually smiled at her, his expression becoming more affable. "But I fear I will have to ask you to embrace that pillar, the one supporting the buttress." He indicated the barrel-girthed pillar with a motion of the muzzle of his pistol.

An orchestra in the back of the choir loft had started playing now. It was a loud and sprightly march composed by a German for the occasion. In the front of the cathedral the mayors of the largest cities were now presenting jewel-encrusted keys to Napoleon. The religious ceremony over, many of the guests felt free to begin talking about what they had just seen and the mur-

mur of the crowd competed with the brassy sound of the orchestra. Victoire knew that if she screamed now, there was a
good chance no one would hear her.

Sackett-Hartley had a leather belt under his sexton's sash.
The task of removing it was awkward, for he kept his pistol
trained on Victoire as he wrestled the belt off. "If you will be
good enough to put your arms around that pillar, Madame
Vernet, as far as you can?" His face was flushed now and he
was becoming visibly apprehensive as he listened to the Coronation. "Just lean against it? If you will?"

"And then what?" asked Victoire, taking as much time as she
dared to do as he ordered.

"Then I will leave. Do be quick. I don't want your soldiers
to find me here. It is enough that they will get Pichegru." As
he said this he secured her wrist in a loop of the belt, then
wrapped her other wrist in a tight knot and tugged at it twice
to be certain it would hold. "Yet I meant what I said: I am
pleased we had the opportunity to meet, Madame Vernet, although I apologize for the circumstances. Perhaps another time
you will have the advantage of me. If that time ever comes, believe me when I say I am always your most sincere admirer."
With that he gave her a quick bow, then fled down the gallery
to the connection with another corridor high over the transept.

Victoire watched him, wanting to cry out even though no one
would hear her in the glorious paeans rising from the musicians
and singers above both sides of the altar. Almost at once her
hands became numb from the belt binding her wrists. Her pa-
tience was exhausted, she was infuriated, and now that she
could do nothing, her fear gained strength and she felt herself
lean against the stone for support. She attempted to console
herself with the reminder that Pichegru was waiting, captive
secure in his bonds, but for Victoire this was a hollow victory

The mayors were finished and the Buonaparte family was
now being honored with the opportunity to congratulate their
brother. Already the clerics gathered themselves to lead the pro
cession to the main entranceway, where a crowd of soldiers and
citizens waited to be the first to cheer their new Emperor.

There was a shout not far away, and then Roustam-Raza ap
peared, a half dozen Guards coming up behind him.

Victoire closed her eyes for several seconds, her sense of hu
miliation increasing at the thought that the stalwart Mameluk
would see her in this predicament. When she opened them
again, a private and Roustam-Raza were only a few steps from
her.

"Allah preserve and—" began Roustam-Raza as he reached Victoire's side. "What has happened?"

"Pichegru," said Victoire as she felt the leather around her wrists ease and the blood flow back into her hands with painful intensity.

"He did this? He is—" Roustam-Raza demanded, only to have Victoire interrupt him.

"No, he did not do this. An Englishman did. Pichegru is . . . well, he may have regained consciousness, but I left him in the northeast balcony over the High Altar, secured." She rubbed her hands together, trying to restore feeling to them without increasing the hurt.

"See to it," ordered Roustam-Raza, and gave the Guards room to move past him.

"He did make an attempt to shoot Napoleon—Pichegru did," said Victoire. "And so did the Englishman, or so he claimed. But fortunately neither of them succeeded."

"The Englishman escaped?" said Roustam-Raza dubiously.

"Unless you detained a sexton with reddish hair and a pair of English pistols, he must have," said Victoire, her thoughts turning giddy now that she was safe.

Already the lesser dignitaries were taking the opportunity to sneak out the cathedral's many side doors. Most were hurrying to the front of the church in hopes of being noticed by Napoleon. Others raced away to final fittings for the uniforms and gowns they would be wearing at the palace that night.

The procession was led by the clerics, followed closely by Napoleon with Josephine on his arm. The rest left in reverse order of their entrance as officers of the Guard cavalry moved along the center aisle, controlling the flow of the crowd. There was a tremendous obligatory cheer when the crowd caught sight of Napoleon as he emerged from the cathedral.

"We discovered no sexton, with or without pistols," said Roustam-Raza heavily. "He will have escaped easily by now."

The Guards were returning now, two of them half-escorting, half-dragging Pichegru between them. The general was not yet restored to his wits, but was no longer insensible.

"What do we do with him?" the nearest Guard asked Roustam-Raza.

"Put him in a cell and guard him," said Roustam-Raza in a tone of voice that made the Guards shiver. "He is a traitor to the Emperor and France."

"He is also a great fool," said one of the soldiers, prodding Pichegru with the butt of his rifle.

Victoire intervened. "Whatever he is, he deserves better treatment at your hands, or it will be said that he acted in just cause." She saw the soldier stare at her in offended incredulity. "You are victorious. You can therefore afford to be generous," she reminded him.

Roustam-Raza gave an emphatic nod of approval. "You have said it right, Madame Vernet." He addressed the rest of the soldiers, "Mind that you conduct yourselves with utmost propriety. Let it be your honor that protects him." He let the prisoner and the soldiers escorting him get by, and then addressed Victoire again. "How is it that you were spared, Madame Vernet?" This was not an accusation but a statement of astonishment.

"Gallantry, I suppose," said Victoire, with a faint smile. "He is one of those English who love the grand gesture, and this was his." She looked down at the wreckage of her gown. "I can't return to Vernet looking like this, not while he's escorting the Spanish."

"It would not be correct," Roustam-Raza agreed.

Victoire sighed. "I'll have to think of something I can do to . . . make myself presentable."

"Where is your cloak? It will cover you well enough," said Roustam-Raza.

"It is in the carriage that brought me," said Victoire, frowning. "Yes, you're right, it would be enough, but look at that crowd. It would take you the better part of an hour to find the carriage and who knows how long to return here?" She was able to laugh once, but her mirth vanished again. "It was a lucky thing for the Englishman that he left the cathedral before the ceremony was completely finished."

"I have no doubt it was part of his plan," agreed Roustam-Raza with a deliberate gesture of condemnation.

"Almost certainly," said Victoire, starting in the direction of the narrow staircase. "He's a clever man, I think."

"And a very lucky one," added Roustam-Raza.

"Luck and planning often march together," observed Victoire, repeating an aphorism she had heard Berthier recite during the return voyage from Egypt. She found her hands were unsteady and she had begun to shiver.

Roustam-Raza glanced toward one of the privates and ordered him to stop. "Give your coat to Madame Vernet, soldier, at once," he ordered. "I will see that you are given a new one for this service."

The private stared at the Egyptian but then shrugged, showing his resignation and shifting the long garment from his shoulders with the same movement. He held it out to Victoire. "It is for your service to the Emperor, Madame," he said with a strong Alsatian accent, turning very red.

"I see," said Victoire as she took the coat, her hands feeling stiff as she attempted to close them on the dark wool. "Thank you, soldier."

"Private Grunne," he said with a half-salute as Victoire pulled his coat around her shoulders.

They had reached the stairs and now conversation was impossible for the tremendous welter of sound that roared like the ocean during a storm.

As she followed Roustam-Raza down the ladder-like stairs—the Mameluke making his way half-sideways because of the narrowness of the treads—she felt a deep, aching fatigue wash over her, as if she had finally put down a pack of such weight that she trembled at the thought of lifting it again.

"Is something the matter?" Roustam-Raza bellowed at her in order to be heard at all.

"No," she answered, shaking her head slowly. "Nothing. In fact, it may be that at last things are all right."

"The word is that Pichegru is dead," Odette said the next day as Victoire lounged in her old-fashioned copper bath. "I've not seen an official notice, but the news is everywhere."

"Did you hear this at the market?" asked Victoire as she felt beneath her for the soap. In spite of her late rising she was slightly bilious from the huge banquet the night before.

"Early this morning," Odette confirmed. "It was believed by everyone. Pichegru has paid for his treason."

"I hope for his sake that he is dead," Victoire said a bit remotely, and looked down at her body through the disappearing bubbles. "These banquets are going to make me stout, I am certain of it. Look at my waist, and my breasts are turning to melons." She sighed. "At least that's fashionable."

Odette chuckled. "Madame Vernet, surely you are joking," she said.

"About my waist? Never!" Victoire sat up suddenly and sent water sloshing onto the stone floor of the kitchen.

"Then you had better resign yourself to it," said Odette, and cocked her head as she regarded Victoire in disbelief. "You are increasing, Madame. You must have settled while you and the Inspector-General were traveling. I thought you knew."

"Increasing?" Victoire repeated as if she had never heard the word, for she dared not hope it was true. "Ridiculous."

Odette sat down on one of the stools. "I do the laundry here, Madame Vernet, and I know when your last courses were even if you do not. You have used no napkins since you returned from Dunkerque. Have you been too busy to notice?" This time she laughed outright.

"Since my return from Dunke—" She broke off as she figured the time in her mind. Slowly color suffused her face. "I thought—" Again she fell silent, afraid to tell Odette that she was afraid she had injured herself in all her activity and was finally barren.

"I assume the child will come in mid-summer, if God is good to you." Odette indicated the ceiling, echoing from the labor of the carpenters on the floor above. "The house is being repaired just in time."

Victoire leaned back in the water, amazed at what Odette said and wishing fervently it was true. Her last courses had been ... when? Three months ago? Was Odette right? There had been disappointments before, and she did not relish having another, not for herself and not for Vernet. She ran one hand lightly over her belly. Perhaps, she thought, and unbidden the prediction of Madame LeNormande came to her mind. What was it she said? There would be three children, although not all of them would survive childhood? And there were two grandchildren at least? Had she remembered this correctly?

"What is it, Madame?" asked Odette, noticing Victoire's deep frown. She had gone to the door to admit the kitchen cat and was bending at the waist, absentmindedly stroking the purring feline.

"Um?" Victoire looked up, coming back to herself and rigorously dismissing what the fortune-teller said as superstition at worst and sophistry at best. "Oh, nothing. I suppose every woman must wonder about an unborn child, and hope that it will thrive."

"Most women, certainly," said Odette. "In a poor family, it might be otherwise," she added carefully.

"And if the woman has no husband, or her husband is cruel," said Victoire. "Yes, there are those who must not welcome children." She recalled a distant cousin of hers who had the misfortune to become pregnant before she was married. The cousin had been sent to a convent in the south as a postulant, and Victoire had never learned anything of the little boy she delivered. She pulled herself to her feet and held her hands out for the warm towel Odette had waiting for her. "Nothing to Vernet yet, Odette. He has had his hopes raised before, and to no purpose."

"Of course, Madame," said Odette as she watched Victoire wrap herself in the towel. "I'll make you broth with good juniper berries it in, and that will strengthen you," she went on. "And I'll stuff a pillow with mugwort, to prevent illness in the night. And then I'll light a candle to the Virgin for you, and to Saint Anne, to protect you." This last was a bit defensive, for she knew that Victoire was not religious.

"That's very kind," said Victoire, trying to determine if she could feel any difference in her body other than a slight heaviness in the abdomen. "I fear it could still be nothing more than too many stuffed loins of veal and collops of pork in pâté and brandy," she admitted.

"You will not think so in another month," Odette warned her. "And in the meantime, you must be careful not to become chilled or to take sick."

Victoire sighed. "Whatever the case, it is probably just as well that I have nowhere to go tonight, but to bed. Vernet is bidden to dine with Fouche and Berthier; no doubt they will discuss Pichegru and the English assassin."

"Has he been caught yet?" asked Odette. "The Englishman'?"

"Not that I know of," answered Victoire, thinking that she could almost feel sorry for Sackett-Hartley if he fell into Napoleon's hands now. "Perhaps I can learn something from Vernet tonight, when he comes home."

"I'm still astonished by his audacity—tieing you to a pillar!" Odette's indignation raised her voice by a third.

"Considering he could have shot me, I must confess I feel a little gratitude toward him," Victoire responded calmly.

"There's proof you are increasing! At such times women always take odd notions into their heads." With that announcement, Odette went to get Victoire's simple housedress, and by the time she returned to the kitchen, Victoire was eager to discuss the ball Murat and his wife Caroline were giving the following evening.

The Emperor's sister Caroline had outdone herself: the hotel where she and her husband Marshall Joachim Murat lived was ablaze with lights, and decorations in the shape of laurel wreaths intertwining golden coronets were everywhere, from the mirrored entry hall to the ballroom to the cavernous chamber where a lavish buffet had been set out for the favored three hundred who were invited to continue the celebration of the Coronation of Napoleon as Emperor of France.

As each person entered they were announced at the head of the stairs leading down into the ballroom. Then they proceeded down a line of important guests to their hosts. While the recognition was often pleasant, this tradition invariably meant that a long line formed waiting to be announced. With only Odette to assist her, Victoire had taken longer than planned to prepare herself. This meant that she and Vernet were trapped far back in the announcement line.

The advantage of this was that from the balcony leading to the stairs Victoire had the opportunity to study the glittering assembly before joining it.

A perversity in her caused Victoire to spot Talleyrand first. Around him gathered a dozen other well-dressed men, all engaged in deep conversation. Talleyrand himself wore a silk coat of bright-blue with lace cuffs. She studied the outfit, aware of what a dandy the Foreign Minister was when given the chance.

Bernadotte and Desirée swept through the center of the room, trailing a number of lesser celebrities in their wake. Eventually they reached the head of the Swedish delegation, who was himself in animated conversation with the British minister.

small orchestra was playing light music, but had not struck up anything suitable for dancing. This would begin when most of the guests had arrived.

Finally the couple ahead of them was announced, the duke and duchess of Klive and Berg. Victoire brushed down the new ballgown and prepared to smile.

When the chamberlain announced Inspector-General and Madame Vernet, Murat stopped in mid-sentence and hurried to the base of the stairs to bring the couple ahead of the rest of the reception line. There was a moment of speculation, considering the Marshall's reputation, but it stopped when he was greeted so affably by both Vernet and Victoire, and Victoire was given three touches of Caroline's cheek.

Murat accepted Victoire's curtsy with a smile. "I'll want a word or two with you later on, when the reception line ends, after my brother-in-law arrives." He glanced at his wife. "She has something to say to you, too."

Caroline Buonaparte curtsied to Victoire more deeply than social convention required, and met Victoire's shocked expression with a direct stare. "I've been told what you did, during the Coronation. All France is in your debt for saving the Emperor, but I am grateful to you for preserving my brother." She hesitated. "I understand why my husband admires you, Madame."

"You're most gracious," said Victoire, dazed, and accepted Vernet's arm to be led toward the ballroom. Her gown, of silk procured from the mercer near Saint-Sulpice, was a gray so pale it was silver, with silver point-lace along the corsage and the open front panel of the robe, which revealed a slip of sea-green brocade scavenged from yet another of her mother's grand toilettes. Her earrings were cascades of black pearls, and she wore no necklace. She whispered to Vernet as they walked into the buffet room, "I don't know what to say to her. She spoke as if I performed a personal service for her, at her instruction."

"Considering the woman's temperament," said Vernet, his eyes narrowing slightly, "she probably assumes that is what you did."

Victoire made an impatient gesture and noticed that there was a slight stain on the fingertip of one of her new long white-kid gloves. Given what they cost, she thought, the least they could do was stay clean for more than an hour. "I hope that the whole family is not going to behave like Caroline," she told her husband. "It would be oppressive to have to deal with so much gratitude."

"From that family, very true," said Vernet, and nodded to Berthier, who came bustling up to them, dusting snuff from his neck cloth with his handkerchief after he wiped the corner of his mouth.

"I'm glad I have the chance to speak with you before the Emperor arrives," he said to Vernet, and glanced at Victoire, favoring her with the suggestion of a bow. "And you as well, Madame Vernet."

Victoire murmured a few polite phrases and listened with intense interest. "I saw the report on Pichegru," said Vernet, "and I am not able to say I am completely in agreement with you."

Berthier looked a bit surprised. "You're not? Why is that?"

"I have not been able to persuade myself that Pichegru was ultimately responsible for the plot. Even possible help from Madame Bernadotte does not account for how close he came to achieving his ends." Vernet touched Victoire's hand. "I discussed this with my wife last night, and she generally agrees with me."

Berthier opened his eyes very wide, and instead of looking guileless he took on the appearance of an oversized dull. "I hope you have not been so indiscreet as to share your speculations with others."

"No; I am aware that it wouldn't be prudent. Still, it troubles me, Berthier, that he allied himself with the English. It is most unlike Pichegru to do that. I recall his low regard for the English and I am shocked to discover he entered into dealings with them," Vernet said.

"And what do you think, Madame Vernet?" asked Berthier with a one-sided smile. "Do you share your husband's opinions?"

"I am concerned, yes, because Pichegru was ill-disposed to the English," she said. "He was outspoken in his distrust of them."

"A smoke screen," declared Berthier. "A clever ruse, so that we would look elsewhere for our traitors and assassins."

"Then it was clumsy, for it didn't work," said Victoire before Vernet could make a more moderate statement. "He was suspected almost at once."

"Because of your perspicacity," said Berthier. "If you'd not been so observant and determined, Pichegru might well have achieved his ends."

Victoire wanted to remind Berthier that luck had little to do with it, but Vernet spoke before she could. "It's well you realize that, Berthier. My wife braved dangers that were not hers to face because you and Fouche were not willing to believe her."

"I realize that," said Berthier with a trace of embarrassment. "It's unfortunate that we permitted our vision to be clouded, but—" He waved his handkerchief in the air, flipping it in the general direction of Bernadotte and Desirée.

"Meaning she was to be protected?" Victoire guessed aloud. "Was that what held you back?"

"Yes," admitted Berthier. "The Emperor ordered that she was not to be made accountable for anything. What could I do but obey? It was his way of showing contrition, I suppose, but it hampered our investigation."

"When did he issue such an order?" asked Vernet, fascinated and vexed at once.

"During the summer, before you were sent north to the coast," Berthier admitted. "Fouche was not given any information, but he was fed early dispatches that made him discount much of what you reported. Fouche saw the information, but Napoleon made certain he evaluated it with a particular slant that served his purpose." He sighed. "I should have warned

Fouche to send another officer, Vernet. He doesn't appreciate your wife as I do."

Victoire shook her head in exasperation, and the black pearls swung and bounced against her neck. "You may tell the Emperor he might have been killed for his show of courtesy to Desirée."

"It wouldn't be permitted," said Berthier firmly.

"And how was it supposed to stop?" Victoire asked. "What if Pichegru had allies other than Desirée and the English?"

"What do you mean?" Berthier rounded on her. "What are you saying?"

"Only that there are others who might seek the Emperor's fall for their own advantage. Desirée is not the only ambitious person who might hold a grudge against Napoleon." Victoire looked around the gathering and at last picked out the popinjay figure of Talleyrand. "For example. And he favors uniting with the English."

Berthier nodded, his face somber. "There is nothing to indicate he participated in any way."

"We have made inquiries, but there have been no discoveries," Vernet confirmed.

"This does not surprise me," said Victoire dryly. "But I cannot dismiss my assumptions, just for that."

"But keep them to yourself," warned Berthier. "And the things you know about Desirée."

Victoire regarded Berthier critically. "I hope you will inform the Emperor that I think he is placing himself at risk, permitting this to remain unresolved."

"You might tell him yourself, if you wish, as he intends to speak with you when he arrives," said Berthier with satisfaction. "Doubtless your husband will relinquish one dance to the Emperor?"

Vernet nodded at once. "If it is his request, then certainly I will offer no objection," he said formally, concealing the rush of pride he felt, knowing that such attention to Victoire at this event would add much to their social standing and increase his own status as well. "An honor for you, my love," he added to Victoire.

"Only if the Emperor has improved his dancing skills," said Victoire before she could stop herself, recalling the last time she had attempted the polonaise with Napoleon.

"Madame," Berthier admonished her.

"My dear," Vernet said.

Victoire smiled, looking from her husband to Berthier and

back again. "Oh, I am fully cognizant of the compliment he offers. But my toes will pay the price."

"Madame Vernet," protested Berthier.

But Vernet was grinning. "Isn't she refreshing? Most women would simper and pout—not my wife. I'm a very fortunate fellow, Berthier. Doubly so, because I have the sense to know it."

Berthier retrieved his snuffbox from his waistcoat pocket and inhaled a pinch of it, holding his handkerchief at the ready in case he should sneeze. "Felicitations," he said, sounding as if he had a head cold. He waved to Inspector-General Suchet and bowed himself away from the Vernets.

"There are times I think Napoleon takes too much advantage of Berthier," said Vernet softly. "The man is so loyal that he is often put in a bad position."

"Berthier is not the only one to have such trouble," said Victoire. "It seems to be the Emperor's gift—and his curse—to inspire profound affections in others." She went with Vernet into the ballroom and took their place not far from the little orchestra of fifteen musicians Murat's wife had hired for the occasion.

"They say that all the music tonight is to be by French composers," said Vernet, passing on what he had been told that morning by Fouche.

"Do they include Lully," Victoire asked, not expecting an answer. "He was born in Florence."

"Mehul has composed a new piece for this evening," Vernet told her. "To honor the Emperor and his family."

"Very wise," Victoire approved. She watched the door as more guests arrived, and after a short time she said to Vernet, "I wish sometimes that I were capable of prescience."

"Why do you say that?" asked Vernet.

"Because . . . I do not trust all this grandeur," she said slowly, selecting her words with care. "I cannot rid myself of the feeling that there is more at stake here than anyone supposes."

"There is the Empire," said Vernet with conviction. "And I share your feeling."

Whatever Victoire might have answered was lost in a sudden blare of trumpets and horns accompanied by a rumble of timpani. Everyone in the ballroom moved back against the walls and stood waiting as the fanfare continued, becoming an entrata for the Emperor and Josephine, falling silent only when the Emperor and his wife appeared in the doorway.

They came in with Caroline and Murat, Napoleon at his most

affable, pausing to speak with various guests and to remark on the wonderful entertainment being offered. As he reached the Vernets, he observed, indicating her gown, "Is it a sea-nymph, Madame Vernet, or one of those Greek storm goddesses?"

"It is a flattering color, or so I hope," she answered as she rose from her curtsy.

"Well, you are in good looks, Madame Vernet. I congratulate you. We will talk later." With that he gave his attention to Vernet. "When am I to see your report of the incidents during my Coronation?"

"I have already presented my notes and observations to—" Vernet began, only to be cut off with an abrupt gesture from Napoleon.

"Not those, you fool, the ones you made for yourself. If I want to see the official records, I need hardly come to you for them. Make me a complete copy of your private notes and deliver them to me yourself." He looked over at Murat. "See that he does it, will you?"

"An honor," said Murat.

Napoleon passed on and was shortly exchanging a few remarks with Berthier.

"He will not like much of what I have to say," Vernet whispered to Victoire as they watched Napoleon make the rounds of the ballroom.

"But he asked—" Victoire reminded him.

"Yes. Yes, I know," said Vernet, softly.

Dancing began almost as soon as Napoleon went into the buffet room, the orchestra striking up a gavotte to begin the evening, very much in the tradition of the royal court of thirty years before.

"Would you like to dance yet?" asked Vernet as the couples took their places on the dance floor.

"Not yet, not if I have to be ready for Napoleon." She listened to the slow, stately strains begin and added, "I trust he won't choose the polonaise. He is a disaster at it."

Vernet could not wholly conceal a chuckle. "If you wish, I will refuse permission for such a demanding dance."

"No, thank you," said Victoire with counterfeit primness. "I know my duty and I shall do it."

In any event, Napoleon selected a cotillion, though he announced that his set would not change partners during the movements, which left most of the rest uncertain of how to proceed. He then paired his wife off with Vernet, put Victoire's hand through his arm, and took her onto the floor. "I have been led to understand you are not wholly pleased with the way this recent contretemps has turned out," he said as he faced her to begin the first figure.

Victoire wanted to look to her husband on her left, but controlled the impulse in order to answer the Emperor. "I think that your sentiments have influenced your judgment," she said, taking care with the first pass so that Napoleon would not tread on the flounce of her skirt.

"I had better inform you that I am adamant on this point, Madame Vernet. There is no question of involving Bernadotte." He missed his timing on the balance and swore softly, not even bothering to ask her pardon.

"A good thing," said Victoire, ignoring his mistake, "for Bernadotte is not involved. It is his wife who appears to have aided Pichegru and the English. If there are others, I have not yet discovered them." She made sure to say it quietly but she could sense the disfavor her remark engendered.

"I will trust to your confidence, Madame, and take comfort in knowing that her participation will never be made public." He said it cordially enough but his orders were clear.

"You are accepting a grave risk," she pointed out as she tried to keep pace with the rhythm of the orchestra and Napoleon's less regular beat.

"I have never turned from danger, Madame, least of all from cowards who hide behind the dedication of others. I respect the English assassin more than Pichegru, I assure you." His bow was graceful enough but at the wrong moment in the dance "He was good enough to spare you, and for that I must thank him."

"I certainly concur," said Victoire.

They went on for a few measures until Napoleon gave a sigh of exasperation. "This is useless. Accompany me off the floor Madame, and we will settle our business together without this endless distraction." He did not wait for her to accept his offer but drew her to the side of the room. "I have had a long talk with my brother-in-law. Murat informed me of your circumstances."

"In what sense?" asked Victoire in an unguarded way. She discovered that this bald announcement annoyed her and she decided she would have to have a few sharp words with Murat later.

"To be blunt, in regard to your need for money. I did not know you or your husband were in such straits, Madame Vernet. No one had mentioned anything about it until this morning." He shook his head. "It does not please me to have my trustworthy officers at hardship. That leads to jealousy and compromise, and ... well, it does neither the officer nor me any good." He regarded her in silence. "Well?"

"It ... it is true that we do not have much money. I have some funds left in trust, but given Vernet's social obligations, it does not stretch as far as I would like." She hated admitting so much, but she did not flinch as she said it.

"Small wonder," said Napoleon, pulling on his lower lip. "I have given orders to Fouche to increase Vernet's salary, in recognition of his superior service. It is to be an annual pension of twenty thousand francs." He said this as if he expected a flurry of trumpets to accompany the announcement.

Victoire stared at him. "Twenty thousand?" she repeated, for the amount was nearly treble what Vernet now received.

"I can't have my brother-in-law underwriting my officers forever," said Napoleon with a faint smile.

For once in her life, Victoire could think of nothing to say.

This satisfied Napoleon immensely. "Oh," he said, as an afterthought. "Fouche informs me that he can discover no link to Talleyrand in the conspiracy." He took her hand, half-bowed over it, not quite kissed it, and then strode away, paying no heed to the notice he attracted.

Victoire stood by herself for a short while, and then blinked as if coming out of a dream. She saw Josephine curtsy to Vernet, then hurry after Napoleon, leaving Vernet standing by himself in the middle of the cotillion. Regaining her composure, Victoire went to his side and picked up the dance where the next pattern began.

"What did you say?" Vernet demanded as the music came to an end.

She repeated what Napoleon had told her about Vernet's pension.

"We're set for life. Lord God of the Fishes," said Vernet, his eyes glazed as if he had been struck a punishing blow instead of rewarded so well.

"Precisely," Victoire agreed, and walked off the floor on his arm before passing on her other, more personal, good news.